STRANGER AT THE DOWER HOUSE

Strangers Book 1

A Regency Romance

by Mary Kingswood

Published by Sutors Publishing

V7

ISBN: 978-1-912167-34-0 (paperback)

Cover design by: Shayne Rutherford of Darkmoon Graphics

Author's note:

this book is written using historic British terminology, so *saloon* instead of *salon*, *chaperon* instead of *chaperone* and so on. I follow Jane Austen's example and refer to a group of sisters as the Miss Wintertons.

Stranger At The Dower House: Stranger Book 1

About this book: *a widow moves into the long disused Dower House and makes a horrible discovery in the wine cellar.*

Thirty-year-old widow Louisa Middlehope is determined to escape from her late husband's family and live life for herself for the first time. The tiny village of Great Maeswood offers her the peace and quiet her heart craves, and perhaps it might provide a little entertainment, too. But the house she has leased has been empty for a quarter of a century and who knows what secrets it holds?

Laurence Gage is still mourning his beloved wife, while raising his two children, and at forty, declining gently into a rather dull middle age. Until, that is, the intriguing Mrs Middlehope arrives in the village and upends his placid life. She's nothing at all like his perfect wife, but he's oddly drawn to her anyway and to his surprise, she seems to like him too. Whoever would have thought it? But what exactly is she looking for? Friendship, marriage — or something else entirely?

This is a complete story with a happy ever after. Book 1 of a 6 book series. A traditional Regency romance, drawing room rather than bedroom.

Isn't that what's-his-name? Regular readers will know that characters from previous books occasionally pop up. Lawyer Mr Willerton-Forbes, his flamboyant sidekick Captain Edgerton and the discreet Mr Neate have been helping my characters solve murders and other puzzles ever since *Lord Augustus*. Michael Chandry, now a crime-solving partner to Captain Edgerton and his pals, was first seen helping after the shipwreck in *The Clerk* and more recently in *The Duke*.

About the *Strangers* series: There's a famous saying attributed to John Gardner that authors like to quote: that there are only two plots - a stranger arrives in town, or a person goes on a journey. Most of my books have been based on the latter, in its loosest sense (sometimes a journey of discovery, rather than a literal journey, but a major change, of death or misfortune or even good fortune which propels the main character in a new direction). So I wondered what the other side of the coin would look like - a stranger arriving in town. And there was my series title - *Strangers*.

Book 0: Stranger at the Parsonage: a new parson arrives at the village of Great Maeswood, and tragedy strikes the baron's family. (a novella, free to mailing list subscribers).

Book 1: Stranger at the Dower House: a widow moves into the long disused Dower House and makes a horrible discovery in the wine cellar.

Book 2: Stranger at the Grove: an estranged brother is forced to return to his home and face up to his past.

Book 3: Stranger at the Villa: a new physician arrives in the village, but is he all he seems?

Book 4: Stranger at the Manor: a destitute man comes looking for help from his cousin, and uncovers some mysterious goings-on.

Book 5: Stranger at the Cottage: an out-of-work governess tries to start a school in the village.

Book 6: Stranger at the Hall: the newly discovered heir to the barony arrives to claim his inheritance.

Want to be the first to hear about new releases? Sign up for my mailing list at http://marykingswood.co.uk/.

Table of contents

The Principal Inhabitants Of Great Maeswood

At Maeswood Hall:

Lady Saxby (47), a baron's widow

Her step-daughter, Miss Cass Saxby (26)

Her daughters, Miss Agnes (20), Miss Flora (18), Miss Honora (16)

Her sons from her first marriage, Mr Jeffrey Rycroft (28), Mr Timothy Rycroft (24)

At the Dower House:

Mrs Edward Middlehope (Louisa, 30), a widow

Marie Fournier (23), her French maid

At Cloverstone Manor:

Squire Winslade (52)

His third wife, Lilian (28), who is ill

His daughter, Miss Susannah Winslade (26)

His son, Mr Henry Winslade (24)

At Lower Maeswood Grove:

Mr Laurence Gage (40), a widower

His children, Henrietta (15), Edward (12)

His sister, Miss Viola Gage (46)

At Green Lawns:

Mr David Exton (28), a reclusive widower

At Whitfield Villa:

Dr Beasley (54), a physician

His sister, Miss Phyllida Beasley (40)

At St Ann's Parsonage:

Mr Theodore Truman (28), a clergyman

At Bramble Cottage:

Mrs Cokely (84), widow of a previous parson to the parish

Her daughter, Miss Lucy Cokely (44), a milliner

Note: Hi-res versions of maps and family trees are available at my website http://marykingswood.co.uk/

The Saxby Family

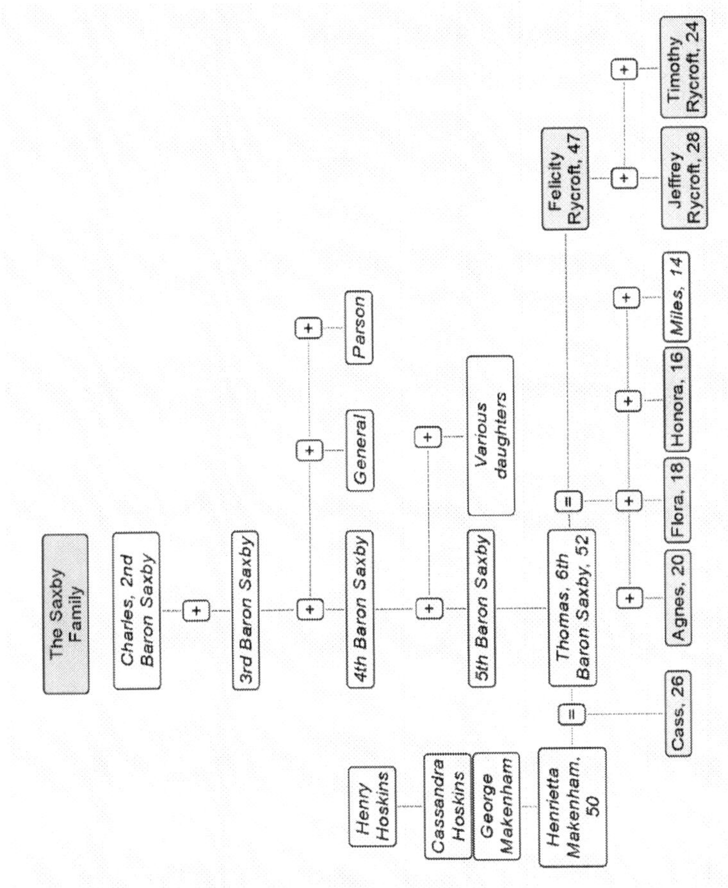

The Gage Family

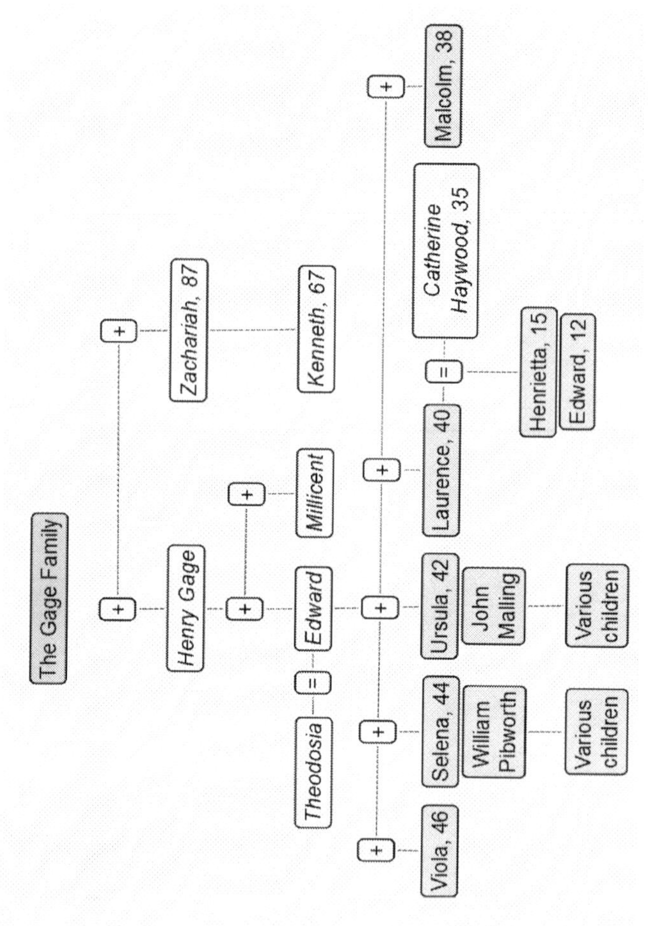

The Middlehope Family

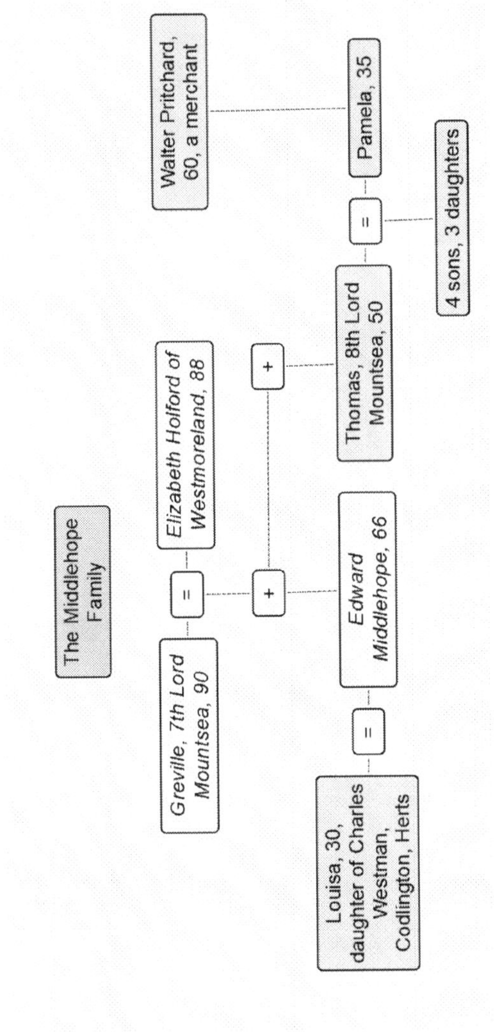

Great Maeswood Map

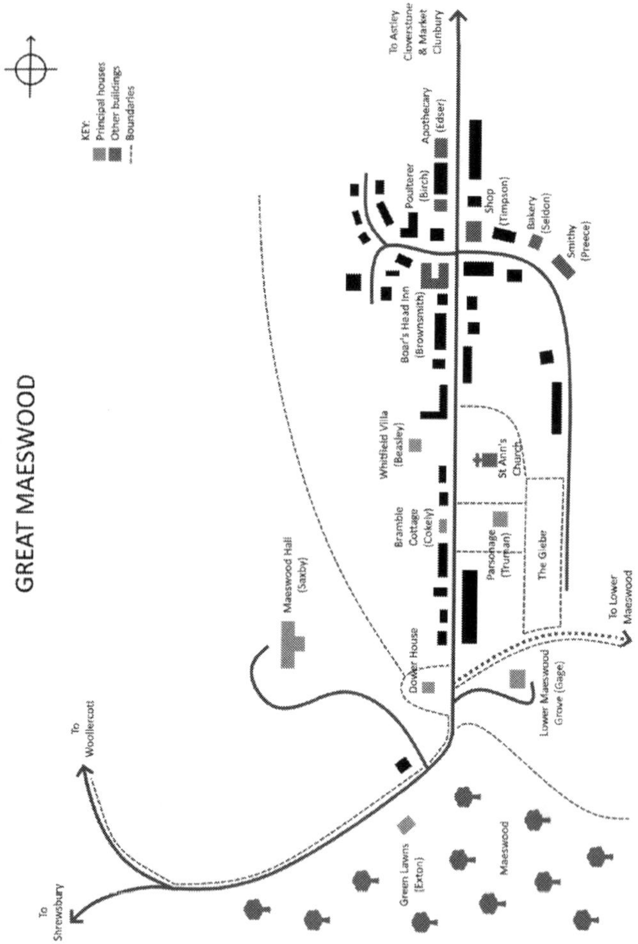

Great Maeswood Environs Map

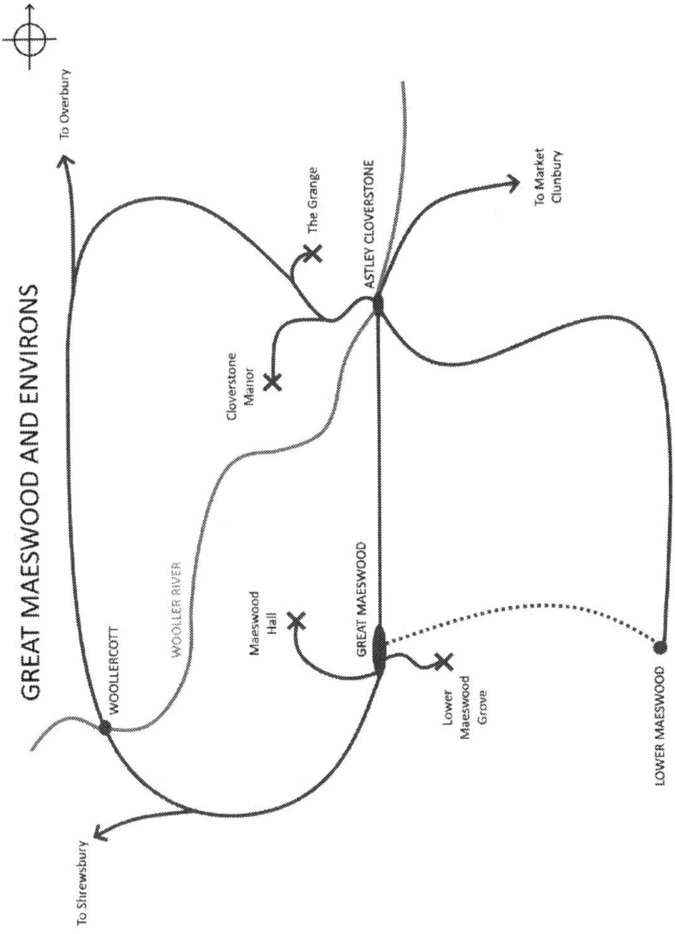

1: The Dower House

MARCH

The post-chaise made a violent turn, throwing the ladies within against the squabs. Louisa gritted her teeth once more, and for about the hundredth time that day wished with all her heart for her comfortable carriage and her faithful, and very gentle, coachman. The chaise made a final lurch before stopping so abruptly that her maid Marie was thrown almost from the seat.

Peering through grimy, rain-spattered windows, Louisa said, "We appear to have arrived."

"Dieu merci!" Marie muttered, through the lavender-scented handkerchief held to her mouth.

"Courage, Marie. No more journeys for a very long time."

Unseen hands turned the outer handle of the chaise door, then rattled it and finally, as if in desperation, heaved it open with a crash. An unknown footman peered in. Hers, Louisa supposed, hired three days before from the agency in Shrewsbury. Well, he looked respectable enough, and he had an umbrella open, so he was not unintelligent.

She stepped down onto a weedy gravel drive, and looked at her new home. "Oh... Palladian. Not bad at all." The classical lines and symmetry, the pedimented door with its fanlight and the arched windows suggested it was no more than fifty years old. "Not the old ruin I was expecting."

"C'est bien petite," Marie said under her breath. *It is very small.*

"Well, yes, it is small, but it is *mine*, Marie. Only mine. Not to be shared with anyone else." *Especially Pamela.* It would do, she thought. It would suit her purposes.

The house looked well-kept, with not a shutter askew or a tile missing, and nothing else amiss that a dab of paint would not fix. The gardens were another matter. Long, desiccated grass stems had been flattened by winter rain, so that the lawns looked like an abandoned hayfield, and beyond were an orchard on one side and a collection of overgrown shrubs on the other, dank and dripping in the drizzle.

Several figures stood awaiting her at the top of the steps. A maid in a neat cap and apron, also from the agency. A man in an atrociously unfashionable coat and buckled shoes — the attorney, she supposed. Crossley. He had said he would meet her here. And two young ladies in black. No idea who they were.

She ascended the steps unhurriedly, so that the footman and his umbrella could keep pace with her.

"Welcome to Great Maeswood, Mrs Middlehope," said the older of the two ladies in black, with a neat little curtsy. "I am Miss Saxby, and this is my sister, Miss Agnes Saxby. We bear greetings from our mother, Lady Saxby, who is indisposed today, but hopes to invite you to dine with us very soon. You know Mr Crossley, I think?"

Louisa reassessed the two ladies. She had not taken much notice of whose dower house she was to inhabit, but clearly these two were from the local big house. The elder was above twenty-five, at a guess, with undistinguished features and a dowdy appearance. The younger, about twenty, was dressed with more opulence but less taste, and was perhaps the plainest girl she had ever seen, poor child.

Nodding politely to the attorney, she said, "Thank you for your diligence, Mr Crossley. Good day to you all, and thank you for your welcome. I would invite you in, but I fear I have nothing in the house to offer you."

"Oh, but there is," said the younger Miss Saxby brightly. "We brought some supplies for you — tea, coffee, sugar, bread, that sort of thing. Oh, and a cherry cake and a lemon cake."

"How very kind of you," Louisa said. "Then I shall be able to offer you tea and cake, but for myself, I think I need brandy after the way the chaise careered through the gates. I brought a bottle with me, and a few other odds and ends, but forgot most of the staples." And wine, she realised. How was she to manage without wine?

"Yes, but do come in," Miss Saxby said. "Mr Crossley has all the keys for you, and then may we show you around? Or would you prefer to be left alone? Travelling is so upsetting to the system, is it not? Mama is always quite overset by it, so we will quite understand if you wish to rest and not be bothered by company."

"Company is never a bother to me," Louisa said firmly, "especially when it comes bearing cake."

The entrance hall was small, and with herself and Marie, Mr Crossley and the two Saxby sisters, not to mention the servants and the boxes now being unloaded from the chaise, it felt uncomfortably crowded. It was the work of a few moments to dispatch Marie upstairs to unpack, the maid downstairs to make tea and Mr Crossley off the premises altogether, his work done once he had surrendered both sets of keys.

"Now, Miss Saxby, Miss Agnes, do give me a tour of the house. It should not take long, I think."

She was quite right. Downstairs there was a parlour, a dining room, a drawing room and a study. Upstairs revealed a large bedroom with a dressing room attached, and two smaller bedrooms. She declined the offer of inspecting either the attics or the basement level, so they returned to the drawing room. Like the rest of the house, it displayed a classical elegance that was very pleasing, and the furnishings, although old-fashioned and a little faded, were of excellent quality. There was a good fire burning, with plenty of the best candles in the sconces, and everything was clean and polished.

While they waited for the manservant to lay out the tea things and the cherry cake, Louisa said, "This is a very pleasant room. I shall call it the saloon, I think. Every house should have a saloon. And a bottle of brandy," she added, spying it already set out on the sideboard, with glasses at the ready. "That will do me more good than tea, I fancy. I had no idea a hired post-chaise could be so uncomfortable."

"Will your own carriage be arriving soon?" Miss Saxby said, taking charge of the tea tray, as Louisa poured herself a generous measure of brandy.

Her own carriage! How she missed it, but she answered gaily, "I shall not need a carriage here, I fancy. I might buy a gig, perhaps. That will do very well."

Miss Saxby said at once, "We have a gig and pony for sale. No longer required."

"Cass—" her sister said, with an anxious glance.

"No longer required," Miss Saxby said firmly.

"That would be most convenient, if we can agree on a price," Louisa said cautiously, detecting undercurrents. "There is no hurry, however. It will be pleasant to drive about in the summer, but it will not be much needed at this time of year. My greatest need is for some more servants — a woman to help with the heavy work and laundry, and a man for the gardens. Have you any suggestions?"

"Mrs Preece's sister will come for the indoor work. You will find her at the smithy on Glebe Lane," Miss Saxby said crisply. "She is a good worker, and reliable. She will do plain needlework, as well — sheets, curtains, nightshirts, that sort of thing. The gardener is more difficult. The experienced ones are snapped up as soon as they become available. You would need to advertise in the Shrewsbury *Chronicle* and see if you can attract an under-gardener looking to move up, unless you are prepared to train one up yourself."

"I should not mind that," Louisa said. "I enjoy nothing better than grubbing about in the earth, so I shall do a great deal of the work myself, but I shall need a man to do the serious digging and scything."

"Oh, in that case, the Timpson twins can help out. Mr Timpson from the shop has a vast brood of youngsters for hire. The twins are only thirteen... no, fourteen, but you pay only one and tuppence a day for the two, and excellent value it is, I assure you. If you want another maid, their sister Tilly is about ready to go into service."

"You are a fount of useful information, Miss Saxby. Just one more question, if you please. Is there an inn nearby where I might obtain a proper meal? For my cook will not be here until next week, and I fear I cannot live on the scraps of food I brought with me and your cherry cake, excellent though it is."

"Oh, you must not eat at the inn!" Miss Saxby cried. "Beth Brownsmith is the world's worst cook." Miss Agnes nodded her head in agreement. "It will do for your servants, but you must dine with us at the Hall. The carriage will collect you at half past five."

~~~~~

Louisa agonised over the choice of gown. Most of her things would come by the carrier whenever her ladyship condescended to organise it. Entirely her own fault, of course, for leaving in such a rush, but as soon as she had received Esther's letter telling her of the Dower House, she had been wild to be gone, to be alone at last, to be *free*. Now she found herself in a quandary, invited to dine at the house of noblewoman Lady Saxby, whose rank would decree a little dressing up, yet the family was in black. Difficult.

She discarded one of her favourite gowns, a deep peach velvet, which seemed too bright a colour for a house of mourning, and the pale green silk was altogether too grand for what she supposed would be a family dinner. Sighing, she allowed Marie to ease her into the dark blue muslin she had worn every evening for a week now.

"Are your quarters satisfactory, Marie?" Louisa said, as the maid laboriously buttoned the back of the gown.

"Pft," was all the response she got.

Louisa laughed, for Marie complained about everything. "Too small, eh?"

"Je ne peux pas respirer, madame." I cannot breathe.

"You will survive. We both will."
~~~~~

"Oui, madame." But she sounded unconvinced.

The carriage was prompt, and deposited her on the doorstep of Maeswood Hall at twenty minutes to six precisely. It was too dark to see much of the exterior, but inside she could see at once that it had been designed by the same sure hand responsible for the Dower House, albeit on a grander scale. From the marble-floored entrance hall, she was led through an inner hall with an elegant double staircase and thence to the saloon, a splendid room worthy of the name. She immediately reduced her own saloon to a mere drawing room.

A woman of middle years rose to greet Louisa as the butler announced her, and despite her age, the remains of great beauty were discernible. She wore her widow's weeds in a fashionably flimsy style, her hair all drooping loose curls, and a fine muslin scarf dangling from her elbows, as if to emphasise her air of delicate fragility.

"Mrs Middlehope," she said unsmilingly. "I am Lady Saxby. Welcome."

"Thank you so much for such unlooked for hospitality," Louisa said, as she made her curtsy. "But I am so glad to be here. This is a lovely house!"

Lady Saxby's face at once lit up. "It is beautiful, is it not? This is the finest room, but the library is much admired, too. Do meet my family, Mrs Middlehope. Cass and Agnes you know already, but this is Flora, and here is my youngest, Honora."

Flora, at least, had benefited from her mother's looks, for she was the beauty of the family, and just as dainty. Louisa felt like a lumbering giant beside her. Honora was not so handsome, but would have been accounted a pretty girl in other company. How unfortunate to have an outstanding diamond in the family, constantly casting her sisters into the shade.

"This is my eldest son, Jeffrey Rycroft," Lady Saxby continued. "His younger brother Timothy is from home just now. He is always from home," she added with a tinkling laugh. "He would always rather be off with his friends doing whatever young men do."

Jeffrey Rycroft, who was a little younger than Louisa herself, looked gentlemanlike enough, and nothing more. The product of Lady Saxby's first marriage, presumably, although she could not quite work it out, since the eldest Miss Saxby looked not much younger than Mr Rycroft. She really should have made more enquiries about the local society before coming here, then she would not be floundering quite so badly. It would be helpful to know who, precisely, was being mourned — Lord Saxby, perhaps? Yet it would be indelicate to ask. She would have to be careful what she said, for it would never do to rampage over the feelings of the recently bereaved.

The meal was excellent, and bespoke a cook almost as accomplished as Louisa's own... no, not her own, *Pamela's* own. Her sister-in-law had inherited the long-fought-for man-cook, just as she had inherited the carriage, the coachman, all the footmen, the well-trained gardeners, her excellent butler and the noble rank that should have been Louisa's. Not that she cared for the title, but she would love to have kept just a few of the servants. Ah well, repining was pointless.

Not surprisingly, Louisa found herself the main topic of conversation. The questions were diplomatically phrased, but she understood what they wanted to know.

"My husband died just over a year ago. He was the eldest son, but we were never blessed with children, so when my father-in-law died last spring, the younger son inherited. They offered me a permanent home at Roseacre, but once my year of mourning was over, I thought it best to move away from Durham."

"Ah yes," Lady Saxby sighed. "That is much for the best. The new mistress will have her own way of doing things, no doubt, and it would be trying for you to see the changes."

That was not the trying part, but Louisa said nothing of that, merely smiling and praising the sauce with which the woodcocks were served, and sighing even more over the loss of her man-cook.

After dinner, the ladies retreated to the saloon again. Lady Saxby and Honora retired to a matching pair of chaises longues, *'to rest a little'*, Lady Saxby said, closing her eyes and settling down more comfortably to snooze. Agnes commandeered the pianoforte, leaving Louisa to the remaining two sisters. Flora was flicking idly through the pages of a journal to find the fashion plates, so it was left to Cass, the eldest, to politely enquire after Louisa's home and family. She was so tempted to say, *'I have no family'*, but that would be too impolite for words. Besides, she was here to forget her losses, after all. So she talked of Roseacre and its multitude of dilapidated and rambling wings, but she could not suppress the sigh of envy as she gazed around the elegantly beautiful saloon.

"Roseacre sounds charming," Cass said. "There is so much history in an older house. I hope you will not miss it too greatly. Are you pleased with the Dower House?"

"Oh yes! Such a cosy little house. I shall be very content there, I am sure. I do love these modern designs. Such lightness and classical simplicity! Such order and regularity, and no danger of going astray and finding oneself in a previously unsuspected wing of the house. Delightful."

With a chuckle, Cass said, "Some would say the Hall is too austere, but it has its charms too. Would you like to see the library?"

She would. They left Flora to her journal, and Cass took a candelabrum and led the way back to the hall and then through a richly appointed room decorated in a deep crimson, to a short corridor. Cass had a pronounced limp, more noticeable this evening, but it would not be polite to enquire what had happened to her.

Cass halted. "I will let you enter first, Mrs Middlehope. You will see why." Then she threw open one of the doors to the library and stood aside for Louisa to enter.

The room was flooded with light. There were deep windows on three sides, and the moon must be full, for it filled the room with a ghostly luminance. And there above the far wall—

Louisa cried out in amazement, for the lunette was filled with colour, a Biblical scene in painted glass that was lit up by the moonlight. "That is astonishing!" she said, as Cass followed her into the room. "How lucky you are to live in a house with such wonders."

Cass grimaced. "Not for much longer, unfortunately. We live from day to day, as we wait for the lawyers to find the new Lord Saxby, who will promptly turn us out of our home."

"So it is your father whom you mourn," Louisa said.

"And my brother, Miles," she said quietly. "A curricle accident, not two months ago. Papa was killed instantly, and Miles... poor Miles lingered for a fortnight."

"My dear, how awful for you all. Your poor mama! And the heir... you do not know who it is?"

"Not the slightest idea. Not a near relation, anyway, for all the uncles and cousins we know of are dead now. The lawyers are going back to the third earl, or even earlier, to find a living male descendant. Mama is certain he will be a disgrace to the family name — a coal miner, or a pie seller, or some such. I think myself he is more likely to be an attorney or a clergyman."

"Yes, very likely," Louisa said. "But what a shock for him! There he will be, stuck in some rural wasteland far from civilisation, struggling to maintain a wife and seven children on a hundred pounds a year, and one day a man in a black suit and a wig will arrive on his doorstep and inform him that he is Lord Saxby, and a rich man, and insist that he must leave his hovel and move into your lovely house. Poor fellow."

"You pity *him?"* Cass said, although she smiled. "We are in worse case, I should have thought."

"No, because you will know how to go on. You will always have a respectable place in society, not just because of your family name, but because you know how to behave. You will be received everywhere, whereas he will be treated with contempt wherever he goes. If he tries to act the great lord, he will be scorned, and if he takes the meat before the soup or prefers ale to claret, he will be mocked. His own servants will bow and *'Yes, my lord'* him, and laugh at him behind his back. Poor fellow, indeed."

"I had not thought of it like that," Cass said slowly. "Yes, he is much to be pitied, whoever he is. Let us hope he may be found quickly so that he can begin to grow accustomed to his new life, and we can begin to grow accustomed to ours. Is it hard, the change from a house like this with a full complement of servants to something much simpler?"

"I cannot tell you," Louisa said with a smile. "I left Roseacre not two weeks ago, stayed a few nights with my friend in Shrewsbury and then — here I am! My first day of something simpler."

"But why here?" Cass said, smiling back in a friendly way. "Great Maeswood is so out of the way, and such a long way from Durham that I cannot imagine what made you choose to settle here."

"No one knows me," Louisa said at once. "I am, if you like, a slate wiped clean, and, perhaps more pertinently, I am free at last of other people's expectations. Consider, Miss Saxby. I spent seventeen years under my father's very careful control. I was married practically from the schoolroom, and spent twelve years bowing to the wishes of my husband and his father, who avoided company. Then there was a year of mourning. I was not at all discontented with my lot, for my path was laid down for me and I knew no other. But now... I am set free, and with only my own wishes to consider, I intend to go out into the world at last and be sociable and *enjoy* life."

"Well," Cass said, eyebrows raised. "Prepare to be gay to dissipation, Mrs Middlehope. On Tuesdays, Miss Gage holds a card party for select friends, with a small glass of sherry on arrival at eight o'clock, whist until eleven, then a cold supper, with a glass of claret. On Thursdays, Miss Beasley returns the compliment, except that we get ratafia to drink and a hot supper with Tokay. Once a month, one or other of the carriage families holds a dinner. And twice a year — do try not to allow your anticipation to overwhelm you — there is an assembly at the Boar's Head, where as many as fourteen or fifteen couples of dairymaids and farm labourers tread on each other's toes. Can you bear the excitement, do you suppose?"

Louisa laughed. "It sounds perfect!"

2: The Widow

"The widow has arrived!"

Laurence looked up from his book. Then, stifling a sigh, he marked his place, closed the book and set it down on the table. When his sister had news of such momentous import, there was no possibility of keeping it for the dinner table.

"Is she old or young?" his daughter Henrietta said, laying down her paintbrush and pushing her sketchpad aside. "Is she very beautiful?"

His son Edward heaved a theatrical sigh. At twelve, the widow was of less interest than the Latin passage he was engaged in translating, but he knew his work would be impossible until the new arrival had been thoroughly discussed.

"Edward, you may take your book next door, if you wish," Laurence said gently.

"It will be freezing in there."

"Well, try the drawing room, and if the fire is not yet lit, you may light it yourself. Tell Skeates I gave you permission."

Edward scooped up an armful of books and papers and writing materials, and trotted out of the room.

"It is not natural, the studying that boy does," Viola said, unfastening her bonnet with nimble fingers. "He will wear himself out."

Laurence smiled, for it was an old argument. "If he enjoys it, there is no harm. You would not have him remain in ignorance of the world, surely, sister?"

"Of the modern world, no, but the ancient Greeks and Romans have been dead for a long time. Henrietta, you have dripped paint on your gown."

"Oh!" She jumped up and dabbed ineffectually at it with a cloth already liberally bespattered with paint.

Viola clucked at her. "Go and find Becky, and get yourself cleaned up. And put that paintbrush somewhere safe."

"May I not hear about the widow?" Henrietta said hopefully. "Papa?"

"You will hear all your aunt's news at dinner. Go along now."

Viola waited until the door had closed behind Henrietta before saying, as she had a thousand times before, "That girl is getting quite wild, Laurence. You spoil her, of course. You spoil both of them, if you want my opinion. It never answers to be too lenient, just because they are motherless. You should marry again so that they would have a proper mother at last. I do my best, but an aunt is not attended to in the same way. But there, they are yours and not mine, so my advice will not weigh with you, I suppose."

"Your advice always weighs with me, Viola, as you well know, but I do not see the faults in them that are so glaring to you. They are children still, and I should like them to remain so for as long as possible."

"Henrietta is fifteen and on the verge of womanhood, Laurence, and how she is to attract a good husband is more than I can tell, when you never stir from your own hearth."

"I am very fond of my hearth, especially with a comfortable chair, plenty of books, my dogs at my feet and a supply of sherry. As for Henrietta, her aunt will bring her out when the time is right, and her godmother will present her at court. Her mother's money will pay the costs and a decent dowry, too, but if she returns home unwed, I shall not be in any way disappointed in her. She may marry for love or not at all, as she pleases, and there is an end to it. Shall I order some tea for you?"

His sister knew better than to argue the point. They disagreed on this, as on most other matters. Viola liked to be busy managing people, and especially children and servants, being quite sure that nothing would get done at all, or at least not properly, if she did not constantly issue reminders. Laurence, on the other hand, was of the opinion that everyone would go along perfectly well without any more than an occasional nudge now and then.

Heaving a reproachful sigh, Viola flopped into a chair. "The tea will be here shortly. I have already suggested to Skeates that you might like some. So..." She settled herself more comfortably into her chair with a wriggle of pure enjoyment. There was nothing Viola liked better than a juicy piece of news. "Let me tell you about the widow. She arrived not an hour since, in a hired post-chaise and pair, and the most disreputable postilion Mrs Timpson had ever seen. Went through the village at a dangerous pace, too, so that all the chickens were a-squawk and one of the

Preece boys was almost run down. Although what he was doing outside the shop I cannot imagine, for he should be making himself useful at home. Mrs Preece is too lax with him by half, if you want my opinion. However, that is nothing to the point. According to Mrs Timpson, there were just two boxes on top and one on the back, but she could not see the widow herself, for the chaise went by so fast. She wore a multitude of feathers on her hat, that much she *could* see."

Laurence was not much interested in feathers. "Has anyone actually seen the lady yet?"

"Well, no, and no one knows much about her, either. The manservant and a maid arrived on Saturday last, and they have been eating at the Boar's Head, but they know nothing. They are from an agency in Shrewsbury, seemingly. All we know is the lady's name, Mrs Middlecott... Middlecombe... no, Middleton, that was it. She has her own maid, but there are no children with her, so she must be an older lady, I suppose. Too old for you, I daresay."

"Or too young, perhaps," he said, smiling at her. "Now, do not be matchmaking, Vi, I beg you. Unless she is as beautiful as an angel and very, very rich, she will not do for me at all. I am very particular as to wives, you know."

"Well, well, Catherine was a paragon in your eyes, we all know that," Viola said indulgently. "You will not find another such, I am sure."

"Certainly not in Great Maeswood," Laurence said equably. "And even if by some astonishing quirk of fate another such should appear, she would hardly be interested in a dull old stick like me. One must not expect two miracles in one lifetime. Ah, there you are, Skeates. I had begun to think you had fallen down the well."

The elderly butler smiled at the familiar sally as he set the tea tray down on the sideboard. He replied, as always, "Not today, sir. Not today."

"What cake have you brought, Skeates?" Viola said.

"Macaroons and lemon cakes, madam."

"No treacle buns? Mr Gage is very partial to treacle buns."

Laurence got to his feet, and the dogs wagged their tails in happy anticipation. "I shall just give the dogs a bit of a run before the light goes."

"Will you not stay for tea? Oh well, I shall just have to drink it myself. It would be a pity to waste it. You will not go far, so late in the day?" She reached for a macaroon as she spoke.

"Not far. I shall see you at dinner. What have you ordered for us today? Something tasty?"

"I have a fine haunch of beef from Mr Vale, and some salmon."

"Excellent, excellent."

The rain had cleared, but the air was still damp and chilly. Laurence did not mind. In some ways, he felt more alive out here, striding about the grounds with the dogs, than he did sitting beside his own fire, despite Viola's words. He could breathe and think and be grateful for all that he had — his house, his children, an income that was... adequate, if no more. And his memories. He had enjoyed seven years of blissful happiness with his wife, and he had thanked God for every one of them. To have known such joy, even for a short time, was more than he deserved, and certainly more than he ever expected to experience again.

The dogs followed their usual evening route, through the shrubbery and then through the gap in the hedge to the lane until they reached the road. They turned at once through the gates onto the drive, but Laurence stopped, gazing across the road at the Dower House. It had not been lived in since he was a boy — getting on for thirty years ago. But now the shutters were open, lights shone out from the windows and smoke rose from the chimneys. The widow had arrived, and the village would be in a bustle for weeks until every scrap of information about her had been gone over and discussed and worried at. And then something else would happen to stir the gossips to action and Mrs Middleton would be forgotten. Poor Mrs Middleton, elderly and alone. He hoped she would like Great Maeswood, and not find it too dull.

Calling the dogs to heel, he turned and made his way home.

~~~~~

Louisa woke early, no doubt because of the unfamiliar bed, or perhaps it was the light that roused her. She was so used to a curtained bed that she had forgotten to draw the window curtains and now the room was filled with the grey light of pre-dawn. Never one to lie abed, she pushed back the covers and went to the window. The view was depressing — a weedy mess where once there must have been a pleasant garden. A few paths were just about visible through the jungle, and she could make out the brick base of what might once have been a glasshouse. An elegant stone wall curved around the perimeter with an intriguing gate set in the centre.

She must explore! At once! Not wanting to rouse Marie, she bundled her hair into an untidy knot, dressed hastily in her gardening gown and travelling pelisse, and sped down the stairs and out through the drawing room door. The garden was an immediate deterrent. From above it had merely looked weedy. Once she had descended the steps to the ravages of a lawn, she could see that the weeds were above her head in places. She
~~~~~

went back inside, through the house and out of the front door, where at least the drive was passable.

The short drive led her to the road, a moderately well-used one, to judge by the width and the copious ruts. The centre of the village must lie to her left and she had no wish to submit herself to the stares of the locals so early in the day, not until Marie had attended to her hair. How vain she was for a widow of thirty years, surely past the age of worrying about her looks. Did women ever stop caring about their looks? Perhaps not. Still, it was always advisable to present one's best face to the world, so she would not go to the village, not yet.

Across the road, however, was a pair of gateposts, each topped with a lion sitting on its haunches, one paw resting on a ball. The words *'LOWER MAESWOOD GROVE'* were engraved on them. Beyond the gateposts, bereft of gates, the drive wound away enticingly between neatly trimmed shrubs, but until she knew the owner, it was best not to venture there. Happily, to one side was a narrow lane, just wide enough for a horseman or a small cart, and that looked perfect for a secluded walk.

She set off at a brisk pace, at first enshrouded in trees and thick hedges on both sides, but after a few minutes gaps in the hedges gave her a view of her surroundings. To one side, the chimneys of the great house were just visible above encircling trees. The chimney stacks suggested a Renaissance style of perhaps two hundred years ago. On the other side was a wide field affording a clear sight of the church and a neat parsonage, and the clustered houses and cottages of the village.

About half an hour further on, roofs and chimneys ahead alerted her to another community, and here she turned back. The clear, cold air and the exercise were invigorating. She had been right, then, to choose a country setting for her new home. It was not, of course, comparable to her own sweet garden and its familiar paths and trees and flowers — specimens she had planted with her own hands and loved almost as dearly as children. But at least she could still enjoy the clear air and open spaces to which she was accustomed. A town home, however practical, would not have suited her nearly as well for her present purpose.

As she passed the field on her return, she saw a man there, engaged in the time-honoured tradition of throwing sticks for his three dogs to return to him. She stopped, leaning on the gate to enjoy the scene. It soon became clear that the man was working his way across the field in her direction, and it was not long before the most energetic of the dogs bounded towards her, scrabbling under the gate to sniff around her feet.

"Well now, my fine fellow, you like my boots, do you?" she said, rubbing his ears gently. "What a handsome chap you are indeed. And here are your brothers to see me, too. Good day to you — to all of you. Well, how friendly you are!"

Their owner arrived moments later, a little out of breath from rushing after them. He was a pleasant-faced man of around forty, and it was impossible to tell his rank from his clothes, for he wore exactly the sort of good quality but worn country clothes that Ned had chosen when he walked the dogs, that she had joked made him look like a gamekeeper.

"I beg your pardon, ma'am. Kenneth, heel, boy. Julian, here boy, at once."

Not a gamekeeper, then. Definitely gentry, by his accent. "Do not apologise, sir. Your pointers have provided me with a wonderfully nostalgic moment, for my husband always had two or three of them about him. This one in particular — Kenneth, is it? Ned had one just like it, exactly that colour. I could almost imagine myself looking at Jupiter now, except that he died... oh, seven or eight years ago now. Lovely dogs, sir. I envy you."

"There is a fellow who breeds them, over Woollercott way. Would you like me to let you know when next there are pups to be had?"

"I should like that very much." A dog! She missed Ned's dogs, which had been banished after his death. She would have a dog... or maybe two. "Dogs are better company than people, very often."

He smiled, so that his eyes lit up with a mischievous twinkle. "Very true," he whispered.

As if at some unseen signal, the dogs suddenly took off across the lane, before disappearing into the grounds of the great house.

The man laughed. "They can probably hear the boy singing in the stables. He only ever sings hymns, and when he gets to *Rock of Ages*, they know it is feeding time."

"What an excellent arrangement," she said, much struck. "It should be employed for humans as well as beasts, I believe. The butler could give a rousing rendition of *Praise to the Lord* when announcing dinner."

"Of course, the choice of hymn might be an indication of the quality of the meal," he said solemnly. "One would be suitably prepared on hearing *Oh God, Our Help In Ages Past.*"

Louisa burst out laughing. "Oh dear! Yes, indeed."

"And now I must join my sister for breakfast, or else I will be eating in the stable yard with the dogs. Enjoy your walk, Mrs Middleton."

With a smile and a wave, he hopped onto the gate, up and over the other side, and would have been gone in a moment. Quickly Louisa cried, "Middle*hope*, but you have the advantage of me, sir. May I not know your name?"

"You will find it out soon enough," he called back, laughing. And then he was gone.

Louisa had no doubt he was right. In such a small village, it would not take her many days to meet everyone of consequence, so she made her way home and tried not to think about the mysterious gentleman with his dogs.

She summoned Marie and allowed herself to be readied to face the world. Today was a day of inspection of her new domain, so she kept on her old, plain gown in case of dust and dirt. There was yet an hour before her usual breakfast time, so she busied herself first with a tour of the nether regions, which were depressingly empty of supplies. There were two bays filled with coal, by the generosity of the Hall, and a few boxes of candles, but no staples like flour, eggs or vegetables, and not so much as a single stray bottle of wine in the large wine cellar. She would have to manage for now with the brandy she had brought with her.

Her inspection was interrupted several times by the arrival of tradesmen hoping for her custom. She took all their names, and the free samples of their wares, and told them she would send orders very soon. Then she breakfasted on tea and the remains of the cherry cake, before settling down in her study — an echoing room containing only a desk, a chair and an empty book case — to begin her lists of essential purchases. Having always lived in well-run houses, she had never before encountered the problem of stocking a house from scratch. It was rather daunting.

The door knocker sounded, followed soon after by the measured tread of William, the footman. Then female voices in the hall. She sighed. Callers, so early in the day! The voices and footsteps disappeared into the drawing room, and a tentative knock on the study door was followed by William's head.

"Sorry, mum. It's a Miss Gage and a Miss Beadley... Beagley... something." He looked at the cards he held in his hand. "Beasley. I put them in the back parlour, if that's all right. Shall I light the fire, mum?"

Louisa smiled, and held out her hands for the cards, scanning them quickly. "What were you before you came to me, William?"

"Under groom at Edgecombe Manor, mum, but Mr Jarrold, what's coachman there, said I were tall enough to go for a footman."

"So you are, and quick enough to learn the job, I am sure. Firstly, I am always *'madam'*, not *'mum'*. Secondly, that room is the drawing room, not the back parlour. Thirdly, always present cards to me on a silver salver... hmm, I shall have to find one of those. And yes, always light the fire if it is cool enough for one. If I have a fire in here or in the dining room, then you should always light a fire for visitors."

"Sorry, mum...madam."

She chuckled. "You will get the hang of it, William. Now then, stand up straight, shoulders back... ah, much better. Always remember that you are a footman now, and not an under groom any longer. So lead the way to the *drawing room*, and open the door for me."

Two ladies of middle years awaited her. Miss Gage was a spare woman nearer to fifty than forty, dressed in a severe style with no concession to fashion or, it had to be confessed, to good taste. Miss Beasley was a few years younger, her gown well-worn, but its outdated style partially concealed by feminine little frills. She had an anxious air and said little, beyond echoing her friend's greetings.

Miss Gage explained at some length about the contents of the basket they had brought — apples, some bottled plums, sugared almonds and preserves, but no wine — and then said, "Now, Mrs Middlecombe... Middleton, since—"

"Middlehope," Louisa said, smiling. "It is an awkward name, and often confused, but it is *'hope'* rather than *'combe'* or *'ton'* or *'wich'*. I am often addressed as Middlewich, for some reason, but that is a town in Cheshire, not me."

"Ah. I beg your pardon. Now then, I understand your cook will not arrive until next week — when do you expect her?"

"Monday, I hope."

"Monday. Excellent. We have drawn up a rota, you see. You were at the Hall last night, and tonight you will dine with my brother and me at the Grove, and if you wish you may stay for the card party afterwards, but everyone will understand if such occasions are a little tame for you."

That was busy, to be organising on her behalf, as if she could not survive on bread and cheese for a week. Bother, she had forgotten to bring any cheese. She had forgotten a great many things, and now she was dependent on the charity of her neighbours. How galling. "I should be delighted," she said politely. "I enjoy card games of all varieties." A card party... was this one of the card parties Miss Saxby had mentioned? Miss Gage... sherry and a cold supper, she recalled.

"Oh! Oh, how delightful!" Miss Gage trilled. "We might manage four tables, if all our regulars come. How splendid! And then on Wednesday you will dine with the Andersons, Thursday with Phyllida and her brother. He is the physician, you know." Louisa thought rapidly — Miss Beasley... ratafia and a hot supper. "Friday is with the Drinkwaters, although you will not get a good meal there, I warn you now. Mrs Drinkwater tries to economise with meat, but that never answers. Then on Saturday it will be Lady Saxby at the Hall again, unless the squire steps in, but he rarely entertains at this time of year. And so on. We will make sure you are well taken care of until your cook arrives."

"How very kind you are," Louisa said. "I cannot express my gratitude. So tonight I shall be with you and your brother. How charming! I look forward to meeting him."

"Oh, but you have met him already," she chirped. "He told me he encountered you this morning while he had the dogs out on the Glebe. Yes, you already know my brother Laurence."

Laurence Gage. It had taken precisely three hours to put a name to the man with the dogs.

3: The Wine Cellar

Laurence had not thought much about the widow since the unexpected meeting that morning, except to be amused that she was not elderly and stout, as he had imagined. It had taken no great perception to work out who she was. Every coming and going in the village was known to Viola and reported over the dinner table at the Grove, and the unknown lady out walking could be no other.

Viola had been quite cross with him for meeting her before she had, and he had endured an uncomfortable half hour over breakfast while she enquired with minute attention to detail into every circumstance of the meeting. Laurence could tell her nothing to the point, except that Mrs Middlehope was ladylike, around thirty years of age and well dressed.

"Well dressed? What does that mean? Expensive? Fashionable? Elegant?"

Laurence pondered that with a frown. "No," he said eventually.

Viola gave a huff of annoyance. "And is she beautiful or plain?"

Another long pause to consider the point dispassionately. "Neither. Just... ordinary."

"But respectable?"

"How can one tell?"

"Really, Laurence! I see I shall have to wait until I meet her for myself."

"Much the best plan, my dear," he said equably, turning back to the book he had propped open on the table.

Naturally, Viola bustled off straight after breakfast to discover what she could about the newcomer, to share her disapprobation of Laurence's lack of information and to visit the lady herself. Her report when she returned was not entirely favourable.

"Her footman is a bumbling yokel, and she did not seem at all pleased at the trouble to which we have gone to take care of her while she settles in."

"She displayed no gratitude?" Laurence said, surprised.

"Oh... well... she *said* she was grateful, but only in the mildest terms. I thought she would be more... effusive. But she seems to be respectable enough."

"How can one tell?" he said, just as he had before. It was a mystery to him how ladies could divine each other's characters at a glance.

"One just knows. Mind you, one can never be too careful with widows. She did not mention her husband to you, I suppose?"

"Only that he liked dogs, so he must have been a sound fellow. What did you think of her person? Fashionable? Elegant? Beautiful?"

"She is nothing special," she said with a sniff. "Quite dowdy, I thought her. Nothing like dear Catherine."

He smiled. "Then we are in agreement. An ordinary woman."

~~~~~

As soon as Mrs Middlehope entered the drawing room that evening he saw his mistake. She was not in the least ordinary, or dowdy either. Unlike her rather down-at-heel appearance that morning, everything about her now spoke of expensive good taste, from the long silk shawl to her delicately embroidered slippers. A velvet gown the colour of ripe peaches draped over an admirably womanly figure, and neat curls framed a face that now seemed so far from ordinary that he felt his eyebrows lift in surprise.

"We meet again, Mr Gage," she said with an amused smile, her dark eyes twinkling merrily at his discomfiture.

"Indeed," he said, momentarily almost lost for words.

"You look very different, dressed for the evening," she said, chuckling. "I wondered if you were the gamekeeper when I first saw you, but now I see that you are indeed a gentleman. My husband was exactly so."

"Ah..." he said, wondering how on earth he was supposed to respond to such an opening. He could hardly tell her that she, too, had looked rather shabby on her morning walk.

With a laugh, she made the point herself. "And so am I — oldest clothes for walking in the mud, and save the finery for evening." Without waiting for an answer, she turned to the children, waiting patiently to be introduced. "And who have we here?"
~~~~~

"Oh... my daughter, Henrietta. She is fifteen, and Edward here is twelve."

"I am pleased to make your acquaintance, Miss Gage, Master Gage," she said gravely, as the children made their courtesies. Turning to Laurence, she said, "Is Mrs Gage here at present?"

"My wife died nine years ago," Mr Gage said, assailed by the familiar wash of grief, still just as sharp as ever. That pain would never leave him.

Before their guest could say anything, Viola said hastily, "You do not mind if we dine *en famille*, Mrs Middleton... Middlecombe? Only we have no tutor or governess just now, and Laurence does not like the children to eat with the servants. It is an indulgence, of course, but—" She broke off with a slight shrug and a glance in Laurence's direction, as if to say, *'You see how it is — their father spoils them'.*

"Middle*hope*, and I have always felt that children should be with their family as much as is possible. Tutors and governesses are not at all the same, are they?" Mrs Middlehope said, with a smile at the two. "Do you have your lessons at home, or is there a school nearby?"

It was Henrietta who answered. "Papa teaches Edward, because he is too clever for school."

"Gracious!" Mrs Middlehope said gently. "I have never met a boy who was too clever for school before."

"He speaks four languages," Henrietta said proudly. "Latin, Greek, Italian and French. All the men in the family are pol... poly..."

"Polyglots," Edward said.

"That is very clever indeed," Mrs Middlehope said. "And what about you? I daresay you are too old for lessons now."

"Oh no, Papa says that ladies must have informed minds, so I study history and geography and philosophy and literature with him, and Aunt Viola is trying to teach me the accomplishments of a lady."

Laurence had to smother a laugh.

Viola, who firmly believed that children should be silent except when reciting their prayers, said sharply, "Trying is very much the appropriate word. How many times have I told you not to monopolise the conversation, Henrietta?"

"Oh, but the fault is mine, for I asked the questions," Mrs Middlehope said mildly. "What a lovely house you live in. Is it Jacobean?"

The discussion of the Grove occupied them until dinner and through most of the first course. Laurence was seated beside their guest, who had Edward on her other side, separating her from conversation with Viola. He knew that it fell to him, therefore, to talk to her. That was difficult, for the question uppermost in his mind, what an exotic flower like Mrs Middlehope was doing in sleepy Great Maeswood, was not one which could be asked directly.

"You are from Durham, I understand, Mrs Middlehope?" he said.

"My husband's family lives near that city, but my father's estate was in Hertfordshire."

"Was?"

"He has been dead for more than ten years. Some cousins inherited, but I have not been back there since I married."

"Do you not miss it?" Laurence said gently. "When you have grown up in a place, the roots can be very deep and it can be a wrench to leave behind the familiar sights and sounds. I came to the Grove every summer as a child, moved here when I was ten years old and cannot now imagine living anywhere else."

"For you, perhaps, such an attachment was possible. No doubt your own son will grow just as attached to his home, and be just as reluctant to leave it. For a daughter, though, putting down roots and developing a deep attachment to any place is a dangerous undertaking. One grows up knowing that one will eventually marry and move away. Fortunately for me, my father did not inherit until I was twelve years of age, and we had lived in three different houses before that, so I never put down any roots. Since the estate was entailed in the male line, I had no expectation of continuing to live there. Mr Gage, this is an excellent claret. Do you have a local vintner? My wine cellar is entirely empty and I should very much like to fill it with wine of this quality. My father-in-law kept an excellent cellar which I greatly miss."

"Ah, now, this is one that was laid down some years ago. I obtain my supplies from a man in Bristol, and although his standards are very high, there is no guarantee of anything quite like this. I shall let you have his latest list."

"Thank you! I should be most grateful. It is not an easy thing, I find, to start up a household from nothing, when every store cupboard, every still room shelf, is empty. It is excessively disheartening."

"We cannot have you disheartened, Mrs Middlehope," he said gently. "I believe Timpson's shop provides most essential foodstuffs, Birch's will supply poultry, meat comes from one or other of the farms and everything else may be had in Market

Clunbury, which is only a few miles away. Or Shrewsbury, for larger purchases."

"It will suit me better to obtain the necessities from local sources, if I can," she said. "Except for wine. Your Bristol vintner will deliver to me, I take it? I shall not be obliged to travel to Bristol?"

Laurence confirmed it, although her aversion to travelling, even for shopping, struck him as unusual in such a stylish lady, whose fashionable gown had the distinctive aura of London about it.

The rest of the evening passed off pleasantly, as usual. They had fourteen for cards, which made up two whist tables and one of loo. There was some masculine jockeying for the places of honour on Mrs Middlehope's table, to Laurence's amusement. It was not surprising that such an attractive widow should draw some attention, for Great Maeswood was unused to women of her sophistication. Laurence himself could admire the lady's charms without being tempted by them.

The women were not pleased. Viola had not shown overt disapproval of the peach velvet gown with its generous *décolleté,* but her pursed lips now were a sign that Mrs Middlehope's respectability ranking had taken a tumble since dinner. Perhaps she had discovered some disreputable aspect of the widow's history while Laurence and Edward had been having their Greek conversation over the port.

It was not until the end of the evening that Laurence had another chance to speak to Mrs Middlehope. Everyone was gathered in the hall making their farewells, but she stood a little apart, gazing up at Catherine's portrait.

"Your wife?" she said. "She is lovely. I see the resemblance to your daughter."

"Yes, Henrietta has something of her mother's looks and temperament, but she will never rival her. No one could, for Catherine was perfect."

"No one is perfect, Mr Gage," she said, her expression one of amusement.

"My wife was," he said firmly.

"Then I am glad of it, for her sake and for yours, but for myself, I far prefer humanity as it mostly is, a swirling mass of quirks and foibles. There is far more of interest in the imperfect, to my mind."

Laurence could not disagree openly, so he smiled and said nothing.

~~~~~

Louisa felt rather beleaguered. She had expected to slink into her little house almost unnoticed and have time to settle in before invitations arrived. This deluge of open-handed hospitality was more than she had anticipated or wanted. She was not at all prepared for it, with little in the house to offer visitors and almost all her good clothes not yet arrived.

On the morning after the Gages' card evening, she walked briskly around the village, looking in at the various shops to surreptitiously inspect the cleanliness of the premises and the freshness of the goods, and, when she had satisfied herself on these points, to assure the shopkeepers of her custom. She quickly came to terms with Mr Timpson to employ his twin sons as gardeners, and agreed to take on his daughter as a maid. At the smithy, she acquired the services of Mrs Preece's sister on two days a week to help with laundry and other heavy indoor work.
~~~~~

Her final visit was to the apothecary to make some trifling purchase, where she found Mr Edser to be a sensible man, tidy in his shopkeeping, and honest enough to point out that the village also boasted a physician.

"Well, as much surgeon as physician — Dr Beasley will do whatever needs to be done, and has been so kind as to share much of his expertise with my humble self," Mr Edser said. "Between us, we cater for all needs in the way of illness or injury. And death, too, when circumstances require it. Dr Beasley is the coroner for these parts and is most skilled at... at..." He tailed off, perhaps realising belatedly that the subject of dead bodies was hardly fit for discussion with a lady.

"Post mortem examination, do you mean?" Louisa said, unruffled. "I have always thought that must be a fascinating field of study. To be able to dissect the human form after death and say, *'Aha! The heart was defective all the time, and the poor fellow might have dropped at any moment'* is a great skill, and a comfort to the bereaved."

"Yes, indeed, madam," Mr Edser said, eyeing her warily.

"When my husband died, it was a relief to know that it was the result of a long-standing heart defect. My father-in-law was about to dismiss the cook for poisoning him."

Mr Edser's eyes widened and Louisa thought it best to say no more on the subject. Poor Ned! He had eaten a hearty dinner, as always, but he had complained that the tongue tasted a little odd. When he simply fell from his chair later that evening, poison had seemed a very likely cause.

"You dined at the Hall on Monday, I understand, madam," Mr Edser said, with a sudden burst of garrulity. "How were the young ladies? And her ladyship, of course. Bearing up nobly in their grief, I expect."

Bearing up... yes, there had been no sign of excessive grief. "They were as well as might be expected under the circumstances," Louisa said diplomatically.

"Did they give any hint as to when they might emerge from seclusion? We miss their smiling faces around the village... we miss them something fierce. Always so cheerful, the Miss Saxbys. Especially Miss Agnes... was she well, Miss Agnes?" His face was eager... too eager.

"She was very well," Louisa said, rather amused at such obvious yearning. An apothecary was ambitious indeed if he dared to lift his eyes to the daughter of a baron. Which was Miss Agnes? The plain one, she rather thought. In which case... but no. Still too unequal.

She returned to the Dower House with the virtuous feeling of having accomplished a great deal. She breakfasted on fresh buns from Mr Seldon's bakery, and then settled down in the study to work on her list of store cupboard essentials. How she wished she had not left Roseacre so abruptly! If only she had taken a little time to consider, she might have compiled a list of staples from the Roseacre household accounts, instead of struggling to remember what might be needed, and with no cook to help with the task. She might even have brought some things with her, instead of scrambling together a box at Esther's. The new maid would be running back and forth to the shop twice a day for lemons or nutmeg or— nutmeg! Quickly she added it to the list.

The door knocker sounded. She listened for William's heavy tread ascending the stairs to answer it, but there was only silence. Probably he was busy in the coal cellar and could not hear. Laying down her pen, she went to the front door herself.

Mr Gage's smiling face peered in at her, doffing his hat with a bow. "Why, good day to you, Mrs Middlehope. I am bound on a mission of mercy — rescuing a damsel in distress."

"Am I in distress, Mr Gage?"

"Certainly you are, for you told me your wine cellar is completely empty. That is a crisis of the first order, I am sure you will agree. And so here I am as... well, not quite a knight in armour, and I seem to have inadvertently mislaid my white charger, but as the bearer of gifts. At least, John here is the bearer."

Louisa now noticed the footman, almost hidden by an overgrown rose bush, struggling under the weight of a wooden box.

"You have brought wine?" she gasped, in disbelief. "Come in! Come in at once. Oh, Mr Gage, you are a prince among men, although the lack of a white charger is a trifle disappointing."

The smile widened. "Shall we take these straight to your wine cellar and bestow them safely?"

She could only nod, chuckling with merriment. Wine! And, she devoutly hoped, of a similar quality to last night's. Pausing only to fetch her keys from the study, she led the two men down the stairs to the servants' quarters and along the passage to the butler's room. It was all ready for her non-existent butler, with a curtained bed area, a cupboard, table and two chairs, and a high window. The small fireplace had a fire laid but not lit. Along the wall were two latticed iron doors which protected the silver store and the wine cellar.

Lighting a couple of candles, Louisa began trying keys in the lock of the wine cellar door. "I have not even bothered going in here," she admitted. "I could see at a glance that the shelves were quite empty. Ah, there we are."

She threw open the door and they all went inside. The footman set his burden down carefully on the floor.

"Well, plenty of room in here," Mr Gage said. "You even have a locked bay at the end there for your special purchases."

Another lattice-work door filled the far end of the little room. Louisa held candle up and peered through. "There is a pile of old sacking in it," she said. She tried her keys again but none of them opened it. "I shall have to get a locksmith to open it before it can be cleaned out. I hope I shall have something special to put in there before too long."

"Nothing I have brought today is quite special enough for such precautions," Mr Gage said. "I may be able to provide a locksmith, however. John, what do you think?"

The footman peered at the lock, and then at the outer lock. "Looks much the same as this one, so I should be able to open it, sir. I'll need my tools, though."

"Off you go and get them, then. Well, where do you want these, Mrs Middlehope?"

"Where I can reach them," she said promptly, picking a bottle from the case. "I brought a tolerable brandy with me, but this will be much better. Is it all drinkable now? What would you recommend for, say, right this minute?"

"This one," he said, laughing. "A good solid claret, nothing fancy."

"Excellent." She rummaged in drawers in the butler's room until she found a corkscrew. "Here you are. Do the honours, will you, and light the fire while I fetch glasses."

And so they sat either side of the little fire, sipping rather good claret and discussing his vintner's list, which he had brought with him. Louisa had not enjoyed an hour so much since Ned had died.

Eventually John returned with a fearsome array of oddly-shaped metal devices and began poking about in the lock for the further door. At last, with a satisfying clunk, he swung it open.

"There you are, madam. Should you like me to pick up a new lock for it next time I'm in Market Clunbury?"

"Yes, if you please. What a versatile fellow you are, John, but I am not sure I should want a footman with the ability to pick locks. How are you with safes?"

"Can't pick a safe lock, madam. Not a decent safe, anyways. These ordinary locks are much easier."

Mr Gage dispatched John back to the Grove with the empty box, but he sat on, talking quite easily about wine and Great Maeswood and footmen and life in general, until somehow most of the bottle was gone. It was very pleasant, and Louisa began to wonder if she had found what she was looking for.

Eventually, with obvious reluctance, he said, "I suppose I had better get back. Edward will be waiting for his Latin lesson."

"Will he be running around breaking things? Boys are prone to that if left unattended, so I am told."

"If I fail to set his Latin text for the day, he will simply find some Greek to read, or French, or Italian," he said cheerfully. "He is not the sort to run around unless ordered to. Oops!"

On rising, he joggled the table, setting the candle wobbling. He caught it in time, but the wavering light caught a flash of something bright in the shadows deep in the wine cellar, something that was out of place in a pile of sacking. Louisa picked up the candle and walked into the wine cellar and then into the bay at the far end, holding the light before her.

"This is not sacking," she said. "It looks like... it could almost be a cloak, the old fashioned kind secured by buttons and a loop of chain at the neck. Old clothes, but what an odd place to put them."

With one hesitant foot, she lifted a corner of the cloak, then gasped and almost dropped the candle.

"Whatever is it?" Mr Gage said.

"It is a person," she said, her voice not quite steady. "A body. It has been here for some considerable time."

4: *The Body In The Basement*

Laurence had to admit that Mrs Middlehope was the most imperturbable female he had ever met. Not for her the screams or vapours or swooning that would have afflicted most women. Instead, after a single sharp intake of breath, she walked out of the inner wine cellar, held the candle out to him and said calmly, "Have a look. Quite skeletal, I should say. A woman, probably, to judge by the quantity of hair remaining."

He went in, bending down to look more closely. The cloak, if that was what it was, was stiff with age, and beneath it was some kind of fabric — the woman's gown, which might have been brightly coloured once, and quite a volume of it. Beneath one corner was a skeletal face, surrounded by wisps of brittle hair. Lifting the opposite corner of the cloak revealed a pair of shoes of a kind his mother had often worn — embroidered, with a low heel and a silver buckle, a style quite gone out of fashion.

"Yes, she has been here for some years. Decades, most likely."

"Whom should we inform?" she said.

How composed she was, and how practical! He admired that. "Dr Beasley, first, as coroner, and Squire Winslade, as magistrate. They will determine whether there is anything further to be done. But I imagine the first task will be to identify the poor woman."

"Someone will have an idea," she said. "A maid who disappeared, perhaps. It is highly unlikely that a stranger stepped off the stage coach, broke into the house, somehow or other, entered a doubly locked wine cellar and then simply lay down and died."

Laurence frowned. "That is a good point. The wine cellar was locked. She was locked in here, by someone. A body in a ditch or in a disused barn could be any itinerant, but this looks more sinister." He picked up the nearly-empty bottle and pulled a rueful face. "Good Heavens, Mrs Middlehope, here we are, half foxed and it is not yet noon." He chuckled. "Whatever will people say?"

"They will say, quite correctly, that you have excellent taste in wine, and that I am a bad influence on you," she said, and the merriment in her expression caused him to burst out laughing. Or perhaps that was just the wine.

After locking up the wine cellar again in case the servants should wander in there, they returned upstairs with the remains of the wine. The hall was unexpectedly crowded. Viola was there with Miss Beasley, and William and another footman appeared to be conducting an argument on the doorstep.

"What a pleasant surprise," Mrs Middlehope said with a calm smile, as if nothing untoward had occurred and she had not just discovered a long-dead body in the basement. "Do come into the drawing room, Miss Gage. Miss Beasley, do you go through too. William, some refreshments for our guests, if you please. Tea and the currant buns."

Miss Beasley followed her into the drawing room, and the footman, having shut the door on his counterpart, disappeared into the nether regions. Laurence found himself alone with Viola in the hall.

"What are you about?" she hissed. "What were you doing downstairs with... with *her?"*

Laurence raised his wine glass with a broad smile. "Can you not guess? I brought some wine for Mrs Middlehope's cellar and she wished to sample it."

"You left the house almost two hours ago. Have you been drinking the whole time?"

"I imagine so. Until we discovered the dead body, that is."

"Laurence Gage, you are *drunk!"*

"No, no. Perfectly... perfectly *not* drunk, actually. But Vi, I have to—"

"I thought you had more sense! To be falling into the toils of a woman like that, and at your age, too. You know what sort of woman she is, I trust?"

He took a sip of wine, then said pleasantly, "No, what sort of woman is she?"

She looked taken aback. "Well... that is the point, we have not the slightest idea, yet here you are, not two days after she arrived, drinking with her before noon and falling under her spell."

"No danger of that. She is a very pleasant woman who appreciates a good claret, that is all. But I have no time for this,

Vi. Go and pay your call. I have to send for Beasley and Winslade."

"Whatever for?"

"To see about this body, of course."

Viola frowned, taken aback. "There truly is a body, then? Whose? And how did he die... or she?"

"That is a complete mystery at the moment. Accident... murder... a poisonous asp... who knows? That is why I need to send for Beasley and Winslade. There will be an inquest and all sorts of unpleasantness."

"Murder? Do you mean there might be a murderer about? How can you be so calm, when we might all be murdered in our beds! Is it quite certain that this person is dead? Might he yet be saved? Beasley is very good at— Laurence, stop laughing at once! This is serious!"

He tossed back the last drops of wine in his glass. "She is well beyond saving, my dear, and has been for many years. Go and eat currant buns and ask Mrs Middlehope to tell you all about it, and tell her, if you please, that I have gone to Beasley's house, and will send word to Winslade. I shall be back directly."

~~~~~

Louisa's life had veered about rather violently of late. From the endless irritations of Roseacre, she had found herself in the stultifying boredom of her friend Esther's house in Shrewsbury. Whatever had possessed her friend to marry such a drainingly pious man as Joseph Deerham was beyond her imagination. Then her planned solitude at the Dower House had been overwhelmed by unsolicited kindness. And now there was a body in her wine cellar. It was dizzying.
~~~~~

She sat in the drawing room awaiting the tea and currant buns, making polite conversation with Miss Beasley, who murmured almost inaudible replies, clutching her reticule tightly, and looking as if she had rather be far away.

When Miss Gage came in, her lips were pursed in disapproval and Louisa guessed that she now knew of the body in the basement. "Come, Phyllida. Your pardon, Mrs Middleton...Middlecroft, but I am afraid that we cannot stay after all."

"Not even for tea and currant buns?" Louisa enquired sweetly, giving up all attempts to correct the name.

"No. Something has occurred... we are having some difficulty with the arrangements we made... the rota for dinners. Most unfortunate. Oh, and Laurence asked me to tell you that he has gone himself to Dr Beasley. About the *body*," she added, oozing disapproval. "Come, Phyllida."

Miss Beasley muttered, "So sorry," and scuttled after her friend, who almost bumped into William bringing the long-awaited tea and buns. He stood gazing after them uncertainly.

"Go and show them out, William," Louisa said calmly. "Yes, put the tray down there."

She was left alone with the tea and currant buns. There was still a half-full glass of wine in one hand and the bottle in the other, she discovered, so she took them through to the study. Then, feeling this to be inadequate to the circumstances, returned for the brandy decanter. The currant buns called to her rather loudly, so she took those, too. Thus fortified, she worked industriously at her lists until Mr Gage returned with Dr Beasley in tow.

Dr Beasley was a spare man in that uncertain age between fifty and sixty, who reminded her a little of Ned. Greying and slightly stooped, but not yet infirm. He greeted her with great enthusiasm — *'You have a body for me, I understand, Mrs Middlehope. Excellent! Excellent!'* — practically rubbing his hands with glee. Louisa left them to their work, having no desire to see Dr Beasley's investigation of the body, which would, she was tolerably certain, be deeply unsettling to watch.

She still had wine left in Mr Gage's bottle as well as several currant buns, so she brought cushions from the drawing room and settled herself comfortably on the window seat, nibbling and sipping, and pondering the strange turn her life had taken. She had just finished the last currant bun when the door knocker sounded again. This time William's slow tread was heard in the hall. Voices, one of them female, then William's apologetic head peered round the door.

"Begging your pardon, madam, but there's a lady outside with a gig."

"I see. Is she coming in? Does she need someone to hold the horse while she visits?"

"No, madam. She wants you to look at it."

"At the horse? Oh, a *gig.* She must be from the Hall."

William blinked at this apparent *non sequitur*, making Louisa laugh. In all the excitement, she had almost forgotten that there was an unwanted gig at the Hall. It was Miss Saxby herself driving a neat little equipage with a sturdy pony in harness.

"How very kind of you!" Louisa cried. "And what a charming little rig. How can you bear to part with it?"

She waited, watching carefully, for it seemed to her that there was something about the gig that she had not grasped. It seemed as if Miss Agnes had been dismayed by the offer to sell it.

Miss Saxby seemed unconcerned. "We have no need for it, and it might as well be used."

"Well then, it will suit me admirably." She rubbed the pony's nose gently. "I have no feed or hay for this little fellow just at present."

"That is no problem at all," Miss Saxby said. "I can bring all you will need to start with, but... do you have a groom?"

"Oh yes. William here will do all that is necessary."

"Excellent," Miss Saxby said. "How are you settling in, Mrs Middlehope?"

"Quite well, I had thought, until I discovered a body in the wine cellar."

Miss Saxby gave a squeak of astonishment. "A *body?* Goodness!"

"A woman," Louisa said. "She has clearly been there for a long time. I wonder if anyone from the village disappeared years ago?"

"I will ask at the Hall," Miss Saxby said. "Mags, our old nurse, has been here for ever. If anyone vanished, she would know."

After agreeing to return the following day with the gig and some supplies for the pony, she drove off again, leaving Louisa amused to consider that the animal would be better provided for than she was. But at least she had wine now!

"William," she said, as they returned to the house, "what was that altercation on the doorstep earlier? Another footman, although I did not recognise the livery."

He went bright red. "Oh, I forgot! He left you this, madam." He fished in a pocket and brought out a small folded letter addressed in a lady's elegant hand.

She broke the wafer and scanned the contents.

'Galtre House, Tuesday. My dear Mrs ~~Middlecombe~~ Middlecross, I regret to inform you that owing to a prior engagement, we shall not be able to entertain you to dinner this evening. Pray accept my apologies for the inconvenience. Jane Anderson'

She laughed, but said, "A letter would not put you so out of countenance. What did the Andersons' footman say to so upset you?"

"Oh... it was all nonsense, madam. I took no notice, but if he says it again, I'll draw his cork, I swear it!"

"No need for that, William. Most undignified, to be brawling on the front step. If any such insult should occur again, lofty disdain is by far the best response, and then shut the door in his face."

"Lofty disdain... shut the door... certainly, madam."

His expression was so fierce that Louisa burst out laughing as soon as he had gone. She was still laughing when Mr Gage and Dr Beasley emerged from the service stair.

"Dear lady, are you all right?" Dr Beasley said.

"Perfectly, I assure you. And what are your thoughts on my unexpected visitor, Dr Beasley?"

"Unexpected and unwanted, eh?" He beamed at her, thumbs resting in the pockets of his waistcoat. "Too soon to say, except that she appears to be quite a young woman — or was, twenty or thirty years ago. And locked in there all that time! Fascinating, quite fascinating. I shall need to do quite a lot more work to determine how this poor girl died, and perhaps discover enough to identify her. Your butler's room would be an ideal place to conduct a more thorough examination... a medical examination, if you understand me. There is light and a table, and the air is both cool and dry. May I, therefore, trespass on your good nature a little further, madam? Will you permit me to leave the young lady where she is for tonight? I shall return tomorrow with all my equipment and take my time to do a thorough investigation. But if it would distress you—"

"No, certainly not. The lady is dead, and cannot hurt anyone. I have only a very small staff, so it will not incommode anyone in the slightest. Have you locked her into her prison again?"

He affirmed it, arranged for her to send the squire to see him if he should arrive and the two men departed, leaving Louisa to her lists, and the tricky problem of how to arrange dinner without any food in the house. For herself, she would not have minded, for there was plenty of wine now, and she thought there might still be currant buns in the kitchen, but she could not live on currant buns for a week and the inn with the world's worst cook was not appealing.

She went downstairs and summoned her French maid, Marie, her Shrewsbury acquisitions, William and Sarah, and twelve-year-old Tilly Timpson, so newly arrived from her father's shop that she still wore her cloak.

"We have a difficulty," Louisa told them. "We shall have to provide our own dinners until Mrs Nokes arrives on Monday. Do we have any meat in the house?"

"Mr Vale sent over a box of things — some cutlets, sausages, a ham, an ox tongue," Sarah said. "Nothing for the spit, but I can griddle the cutlets and sausages."

"That is a start. Any vegetables?"

"Carrots and tatoes, mam."

"Well, we ought to be able to make something with those and the ham… a soup, or some such," Louisa said optimistically. "The ox tongue… Marie, you are French, you must know how to run up a ragoût."

"Moi? Mais non, madame! Je comprends les vêtements mais pas la cuisine. C'est quoi, un ragoût?" I understand clothes but not cooking. What is a ragoût?

"I can cook a bit, mam," Tilly said. "If I can run home and ask Ma if I can borrow Leah — she's my oldest sister — she can give me a hand. I can mebbe pick up a few things from the shop, too, if you like."

"Excellent girl! Yes, please."

It was, perhaps, the oddest dinner Louisa had ever had. She sat in state in her dining room, at the head of a table long enough to seat twenty people, eating the strange assortment of dishes her servants and Tilly's sister had managed to concoct. The soup was rather good, the cutlets came in a tasty sauce with dumplings, and there was an apple pie, but naturally there was no fish and little fresh meat or vegetables. She kept paper and pencil beside her as she ate, to jot down notes of all the omissions. At least there was wine, and Tilly had provided both cheese and nuts from the shop. It was a dinner, of sorts, and she was in her own house and would now, it seemed, be able to pursue her objectives discreetly without undue attention from the locals.

Apart from the small matter of a body in her wine cellar, of course.

~~~~~

'The Dower House, Great Maeswood, nr Market Clunbury, Salop. 28th Feb. My very dear Esther, My quiet little backwater has not performed to my expectations in the least. To start with, the local ladies at first saw in me a suitable case for charity, taking pity on my lack of a cook, and therefore invited me to dine with one or other of them every day until my cook appears. I enjoyed two rather good dinners on this basis before this largesse was abruptly withdrawn, although I am at a loss to know what my transgression might have been. I did not, that I can recall, spit or drool or fail to thank my hostess, so I am quite mystified. However, hearing me praise his excellent claret and bemoan the emptiness of my wine cellar, my host of last night arrived on my doorstep bright and early this morning to rectify the latter with supplies of the former. I expressed my gratitude at some length, as you may suppose, and he was so willing to hear his praises sung that we found ourselves depleting the stock perhaps rather more than the early hour warranted. In our excuse, it was an extremely good claret, and it would be an insult to such a fine wine to merely sip it, do you not agree? The agreeable Mr Gage agreed, in any event. While we were thus pleasantly engaged in the butler's room, having not managed to stray very far from the wine cellar, by chance we discovered that the supposed pile of sacking in one corner was in fact the body of a woman, who had been concealed down there for some years, to judge from the state of the corpse and her clothes. And she had been locked in, my dear Esther! You may imagine how my mind whirls with
~~~~~

speculation about that! I am sure I need not ask Dr Deerham to employ some of his prayers on behalf of a stranger whose life came to such a tragic end, quite unnoticed by the world. So you see, my dear friend, all my hopes of a retired life are set at naught, and, which is perhaps far worse, my cook does not arrive until Monday and if she is as untrained as my footman and maid, I shall be in dire straits indeed. My respects to Dr Deerham, and I hope Milly's tooth is better. Your affectionate friend, Louisa.'

5: A Geography Lesson

Laurence spent the evening fending off a deluge of recriminations from Viola. He could not quite decide whether she was most incensed by him spending half the morning drinking wine with the widow, or his lamentable want of good taste in discovering a dead body. It soon became clear that it was Mrs Middlehope preoccupying her.

"She is *nobody!"* she said in outraged tones, as they gathered in the drawing room before dinner. "We thought that she was related to *Lord* Middleton... but she is not a Middleton at all and there is no Lord Middle... Lord Whatever-she-is. Jane Anderson thinks— Really, Laurence, you should not laugh at me in that vulgar way."

At dinner, as soon as the soup had been removed, she went on, "When I talked to her yesterday, I could not find out that she is connected to anyone of importance at all."

Laurence did not care for this line of thought. "Does that matter, sister?" he said, in his mild way. "You agreed that she is a respectable person, and she is a gentleman's widow, after all."

"Seemingly so," she conceded, although her tone was reluctant. "Her father had an estate in Herefordshire—"

"Hertfordshire," Laurence said. "An estate called Codlington."

"Oh... well, that is near enough, and her husband's people are from Derby or somewhere like that."

"Durham. Roseacre, County Durham."

"Ah. Where precisely is Durham?" Viola said.

Henrietta wriggled with pleasure at this opening. "The county of Durham lies between the North Riding of Yorkshire and Northumberland," she said. "It has Cumberland and Westmoreland to the west and the German Ocean to the east. Its capital is the city of Durham. The principal rivers are the Wear, the Tees, the Tyne and... and one beginning with D. The principal industries are wool, sail-cloth, steel, glass and iron, as well as agriculture. There is an abundance of coal, iron, millstone grit and limestone."

"What is millstone grit?" Edward said.

Henrietta frowned. "I have no idea. Something used to make millstones, I imagine. Oh, Derwent! The fourth river."

Viola blinked at this outpouring of knowledge. "How well informed you are, Henrietta dear, but be sure not to talk so when you are in company because—"

"Gentlemen dislike ladies who are blue-stockings," Henrietta chimed in. "Yes, I know. When I am with a gentleman, I shall do all I can to pretend to know nothing."

"It is not pretence," Laurence said gently. "At fifteen, you have seen nothing of the world. All you know of it is what you have read in books — rivers and industries and capital cities.

Knowing so much of the county of Durham, could you have held a conversation with Mrs Middlehope about it? Could you have talked to her about anything beyond millstone grit? What about the architecture of the city, the cathedral, the principal buildings? Who are the great families nearby? What are the natural attractions of the area, the mountains and woodlands? That is what your education is for, to enable you to move through society and be able to hold a conversation with anyone."

He thought he had successfully diverted Viola's attention from the question of Mrs Middlehope, and for a while the discussion was all on the subject of education. When the children had gone to bed, however, and Laurence had optimistically poured himself a large Cognac and picked up his book, she began again.

"I hope you will exercise extreme caution around Mrs Middlecombe… Middlehope, dear. You know what young widows are like."

Stifling a sigh, he laid his book down. "What *are* young widows like?"

"One never knows for sure until they pounce," she said at once, providing Laurence with an image of Mrs Middlehope as a cat, tail twitching, waiting at a mouse hole for some hapless gentleman to emerge. "Most likely she is on the search for another husband. As a wife, she was well off and now she is poor."

"We cannot guess her circumstances," Laurence said mildly, recalling the expensive evening gown.

"If she had an independence of any sort she would go to London or one of the spa towns and make a splash, but as she has not, we must assume her to be poor and desperate for a husband to support her expensive ways. Since you are quite the most eligible single gentleman in the vicinity, naturally she will set her cap at you."

"I am not much of a catch, my dear. An estate that needs more work than I can well afford, an income considerably less than it was and Edward's education still to be paid for... and I am far too dull for a lady like her. No, she could do much better, if a husband is indeed her aim."

"Nonsense! You are not as well situated as you were when Catherine was alive, it is true, but our needs are modest and there is no one else with a better income this side of Market Clunbury."

"Beasley is comfortably off, I believe."

"He is too old and staid to consider marrying now," she said.

"The parson, then. He has an excellent income for a man of the cloth, and he is a fine figure of a man, too."

"Ah." Viola looked smug. "A little bird told me, quite in confidence, you know, that he is dangling after one of the Saxby girls. Flora, probably. He will not settle for an impoverished widow. And as for Mr Exton, he is reputed to have a very good income too, but he secludes himself in his villa, going nowhere. The widow will have no opportunity to meet him. I have only met him twice myself, and that by chance in Mr Edser's. You did not mention the apothecary, either, but he dreams of Agnes Saxby, poor man. *That* will never fly. The Rycrofts are penniless, and Henry Winslade not much better. No, it is you that the widow is after, you may be quite certain, so be sure to be on your guard. It will be a dark day indeed if ever you replace dearest Catherine with a woman of no family and no breeding."

"There is no danger of that," he said equably. "I shall never marry again."

After that, she subsided and, to his relief, let the subject drop. He had no intention of making Mrs Middlehope his wife, but he very much hoped to retain her as an acquaintance. Nor could he quite agree that she was in any way under-bred. Her manners and ease in company bespoke a woman who had moved in a high level of society, and while her day gowns might be somewhat dowdy, her evening dress gave off clear signals of a fashionable and expensive *modiste*.

When Viola had gone to bed, he retrieved *Paterson's Roads* from the library and looked up Mrs Middlehope's two previous homes — her father's, Codlington, and her husband's, Roseacre.

'Codlington, Hertfordshire, Thomas Westman Esq. A well proportioned brick structure comprising a central block and two wings of pleasing design. Within are many elegantly decorated apartments, and a good gallery that runs through the house with some fine paintings. The park has a circumference of four miles, and contains much fine woodland, a large deer park and a splendid body of water of a serpentine construction, crossed at its centre with an elegant stone bridge with two arches.'

A gentleman's estate, then, and rather a good one, by the sound of it. But what of the family she had married into? What of Roseacre?

'This large edifice is of considerable antiquity, having been much improved and extended by many generations of the family into its present imposing condition, and now comprises several wings, each in its own way as beautiful as another. The hall is a noble room, having in its windows and walls the arms of all the matches in the family, with many other apartments of splendid decoration. The house stands on an eminence from which the views are extensive and beautiful. The large park includes woodland with magnificent stands of pine and birch, and pleasure

grounds recently subject to much replanting and additions, so that they are now acclaimed as some of the finest in the country.'

At the top, in neat print, were the words that made him laugh out loud in delight. *'Roseacre, co Durham, seat of Lord Mountsea'* A baron! And Mrs Middlehope had married the eldest son — the heir. He had died before his father, and the younger brother had inherited, yet if the gentleman had but hung on a little longer, then the widow would now be Lady Mountsea, and Viola would not be talking about her lack of breeding, of that he could be sure. It was a sad fact, but his sister was too high in the instep by half.

~~~~~

The following morning, Laurence optimistically exercised the dogs on the Glebe, but for the second day Mrs Middlehope did not come. After breakfast, he took a gun out and then, having dropped off the dogs at the Grove, he selected some of his haul, plus a capon from the kitchen, and walked down the drive and across the road to the Dower House.

It was pleasant, he thought, to see the place alive again. A maid was polishing one of the upper windows and in the garden the Timpson twins were hard at work, scything and raking the unkempt grass that had once been lawn. Round at the side of the house, he could see activity in the stable block, where he discovered Cass Saxby, her groom and the widow's footman busily disposing a gig, pony and quantities of hay and feed about the place.

"Miss Saxby. How are you?" he said, making her a bow.

"I am well, as you see, Mr Gage. Have you brought those for Mrs Middlehope? There is a game store just through that door there. William will take them from you."
~~~~~

"Is your mistress in, William?" he said as he handed over his burden.

"Aye, sir. In the... in the room at the front, the... the study!" He grinned in triumph at remembering the name, before disappearing.

Laurence left Miss Saxby in the stables and walked towards the house. There was no point going to the front door, since the manservant was not there to answer it, so he entered the house through the basement door to the kitchens. No one was about, but he heard low voices not far away. Beasley, he thought.

Following the sound to the butler's room, he peered through the open door. Beasley and Squire Winslade, huddled over an assortment of bones spread out on the table, looked up at him.

"Come in, come in, Gage," Beasley said, waving his hands excitedly. "This is fascinating. Do have a look."

"Thank you, but you may give me a summary later," Laurence said with a laugh.

Upstairs, there was still no one about. There were four doors, but only one was slightly open and when he peeped in, there she was, sitting at her desk with her back to him, head down as she wrote steadily. Beneath a frothy little lace cap, loose fronds of hair curled onto her bare neck in pleasing disarray. Then he wondered why he found it pleasing, he who had so loved his wife's neatness, with never a hair out of place. It was not like him, and yet it amused him, too. How long was it since he had admired a woman's feminine charms? There was life in him yet, even a dull old dog such as he was.

She must have heard a sound, or sensed his presence, for she half turned her head, and said, "Yes, William, what is it?"

"Not William, I am afraid. It is only I."

She turned fully round, her face alight with amusement. "Why, Mr Gage! What a pleasant surprise. But oh dear! After mistaking you for a gamekeeper on our first meeting, now I am confusing you with the manservant. How dreadful. But do come in. There is Madeira on the sideboard there, so please help yourself. It is from your own cellar, after all."

He laughed, saying, "Shall I pour for you, too?"

"Why not? Do sit down, Mr Gage. I told William I was not at home today, but you are always welcome, even without gifts."

"Ah, but I do indeed bear gifts," he said, rather pleased to be singled out as an exception. Although perhaps she would say as much to anyone. "There are several pigeons and rabbits hanging in your game store at this moment, and a capon, too. I might take myself down to the river this afternoon and see if I can catch something for you."

"This is generosity indeed," she cried. "How very kind you are, but you must not deprive your own table on my account, especially as I have no cook to take advantage of fresh fish. I am not confident that my makeshift arrangements would do it justice. I am very glad of the game, however. But please, do sit down and then we may be comfortable. Pray excuse the disorder, but my footman has been diverted by the arrival of the gig."

The room looked as if it was in the middle of a rearrangement. A chaise longue was seemingly abandoned in the middle of the room, and two pairs of stacked chairs stood beside it. A matched pair of armchairs stood back to back on one side of the fire. She spun them round and pushed them here and there until they were positioned one either side of the fire.

"There, that is better," she said, settling into one of them and taking her glass of Madeira from him. "Please, sit. As you see, I am in the process of making this room a little more comfortable. I shall likely spend my mornings in here, so it will suit me to receive callers here as well. That way I need not light the fire in the drawing room until the evening. It is not an easy thing, I find, to arrange a house to suit one. I have always previously lived in houses where the proper room for each purpose had been determined three generations ago at least, and therefore no consideration need be given to the matter."

"I had never thought of that," he said, sipping his Madeira. "I should have supposed that each new mistress would make changes."

Her face clouded momentarily. "Perhaps some do. I certainly never did at Roseacre, but then, even after my husband's mother had died, his father was still alive, and liked everything just as it always was."

"That would be Lord Mountsea."

Her eyes crinkled in amusement. "Now, how did you know that? I have not mentioned it to anyone here."

"I looked up Roseacre in *Paterson's Roads*. Is it a secret? I shall not mention it to anyone, if so."

"Not a secret, exactly, for it is easy enough to find it out, as you have discovered, but the connection is hardly relevant to me now. My husband is dead, and my rôle in his family is over. It is in my past, and I do not wish to drag it with me wherever I may go."

"Like a millstone around your neck... yes, I can see that it might be a burden," he said thoughtfully. "Yet your husband was the heir. Had matters fallen out otherwise, you would have been

Lady Mountsea now, and your place in the family would be unavoidable."

She gave a burst of laughter. "Yes, and I thank God for my narrow escape! Three months, that was how close it came! Poor Ned, he was so cross about it, when he realised that he would not outlive his father and could not, after all, bestow the title upon me. *'I promised I would make you a lady,'* he said, *'and you have waited so patiently and now* she *will have it and not you.'* By *'she'* he meant his brother's wife, of course, but we had known for years that there would be no son and that Pamela would one day displace me. I was quite accepting of it, and it was entirely my fault, after all. I had but one duty — to provide my husband with an heir, and preferably two or three. Unfortunately, I failed dismally, whereas Pamela, bless her, has presented her husband with four sons and three daughters, so she quite deserves her title and frankly, she is welcome to it."

Her tone was light-hearted, and he could detect no bitterness, but he wondered just how easy it had been to give way to the new Lady Mountsea. He had looked up the barony in *Debrett's Peerage*, and seen much that intrigued him.

"Even if you never much cared about the title, it must have irked you to surrender the house to your sister-in-law, and yield to her wishes in every matter."

"Oh no, if she had had any wishes, that would have been easier to bear. The trouble was, she had no idea what she wanted. She would ask my advice on a matter, and then she would ask the housekeeper, and then she would ask me again, and then she would ask her husband, and then she would ask me yet again, and all the while the cook or the butler or the coachman, whoever was waiting for a decision, was kept hanging about not able to proceed. And then she would decide, and everyone would breathe a sigh of relief and set about doing whatever she had ordered and at the very last moment—"

"She changed her mind!"

"Yes!" she said, laughing. "The poor servants never knew what they were supposed to be doing. Sometimes she would send all the footmen off on one errand or another, and wonder why no one came when she rang. And then—" She stopped, and drained her glass. "Well, that is neither here nor there. Changes happen, one must accept that."

Silently, he rose, took her glass to the sideboard and refilled it. Resuming his seat, he said gently, "Tell me. I am the soul of discretion."

She sighed. "For twelve years, Roseacre was a place of calmness and tranquillity. Then Tom and Pamela arrived with their seven children, and suddenly the house was filled with bustle and running feet and squealing children. They brought friends, too, and a multitude of Pamela's relations. Her father practically lives there now. It was uncomfortable for me, frankly. I had grown very accustomed to my quiet life, and I very much hope to rediscover it here, with no husband, no relations, just myself."

A quiet life… that was interesting. "The father would be Mr Walter Pritchard of Hartlepool, I think. *Debrett's* was rather reticent about him. Not even an esquire after his name. Not a gentleman?"

She raised her shapely eyebrows. "I am not quite sure what he was. A merchant of some kind… a dealer. He never explained about his *'endeavours'*, as he called them. He was always dashing here and there to see about *'one of my endeavours, Mrs M',* as he would say. He was seldom at Hartlepool, and Pamela used to go with him, as often as not. A restless pair, the two of them.

Tom and Mrs P stayed at the Hartlepool house with the children. He always called his wife Mrs P, I was Mrs M and Pamela was Mrs Tom. He was a bit rough, but I rather liked him. I often stayed with them at Hartlepool for a week or two."

"What is Hartlepool like?" he said, mindful of his discussion with Henrietta.

"Oh, a tiny little place, barely bigger than a fishing village, and very bracing, owing to its position on the German Ocean. A spa town, but a pale imitation of the more famous ones, and the waters are particularly nasty. There is some nervousness there in anticipation of an invasion from France, but Mr Pritchard says that Bonaparte has more sense than to come to Hartlepool and if he does, the locals will invite him to drink the waters and he will immediately turn round and go home."

"Is that its strongest claim to infamy, the nastiest spa waters in England?" Laurence said, chuckling.

"No, indeed, for there was a murder there last year," she said triumphantly. "It was deliciously shocking. One of Pamela's aunts, in fact."

"Was murdered or did the murdering?" he said innocently.

She half choked on her Madeira. "How wicked you are, Mr Gage! She was the victim, of course — money stolen, too. It was a great mystery until some people came from London and realised that she had owed her milliner a great deal of money, and when they examined the body carefully, they found the tiniest pin prick above her heart. Killed by a hat pin, you see. The milliner was hanged."

They were on their third, or possibly fourth, glass of Madeira when Beasley and Squire Winslade emerged from below stairs, grinning with satisfaction.

"Most interesting!" Beasley said. "A most intriguing case. Never dealt with anything of the kind before, so most grateful, Mrs Middlehope, most grateful. A young lady, we cannot be sure as to age, but perhaps twenty-five or thirty, something of the sort. No wedding ring, and yet — she was with child! What do you think of that."

"Aha!" Laurence said before he could stop himself. "Then her lover murdered her! How fascinating!"

Beasley's face fell. "That would indeed be fascinating, but unfortunately the story is sadder than that. No doubt there was a lover, but clearly she had no hope of aid from that direction. You see, we found this in her clothing." He pulled a small object from his waistcoat pocket, and handed it to Mrs Middlehope. A key. "The poor girl was so distressed that she locked herself in the wine cellar to die."

"But how did she die?" Laurence said. "Did you find a knife with the body? An empty poison bottle? Rope to hang herself?"

"As to that, nothing was found, so we cannot say precisely how she died," Beasley said uncomfortably.

"No doubt she took poison before she entered the wine cellar," Squire Winslade said. "It is of no consequence. We will try to find out who she is, but I do not think we need look too far for a reason for her death."

"You have it all worked out," Laurence said. "I suppose it makes sense."

"Of course it does. Such things happen all too often, unfortunately," Beasley said. "Let us restrict ourselves to the ordinary world, Mr Gage, and not stray into the fanciful realm of murder."

6: Worthy Of Notice

Louisa listened to the discussion in silence. She was not convinced for one moment by the argument for suicide, for who, in such distress, would take the trouble to lock themselves in? Nor did Mr Gage look convinced, either, for although he put forward no further arguments, there was a frown on his face that gradually deepened.

Before long, Dr Beasley and Squire Winslade rose to arrange to transport the remains to the squire's ice house, to preserve it for further examination later, although it was hard to see what there was left to preserve.

"I shall see you this evening, Mrs Middlehope," Dr Beasley said, as he made his way to the door.

"Will you?" Louisa said, rather startled. "How so?"

"Why, you are joining us for dinner and staying for cards afterwards, I trust. It is all settled. We are all to take care of you until your cook arrives."

"Oh. I understood there was some... difficulty with the arrangements."

"Take no notice of that. We dine early, so come round at half past four."

"You are very kind, but I do not believe Miss Beasley is expecting me, sir. You may wish to check with her."

He grunted, and departed with the squire. Louisa was left with Mr Gage. Silently, she rose, took both their glasses to the sideboard to be refilled, and returned to her chair.

"I daresay my sister will ring a peal over me when I return home in my cups again," he said cheerfully, raising his glass to her in a toast.

That made her laugh. "Do you care about that?"

"Not a great deal, but—"

"But you do not like to distress her."

"I do not," he said. "Viola has a certain way of looking at the world, and she likes it better if I conform to her ideas, and mostly I do so. However, it is a pleasant thing, I find, to enjoy a fine wine with someone who also appreciates it."

"As I suspected," she said, chuckling. "I am a bad influence on you, leading you into bad habits. Admit it, for I know Miss Gage disapproves of me mightily. Not at first, to be sure... she was very welcoming at first, but now—"

"She believed you to be connected to Lord Middleton," he said, eyes twinkling. "When she discovered her mistake, and not knowing how close you came to a real title, she decided you were not to be encouraged. It is not you personally of whom she disapproves, you must understand, it is all beautiful young widows, whom she supposes to be predatory creatures on the prowl for a second husband. Naturally, she fears that I shall fall into your toils."

Beautiful! A casual compliment, but it was a promising sign. "Of course she does! But pray tell her, if you please, that I am *not* looking for a husband. I have been a daughter and a wife, and chafed just a little under the restrictions of both. I look forward to a long and very happy widowhood, with no one to please but myself. Besides, I should not marry you if you were the last man alive, for your first wife was perfect and who could compete with that?"

For a moment, she wondered if her levity had carried her too far, for she saw surprise written on his features. But then he burst out laughing, shaking his head. "Indeed, it is a good point, one which poor Viola can never understand. It is an odd thing, but she has been telling me for ever that I should marry again, if only for the sake of the children, yet when a highly suitable lady appears, she sets her face against it. I wonder why that should be?"

A sharp knock on the open door was followed immediately by Miss Saxby's smiling face. "May I come in? Goodness, you two look cosy! I had hoped to catch Dr Beasley and the squire."

"They have just this minute left."

"No matter. I shall send a message. I have a name for them — Dilys Hughes, a junior housemaid at the Hall years ago. She got into a spot of bother and was given notice, and supposedly sent home. She did not get far, did she? The pony is settled in your stable now, Mrs Middlehope, and I have explained to your man how to care for him, but he seems very competent and Goronwy likes him."

"Goronwy! Strange name," Louisa said.

She laughed. "He is Welsh. I must go. Good bye!"

Louisa sipped her wine thoughtfully once they were alone again. "Well, it is a great relief to find that William is competent at something, for as a footman he is sadly deficient. I have never had to train servants before, Mr Gage, and I am finding it a tiresome business."

He frowned as if finding the point difficult to grasp. "How did you manage?" he said eventually. "Did they always come to you fully trained?"

"Generally speaking, they were born on the estate or one of the neighbouring estates. They went into service at the age of ten or twelve, and then the butler trained them up, or the housekeeper or the head groom or the cook. The family never even saw a footman until he was proficient. Now I have a footman who used to be a groom, and no butler to teach him how to behave. The maid was a third housemaid somewhere, and I have no doubt that she was an excellent third housemaid, for her polishing and dusting is exemplary, but now I need her to be everything from scullery maid up to housekeeper, and to do what needs to be done without being told, and it is a challenge for both of us."

"Ah, the trials of the mistress of the house," he said lightly. With a frown, he went on, "Dilys Hughes, a housemaid in a spot of bother. It could be, I suppose."

"With shoes like that? No housemaid ever wore anything so fancy, and the cloak had silver fastenings. I should very much like to see the rest of her clothes. Sometimes the outer garments are the mistress's castoffs, so the cheap shift will give it away. And her hands... a housemaid would have roughened hands, although perhaps that could not be discerned, given the state of the corpse."

"I wonder why she came here?" he said thoughtfully. "That is the part I find odd. If she worked at the Hall, and wanted to kill herself, why come here to do it, and lock herself in? It is very strange."

"Perhaps because the house was empty?" Louisa said. "Was it empty then?"

"I cannot remember. There was a very elderly lady living here when we first came to the village, about thirty years ago, but she died not long after and the house has been empty since then. I expect Winslade will check the precise dates."

The door knocker sounded, and a thunder of feet on the service stairs heralded the arrival of William to answer it. The front door opened, a few words were spoken, the door closed again. A moment later, he stood hesitantly in the door.

"Letter for you, madam."

"Then bring it to me," she said. "I have still not found you a silver salver for this sort of thing, have I? Who brought it, a footman?"

"Maid, madam."

"Is an answer expected?"

"No, madam."

"Then you may go."

Mr Gage smiled, shaking his head. "I see the problem. One takes one's servants for granted rather."

"Indeed. How he will manage when my wine arrives I cannot imagine. I wonder if I might presume to send him to your butler for instruction? I do not care if he addresses me as *'mum'* and calls the drawing room the back parlour, but I care very much about racking and sulphuring, and the proper management of my cellar. Oh, this is from Miss Beasley. *'So sorry for the confusion… most happy to invite you… look forward to seeing you…'* I am to get my dinner and cards at the Beasley's after all. How delightful. Is Dr Beasley a connoisseur of wine also?"

"You will get Hock with the dinner, I expect."

"What a pity. And ratafia with the cards and Tokay with supper. Your sister warned me of those. I shall endeavour to conceal my disappointment."

He laughed and drained his glass. "Just one more before I go?"

~~~~~

It would be stretching a point to say that Louisa settled into a routine, but the days began to show some semblance of order. Each morning she strode briskly down to what might loosely be described as the centre of the village to buy bread and buns for her breakfast from Mr Seldon, and to leave her letters at the inn. Quite often she would call at Timpson's, a general store where might be bought almost anything from butter to buckets, and from dried peas to pins, and a great deal more besides. There were other more specialised shops, but there was something peculiarly satisfying about a shop that stocked absolutely everything. Several times in that first, rather fraught, week she would say to Mr Timpson, "I suppose you have no ink… or gelatine… or rose water…?" and he would reply, "One moment, *if* you please, madam," and there it would be, the thing she wanted, often a little dusty or faded or dried up, but perfectly sound, and for considerably less than she would have paid in Durham.

She found herself a person worthy of notice again, but she was as yet undecided as to the benefit of this. Her evening with the Beasleys was pleasant enough, although Dr Beasley was
~~~~~

rather too inclined to beguile the dinner table with every tiny detail of his discoveries regarding the wine cellar body. However, this was followed by two evenings of bad dinners and stultifying boredom with the Andersons and the Drinkwaters. Mrs Anderson was shocked to find that Louisa had not been to London since her come out. "Oh, but the season!" she twittered. "How can you bear to miss the season? It is so important that our leading families set the tone, do you not agree?" Mrs Drinkwater was even more direct. "Surely Lord Mountsea wished his heir to show himself at court?"

So that accounted for her return to popularity. They knew she had nearly become a baroness. Ah well, so much for her quiet, discreet life in the shires. Still, she was optimistic that her plan would eventually come to fruition.

Sunday took her to church, where she found herself sharing a pew with the Beasleys, and discovering that the parson was an excessively personable young man of much her own age, with a well-honed and muscular figure, and a decided air of fashion, only partially concealed by the vestments. Louisa had never met a clergyman before who was neither dowdy nor elderly nor pious, and more usually all three, so Mr Truman was something of a revelation to her.

"He is wasted in the pulpit," she murmured to Marie, as they joined the throng outside the church.

"Il n'est pas marié, madame," she said, with a knowing smile. *He is not married.*

"Not... um, *marié?* A bachelor, is he?" Well, that had possibilities, certainly.

That evening, she dined at the Hall again, and to her delight, the attractive Mr Truman was there too, having set aside his sober Sunday blacks for a well-fitted coat of blue superfine and silk knee breeches that displayed his shapely legs to perfection. She was rather glad that she had decided to abandon the tired blue muslin and wear the pale green silk this time.

Mr Truman's manners were exquisite, bestowing his perfect form and well turned phrases liberally on the company in equal measure. Louisa detected a certain excitement amongst the young ladies — Miss Saxby in particular wore a little glow of pleasure whenever the parson addressed her, and she was old enough to be past the awkward stage of blushing over every personable young man. But then some women never quite grew into composure until they married, and perhaps she was in love. It could happen to anyone, she supposed.

She had her share of his attention at dinner, where she found herself seated next to Mr Truman and discovered, rather to her surprise, that he was from Shrewsbury and knew Esther and her husband.

"Dr Deerham is very highly regarded, Mrs Middlehope," he said. "Most highly regarded. Have you read his book of sermons?"

"I have tried," she said, with a laugh. "They are a little too dry and scholarly for my taste. It rather defeats the point if one has to struggle to understand the moral being imparted, do you not think? Your sermon today was very effective, I thought."

"Why, thank you! Its effectiveness is in opposing proportion to its length, I suspect. My father always said, *'Keep it short, and speak loud enough to keep the congregation awake.'* His advice has stood me in good stead. I find Dr Deerham's sermons rather dry myself, but there is no need to mention that when next you see him."

She laughed again. "I will not do so, but whatever our opinions, the book must sell rather well, for his publisher has asked him to compile another volume."

Louisa had refused the use of the carriage, since it was a fine, dry evening with the waxing moon providing enough light, and now she was glad of it, for it meant that she had the company of Mr Truman on her walk home. He was an excellent conversationalist, and they managed to range over poetry, modern architecture, the fall of Rome and the Emperor Napoleon before they reached the Hall gates and turned into the lane. Before long they had reached the Dower House gates, and the welcome sight of the lamp above the door.

"This is where we part ways, Mr Truman," she said.

"By no means," he said. "I shall escort you to your front door, for I do not like to leave a lady to make her way all alone at night, even for so short a distance."

She was not averse to prolonging his company, so she acceded to it graciously.

"In fact," he continued, "it does not sit well with me to see a lady alone in any circumstance. I do hope you will not be too solitary living by yourself in this way. I can tell that you are a lady with many resources, and will find much to occupy your mornings, but the evenings… ah, that can be a lonely business, as I know only too well. My duties during the day are many, and leave me no time to repine, but unless my neighbours are so kind as to issue an invitation, my evenings stretch before me, long and empty. Do you not find it so, Mrs Middlehope?"

"I confess, I rather enjoy long, empty evenings, sir, when I can put my feet up and read for hours. I never notice that I am alone when I have a book to read."

"Ah yes, but when you lay down your book, with whom will you share your reflections? Who will discuss the finer points of the ideas contained within its pages if you have no companion beside you?"

For some reason, the image of Mr Gage rose to her mind, a glass of wine in his hand, his face alight with enthusiasm for the subject — any subject, she had discovered. He was the perfect companion for the evening hours, for he could talk knowledgeably about anything. As could Mr Truman, she realised. Yes, he was definitely a possibility.

"I keep a journal for such a purpose," she said cautiously. "Naturally it is pleasant to discuss points of contention with a friend, but failing such a person I will write down my own thoughts."

"Did I not say you are resourceful?" he cried, pleased with his own perspicacity. "That is exactly as I should have expected of you."

"Oh, you understand me so well, do you, sir?" she said, amused.

"I begin to understand you, a little. You will not repine — you will never repine, no matter the circumstances, but I do not think you were made to be solitary. Perhaps you have plans for a female companion to join you in your pretty little house? Or you might, one day, consider the possibility of placing yourself in the care of a man once more?"

"Neither a female companion nor a second husband is likely to feature in my plans, Mr Truman," she said crisply. "I have been looking forward to living alone for some time now."

"Ah," he said thoughtfully. "But that does not preclude the possibility of... friendship, does it? A congenial companion to while away a few hours now and then, and keep loneliness at bay for both parties? You are such an affable and open-hearted woman that I am sure it will not be long before you make such a friend."

Louisa did not quite know what to make of such a remark. Was it a bland expression of good will from a clergyman, or was it a subtly worded proposition from a single man? Impossible to tell. She made some non-committal reply, and, since they had now reached her front door and William was holding it open for her, she bade Mr Truman good night.

"There's a fire in the front room... the study, madam, and I decanted the wine very carefully, just as you told me."

"Excellent. Thank you, William, and you were on the watch for my return, too. Well done. You are coming along very well. Now you may lock and bolt the front door, check that the drawing room door is locked and all the windows are closed. Then you may go downstairs, check the kitchen door is locked and bolted, and make sure the kitchen fire is banked for the night."

"That's Sarah's job, isn't it, the kitchen fire?"

"Yes, but you are the senior servant in the house, so it is *your* job to ensure that the servants under you are doing their work properly. It is also a question of safety, in ensuring that an unattended fire does not burn the house down. After that you may go to bed. I will attend to the fire and candles in the study."

"Very good, madam."

She entered the study and shut the door behind her with a sigh of relief. A glass of something and a few minutes of quietude before bed would settle her. She had no books to read until her things arrived from Roseacre, but it would be pleasant to ponder her options. For now she had two possibilities, Mr Gage and Mr Truman. An interesting choice.

7: A Visit From A Friend

Monday brought Louisa a welcome visitor, her friend Esther Deerham from Shrewsbury. Esther was a former neighbour from Hertfordshire, whose high spirits had precisely matched Louisa's own, engendering a close and deep-rooted intimacy. Even when Esther's father had inherited a modest property in Shrewsbury, their friendship had survived the separation through long and frequent letters, and regular visits. It had even weathered their marriages, each of them disapproving of the other's choice of husband, but their affection was so strong that after the initial shock, they never did more than tease each other gently on the subject.

Esther brought not only the long-awaited cook with her, but also a large parcel of books. Leaving William and Sarah to take care of the cook, Louisa took Esther straight into the study and gleefully unwrapped the parcel.

"Wonderful! At last I have something to read."

"You ordered them and then vanished, and Mr Moffat delivered them last week and was astonished to hear that you had gone. I believe he thought to make his fortune from you, for no one else buys books twenty at a time. He has enclosed a list of more that you might like, but I was not sure what to tell him. Do you always buy so many books at once?"

"Only when I find myself without a library at my disposal. Once Pamela sends my things to me, I shall be better placed, but I shall continue to buy from the obliging Mr Moffat."

"Oh yes... Pamela," Esther said. "That reminds me that I have letters for you."

She reached into her reticule and pulled out a handful of letters, tipping them onto the desk. Another probe produced more. A third rummage brought forth several more.

"Good gracious!" Louisa said. "These cannot possibly all be from Pamela. Oh, but most of them are. She must have been writing to me every day, or even more often. I shall read them later."

"Oh, do read them now! I cannot wait to find out what is so urgent."

"I shall need to fortify myself for so much of Pamela all at once," Louisa said. "Will you have something? I have brandy or sherry, or a very good Madeira."

"Oh, sherry, if you please. Such a treat for a Monday."

Louisa poured, saying in amused tones, "That is what comes of marrying a righteous man, my dear friend, he expects you to be righteous too. It was fortunate for me that Ned was more tolerant of my foibles." She sat in one of the chairs beside the fire, waving Esther to the other, and began opening the letters and arranging them in date order. "Heavens, why must she cross her lines so! I can barely read this. Oh, I see, she is waiting for me to send my direction. But I told her to send everything to you, and you would see that it got to me. But no, she has changed her mind and is sending everything to you... but when the wagons came she sent them away! She would not trust my things to the common carrier, and is to send them in the Roseacre travelling coach, but there is some difficulty with it, something broken. As soon as it is mended, she will send my things. Oh, Pamela, Pamela! And all this time I am without my pianoforte, my pictures, my books and most of my gowns. I have precisely three day gowns and three for evening, and I am heartily sick of all of them. I must write to her, I suppose."

"Louisa! Have you not written at all?"

"I sent her a note to say I had arrived safely when I reached Shrewsbury, and I planned to write and thank her when everything arrived. What more is needed?"

Esther snorted with unladylike laughter, and instantly covered her mouth with her hand in embarrassment. "But you have written three times to me, telling me in great detail of all your adventures here."

"Yes, but you are my *friend,"* Louisa said tartly. "Pamela is not and never will be my friend, no matter how much she encroaches."

"Oh, Louisa, you are wicked!" Esther said. "Does she encroach? Can a baroness encroach?"

"She can indeed. I had my own apartments at Roseacre where I could retreat when the combined mass of Middlehopes and Pritchards became too much for me, and I was very glad of it, for I should have decamped long since without that refuge. Pamela, however, never once waited to be invited there. She would knock on the door of my boudoir and then come marching in as if she owned the place... well, I suppose she did, if we are being strictly truthful, but that is neither here nor there. In she would come, saying, *'Oh, so this is where you are hiding away, you naughty creature. Are you avoiding us?'* I so badly wanted to answer that truthfully, but good manners are wretchedly inhibiting and I was never able to, so I had to listen to her twitterings for an hour instead of reading. And she scolded me constantly, far worse than my mother ever did."

"Scolded you! On what grounds?"

"I eat too much, drink too much, spend too much money… all of which is doubtless true, but at my age these are my choices to make. That I am too sociable, or not sociable enough. Also that I take no interest in her children, although why I should is beyond me. It would be good for me, she opined, while graciously telling me that she quite understood how painful it must be for me to be daily confronted by such an abundance of offspring. And again she is right, but for the wrong reason. If her children screamed less or could stay in one place for more than two minutes at a time, I might have found them more appealing. Now *your* children are lovely. If I had ever had any myself, I should have wanted them to be just like that, quiet, respectful and above all intelligent."

Esther smiled. "I will not tell you that you wrong your sister-in-law, for I am sure you know it already. Perhaps distance will lead you to a kinder view of her."

"A very great distance, and no possibility of reducing it, preferably. Shall I confess the worst of my fears to you? I shall, I think. The reason I have put off sending Pamela my direction is that I have a terrible fear of finding her standing on my doorstep one day. She and her father are great travellers, perpetually leaping into the carriage and haring off about the northern counties. If she knows where I am, perhaps she will have a yearning to hare off to Shropshire, and I am not sure I could cope with that. Oh, let us not talk about Pamela! Even from two hundred miles away she rubs me the wrong way. I am the most placid person as a rule, but she is like a burr under my saddle, making me unreasonably wild. Let us speak of less contentious matters. Tell me of my new cook."

Esther avoided her eye, pleating her gown nervously. "Now, you must not be cross, Louisa, and truly she sounded most promising. But when I questioned her, she said that she is a good, plain cook."

"Oh dear! We had better have her in, I suppose."

Mrs Nokes was a solidly built woman of indeterminate age. She looked clean and depressingly respectable to Louisa, who had harboured hopes of finding her instantly unsuitable.

"How do you find your quarters, Mrs Nokes? Are you pleased with your accommodation?"

"Room's fine, thank you, mum."

"And the kitchen? It is rather old-fashioned, I am afraid, although I plan to get a range installed."

"It's fine, mum. It's just as I'm used to, and the girl seems willing."

Louisa read Mrs Nokes' sole reference from the niece of her last employer, finding nothing terribly alarming in it. "You have had no other employers beyond this Mr Langridge?"

"No, mum. Started there as kitchen maid, bin cook these last fifteen years, but he died a month since, so I gotta look elsewhere."

"And what did you cook for Mr Langridge?" Louisa said.

"Gruel, mostly, mum, the last year or two, and beef tea. Poultices for his leg. His leg was real bad at the end."

"Well, I shall want something a little more fortifying than gruel and beef tea," Louisa said. "If I dine alone, I shall want about six or eight dishes, just the one course. What would you prepare for me, if you had a free hand?"

"Spit-roasted mutton, mum, and a clear soup."

"Vegetables?"

"Boiled tatoes and whatever's in season."

"Boiled potatoes. I see. What about fish?"

"Don't hold with fish, mum. Too many bones, but if you insist, I'd fry it in butter."

"Suppose I have two or three guests, and would like to impress them with two courses?"

"Spit-roasted mutton, boiled beef, and an ox-tongue in aspic. A pigeon pie, mebbe. Fried fish if you insist. Vegetables."

"Boiled potatoes again?" Louisa said. "What about something sweet, a blancmange, say."

A long pause. "I could try. Apple pie... I can do an apple pie."

"Meringues? Soufflé?" A very long pause. "How would you cook pheasant?"

"Spit-roast, mum."

"Woodcock? Larks? Swan?"

"Spit-roast."

From her corner of the room, Esther's giggles were audible.

"Thank you, Mrs Nokes. You may go and begin work now. I shall dine at six o'clock."

"Six o'clock!" the cook said, in outraged tones. No doubt her elderly employer had still dined at three, in the old manner. "Well, as you please, I daresay." And out she stumped.

The door was barely closed before Esther burst out laughing. "Oh, Louisa, you will never stand for mutton and boiled potatoes every day! I give it a week."

"Oh, but *spit-roasted* mutton... and woodcock and pheasant. And do not forget the ox-tongue in aspic." She groaned. "Oh, how I miss Chambers! It took me five years — five years! — to persuade his lordship to engage a man-cook, and another two to find one who was not French, for heaven forfend that the sacred halls of Roseacre be darkened by the presence of The Enemy. Fortunately, I kept Marie well out of his way, and he never realised that she is French. And now I am reduced to boiled potatoes and fried fish."

"Well, if Mrs Nokes does not work out, then you can engage a French man-cook if you wish, for you do not need to persuade anyone now."

"Very true," Louisa said, brightening. "A *French* man-cook — that would be just the thing. Come, let me show you around my humble abode."

The house was quickly shown, and Esther soon abandoned the attics — "Too many cobwebs, but there are all sorts of intriguing boxes there" — but she insisted on being shown the site of the gruesome discovery in the wine cellar, and every minute detail recounted.

"And she was just... lying there?"

"Covered by her cloak, but yes, just lying there, all curled up."

"Curled up how, precisely?"

After a moment's hesitation to remind herself that Tilly had scrubbed the whole floor very thoroughly, Louisa lay down and positioned herself as she remembered the body to have been.

"Ha! Then it is as I thought," Esther said with an air of triumph. "Nobody sleeps so tightly curled like that. I wager you anything you like that she was murdered elsewhere and then brought here to be concealed."

Louisa laughed and shook her head, as she rose and brushed herself down. "A very imperfect concealment, when the door is merely latticed metalwork. Better to have hidden her behind a wooden door, surely. Besides, she had the key in her pocket."

"The key is only to make it look like suicide," Esther said eagerly. "And look, she *was* hidden behind a wooden door — the door to the butler's room is solid enough, and you unlocked it for us to enter, then the wine cellar door and then this inner door. Three separate doors, all locked."

"They are all locked *now* but—" Louisa frowned, trying to remember. "No, you are right. When we first came down here, Mr Gage and I, and the footman, I had to unlock every door. I had keys for the outer wooden door and the wine cellar, but not this inner door. Mr Gage's footman had to pick the lock to open it. He has replaced it now, for there is the lock on the sideboard there. Everything was locked, but only one key was found on her. Wait a minute... there are two sets of keys for the house. I wonder if there is a key for the inner door on the other set."

But rapid investigation showed that there was not, and Esther immediately pounced on this evidence. "There you are! Someone murdered her, placed her very carefully inside the inner door with the key in her pocket, and then locked the outer doors as he left. He will have thrown away the second key for the inner door."

"He?" Louisa said, amused by her friend's imagination. "Must it be a man? Not an irate mother or employer?"

"Pft! Of course it was a man!"

Esther wanted to see the gardens, too, so they donned pelisses and bonnets, and set out to brave the sharp wind. The Timpson twins had scythed and raked the lawns into submission, and were hard at work creating some vegetable beds. Their tidying had revealed a series of neat paths, one leading directly to the intriguing gate at the bottom of the garden and one meandering round the perimeter. The gate was locked and none of Louisa's keys fitted, so they could do no more than peer through the latticework at the wooded grounds of Maeswood Hall beyond.

"There may be a key at the Hall," Louisa said, and they continued their perambulations. "If not, I shall get Mr Gage's enterprising footman to pick the lock. It will be very pleasant to have the grounds to walk about in."

"You do not suppose they might mind?" Esther said anxiously. "Is Lady Saxby very starchy?"

"A little," Louisa said. "I am renting her house, though, so why she should object to my walking about this end of her vast estate I cannot imagine. It is not as if I shall be strolling on her terrace. What a pleasant little arbour! Shall we sit for a while?"

It was a simple stone shelter with a seat inside, built in the same style as the house, and angled so that it caught the late afternoon sun. Louisa immediately decided it would be the perfect spot to avoid the summer heat and hide away with a book. Dusting off the stone seat as best they could, they sat to admire the view across the gardens to the house.

"It is very pretty, your new home," Esther said, with just a hint of envy in her voice. "So modern and elegant. Not like the Rectory! We have dry rot again, did I tell you? There is no end to it." She sighed. "But this is lovely! Shall you be happy here, dear, do you suppose?"

"I cannot see why not," Louisa said robustly. "It is very peaceful, which is exactly what I need just now."

"Have you made any progress with your little project?" Esther said. "You say nothing of it in your letters but then you are always so discreet when you write."

Louisa did not mention that her discretion arose entirely from the fact that Esther's husband liked to read all her correspondence. No power on earth would bring her to disclose her innermost thoughts to a man as pious and censorious as Dr Joseph Deerham. She had never understood Esther's choice, but then Esther had never understood why Louisa had married Ned.

In person, however, there need be no restraint, so she chuckled and said, "I am progressing, although with due caution. It is a risky endeavour and I must not be precipitate. At first I was sure I would be out of luck, for all I found were callow young men or greybeards or married men, which would not suit my purposes at all. But I now have two possibilities in mind. One is the wonderfully generous Mr Gage, who brought me an emergency supply of wine — and helped me drink some of it."

"Ooh!" Esther said, eyes wide. "Tell me all about him, for I have forgot what you said of him in your letters. He is an older man, I think you said? A widower?"

"He is, and still deep in love with his late wife, so there will be no likelihood of complications. He is... oh, perhaps forty but still very youthful in body and mind. Not fashionable! I daresay he buys himself one new coat a year because he feels he ought to, even though there is plenty of wear in the old one yet. He reminds me a little of Ned, in that respect."

"Is he handsome?"

Louisa considered the point dispassionately. "Not handsome, exactly, but there is no displeasing irregularity in his features. He seems very open and friendly towards me, so I am optimistic. The other possibility is a fine fellow indeed, very handsome and his clothes all in the first style of elegance — complete to a shade. He is the clergyman here, and he knows you and Dr Deerham, for he is from Shrewsbury too. Truman is his name."

"What, Theodore Truman?" Esther's eyes widened. Was that dismay in her expression?

"Oh, do tell," Louisa said easily. "He seems to be highly regarded here, but if you know of something to his discredit, I should prefer to hear of it from you, rather than find it out later."

"Oh, no, no, nothing... nothing bad, but... my brother was at school with him, for they are the same age, eight and twenty, and Norman said he was not well liked. Kept himself to himself. You know how it is with boys sometimes... well, I daresay you do not, having no brothers, but some boys are popular and some are... just not, and there is no obvious reason for it."

Louisa frowned, considering that. "Nothing more? Just... he was not popular when he was at school?"

"Oh, well, he was always running about for the masters, you know... a bit of a toady. And then later, there was a very elderly man, a deacon, I believe, and Mr Truman was very... *solicitous* of him, and the old gentleman left him all his money. Twenty thousand pounds, I believe. And this living—" She stopped, biting her lip.

"Go on," Louisa said.

"It is all gossip and hearsay," Esther said. "You should not regard it, I daresay, but it is rumoured that Mr Truman bought the right of first presentation a year or so ago, and then recommended the previous incumbent for a position at Lichfield, so that he might be put in as curate. He was something of a favourite with the Archdeacon, so he got his wish, but there was some grumbling about such manoeuvring. And then the poor fellow died of a seizure not a month after he went to Lichfield, so Mr Truman got the living in full, which was a great piece of good fortune for him." She paused and then said in a stronger voice, "It is all jealousy, I expect, if he is so fine a young man as you say. I should not give it another thought if you like him."

Louisa smiled and nodded, but it gave her pause. Mr Truman was certainly very handsome and agreeable, but he was younger than she would like, and a bachelor, too. No, it would have to be Mr Gage after all. Oddly, the thought made her smile. Perhaps she had preferred Mr Gage all the time.

8: Dinner For Twelve

Laurence found his thoughts returning often to Mrs Middlehope. With her womanly curves and hedonistic ways, she was the very antithesis of his beloved Catherine, yet he felt the strongest affinity towards her. It was inevitable that they would meet often, at the card evenings on Tuesdays and Thursdays, at church, and occasionally on his morning outings with the dogs. Now that she had her own cook, however, he no longer had the opportunity to invite her for dinner and he rather missed the gown of peach velvet that draped itself around her so enticingly. Even though he laughed at himself for having such thoughts, and at his age, too, he could not help a twinge of disappointment when she had arrived for their card party in a rather plain blue muslin gown. So his thoughts began to turn in a different direction.

"Is it time for us to have a few people round for dinner?" he said to Viola one morning at breakfast.

"It is not so long since our last dinner," she said, looking at him with suspicious eyes.

"We must owe a few people," he said. "I feel sociable. How about next Wednesday?"

"Very well, if you wish. I shall talk to Mrs Rogers about it."

"Who shall you invite?" he said.

She gave an impatient lift of one shoulder. "Oh, do give me time to think about it, Laurence. I shall have to see who has invited us recently."

He hesitated, knowing that she was perfectly well aware of his purpose, but unwilling to mention Mrs Middlehope by name and invite a lecture on the subject of rapacious widows. Fortunately, Henrietta rescued him.

"Will you invite Mrs Middlehope?" she said. "She is all alone, and would enjoy the company."

Viola looked even more suspicious, looking with narrowed eyes from Laurence to his daughter as if considering whether they had cooked up the whole scheme between them.

"And Mr Truman," Henrietta added, going very slightly pink. "He is alone, too."

"Not forgetting Miss Cokely," Laurence added. "One does not like to leave her out, even though she cannot return the invitation." Then he held his breath while Viola considered her response. She was perfectly capable of making an issue of it, and he was quite prepared to insist — he was the head of the household, after all, and entitled to choose whom he entertained in his own house — but Viola could make life deuced unpleasant if she chose to.

She did not. "Very well," she said, although her lips were pursed in disapproval. "Shall we say twelve? Mrs Middlehope, Mr Truman, Miss Cokely. The Manor family is due a dinner, too, and I shall see who else we might ask. It is too early in the year for the Woollercott people to venture so far, but the Whittels might come, if Mr Whittel's dyspepsia is a little better. If they fail, the Platts will come. They always come. Very well, leave it to me. "

"May I come?" Henrietta said brightly.

"No," Viola said.

"Yes," Laurence said at the same time. "Why not?"

"Laurence! She is too young!" Viola said. "Family dinners only until she is out."

"She is a very sensible fifteen, and behaved with the utmost decorum when we had Mrs Middlehope to dine. It will do the child no harm to spend an evening amongst our good friends."

Henrietta jumped up, raced round the breakfast table and flung her arms around Laurence, planting a kiss on the top of his head. "Thank you, thank you, *dear* Papa! You are a prince among men!"

He laughed out loud, remembering another woman using those exact same words. So many things made him think of Mrs Middlehope. "Well now, no need to be quite so much in alt. You will find it all very dull, I daresay."

Viola's expression darkened and he knew he was in for a storm. Hastily getting to his feet, he clicked his fingers to the dogs under the table and beat an orderly retreat to his study. He knew he would be safe there, for Viola would be caught up in domestic matters for an hour or two, and then she would be sitting in the Roman Saloon with Henrietta entertaining callers, for today was the ladies' day to be at home. He and Edward settled comfortably to some mathematics, or at least, Edward was entirely comfortable with it. Laurence struggled rather to keep up with his brilliant son. Eventually, he gave it up.

"You have gone far beyond my abilities with numbers," he said sadly. "I shall engage a tutor for you, I think, someone who understands the subject better than I. Languages I can help with, and history, philosophy, even literature. But numbers and the mysteries of science — I cannot teach you those. Should you like to try school again? Not necessarily Shrewsbury... you could perhaps try Eton or Winchester. Plenty of clever boys go there, so the masters must be clever enough to keep up with them. What do you think?"

"What about Harrow?"

Laurence shivered. "*Not* Harrow. What about one of the others?"

But Edward shook his head.

After setting Edward some work to be followed on his own, Laurence poured himself a glass of sherry and settled with a sigh into his chair to read the latest London newspapers. Beside him on the table were several books newly arrived from Shrewsbury. Books were such an extravagance, but he could not find it in him to cut down his expenditure. Books and wine were as necessary to him as air to breathe.

For some time, there was no sound in the room but the shifting of coals on the fire, the slight rustle of the newspaper or the scratch of Edward's pen as he made notes. From outside, the occasional crunch of carriage wheels on gravel suggested that callers were arriving or leaving, but that did not concern Laurence. Mostly it was Viola's female friends, and he was happy to leave them to gossip away uninhibited by a masculine presence. He knew he would be summoned if their social superiors from the Hall called, or if there should be a gentleman visitor.

John, the footman, came in to tend the fire. “Been busy today, sir,” he volunteered, as he raked the coals. “Quite a few callers.”

It was so unusual for John to offer such information unsolicited that Laurence laid down his newspaper in curiosity and waited.

“I see that Mrs Middlehope just a-comin’ up the drive, sir,” he added.

“Is that so?” Laurence said. “Good. I should like a word with her… about her wine order.”

John grinned, and reached for the coal scuttle.

Laurence ambled across the entrance hall, where Skeates waited patiently for visitors, and entered the Roman Saloon, so called because it boasted several busts of Roman emperors in niches around the walls. He had never liked the room, but that had more to do with the many hours of boredom spent in there while his mother had entertained a succession of dull matriarchs and their even duller daughters. As soon as he had married, he had said very firmly that he was happy to attend if courtesy demanded it, but otherwise receiving callers was ladies’ business. Catherine had laughed and said that of course it was, and he should run away and hide in his study like a true gentleman. His mother had not minded either. She had got on so well with Catherine. Now they were both gone, and he had Viola to do the honours. But there was no point being maudlin.

Miss Beasley was the only caller when he arrived, but he had barely made his bow and enquired how she was than Skeates arrived.

“Mrs Middlehope, madam.”

She was pleased to see him, he was sure. She smiled at all of them, but he was certain her smile was a little warmer for him. How pleasant it was to know that an attractive young woman was happy to find herself in his company, as he was happy to be in hers. And how wonderful to have such a woman as a friend, without the slightest thought of matrimony on either side.

"You may be the first to know, Mrs Middlehope," Viola said with tight lips, "that we are holding a dinner for a few friends... and *acquaintances* next Wednesday, and you will be receiving an invitation."

"How delightful!" Mrs Middlehope cried, seeming quite sincere. "I shall look forward to it with the greatest pleasure."

"I am to be there, too," Henrietta said with shining eyes. "My very first formal dinner."

"But how exciting!" Mrs Middlehope said. "Have you decided what you will wear?"

"No," Henrietta said, her face falling. "I have nothing suitable."

"Your white muslin will do very well," Viola said.

"But I wear that almost every night," Henrietta said in despairing tones. "Is it too late to have something new made up?"

"Was that the one you wore when I dined with you last week?" Mrs Middlehope said. "I thought it was charming, and admirably suited your colouring."

"Oh... do you think so?"

"I do, and it is always possible to give an outfit a new touch through one's accessories. A scarf, a little bit of lace, a ribbon or two, or silk flowers, if you have them. And the choice of jewellery makes a great difference."

"But I have no jewellery," Henrietta said mournfully.

"Yes, you do," Laurence said. "Your mother's jewels are yours now. You have never needed them before, but you may choose something to wear for the dinner." Then, seeing her face light up, he said gently, "Would you like to see them now?"

"May I?" And then, to his surprise, she added, "Perhaps Mrs Middlehope might advise me on what to choose."

"That would be a matter for your aunt, Miss Gage," she said at once.

But Viola shuddered. "Oh no, no, no! I cannot look at dear Catherine's things. Pray do not ask me."

"Then perhaps Mrs Middlehope would be so good as to advise us," Laurence said at once, and was out of reason triumphant when she rose and followed him and Henrietta out of the room.

She and Henrietta both looked round with interest at Catherine's bedroom, as immaculate as the day she had left it. So tidy, his wife! She never left a thing out of place, her sewing things always put neatly away before she left her chair. He crossed to the rosewood davenport, Catherine's elegant little writing desk. Unlocking and lifting the lid, he opened a drawer and found the key to the side drawers. Mrs Middlehope cried out in amazement at the book inside.

"Oh, such exquisite needlework! Your wife made this cover, I assume?"

She picked up the book, its silk covering embroidered with the words *'Catherine Gage ~ Her Diary ~ Volume IX'* and a pattern of flowers, touching it almost with reverence. To his surprise, he found he did not mind. He felt he should have resented any handling of Catherine's things, but Mrs Middlehope was so respectful that he could not object.

"Mama was very good at sewing," Henrietta said. "She made these cushions, and all the fire screens in the house."

"How very accomplished she was," Mrs Middlehope said, laying the diary down again, and straightening it carefully so that it lay just as it had before. "I am ashamed to admit that I never sew at all now if I can help it, and even when I made the effort I could never have created anything so wonderful."

"I dislike sewing, too," Henrietta said. "And music. I practise, but I am not a very good performer."

"Ah, now, music is perhaps my one accomplishment," Mrs Middlehope said. "Not that I have any great talent, but I love to play and I have never let my lack of skill stand in the way of performing when asked."

"Then we must be sure to ask on Wednesday," Laurence said, with a smile.

"I should enjoy that very much," she said at once, with an answering smile. "My own instrument is still somewhere between here and Durham, so I shall be grateful for a chance to exercise my fingers once more. And perhaps Miss Gage will play for the company, too?"

Henrietta gulped, but nodded gamely.

"Here is your mama's jewel box," Laurence said, lifting it out of its drawer. "These are just the trinkets. The serious jewellery is at the bank, safely locked away, and most of it you will not need until you marry, but there are some diamonds and garnets you might wear when you go to town for the season, and a very pretty pearl set." Henrietta's eyes widened at the mention of serious jewellery. He had always assumed that she knew about all that, but perhaps he had never quite mentioned such things explicitly. "It is all yours," he said gently. "She left you everything of that kind — her clothes, hairbrushes, perfume bottles, fans, all her personal effects. Even the fire screens," he added, making her laugh. "Now then, have a look through and see what you would like to wear on Wednesday."

It was a large box, and so there were numerous necklaces, bracelets, combs and aigrettes to be sorted through. He stood aside as the ladies opened every tiny drawer and exclaimed over the treasures within.

"With a white gown, you will want a bit of colour," Mrs Middlehope said, lifting up a necklace studded with tiny sapphires. "This is very pretty... oh but this would be better with a square neckline. Something round, you see." She held up a pendant with amber and diamonds. "There is a pair of bracelets to match. I would wear just one of those. You will not need this headpiece, which is rather too heavy for a quiet dinner with friends, but this comb at the back, like so, and an orange ribbon threaded through to match the amber, and curls just here... and here... That would be charming, and very suitable, in my opinion, but of course, you will discuss it all with your aunt. She is the best person to guide you in such matters."

"Oh, but you are so... so *stylish*," Henrietta said. "Aunt Viola likes everything very plain."

Mrs Middlehope nodded sagely. "There is something to that. Your aunt must decide how best to show *herself* to the world, but you are your father's daughter and must represent him when you move in society. Always remember that you are Miss Gage of Lower Maeswood Grove and have a position to uphold. You must be a credit to your papa, and to your mama, as well."

Henrietta lifted her chin and straightened her back a little. "I shall do my very best, but what shall I do if Aunt Viola thinks the amber is unsuitable?"

"Then you will accept her guidance with a good grace, like the well-brought-up young lady you are," she said.

Solemnly, she nodded, and Laurence could see that she understood. How wise Mrs Middlehope was! And it crossed his mind that she would be a much better chaperon and companion for Henrietta than his rather stiff and censorious sister.

~~~~~

Louisa dressed with care for Wednesday's dinner engagement. There was no need to agonise over her choice of gown, for having worn the peach velvet for her last dinner at the Grove, she must necessarily wear the green silk, but she spent some time pondering her accessories. The silk shawl that precisely matched the gown was still in transit, so she had to use the cream one, but jewels were problematic. Her best items were still in the bank in Shrewsbury, and would stay there until she had installed a safe. In the end, she settled for the same diamond pendant and aigrette she had worn to the Hall, although it pained her to wear precisely the same outfit twice.

The weather was still fine enough for her to walk, and since the charming Mr Truman had offered to escort her for the ten minutes it would take to reach the Grove, she enjoyed a pleasant stroll. He was excellent company, and she arrived at the house in good spirits. The company assembled in the saloon, a splendid chamber two stories high, with magnificent plasterwork on the ceiling. Once dinner was announced, they processed up a spiral staircase and then along the balcony which ran round the upper
~~~~~

level, admiring the many paintings adorning the walls, before entering the large and elegantly appointed dining room.

Louisa was invited to sit beside Laurence in the guest of honour's position, which at least guaranteed her some stimulating conversation, and perhaps more wine than was usually offered to ladies. On her other side was a Mr Platt, the oldest of three siblings from Astley Cloverstone, a rather impoverished family, to judge by the shabby nature of their clothes. The squire and his son she had encountered before, but this was the first time she had met Susannah Winslade, a pleasant, sensible woman a few years younger than Louisa, whom she had heard spoken of sadly as *'A most capable woman, but such a pity she is so dreadfully plain!'* She was indeed plain in repose, but when animated her sparkling eyes and generous mouth gave her an aura of prettiness. The final member of their company was Miss Cokely, usually mentioned as *'Poor Miss Cokely',* a woman in her middle years who had come down in the world lately, and now supplemented her elderly mother's meagre annuity by making bonnets. She was reputed to be a very skilled milliner, so Louisa was very happy to make her acquaintance.

By the time the covers were removed, the Mr Platts and Mr Henry Winslade had begun to be rather loud, and were monopolising the rest of the table. Louisa felt it safe, under cover of the noise, to talk more freely to Mr Gage on a matter which intrigued her.

"Now that I understand your wife's talent with a needle, I have been seeing examples of it everywhere," she began cautiously. "Every room has one of her beautiful fire screens, and there are cushions and cloths and framed pieces to admire. They are works of art."

He beamed at her. "They are wonderful, are they not? She had such a delicate hand, and such fine work, although I used to worry about her bent over her embroidery frame. It would have ruined her eyesight, in time. I used to tell her so, but she laughed and said she loved to do it and would continue as long as she could."

"The covers on her diary are a particularly beautiful example," Louisa said, venturing a little nearer to her object. "I should never have thought of covering a book so. Are all her diaries enhanced in that way?"

"Every one, although the earlier ones are not so elegantly executed. The first was begun when she was just sixteen, on her birthday, in fact, and she continued right up to the day she died."

"Did she keep a proper diary, with an entry for every day?" Louisa said, pleased to find him willing to continue the subject. "Like most women, I keep a journal of sorts, but I add to it very sporadically, only when my mind is overfull of thoughts and I have no one with whom to share them, so they spill into my journal. I write about books I have read or interesting conversations that I continue to ponder. But many women like to write about their everyday lives — calls made and received, the children's activities, that sort of thing. Or secrets! Sometimes a diary is the repository of thoughts and inclinations that cannot be shared with anyone. But I do not suppose Mrs Gage had any secrets to be concealed."

"I do not imagine that she did," he said, smiling softly, clearly enjoying fond remembrances. "She wrote in it every day, that much I know for she told me so, but as to what she wrote about I can tell you nothing."

Louisa raised her eyebrows. "You have not read them?"

"Naturally not," he said, with a sudden shuttering of his open countenance. "I would not dream of intruding upon my wife's private thoughts."

That surprised her. No wonder he thought his wife perfect if he had never ventured beyond the mask she presented to the world. "Have you never wanted to?" she ventured. "Obviously you would not while she was alive, but now—"

"It makes no difference," he said, in some agitation.

"But do you never wonder what was hidden inside — the hopes and dreams, her resentments and discontents, the untamed corners of her mind?"

"There was no untamed corner of her mind," he said firmly. "Nothing was hidden with Catherine. She was just as she appeared to be — a tranquil and contented wife and mother, with nothing concealed."

"There is always something concealed," she said. "Every one of us has feelings and needs that we share with no one. To have secrets is to be human, Mr Gage, in my experience, and if your wife had none at all, then she was very much an exception."

"She was exceptional," he said quietly.

There was no possible answer to that.

9: A Mystery

Laurence decided this was exactly how a dinner for friends should be. There was lively conversation, good food and wine, an amicable atmosphere with everyone ready to be pleased, and a beautiful woman to add spice. Actually, there were three beautiful women. Mrs Middlehope took the palm, naturally, but Miss Platt was in bloom, too. And then there was Henrietta. When had his little girl turned into a beautiful young woman? Even with a gown she had worn a score of times before, she looked quite different.

There had been a fuss from Viola as soon as she heard what was proposed, but he had expected that and simply told her exactly what Mrs Middlehope had said — that Henrietta was Miss Gage of Lower Maeswood Grove and must dress according to her station in life. Then he had gone to see Hannah, Catherine's lady's maid, kept on after her death to take care of Viola and then Henrietta. He told her all that Mrs Middlehope had said, and apart from asking him precisely how she had described the hair, she understood it all at once.

"Just what I would have suggested myself, sir. Miss Henrietta's been ready for something a little more grown up for a while now. Do her good, it will, to be in company now and then."

A little more grown up? He could hardly believe the transformation when she entered the saloon, her head diffidently lowered. There was the amber pendant and bracelet, the comb in the hair with some ribbon and artificial flowers, and the curls around her face. He recognised one of Catherine's shawls draped over her arms, and perhaps the gloves were hers, too. Henrietta looked enchanting, and so he told her.

She instantly went pink. "Do you like the way my hair is done? Hannah spent ages curling it."

"I do. It suits you very well."

Mrs Middlehope thought so too when she arrived. "How well you look this evening, Miss Gage. What lovely curls! You have the perfect type of hair for the current styles, you lucky creature."

Laurence was momentarily disappointed not to see the peach velvet gown, but when he observed how the pale green silk she wore clung to her hips while foaming gracefully around her feet, he felt himself adequately compensated. Again her shoulders were almost bare, but they were admirable shoulders, smooth and white, and no ugly bones protruding. He so disliked the sight of collar bones. A woman needed a bit of flesh, he decided. Then with a twinge of guilt, he remembered Catherine's slender frame. She had not needed a bit of flesh to make her womanly… but she was different, queenly and composed, not a bit like Mrs Middlehope, who was… curvaceous? Alluring? Voluptuous, he decided. Yes, very different from his dear Catherine.

There had only been one awkward moment, when Mrs Middlehope had wondered if he had ever read Catherine's diaries. As if he would! Not that there would be anything to dismay him within their covers, but still it would not be right to pry.

But the rest of the evening was pure delight. Henrietta behaved with maidenly poise, and managed not to spill or drop anything except a glove as she rose from the table, which the youngest Platt boy rushed forward to retrieve with an energy which made both of them blush. There was the pleasure of listening to all the young ladies performing on the instrument, and there were songs, too, for Mr William Platt had a fine baritone which he exercised with enthusiasm. Then there were cards and supper, and all too soon they were in the hall awaiting the carriages.

"Gage, are you free tomorrow?" the squire said. "Beasley and I would like to discuss our findings with you and Mrs Middlehope. I have already asked the lady, and she said she will make herself available whenever convenient, so it is up to you."

"I am not otherwise engaged tomorrow," he said, rather pleased to be included in such a meeting, although perhaps his status as one of the finders of the body gave him a claim.

"Noon, then, at the Dower House," he said.

"Noon at the Dower House," he repeated, smiling at the prospect.

~~~~~

Laurence strolled down the drive to the Dower House at half past eleven, for it would not do to be late. He carried a bottle in his hand, for when he reflected over his previous wine offerings, he realised that he had not given her any Canary. The dogs had not
~~~~~

been invited, but they had decided to accompany him anyway, the younger two chasing each other through the shrubbery, and the oldest trotting sedately at his heels.

The footman saw him coming and had the front door open. "You are expected, sir."

"But the dogs are not. Will you enquire if they are welcome?"

But they were, and in they bounced, running up the hall and back again before following him into the study. It looked less like a study now and more like a lady's boudoir. The dark rug had gone, replaced with something brighter, and a round table and a davenport stood in place of the heavy desk. Vases of daffodils added colour, and there were two small pictures on the walls.

"Codlington and Roseacre," she said, in answer to his questioning look. "Very inferior, since I painted them myself, but my husband liked them and had them framed, so they have sentimental value to me." She bent to scratch the dogs' ears. "Now you three will have to behave, for my house is not so large as yours. You may sit by the fire while the humans are talking." Then, looking up at Laurence with a mischievous grin, "Shall we try the Canary at once?"

"I was hoping you would say that."

With a chuckle, she said, "I am not at all sure whether I am a bad influence on you, or you on me."

He laughed easily. "We are *good* influences on each other."

They had barely got the bottle open and taken the first sip when the knocker sounded again, and the squire and Beasley were shown in. They were early, too. More Canary was poured, chairs arranged in a ring and they all looked expectantly at Beasley.

"We have a name," he said slowly. "Dilys Hughes, a housemaid at the Hall, who got herself in the family way and was sent packing. She agreed to go home, and was given her pay to the end of the year and her fare for the stage coach, pretty generous treatment. Two of the servants at the Hall helped her pack and saw her onto the stage for Shrewsbury. They are still at the Hall and we have spoken to them, so there is no doubt at all that she boarded the stage. We cannot say what happened to her in Shrewsbury, but certain it is that she never arrived at her home, for we have been there and talked to several members of her family. It is a tiny Welsh village, so everyone would have known if she had turned up, but she never did."

"Did she not let them know of any change of plans?" Laurence said. "Were they not concerned?"

"None of them could read or write, so they had not seen or heard from her for years," Beasley said. "She went into service at ten years of age in the local manor house, but the old gentleman died and she went to Shrewsbury to find work, ending up at the Hall. Her parents never expected to see her again after that, so they knew nothing of her disgrace. And we are left with a puzzle. Did she get off the stage before it left the village? Or did she go all the way to Shrewsbury and then, for some reason, return here? And in either case, why?"

"What about her lover in all this?" Mrs Middlehope said. "Presumably there was no possibility of marriage?"

Beasley shrugged. "There were a number of possibilities. Dilys was one of those girls whose morals were somewhat suspect. No one seems to have been terribly surprised to find that she was with child. She herself accepted it calmly. I daresay her plan was to go home, have the child, foist it on her hapless parents and then go back into service, but something happened to prevent it."

"Or some *one*," the squire said grimly.

"Perhaps," Beasley said. "Impossible to say. All we know for certain is that she died very shortly after she left the Hall."

"How can you be sure of that?" Mrs Middlehope said.

"Ah, now that is the interesting part," Beasley said, leaning forward in sudden animation. "The skeletal remains of the child within her, combined with the information we have from the Hall, enable us to estimate the date with some precision. You see, the development of the unborn infant is such that—"

"We will take your word for it," Mrs Middlehope said. "For myself, the precise details are unnecessary. Have you any idea as to how the poor girl died? Poison, perhaps?"

Beasley shook his head. "The manner of her death, and whether it was by her own hand or otherwise, or even an accident cannot be determined, but..." He frowned. "I am not happy about it, not happy at all."

"I would go further," the squire said. "That girl was murdered, I am convinced of it. Locking herself into the wine cellar? Nonsense! Besides, when all this happened, the Dower House was still lived in. A very elderly relation — Great-aunt Elizabeth, Thomas used to call her — had the place then, with a full staff, so how she got inside unobserved is beyond me."

"Who is Thomas?" Mrs Middlehope said.

"Lord Saxby, the recent one. What was he, the sixth? Yes, the sixth. He called her Great-aunt, but I think she was a Great-great-aunt, in fact. The point is that the house was inhabited."

"I can quite easily believe that she got in, for working houses leave doors unlocked and windows open all the time," Mrs Middlehope said. "What I can *not* believe is that she lay down in the wine cellar and died, and no one noticed anything odd. We once had a pigeon fall down a chimney and get wedged in, somehow, so that the creature perished. We could not see it, but we knew it was there — the smell was abominable. If Dilys Hughes lay dead in that basement, someone would have found her."

"That is a good point," Beasley said, finishing the last drop of Canary in his glass and setting it down on a table. "However, Great-aunt Elizabeth died twenty-eight years ago and Dilys Hughes conceived her child twenty-nine years ago, and there is no getting around that. If it is indeed Dilys Hughes who was lying in that wine cellar, then she must have died there when the house was occupied."

"Is there any evidence that she died elsewhere and was brought here only after the house was empty?" Laurence said, frowning as he tried to work it out.

"No evidence that I can detect," Beasley said. "That would also raise the question of just where she had been for at least a year."

"And who brought her body here," Mrs Middlehope said. "Which brings us back to the matter of her lover. If she was murdered, or even if she died by her own hand somewhere else and was brought here, then there was another person involved and who else could it be but her lover?"

A silence fell on the room. The dogs were dozing by the fire, but the four humans were far from asleep. Laurence could not make head or tail of it. Why would anyone, no matter how desperate, sneak into an inhabited house, lock herself into the wine cellar and then die? Or if she died elsewhere and someone came upon the body, why move it to the Dower House? It made no sense. He latched on to some words of Beasley's...

"You said *if* it is Dilys Hughes... but what if it is not?" He had a sudden vivid memory of embroidered shoes with a silver buckle. "Those were not housemaid's shoes — and the cloak with silver fastenings! That is no housemaid."

"You see, Beasley?" the squire said with a note of triumph. "Exactly what I have been saying myself, Gage. The shoes, the cloak, the quality of the clothes generally all suggest someone other than Dilys Hughes. If it were some other woman, it could have happened later when the house was empty and it would be a lot less puzzling."

Beasley shook his head. "It is highly improbable that there were two such women in the same village, both with child, both disappearing from the face of the earth. For if that body is *not* Dilys Hughes, then what happened to her? Where did she go to? No, it makes far more sense if it is her. A pregnant woman vanishes — the body of a pregnant woman is found many years later. It *must* be her. But as to how she died or why she was locked in your wine cellar, Mrs Middlehope, I cannot say, and I do not feel I can pursue the matter any further."

"But there is much more that could be done," Laurence said. "Have you asked, for instance, if any other women disappeared at that time? What about the stage? It might be possible to trace the coach driver and guard, who might remember something. It is a long shot, I agree, but something might be discovered."

"That is what I should like to do," the squire said, "but neither I nor Beasley can give up any more time to it. What we need is someone like Miss Saxby. You will not know this, Mrs Middlehope, but when Lord Saxby died in January, there was a rumour that his end had been hastened by someone driving a stake through his heart, and the simple-minded boy who sharpens knives was arrested for it. He could not say where he had been that day, you see. But Miss Saxby set out to discover it all, and found people who would vouch for him being out at Overbury that day, so that he could not possibly have been anywhere near Lord Saxby. Clever girl, Cass Saxby, but she must not do so again. It is not fitting. However, I do not see what is to be done. If the girl had relations who were willing to pay for an investigation, we might get a Runner up here, but as it is—"

"I can pay," Laurence said at once. "I have no idea how to engage a Bow Street Runner, but I can certainly pay if one can be found."

"Now that is something that I might be able to help with," Mrs Middlehope said. "Not a Runner, but there are some people in London who are very experienced at this kind of investigation — murder and so forth. They solved the hat pin murder in Hartlepool last year."

"I remember that," Beasley said, pleased. "Very ingenious, both the murder and the resolution of it. It was very well covered in the London newspapers. Well, if Gage is prepared to pay the costs, then perhaps you will be good enough to write to these people, Mrs Middlehope."

Beasley and the squire took their leave, but Laurence stayed on. Mrs Middlehope refilled their glasses and they removed to the chairs by the fire, the dogs at their feet. And they talked. It was an odd thing, but he could talk to her about anything. Dilys Hughes occupied their thoughts at first, naturally, but when that had been gone over they moved on to the dinner the previous night, and how pretty Henrietta had looked, and how rowdy the Platt brothers had been, and how pleasant Susannah Winslade was.

"But I hardly got to talk to Miss Cokely at all," Mrs Middlehope said. "We exchanged three sentences before dinner, and afterwards by the time I had left the instrument, the card tables were being arranged. However, her little headband was adorable. I shall go and see her as soon as I may to get one just like it. And what is your opinion of Mr Truman? Everyone seems to think well of him."

"Not as well as he thinks of himself."

"Oh! You dislike him."

"He is... oily. A little too puffed up in his own importance for a clergyman. But I know no harm of him, except that he is excessively handsome and has all the ladies in his pocket, but I suppose he cannot help that."

She laughed. "Not *all* the ladies, surely?"

"Even Henrietta becomes a little tongue-tied in his presence," he said soberly. "I should not like to see her in thrall to such a man, even though she is too young to attract his attention."

"That is fortunate, for he is the sort of man who could be devastating to a woman's heart if once he turns his charm on her. Personable, sensible, well mannered and with an independent fortune — and very, very charming."

"A paragon of his sex, then," he said, aware of a certain sourness in his words.

But she only laughed again. "Certainly, for he embodies every masculine virtue, perfection personified."

"So *you* are in thrall to him, too," he said, unreasonably downcast by the thought.

"I may have mentioned to you before that I find perfection uninteresting," she said, smiling at him with such warmth that he was heartened. "Human foibles are far more to my taste, and, in my experience, even the most perfect of men has some flaw concealed within. Your wife may be a noble exception, but for myself I never knew anyone so perfect as to have no fault at all. My friend Mrs Deerham knew Mr Truman in Shrewsbury, and she says that he was not well liked at school and that she fears he is ambitious, but that could be said of any number of men, I daresay."

"Ambitious? Hmm, it could be. It is widely believed that he is hanging out for a wife, and when he arrived last year he was definitely dangling after Agnes Saxby."

"The plain one?"

He chuckled. "That is the one. A good-natured girl, and got herself entangled with Edser, the apothecary, at one time, but her father put a stop to that. She is very keen to marry, and Truman was definitely prowling round her. Then her father died, it was discovered that her dowry was far less than supposed and suddenly he has veered away. Agnes herself says she has no expectations in that quarter. So he is ambitious, yes, and avaricious, too. If ever he starts making up to Cass Saxby, you will know the truth of it, for she was thought to be penniless and a settled spinster at six and twenty, but when her father died it was discovered she is an heiress to the sum of seventy thousand pounds. A fine prize for a country parson, no? Is that Hugh Blair's sermons I see on the table? What do you think of him?"

And so they talked on, until half the day was gone. William came in once with cake and buns, and to tend the fire, but otherwise nothing disturbed them. It was the most comfortable thing in the world to sit like that, the dogs around their feet, a glass of Canary on the table beside them, not often touched but reassuringly there, and simply talk without any reserve.

It had not been so with Catherine. She had always been working on one of her complicated embroidery patterns and needed to concentrate, so when they were alone they had sat companionably enough, but in silence, he reading and she sewing, and he had never felt there was anything lacking. But of course that was different. Catherine was his beloved wife, his *perfect* wife, and he had not needed anyone else, not then.

Now he was alone, and although he would never insult Catherine's memory by marrying again, it pleased him that he had found such a good friend.

~~~~~

'The Dower House, Great Maeswood, Shropshire. 20th March. To Msrs Edgerton, Chandry & Associates ~ Sirs, We have never met, but relations of mine had the privilege of witnessing your skill at Hartlepool last year. Now I find myself with a similar mystery. My new home, having been empty for more than a quarter century, proved to have an unexpected tenant - the body of a young woman who had seemingly locked herself into the wine cellar and then died by some means. It is also possible that she died elsewhere and was subsequently moved to the cellar. Her identity has been guessed to be that of a housemaid from the adjoining house, but the dates and her clothing dispute this. Neither the reason for her death nor the manner of it have been determined, despite thorough investigation by the coroner and magistrate. They can do no more, but if you are willing to investigate further, your fees and expenses will be met in full. I am willing to furnish additional details, or supply the directions of the coroner and magistrate if required. I am sure you will agree with me that every untimely death, even one from so long ago, must be investigated and brought to a just conclusion if humanly possible, and I very much hope that you will undertake this commission. I
~~~~~

look forward to your early response. Yours, Mrs Edward Middlehope.'

~~~~~

'Oxford Street, London. 21st March. How fascinating! We are on our way. Captain M Edgerton.'
~~~~~

10: Edgerton, Chandry And Associates

Louisa had been informed by Miss Gage that she was to be at home to receive callers on Thursdays. She had also been provided with a helpful list of all the ladies of Great Maeswood and the surrounding villages, and the days on which they would be receiving callers. Although there was something horrifying about being so regimented, she found it amusing too, for she had no intention of being constrained. She might, perhaps, be at home on Thursdays if she felt so inclined, but otherwise she would do exactly as she had in County Durham — if she liked a person, she would call upon her when she felt like it and if she was not at home, then so be it. But if she was not interested in a person, however grand she may be, then she would not bother to call at all. There was no point, to her mind, in diligently cultivating acquaintances whose company gave one no pleasure.

On the Monday following, she found herself at liberty to walk about the gardens and see what needed to be done. The Timpson brothers were making good progress on the vegetable beds, and had already begun sowing and planting, although when she enquired as to the delights in store for her, they unpromisingly replied, *'Tatoes'*. She stifled a sigh, for she was getting very tired of boiled potatoes.

Leaving them to it, for vegetables, even such boring ones as potatoes, were more important than flowers, she wandered around what had once been pleasure grounds, assessing the weedy borders and wildly overgrown shrubs to see what she might be able to do herself. She had never minded getting earth on her hands, and the weeds were crying out for the attention of a patient lady with a trowel, but there were more urgent matters. A number of roses stood in need of hard pruning, and she would start with those beside the front door. Borrowing a pruning knife from the Timpsons, for her own was still in transit, she began cutting.

She had not made more than half a dozen cuts before a post-chaise and four turned into the drive, the horses lathered and near to exhaustion. It came to a halt, the door opened and a small man, swaddled in a greatcoat adorned with a vast number of capes, jumped down. Beneath the greatcoat, she caught a glimpse of a garish blue and yellow striped waistcoat, and was that a sword he was wearing? It was!

"Have I the honour of addressing Mrs Middlehope?" he said, whipping off his tall beaver hat with a flourish.

"I am she."

"We are come to solve your mystery!" he cried melodramatically, making her an elaborate bow. "Captain Edgerton at your service, madam. Allow me to present my colleagues." Two more men descended, one a handsome fellow with a roguish smile, the other looking as if he had come directly from Bond Street. "This is Mr Willerton-Forbes," he said, gesturing to the fashionably dressed man. "And this is Mr Chandry." The roguish man grinned and bowed.

"How do you do, gentlemen," she said politely. "I had no expectation of seeing you for days yet. The lady in question has been dead for a great many years, after all, so the matter is hardly urgent. However, you are most welcome. I only hope the matter to be investigated will prove worthy of such enthusiasm."

"We had no other case of interest," Captain Edgerton said. "A couple of pickpockets, a common assault... all very boring. Whereas a lady in a locked wine cellar... now that is intriguing! We could not wait to get here. But first things first. Is the inn here tolerable, would you say, or must we go on to Shrewsbury for accommodation? For myself I do not mind bed bugs, but Willerton-Forbes here is the Earl of Morpeth's son and therefore has higher standards than we plebeians."

Laughing, Louisa said, "We can do a little better than the Boar's Head, Captain. You are invited to stay at the home of Mr Gage, the gentleman who has undertaken to pay your fees. You will find the entrance to Lower Maeswood Grove directly opposite this drive."

All three men expressed their pleasure at this arrangement, and went off at once to make themselves known to their host. Louisa could only hope that the household would not be too dismayed by the unexpected arrival of so many people, and one of them, at least, looking as if he needed his valet with him at all times.

They returned within the hour, bringing with them Mr Gage and Dr Beasley.

"You may leave your sword at the door, Captain," Louisa said. "I cannot feel it will be necessary for our discussions."

"One must be prepared for all eventualities," he said with a grin, producing a pistol from each pocket.

"Good heavens! Are they loaded?"

"They would be of little use in an emergency if they were not," he said affably.

"True enough. May I look at one?"

He only hesitated for a moment before handing it over, although she was aware of Mr Willerton-Forbes and Mr Chandry surreptitiously moving out of harm's way behind her. Only Mr Gage stood his ground, smiling. He knew her well enough to be sure that she could handle the gun safely. She took it carefully, pointed towards the floor, feeling the weight of it and admiring the craftsmanship.

"Very well made, but then Manton's work always is," she said, handing it back. "Not his fanciest effort, but more serviceable for your purpose, I should imagine. I have something similar myself, although a little smaller. However pleasing the design, I should still feel happier if these beauties were left here with your sword, or better still, in the parlour there. William will make sure that no one touches them."

He complied at once, and then helped William fetch extra chairs to accommodate so many people in the study. After that there was the business of refreshments — Mr Gage, bless him, had brought another bottle of Madeira — before they could settle to discussing Dilys Hughes. The three Londoners' eyes gleamed with excitement as Dr Beasley told of his findings and all his concerns.

"It seems to me," Captain Edgerton said thoughtfully, "that there are two lines of enquiry to pursue. Firstly, Dilys Hughes. She left here on the stage coach, but where did it take her? We might be able to track down the coachman or guard, and we can enquire in Shrewsbury and the coaching inn, although it seems unlikely anyone would remember something after all this time. The second question is whether this body is Dilys Hughes at all, so we must ask everyone in the village if any other young lady went missing. Mr Gage, we shall need letters of introduction from you, so that we may approach people who would otherwise not talk to riff-raff like us."

"I'm the only riff-raff here, Michael," Mr Chandry said with a soft accent — the West Country, perhaps. "You and Pettigrew are definitely quality. Well... Pettigrew is, at any rate. Not sure about you." To Louisa he said, "He was in the East India Army, ma'am, and you know what they're like."

"Adept with swords and pistols, I expect," she said, chuckling. "Is there much call for such weapons in your present line of work, Captain?"

It was Mr Willerton-Forbes who answered. "You would be surprised, Mrs Middlehope. Murder is a nasty business and when cornered, a man who has already killed once will not hesitate to do so again. On such occasions, one needs to have one's defences at the ready. As a lawyer, my preferred weapons are words, and Mr Chandry is a useful man in a fist fight, but in a crisis there is no substitute for lethal weapons and a man with the battle skills and experience to use them."

"Let us hope we encounter no crises, then," she said lightly.

"Unlikely, one would suppose," Mr Willerton-Forbes said. "However, one never knows what may be stirred up from the past. And speaking of the past, we shall need to know a great deal more about this body. Dr Beasley, you have a detailed report which we may examine, I trust?"

"Ah, I have something even more useful to you — I have the body itself. Squire Winslade is helpfully preserving it for us in his ice house, although it is probably beyond the need for such preservation. Shall we go and have a look?"

The Londoners jumped up eagerly, and went off with Dr Beasley to fetch his carriage.

"They will be gone for the rest of the day," Mr Gage said, picking up a chair to carry back to the parlour. When he returned, he said, "Will you come for dinner tonight, Mrs Middlehope? You will want to hear their findings, I am sure."

"Your sister will have all too many unexpected guests to attend to without adding me to the number. I would not impose on her good nature by asking her to entertain an extra lady as well."

"Oh." He looked pleasingly disappointed. He picked up another chair. "That is a pity. Your thoughts would be most welcome."

"I think Captain Edgerton and his colleagues are the experts," she said.

He carried the chair away, then returned and picked up his glass of Madeira, not yet empty, twirling it pensively. "I think you should come tonight, whether Viola likes it or not," he said abruptly. "Edgerton and his friends are very enthusiastic, but I am not comfortable with a man who goes about with loaded pistols in his pockets. It seems to me to be looking for trouble, and those who do that tend to find it. I am not sure that I am sufficient to rein in his wilder starts, but a lady's presence would certainly have a restraining influence."

She laughed, shaking her head at him. "You sound very determined to have me there, whereas I am almost equally determined not to go."

"Almost?" he said, his eyes crinkling with amusement.

"You know my weaknesses, Mr Gage. I am sure you can find a way to tempt me."

"Let me see... how about a Château Latour, laid down by my father twenty years ago?"

"Done!" she said promptly. "There, that was easy, and you have saved me from mutton and boiled potatoes."

"Is that what your new cook serves you?"

"It is all she knows how to prepare. Boiled potatoes are a very depressing vegetable, I find."

He laughed. "Then at all costs we must preserve you from the depressive effects of boiled potatoes." Draining his glass, he set it down on the sideboard with what sounded like a sigh. "And now I must away, for my steward has been awaiting me this half hour past. I shall see you this evening, Mrs Middlehope."

Louisa was greatly cheered by this invitation, and promptly sent word to Mrs Nokes that she would be dining out that evening. One meal, at least, which would offer her something more interesting than boiled beef and potatoes. It was such a fine day, and so mild for late March, that she was tempted to make an expedition and explore the surrounding lanes and villages. She had been told of a fine haberdashery in Astley Cloverstone, which was reason enough for an outing, so she ordered the gig brought round and changed into her travelling gown and pelisse, the only outfit she had that was suitable for driving in.

The pony was full of energy after several days of idleness, and set off at a good speed down the drive. Louisa had to restrain him through Great Maeswood, but with the village left behind, she came to a long stretch of straight road, smooth and well-maintained, where she could give him his head. About a quarter of a mile outside the village, she came to a group of men labouring to erect a tall stone at the side of the road, so she brought the gig to a halt.

"Good day to you! What is your enterprise here?"

"G'day, mum," said one of the men, stepping forward and removing his hat. "G'day, Goronwy. 'Tis a monument to Lord Saxby, who died in this very place at the turn of the year, mum. The 'orses musta took fright at somethin' and tipped 'im out, and the young master too. Terrible tragedy, it were. Thought it right to mark the spot. We took the 'at round and all o' us put somethin' in, all 'is lordships tenants and workers."

"That is commendable," she said. "He was well liked, then, the late Lord Saxby?"

"Aye, 'e was that," the spokesman said, but the other men exchanged glances and Louisa drew her own conclusions. She drove on, the straight road permitting an exhilarating pace. It was easy to see how his lordship might have come to grief — a fast drive, a rabbit startled into motion, the horses spooked... It would not have taken much.

She slowed for the village of Astley Cloverstone, which was smaller than Great Maeswood, with no properties of substance, yet it looked to be better cared for, and perhaps more prosperous. She easily found Mr Whiteway's haberdashery and was delighted to find that he was also a draper and hatter and much more besides. She spent an hour and a great deal of money there, the entire family emerging from back rooms to stow her many parcels in the gig and wave her off.

From there Louisa turned west, passing two substantial properties on the outskirts of the village, Cloverstone Manor and the Grange. After that, the road narrowed and meandered through pretty woods, barely tinged with green as yet, a few scattered hamlets and a stretch of river before turning south again. Her route ran through a maze of narrow, criss-crossing lanes. She had checked the map before leaving, but even so she had to ask directions twice.

She passed through another large village, Woollercott, a substantial habitation with several good-quality houses, and thus came once more to the main road between Market Clunbury and Shrewsbury, where she turned for home. She came back into Great Maeswood almost before she was aware of it. Only one house, half-hidden amongst trees, gave warning of the approaching village and almost at once she rounded a bend and saw the entrance to Maeswood Hall.

The pony never broke stride, but even sped up a little as he turned into the drive. Louisa laughed out loud, realising the creature's mistake. He was so used to returning to the Hall that he did so automatically, even though his home was now at the Dower House. The drive was too narrow to make a turn, so she allowed the pony to take her all the way to the house. He turned aside before that, however, and thus she found herself arriving at the stables, where the pony stopped.

Two grooms ambled out, saw the gig and laughed. "Well, Goronwy, have you come home, you daft thing?"

"It was my fault," Louisa said. "I was inattentive, and he had turned in before I knew what he was about. Will you help me get him facing about? I had hoped to turn him in front of the house, but he had other ideas."

The grooms persuaded the pony to reverse enough for Louisa to set off again, back down the drive, onto the main road and then into her own drive. He seemed a little reluctant, but she eventually got him to the stables and carried her parcels into the house in triumph. Marie was summoned at once to unpack and inspect.

"There now, have I not done well? Gloves, ribbons, buttons... do you not think these silk flowers are pretty? And what about this spotted muslin? It will make a very pretty gown. They had plenty of cotton, and a few lengths of satin, but I am not a satin sort of person, I feel."

"Vous êtes de la soie, madame." You are silk.

"*La soie?* Silk? Oh yes... silk, velvet, swansdown... but we must make do with what we can get, must we not? Can you do something with the muslin and this jaconet? Day gowns... something different. I am so bored with the three I have... round and round they go. Monday, Tuesday, Wednesday, then start the cycle again on Thursday."

"Vous aurez besoin de robes pour le soir aussi." You need evening gowns, as well.

"Evening robes?" she said, grasping at the few words she understood. "The only occasion requiring an evening gown is a dinner engagement, and there are all too few of those," Louisa said sorrowfully. "No, let us not worry about evenings, but I am sure your nimble fingers can contrive something for mornings."

"Mais bien sûr, madame. Le décolleté comme ça, et les manches... voyez-vous? Deux jours." But of course. The neck like so and the sleeves... you see? Two days.

"I did not quite catch all that, but I am sure it will be wonderful. How clever you are, Marie! What would I do without you? How old are you now?"

"Vingt-trois, madame."

"What is that in English? Hmm... twenty... three. Yes, it must be, for you were eighteen when you came to me, and that was five years ago. I thought then that you were far too pretty to be a lady's maid, and that some observant young man would snap you up. Both my previous maids left me for husbands, but happily for me you have not done so yet."

"Mariage? Moi? Jamais! Les hommes sont abominables, madame. Je ne veux rien à faire avec eux." Marriage? Never! Men are abominable. I want nothing to do with them.

"I wish you would not speak so fast, Marie," Louisa said. "I get the gist of it... you dislike men and have no wish to marry, but that is very sad. Not all men are abominable. Thoughtless, some of them, boring and selfish, on occasion, but not abominable. Not *all* men, surely."

"Tous les hommes," Marie said firmly, and then, emphatically, "All men."

Louisa gave it up. It was sad, but at least she would never lose another maid to a lovestruck suitor.

~~~~~

Laurence had been forced to endure a long lecture from Viola on the subject of wily widows, but she could not rescind an invitation already given, much as she would have liked to. She took her revenge on the children, deeming the company too adult for a boy of twelve and a girl not yet out. Henrietta had been disappointed not to hear more about the dead body, but Edward, who was not as ghoulish as his sister, accepted the
~~~~~

rebuff without demur. Laurence knew that they would eat the same dishes in the nursery, so they would not miss a great deal and he chose not to contest the ruling. Viola had enough to deal with, what with three very stylish young men arriving on her doorstep days earlier than they were looked for, and then having Mrs Middlehope foisted upon her.

He was rewarded by the peach velvet evening gown, which warmed him inwardly, and clearly warmed Captain Edgerton, too, judging by the gleam in his eye and the alacrity with which he swept Mrs Middlehope away from Laurence. Mrs Middlehope threw him an amused glance as she allowed herself to be drawn away.

At least he was able to claim her for dinner, and keep some of her conversation exclusively to himself. The London gentlemen were well-bred, and kept the table amused for the whole meal. Mr Willerton-Forbes talked glibly of his high ranking acquaintances, like the Duke of Dunmorton and the Marquess of Carrbridge. Mr Chandry was from Cornwall, and able to make the adventures of dashing smugglers sound almost heroic. As for Captain Edgerton, his tales of life in India were a great deal of nonsense — elephant stampedes and tiger-shooting females, indeed! Still, Viola was enthralled with it all, and by no means impervious to the delicate flattery of the gentlemen.

When the ladies rose to withdraw, Laurence put in hastily, "Mrs Middlehope, will you not stay a little longer, for our intrepid investigators are bursting with news, I can see, and the business most nearly concerns you, since the lady was found in your house. Viola is welcome to stay, too, if she pleases."

"It is all too horrible for me, Laurence," Viola said firmly. "Mrs Middlehope?"

"If you will indulge me, Miss Gage, I should like to stay for a short while, just to hear of Captain Edgerton's discoveries."

Viola could not object to such a request from a guest, so she nodded and passed through the door Mr Chandry was holding open for her. The gentlemen re-seated themselves, shifting their chairs a little closer together.

"Will you try a little port?" Laurence said to Louisa. "You will like it, I believe."

"I should love some," she said at once. "I very often took a glass at home, for once my mama-in-law died, I was generally the only lady in the house and I so hated to miss all the interesting conversation."

"Just you, your husband and your father-in-law?" Laurence said, as he poured her a glass and slid it to her.

"And the chaplain and the secretary, and occasionally the steward or attorney, too. I was quite outnumbered. Oh, this is excellent! So smooth!"

"It is something to do with when the brandy is added," Laurence said. He would have liked to enter into a longer discussion of the fortification process, but he could see Captain Edgerton was impatient to talk about the body, so he yielded to him.

The captain leaned forward eagerly. "We now know that this is *not* Dilys Hughes at all. You suspected it, Mr Gage, because of the clothes, but today Dr Beasley took some additional measurements to confirm it. Dilys Hughes was small, not much above five feet in height, whereas our mystery lady is about five foot six inches tall. So now we must start a full enquiry to find out just who she is."

He rubbed his hands together in glee.

11: Books, Gowns And A Square Pianoforte

Louisa did not stay long with the gentlemen, for they began to talk about ways of identifying the mysterious body from the wine cellar, and the details of that did not interest her. So she returned to the drawing room and virtuously made herself agreeable to Miss Gage. Knowing her to be an inveterate gossip, Louisa allowed herself to be drawn into a discussion about the Roseacre family. She was too polite to relate the more opprobrious tales of Pamela, but there was no hiding her background, and it was amusing to watch Miss Gage attempt to reconcile the deference due to a baroness with her contempt for the merchant class. And somewhere at the back of her mind was the thought that if ever Pamela should encroach herself all the way to Shropshire, preferably with her delightfully vulgar father, the ghastliness would be greatly ameliorated by observing their encounters with Miss Gage.

The gentlemen lingered so long over their port that Miss Gage was visibly yawning and even Louisa's good manners were stretched to find sufficient conversation to keep her awake. But eventually they came, the four gentlemen settling down for whist and Miss Gage, who was clearly determined not to leave Louisa alone with them, insisting on a game of cribbage, even though she was visibly dropping from tiredness.

Louisa took pity on her and left rather earlier than she would have liked, escorted on the ten minute walk by Captain Edgerton and Mr Chandry, irrepressible rogues the pair of them. She would have preferred Mr Gage's company, in the interests of advancing her project, but she could wait. She was a patient woman, and she was finding the chase just as enjoyable as the anticipated reward.

~~~~~

Three days of continuous rain kept Louisa trapped at home. She was not such a delicate flower as to shun wet weather, but her lack of changes of clothes prohibited it for the moment. Instead, she made good use of the time by trying to teach Mrs Nokes some receipts more sophisticated than mutton and boiled beef. The result was a tolerable ragoût and a blancmange, three new soups, one of them rather good, and some pigeons in a wine sauce, which Mrs Nokes thought a shocking waste of good Madeira. There was also an almond pudding that was almost of a standard to serve to guests. Perhaps in another year or two there might be hope of a soufflé. Or perhaps she should simply be done with it and request the agency in London to find her a man-cook. A *French* man-cook.

Finally the sun came out and Louisa felt able to brave the puddles and walk to the centre of the village. She no longer needed to patronise the bakery, for Mrs Nokes was competent enough with bread and buns, but Mr Timpson might have some interesting spices to liven up one or two dishes. How she longed for a proper curry, but that was not part of Mrs Nokes' repertoire and Louisa was not familiar enough with the necessary
~~~~~

ingredients to teach her. She would have to write to the ever-helpful Mr Moffat for a cookery book. She could not find spices, but Mr Timpson had newly-arrived supplies of quills, of which one could never have too many, and a box of parasols, just arrived from London in all the most fashionable styles, he assured her. Louisa could not quite agree, but she found one that would match a summer gown she owned. The gown itself was still presumably on the road somewhere, but it would no doubt arrive before summer, next year's if not this.

A visit to the Boar's Head brought forth many treasures — half a dozen letters, happily none of them from Pamela, and a large parcel of books from Mr Moffat. When she returned to the Dower House, she was delighted to find even more treasures being unloaded from a large wagon — her first consignment of wine from William Matley and Sons, wine importers and vintners of Bristol.

The wagon had only just lumbered down the drive and onto the road when a smart carriage turned in, a very elegant and very *familiar* carriage, now bearing a nobleman's coat of arms on its door. Behind it, a larger, more elderly conveyance, piled high with luggage. Louisa groaned so loudly that William and Sarah, engaged in shifting barrels of wine, looked at her in alarm.

"Well," she said, struggling to regain her composure. "It seems we have visitors."

Then, affixing a smile to her face, she stepped out of the front door to greet the arrivals decanting from the carriage.

"Pamela. What a surprise. And Mr Pritchard, too. How... how unexpected. The letter bearing notice of your arrival must have gone astray."

"Oh, it wouldn't be near so much fun if we'd told you aforehand," the lady trilled happily. "We was packing up all your things, you know, and I was fretting over sending them such a distance, and what would happen if there was some mishap and your lovely things got lost or damaged, and Pa said *'Why should we not go ourselves, to keep an eye on them?'* Well, I was not sure, because Lottie had such a bad earache that I hardly liked to leave her side, but I've been that worried about you, stuck here all on your own — Shropshire! Why, it's practically in Wales! So far from anywhere, and not a soul here that you know. So lonely you must be, you poor thing. And your letter — so short and not a word about friends or company. I was that upset to read it, but Pa said, *'Let's go and cheer her up',* and that settled it. So here we are, although we cannot stay more than a few days, so you must try not to be too upset when we leave."

Lady Mountsea was a dumpy woman who had once been pretty but had lost her bloom early and was descending rapidly into her matronly middle years. Once her daughters were old enough to go into society, she would blend effortlessly into the ranks of gossipy, optimistic mamas on the chaperons' benches. Her father, Mr Pritchard, was a jolly man with a penchant for vivid waistcoats and a multitude of gold fobs. He beamed genially at Louisa.

"There now, isn't this a grand surprise, Mrs M?"

"It is indeed a surprise," she murmured. Then, catching sight of the coachman smiling and nodding at her, she said, "Whitmer! How are you? And Mrs Whitmer? Is her leg better? And Sally... has she had her baby yet?"

He chuckled. "Aye, we're all fine, ma'am, thank you for asking. Our Sally had a boy two weeks since, a fine lusty little chap. Just like his grandad he is, and just as bonnie a head as me." He lifted his wig to show his bald pate, making her laugh.

Spotting the two footmen unloading luggage and the under-coachman and a groom on the luggage coach she waved to them, but said, "I am very pleased to see you all, but you will have to put up at the inn, I am afraid."

"Aye, we expected that, ma'am."

"Nonsense," Pamela said. "You must have plenty of room here, a house this big."

"The house is certainly big enough," Louisa said, "but the stables are not, and my cook can barely cope with feeding me and four servants. You and Mr Pritchard and your maid and valet may stay here, but the rest must go to the Boar's Head with the coaches and horses. They will be very comfortable there. Do come inside, Pamela. You will want some tea, I am sure."

The hall was still cluttered with wine and Louisa's parcels from the village, and the two Roseacre footmen were piling boxes and oddly shaped packages in every available space. Louisa looked around for her own footman, hovering uncertainly by the service stairs.

"William, Lady Mountsea and Mr Pritchard will be staying for a few days. Tell Mrs Nokes there will be two extra for the dining room and two more below stairs, and bring some tea to the drawing room. Ah, Sarah, there you are. The two front bedrooms will need to be prepared. Broughton and Harvey will tell you what their master and mistress require for their comfort, but get fires lit as soon as you can. John, Matthew, do not bring any more boxes in until we have cleared what is here. Get this lot down to the wine cellar first. William has the keys. After that, anything that is for me can go into the parlour here. Move the furniture aside to fit it all in, if need be. Pamela, Mr Pritchard, do come into the drawing room until order has been restored. It is a pity you gave me no warning of your coming, for I am not at all prepared for you."

"Is this wine? All of it?" Pamela said in astonished tones.

"It is," Louisa said curtly, not feeling any necessity to explain herself.

"Good heavens, Lou, and only you in the house! How will you possibly drink so much?"

"One glass at a time, savouring every mouthful. And I shall entertain my friends, if ever my cook is up to the task."

"Oh, you have friends, do you? Well, that is a relief." But she sounded rather cross about it.

"Naturally I have friends. I am not a hermit, and have dined out several times since I arrived, not to mention card parties twice a week. Do come into the drawing room, Pamela, and take off your bonnet. Have you come far today? What are the roads like after the rain?"

"Yes, but— Careful with that, Matthew! No, that one is for my room, but not the other. Do you have a box room, Lou?"

"Only the attic, but no one has been up there for twenty-five years, at least," Louisa said. "Put it in the parlour, Matthew. Oh… is that my pianoforte?" She shivered with excitement. At last, she would have music again. How much she had missed it! "In the drawing room, if you please, and unwrap it at once. I have just the space for it. Mr Pritchard? That is the dining room. The drawing room is in here."

Finally she got Pamela and Mr Pritchard into the drawing room, while the footmen gently carried the instrument to the place she had set aside for it. It was a little bigger than she remembered and only just fitted, but perhaps that was the quantity of felt and sacking that protected it. Not until all the wrappings were removed did she realise the truth.

"This is the clavichord, Pamela, not the pianoforte."

"It is the Broadwood, the square Broadwood — that was what you asked for, wasn't it?"

"The square *pianoforte* from the winter parlour. There are three Broadwoods at Roseacre, and this is the clavichord from the music room."

"Oh. Well, it is just as good, I am sure. Is that your garden? There is not much growing in it. The children send you their best love, and are wild to hear how you go on. I was a bit surprised you made no mention of them in your letter, but there, I suppose it distresses you too much. Ah, tea! How lovely. Goodness, I am thirsty."

"Did you have room for all my boxes of books, and my clothes?" Louisa said in some trepidation. She had left very clear instructions about what to pack, but she no longer had any confidence that they would arrive.

"Oh, your clothes, certainly, but the books... it would have depleted the library considerably to send all that you asked for. It must have been a quarter of the entire collection!"

"But they are mine," Louisa said resentfully. "Mostly my father's but also those I have bought with my own money. I *will* have them, Pamela, and the square pianoforte, which was a wedding gift from Ned. What about the pictures? Have you brought those? Ned left me those in his will, you know that perfectly well."

"Aye, we brought those," Mr Pritchard said, looking up from the newspaper he had picked up. "Lord M right down insisted. And your horse. Said that was yours, too. He didn't know about the books, I'll wager, but I'll make sure he knows and sends what's yours."

"My horse? You have brought Gaius Valerius?" Without warning, her legs weakened, she collapsed into the nearest chair and burst into tears. Such an unlooked-for kindness!

"Aye, Spencer's bringing him," Mr Pritchard said. "He just stopped at the inn to bespeak accommodation, in case you couldn't cope with us all here. We had no idea how big the house was. Lord, Mrs M, don't cry. Have you any brandy in the house? Any that's not still in the barrel, that is." He chuckled at his own wit, and went off to find William.

Gaius Valerius! He was not, strictly speaking, hers, for Ned and his father had always said that whatever was in the stables was for anyone to use, family and guests alike, and her previous mount, a placid mare, had been ridden by a great many ladies over the years. However, when Pulcheria had grown too infirm to carry her, her father-in-law had bought Gaius Valerius, and no one had ever ridden him but Louisa, and Spencer, her groom.

Mr Pritchard put his head round the door. "Here's your horse arriving now, Mrs M, and your man's finding some brandy."

"Never mind the brandy!" Louisa cried, jumping to her feet and dashing away her tears impatiently. "Just let me see Gaius and I shall be better."

She rushed through the obstacle-strewn hall and through the open front door, and there he was, her magnificent grey, and Spencer on his own horse, leading him. Gaius Valerius whickered with delight at the sight of her, and tossed his head. Louisa raced down the steps and buried her face in his soft mane. *"Quomodo es, amica mea? Beati estis ad me? Ego sum gauisus ut vos." How are you, my friend? Are you pleased to see me? I am happy to have you.*

And she sighed with pleasure.

~~~~~

"Mrs Middlehope has visitors!"

Laurence marked his place and closed his book. "Anyone exciting?" He was alone in the study, the children having been drawn into helping Captain Edgerton in his enquiries around the village, and for once he was interested in Viola's gossip.

"Lady Mountsea! There now, what do you think of that? All the way from Derbyshire to see—"

"Durham."

"—her sister-in-law, and brought such a quantity of luggage, Mrs Timpson says, so they must be staying for a while. Oh, and a horse, rather a fine one, by all accounts, a big grey creature, not at all a lady's horse so it must belong to the gentleman who is with Lady Mountsea, whoever he is."

"Lord Mountsea, conceivably?" Laurence hazarded.

"That was what Mrs Timpson thought at first, but Beth Brownsmith said not. The groom went in there to ask about accommodation, and bespeak two good rooms for Lady Mountsea and the gentleman, and Beth asked outright if it was Lord Mountsea, and he said not. A Mr Richard or some such. Ditchford... something of the sort. I did not quite catch it. But they are not to stay there after all, they will stay with Mrs Middlehope and only the coachmen and footmen will stay at the Boar. What do you think of that? Another baroness in Great Maeswood! Although her origins— But then nobility is still nobility, no matter who her father is. I wonder if I should pop over to the Dower House and ask if they need anything. Imagine, two distinguished visitors descending unannounced and who
~~~~~

knows if poor Mrs Middlehope has all she needs for their comfort."

"By *unannounced*, I presume that you mean that *you* were unaware of it," Laurence said, amused. "Mrs Middlehope may have known all about it. Besides, if these visitors are so distinguished, they will travel with their own sheets."

"Oh, sheets! It is not sheets I am thinking of, it is... it is... well, I cannot say what she may need."

"Whatever it is, she knows us well enough to ask for it," he said mildly. "I will send John over with some of the fish. There is too much for us anyway."

"At least she will not be short of wine," she said acidly. "Phyllida says the Matley cart went by earlier, and it did not come here, and the Saxbys order from that fellow in Market Clunbury. I think I *will* just pop across and see if Mrs Middlehope needs any help."

Laurence hesitated, and then wondered why he should do so. He need not be browbeaten by his own sister. "If they are to stay with Mrs Middlehope for a few days we might invite them for dinner. Her cook's repertoire is limited to mutton and boiled potatoes, apparently, so it would be a kindness."

Viola narrowed her eyes in suspicion, and for a moment he could almost see her weighing the advantage of entertaining a baroness to dinner against the disadvantage of encouraging what she saw as the widow's pretensions. Abruptly she sat down, then blurted, "Laurence, are you... have you formed an *attachment* to Mrs Middlehope?"

He had picked up his glass of Madeira from the table beside him, but now he set it down again and steepled his fingers. Such a question deserved an honest answer, so he said carefully, "I enjoy her company but there is nothing more to it than that, Vi. I have told you before that I have no intention of marrying again, and, despite what you may think, nor has Mrs Middlehope. She has told me so explicitly. You need have no fears on that score."

This reassurance did not have the expected effect on Viola. Her face remained anxious, and she chewed her lips fretfully. "But that is not the only possible outcome," she said hesitantly. "I know you see nothing wrong in her behaviour, brother, and to be sure a married woman is permitted far greater freedom, but to my mind she is a little too forward with gentlemen, and especially so with *you*. My real fear… the worst that could possibly happen… is that she might draw you in to… to a *liaison*, and that would be too dreadful to contemplate. The disgrace! The humiliation! I should have to leave this house, leave you and the dear children, and what would become of them? It would be the ruination of Henrietta."

"Sister, you refine too much upon Mrs Middlehope's natural liveliness," he said gently. "You insult her, and you insult me, too, in imagining either of us capable of such behaviour."

Her face brightened. "Then… you would not do it?"

"I give you my word as a gentleman that I would never, ever do anything of that nature. I would not cause you such hurt, nor would I so dishonour Catherine's memory."

He meant it, too, every word. And yet there was something, some tiny niggle at the back of his mind that felt suspiciously like disappointment.

12: Cooks And Grooms

APRIL

Louisa could not wait for Pamela to leave. Since she had travelled two hundred miles and could not be expected to set off again immediately, she knew she would have to suffer her sister-in-law for several days. Mr Pritchard was no trouble, for Mr Gage swept him off to shoot and fish and visit other gentlemen, but Pamela was another matter. Whatever Louisa did, Pamela would be there. If she walked into the village, Pamela went too, chattering away volubly to everyone they met. If she tried to do some gardening, there the woman was again, rattling on and on about her own garden at Roseacre — which Louisa had largely created — or her multitude of children or some boring detail of one of her army of uninteresting relations, until Louisa wanted to scream.

And then Pamela saw it as her sisterly duty to try to persuade Louisa to return to Roseacre. "You must be so lonely here in this tiny village, so far from your family," she said over and over. "I'm glad you have friends but it's not the same, is it? I hate to think of you dwindling away here when you could be at home, and surrounded by your nearest and dearest."

Louisa had to bite her tongue not to point out that in some cases one's nearest were not necessarily dear at all.

Happily for her sanity, her friends in the neighbourhood rallied round. On Saturday, the Gages invited them to dine at the Grove, along with the three London investigators and Squire Winslade and his family. Captain Edgerton and Mr Chandry exerted their considerable charms on Pamela, Mr Pritchard and the squire struck up an odd rapport and Louisa was left to savour the delights of good food and wine, while progressing her project with Mr Gage.

There was only one sticky moment, where the squire said loudly, "I hope you will stay until after Easter, Lady Mountsea, for then you will be able to join us at the Manor for our ball. Always the first Saturday after Easter, and everyone stays until Monday. A most enjoyable occasion. Do say you will come."

The Saturday after Easter! Louisa held her breath in sheer terror, until Pamela tittered and said, "Oh, how kind, but I cannot leave the dear children for so long. What a pity."

What a pity? What a relief! Sunday was another good day, for both her guests enjoyed showing themselves off at divine service, and Lady Saxby extended the courtesy of her table to a fellow noblewoman. Another good meal to be had.

On Monday, however, they were back in Mrs Nokes' hands.

"It is not quite up to the standards of Maeswood Hall or Lower Maeswood Grove," Louisa said apologetically, as they took their places and looked at various dishes laid out before them. "I hope you will find something to tempt your appetites, however."

"Splendid array, Mrs M, quite splendid," Mr Pritchard said, as he carved the mutton with vigour. "Mmm, lovely piece of meat."

"Oh yes, this is lovely," Pamela said. "So much more appetising than all those strange things in sauces that Lady Saxby served. Lobster! Eww! Horrid stuff. She offered me some and I felt obliged to take it but I left it on my plate, hidden by some of that peculiar vegetable. Are those boiled potatoes? Such a treat to have food that hasn't been messed about and mangled. Chambers never does anything of the sort, and he is so expensive. Have you any idea how much we pay him? Well, I daresay you have, since you engaged him, but it is not worth it for no matter how much he tries he cannot make a good gruel. Poor Pa is a martyr to his dyspepsia, you know, and a dish of gruel at bedtime sets him up wonderfully. Your Mrs Nokes makes a lovely gruel, doesn't she, Pa? He has been so much better since we've been here, and all because of Mrs Nokes' gruel. If only Chambers could make gruel."

Louisa could think of no sensible response to this. Her wonderful man-cook, so hard fought for and long awaited, so carefully chosen and greatly prized, set to making gruel! It was unspeakable.

"He is quite good with pastry, however," Pamela rattled on, oblivious. "His pies are lovely, aren't they, Papa? But he will never do a boiled chicken, just as I like it, and I think he should cook what I tell him, don't you, Lou? So I've had to let him go. Mm, this cabbage is delicious."

Louisa squeaked, and dropped her knife. *"Let him go?* You have dismissed my man-cook?"

"Well, strictly speaking, he is *my* man-cook now, and I do not find him satisfactory. I have given him notice, but he may stay until I've found a replacement."

"Send him to me," Louisa said urgently. "Send him here and you can have Mrs Nokes, with my goodwill."

Pamela looked at her in surprise. "Can you afford him? I mean, you're an impoverished widow now, aren't you?"

Mr Pritchard chuckled. "Didn't you listen when Mr M's will was read out? Very handy jointure Mrs M has, and no sticky conditions about remarriage, either. Your sister-in-law is a wealthy woman, and even Chambers' extortionate salary is well within her means."

"Oh. Then you can have him, I suppose," she said, huffily. "Are you sure you will not come home with us, Lou? I shall worry about you, all alone here, and it is not as if we were just down the road. You should be close to your family."

"I am very content here," Louisa said. Or she would be when Pamela had left and Chambers had arrived. She had her gowns, her horse, some of her books and very soon she would have her man-cook. And perhaps, if her project came to fruition, she would have Mr Gage as well. And then she would be perfectly content. For a while, at least.

~~~~~

Laurence was worried about Louisa. Louisa! There was a thrilling frisson to using her name, even in the privacy of his own head, but he had heard Lady Mountsea address her so, and now he could not think of her any other way. Louisa… Louisa entering his drawing room in shimmering gold, making all of them look dowdy. Well, perhaps not Mr Willerton-Forbes, who was a very fine dresser, but everyone else. Lady Mountsea looked like a veritable drab beside her glorious sister-in-law.

But there was a definite strain on her lovely face, and it was not hard to work out why. Pritchard was in trade, and although Viola as good as held her nose while conversing with him, Laurence found him a straightforward man, not well-educated perhaps, but sharp as a needle and not at all pretentious. His
~~~~~

daughter was another matter. She displayed all the sensitivity of an ox, insisting that Louisa must be lonely, even while she saw her surrounded by friends. Nor had she even done the one thing required of her, and brought all Louisa's property from Roseacre. The wrong instrument and only a small portion of her books.

"But at least I have enough clothes now," Louisa had said with a wry smile, as the dinner wound to a close. "I was so tired of the few I had brought with me. It is excessively dispiriting to rotate the same three gowns for morning and three for evening, day after day. Is it so for men, too? Do you like to put on a different coat every day, Mr Gage?"

"I cannot speak for the whole of my sex, but for myself three coats for morning and three for evening gets me through most weeks. The first coat is for Mondays, Wednesdays and Fridays, the second for Tuesdays, Thursdays and Saturdays, and the third for Sundays. I am very dull, where coats are concerned."

"And you have old coats that you wear when you take the dogs out," she said, smiling.

"Which make me look like a gamekeeper. True enough."

That made her laugh. She was so beautiful when she laughed. It was not Catherine's exquisite perfection, but a different, more approachable type of beauty. It had been enough to admire Catherine, to worship her from afar, but with Louisa there was an almost overwhelming desire to touch — to stroke her lush hair, to hold her, to kiss those ripe lips. Such nonsense, of course, but it was enjoyable to sit beside her, to share the choicest dishes with her, to savour the wine with a fellow connoisseur and to talk to her, all the while wondering just what it would be like to kiss her.

Lady Mountsea had exceeded expectations in one direction, by bringing Louisa's horse all the way from Durham. It was a subject which animated the whole table, or at least the male portion of it.

"The finest grey you ever saw," Chandry said, his enthusiasm a marked change from his usual easy-going manner. "Fifteen hands and a quarter, the groom told me, and such a sweet stepper. He walked him round the yard for me, to show off his paces. Splendid back on him, and deep through the girth. Not a hunter, though he looks as if he'd be up for it."

"He would certainly be up for it, but I am not," Louisa said with a laugh. "I will jump if I know the terrain, but I dislike the helter-skelter atmosphere of the hunt."

"If ever you want to sell him, let me know," Chandry said.

Louisa smiled but shook her head, and when the conversation had moved on and the attention was no longer on her, she said in a low voice to Laurence, "He is not truly mine, Gaius Valerius. Not a personal gift, not bequeathed in anyone's will. I am very glad to have him, but I shall have to buy him from my brother-in-law, and then I shall need another horse and a groom, and it is more than I bargained for just now."

"Then leave him here," Laurence said promptly. "I have more than enough space, and grooms, too. We will treat your Roman very well. Is he named for the consul or the poet?"

"The poet."

"Ah, the *Argonautica.* I have not read it for years, but it is worth rereading I think. Please do bring Gaius Valerius to me."

"How kind you are! I may avail myself of your generosity briefly, perhaps, but it would not be a permanent arrangement. I am hoping to persuade my sister-in-law to let me keep Spencer, his regular groom, but if she will not agree to it, I shall send Gaius Valerius to you for a while. He needs expert handling and although my footman was trained as a groom, I would not entrust him with a beast of Gaius Valerius' mettle."

"Will Gaius Valerius take kindly to a dog? Because my breeder at Woollercott has a litter which will soon be ready."

"Oh, yes, the Roseacre dogs often came out with me when I rode. That would be lovely! Could he spare me two, do you think? They are always better with a friend."

"Just like humankind," Laurence said, and she smiled in acknowledgement. Although he had not realised it, he had needed a good friend, and now he had one.

And then had come the difficult moment. Squire Winslade had invited Lady Mountsea to his Easter ball, and for a second Louisa's face had registered pure terror. She had quickly schooled her features into neutrality, but Laurence had seen it and it made him long to protect her from her dreadful relations. A strange marriage she must have had, and now she was left with this vulgar, intrusive woman as almost her only family. It was abominable.

On Sunday he had briefly glimpsed Louisa at church, but had no opportunity to speak to her. On Monday, he had not seen her at all, and was left fretting and wondering how soon he might call to see how she did. Then on Tuesday came the glorious news that Lady Mountsea and her merchant father were leaving, the coaches sent for and the servants busy loading the luggage. Viola, too excited by the spectacle even to walk to the village, spent half the day running back and forth to the gallery above the saloon, which was high enough above the shrubbery to give a clear view to the Dower House. By the time the two carriages departed, she could list the exact number of boxes on top and the passengers inside each.

"Did the groom go with them?" Laurence said. "He would have been riding his own horse."

"No, there was no other horse but the carriage horses."

"Ah. Pity," he said. Now Louisa would have no excuse to leave her beautiful animal at the Grove.

At least he would see her again that evening, for it was their card party, and she had never missed one yet. All afternoon he was in a pleasant glow of anticipation, wondering what gown she would wear now that she had her full wardrobe and hoping to see her face with its usual contentment. Even at dinner he was in an unusually good humour, venturing the odd joke now and again.

She did not come.

At first he assumed she was just a bit late. But then the tables were set out and play began and still she had not come, and he was aware of a heaviness inside like a lump of lead. The degree of disappointment he felt took him by surprise, and he could hardly gather his scattered wits to concentrate on the play.

After supper, a few people departed but the serious players reformed into three whist tables, leaving Laurence to sit out.

"Do take my place, Mr Gage," Willerton-Forbes said. "I am perfectly content to watch."

"By no means," Laurence said at once. "I have a letter to finish, so I will bid you all a goodnight."

He collected a fresh bottle of Cognac from the cellar and then made his way across the saloon to the spiral staircase and up to the gallery. His eye was irresistibly drawn to the Dower House, where the shutters and curtains were open and lights still burned in Louisa's study. She was still up, then.

From there, he went through his wife's bedroom and dressing room to reach his own bedroom, for the principal rooms all connected one with another, in the old manner. When Catherine was alive, he had always reached his room the other way, never venturing into her rooms unless invited, but since her death it had comforted him a little to pass that way. It was almost as if she were still alive.

In his own room, he stopped, irresolute. He could not settle to letter-writing when he was so uneasy. He turned, went back, all the way to the window in Catherine's bedroom. For some minutes he stood, watching the glow from Louisa's window, puzzled and hurt by her non-appearance that night, needing her company. The brandy bottle was heavy in his hand.

Impulsively he fetched a greatcoat and slipped the bottle into a deep pocket. Then he went down to the hall, where Skeates was lurking.

"I am going out for some fresh air. Make sure you do not lock me out."

"Very good, sir."

The air was crisp and cool, with just a hint of dampness. He made his way down the drive and across the road. Inside the Dower House grounds, he stepped off the drive onto the lawn to move soundlessly up to the house. There was no point in alerting the servants if she was not receptive to an evening caller. Or perhaps she had long since retired, leaving the candles burning. Silently, he drew near the study window, pushing through a flowerbed as he did so. Roses, but fortunately well pruned, or he would never have got through. He went right up to the window and peered inside.

She was stretched out on a chaise longue near the fire, a book in one hand while the other played idly with a stray curl of hair. On a table beside her was a plate and a glass of something dark and red. Smiling, he tapped on the window.

With a startled look, she raised her head. At first, she looked at him unseeingly, then abruptly she smiled, set down her book and rose to her feet. He held up the bottle, as a token of his good intentions. Laughing, she nodded, then pointed in the direction of the front door.

He pushed his way back through the roses, and by the time he reached the door she was already drawing back the bolts inside.

"Good evening, Mr Gage! What have you brought me?"

"Cognac."

"Then come inside at once. It is the one thing I forgot to order from the estimable Mr Matley. Some ordinary brandy but no Cognac. William has gone to bed, worn out by my exhausting relations, so leave your coat over the chair there and let us sit by the fire. Would you be so good as to add a few coals while I fetch glasses? How did the card party go? I was very sorry to miss it."

"I was sorry you missed it, too. Were you too tired? It would be understandable, if so. You have had a busy day."

They fell silent for the ceremony of opening the bottle and pouring the golden liquid, then, flopping into her chair, she said, "Busier than you can imagine. Along with all her own multitude of boxes and the unwanted clavichord, Pamela took my cook with her, which is not a tragedy by any means, for I shall have my wonderful man-cook in exchange, but it did leave us dinner-less tonight."

"You could have come to us. One extra would be neither here nor there," he said.

"You are kindness itself, as always, but it would not have done, for it would still have left the servants scratching round for a meal. There is food in the house, so it would not seem to be a hard task to create a simple and nourishing meal, would it? I can tell you, Mr Gage, it is harder than it looks. There we were in the kitchen, all six of us, and at the end of it we had a passable soup, a haunch of beef that was half burnt and half raw, and an assortment of sad, wilted vegetables. Have you any idea how hard it is to keep a spit turning regularly? We would set the mechanism going and then go off to do other things, and turn round to find the meat stationary and blackened."

He laughed. "You should indeed have come to us! We would have fed you better than that, and a few more in the servants hall would not be a problem either. You must dine with us every night until your man-cook arrives."

"No, indeed! There is not the slightest need, for tomorrow Tilly's sister will be back from Market Clunbury and will help out. Oh Mr Gage, this Cognac is wonderful. What a generous man you are. I was never allowed to drink Cognac at Roseacre, or Armagnac either. My father-in-law was sternly opposed to anything French."

"What, nothing at all? No claret?"

"Oh, we had claret, but we told him it was Spanish wine. Once it was decanted he never knew, except to say that it was remarkably good for a Spanish wine."

Laurence spluttered a mouthful of Cognac. "The devil you did! 'We' being you and your husband of course."

"Yes. Ned understood my appreciation for good food and fine wines. My life was tedious enough without depriving me of those little pleasures too."

A tedious life... she had never been so open before, and because he was desperate to know, he blurted out, "Why ever did you marry him, Louisa? Why marry a man old enough to be your grandfather?"

And then he could have bitten off his tongue for the hurt look on her face.

13: Cognac And Confidences

Louisa got up to fetch the brandy bottle, to give herself time to consider her reply. At first she was disappointed in him. Such an intrusive question, and one that was still difficult to answer, even after all these years. But by the time she had refilled both their glasses, she acknowledged that their friendship had reached a point where such questions were bound to arise. If her project should ever come to fruition, such intimacies were inevitable. Besides, she was curious about his marriage, and naturally he was equally so about hers.

"You looked him up in Debrett's, I suppose."

"I did, yes." No apology. Actually, she rather liked that. It was a straightforward question, and she could answer it or not as she chose.

"You find it difficult to understand." A statement, not a question.

"I think you must have had good reason for the decision," he said slowly.

"My friend Esther Deerham finds it just as hard to understand," she said. "In fact, it nearly drove us apart until better sense intervened. I find her marriage just as inexplicable, but I accept that it must satisfy some need in her that I had not divined. She is content... as was I. You must not imagine that I was forced into it, or anything of that nature. I was seventeen and he was fifty-three, but I went into it willingly. It suited us both."

For a moment she stared into the fire, remembering, then she leaned back in her chair and went on, "My parents married late in life, not expecting children to be any part of it and for three years they were correct. To their bemusement, I happened along when my mother was forty-five, to upend their quiet, studious life. They never quite knew what to do with me, and when I was little there were whole days at a time when I am quite sure they forgot my existence until I materialised in the drawing room before dinner. But as I grew older and showed that I had inherited their love of reading, they took a keener interest in me, and admitted me to their little circle of study.

"By the time I was ready to enter society, my father was very frail and clearly not long for the world, and my mother not in much better case. They fretted over me, to be left alone with only distant relations upon whom I had no great claim. I went through a spell of wildness for a while, too. I had always had a wilful streak, but Esther was my very good friend and she kept me from serious mischief, and occasionally took the blame on my behalf. Everyone should have such a heroic friend! But when she moved to Shrewsbury, I had no close friends and there were one or two scrapes, I confess. My parents worried a great deal about me.

"Ned's father was an old friend of my father's, with similar bookish tendencies. Ned had visited once or twice a year for longer than I can remember, first with his father and later alone, so I knew him well and we got on together. He had a problem, too. His family was gentry, but at a very modest level. There was a small estate, which Ned would inherit, but he had never married. He had come close to it twice, but it never happened and nobody worried too much about it, because his younger brother Thomas had married Pamela and her vast dowry, and produced an army of children to maintain the line. But then the unthinkable happened — Ned's father inherited Roseacre and the barony.

"You have never seen Roseacre, but it is vastly different from the old house, which was not a great deal bigger than this. Roseacre... a wonderful old house, magnificent grounds and a barony — all of which would descend to Thomas and Pamela, unless Ned married. Perhaps it was wrong of them, but they did *not* want Pamela to become a baroness. Mistress of a small country estate, yes, but not Roseacre.

"Ned and my father had some correspondence on the matter, and then he came to see me, to determine my feelings. I will not pretend that I was in love with him, or he with me, but there was a degree of affection between us, as between friends. We were both startled to find ourselves considering matrimony, he because he had long since given up the idea and I because I had expected to have many more years under my parents' sheltering wings. But he needed a wife and I needed a safe haven, and so it suited us both. I had a month in London with a cousin, who presented me at Court and took me to Almack's, after which I turned my back on the *beau monde* with some relief, married Ned and went to Durham."

She stopped, aware that there was much unsaid, much that she could not explain even to herself. At a time when she should have been looking life in the eye and leaning towards adulthood, she had deliberately run away to hide in the north with a man who wanted nothing more than to sit by his own fire. Why had she done it? Had her courage failed her? Perhaps, but there was also her ignorance of the world. Having grown up with her head in a book for much of the time, she knew little of society. Her ventures into independence had not gone well. Ned had offered her a refuge.

"But you found it tedious."

She jumped at the sound of his voice. It was so long since he had spoken that she had almost forgotten he was there. "Not at first. I loved Roseacre, loved the garden, loved the peacefulness of it. There was a good library, several excellent instruments, there were dinner engagements and visitors, even the occasional ball, although I am not much of a dancer. But gradually it dawned on us that there would be no children, and there came a point when Ned simply... gave up. He never treated me any differently — none of them did — but there is no escaping the fact that I failed in my most fundamental duty."

"Such things are in God's hands," Laurence said with sudden passion. "You cannot be blamed."

"I blamed myself, of course, and my physician confirmed it, but Ned never spoke one word of reproach. That made it worse, somehow. We went on just as before, but it hung between us, this monstrous void, the silence of the childless house, the empty nursery. It was almost a relief when he grew sick, and I could become his nurse and not pretend I was any sort of a wife. Oh Lord, do I sound bitter? I assure you I am not. What we did was the right choice at the time, and I do not regret it."

Laurence swirled the Cognac in his glass, then looked up with a mischievous glint in his eye. "And so the delightful Pamela became Lady Mountsea after all. Has she refurbished Roseacre to her own taste yet?"

"Not quite!" She could not help laughing. "Roseacre is rather resistant to refurbishment. It was too daunting a task for me. Whenever a room required attention, I had it redone in exactly the same manner as before. It was easier than trying to impose new ideas on a venerable old building. The garden was where I tinkered, in my amateurish way, for although it had been well designed, it had been much neglected. A little renovation, a dab of replanting, a touch of careful pruning... I spent a great deal of time in the garden, latterly."

"Shall you do the same here?" he said. "You could have a pretty free hand, for it has not been touched for decades."

"I might," she said, knowing that she was being evasive. There was no need for him to know that she had no plan to be in Great Maeswood for long. "I have been doing some pruning, but when the weather is warmer, I shall look at the structure and see if there is any improvement that seems good to me. Heavens, all this talking is making me hungry. Do you want something to eat? After the disaster of dinner, William put up a supper tray for me. It is not exciting, just cold chicken and cheese and cake... oh, and pigeon pie. One of the few things Mrs Nokes could cook well."

She jumped up and fetched plates of this and that from the sideboard, and brought them back to the fire. There was no table large enough to contain them, so she set them down on the floor and sat on the rug, her back against the chaise longue. He laughed and joined her on the floor, the plates between them, their feet stretched out side by side towards the fire. They nibbled chicken and bread, sipped warming Cognac and talked about cooks and pies and disastrous dinners and then, when he picked up the volume of Boswell she had been reading, of Scotland and the wildness of its mountains and the independence of its people and the advancement of science and literature in Edinburgh.

It was a little like being married, she decided, except that she had never quite had this kind of intimacy with Ned. They had sat with their books of an evening in companionable silence. There had been conversation over dinner, of course, but it had been of a more impersonal nature, the minutiae of domestic life or the news from faraway London, or even farther away France or Spain or Argentina. After dinner, they had played cards or chess, in the early days, and latterly they had hidden behind their books. There had never been much talking. With Laurence, though, there was an almost unstoppable flood of words. The hands of the mantel clock passed midnight, and still he sat beside her, showing no inclination to leave. A very promising sign.

After a while they lapsed into silence. He reached for the bottle and replenished their glasses. “Were you disappointed for yourself?” he said pensively. “The lack of children, I mean. Quite apart from the son and heir business, should you have liked to have children?”

“Of course, for what else is a woman for? That is our sole purpose, is it not? From the moment of our birth, females are directed towards marriage and motherhood. What else are we to do with our lives?”

“Many things, I should imagine,” he said mildly. “If God has denied you motherhood, then he has some other purpose for you.”

“But what? Of what use is a barren woman?”

“That you will only know when the time comes, but do not feel your life is wasted because you have no children to comfort you. At least you still live. A child is a great blessing, but that which is conceived in exquisite joy may also lead to the utmost anguish.”

She could not miss the bitterness in his voice. "Is that what happened to your wife?"

He nodded. "The third child. Two babes brought into the world without the least difficulty, but the third arrived too soon and was born dead, and a day later... there was fever. The physician could do nothing for her. We were visiting my sister at Bristol, and she called in the city's most experienced doctor as soon as we understood the urgency, but he could not save her or the babe. My poor Catherine!"

"What a sad journey home for you," she said, reaching across to touch his hand. "How old were Henrietta and Edward then?"

"Six and three. Henrietta remembers her mother a very little, but Edward has never known any other mother-figure than Viola. My sister has her faults, I do not deny, but she came at once and has done her very best to be a second mother to the children, even though it does not come naturally to her. She is one of life's born spinsters, and would disagree very strongly with your assertion that all women should be mothers."

Louisa gave a little laugh. "You are quite right to chastise me, for there is much of good that may be accomplished by a childless woman, especially one with an independent income. I hope in time that I may accomplish some good, too, for Ned left me very well provided for."

"Then you are lucky. So many widows are left in desperate straits, and are forced to marry again. I suppose I should have married again, too, to provide the children with a mother, but I could never bring myself to do it. And then there is all the awkwardness of searching for a suitable woman, of going into unfamiliar society with the express purpose of selecting a helpmeet. I have never been good at mingling with strangers."

It seemed such an obvious question to ask, so she said, "Then however did you meet your wife?" Then she held her breath. Was this the point where the confidences ceased? Would he make some excuse and leave?

To her surprise, he laughed. "Yes, extraordinary, is it not? However did dull, reclusive Laurence manage to entice beautiful Catherine Haywood to marry him?"

"That is not what I meant!"

"No, you did not," he said, eyes crinkling as he smiled at her. "You should have, though, for it is a thing which has puzzled me for years. Why did she marry me when she could have had—?" He stopped abruptly, a frown on his face. "So long ago! Somehow, it no longer hurts. Shall I tell you the whole story? I think I shall."

"I should love to hear it." She picked up a slice of pound cake and pulled off a corner to eat.

"Let me start with my grandfather. He was one of those men who did everything to excess. Eating, drinking, gaming, women... all of those and more. Fighting, too. Seven duels, according to family legend. Allegedly he killed his man once, but it was all hushed up. Well, he was the local magistrate, so it was not surprising. The poor fellow was dumped in woodlands known to be frequented by poachers, and no one asked any awkward questions. Grandfather loved to entertain, too, so the house was always full of people eating their fill at his expense. By the time he died, the estate had been left to go to ruin, but Father was no better at management than Grandfather. He was a timid soul, who hid away from his money troubles for ten years. Then one day he suffered an apoplexy. He rose from the breakfast table and just dropped where he stood. The whole of his left side was frozen, he could not move or speak... he was carried to his bed and never left it from that day forth. He lived on for two years, but he gradually dwindled into nothing."

"The poor man!" Louisa said. "Apoplexy is such a distressing illness, and there is little to be done about so severe a case. How old were you when this happened?"

"Four and twenty. My sisters were all gone from home by this point, Selena and Ursula married and Viola a companion to an elderly aunt, but my brother Malcolm was here. He was two and twenty at the time. We had to take over Father's financial affairs and that was when we discovered just how desperate matters were. Half the estate's land had been sold off or mortgaged, and Father had been quietly selling off paintings and silver and jewels to stay afloat. We could not see any way out except for me to find myself an heiress and marry at once. London was too big and expensive a stage for shire gentry like us, so we took ourselves to Bath, and went directly to the Pump Room and the very first person we saw was Catherine Haywood."

"How amazing!" Louisa said. "And you fell in love with her on the spot."

"Well, I did, yes, but I was not so foolish as to set my sights on her instantly. I needed an heiress, and could not settle for a dowry-less wife, no matter how beautiful. We made discreet enquiries, and discovered that — miracle of miracles! — she was an heiress to a fortune of one hundred thousand pounds. If I could secure her, the estate would be saved and I should have such a wife as I could scarcely dare to dream about. And so I set out to court her. Everything was done properly by way of her mother, but she gave her permission and Catherine seemed amenable. She did nothing at all to discourage me, in any event."

He paused, his expression disturbed as if he wrestled with some severe emotion.

"But there was something wrong?" Louisa prompted. "I feel sure you are about to tell me of some obstacle."

"Oh yes, there was an obstacle," he said grimly. "Malcolm was the obstacle. He fell in love with her too, and he did not see why he should not have his chance to win her. He would use her dowry to restore the Grove, just as I would, he said, so what was the difference? That was his contention, and no argument of mine could sway him. In vain I pleaded that only the eldest son had the duty of repairing the damage to the estate, in vain I pointed out that it was I who had been granted permission to court Catherine. He would not listen. And he had an ally. Mrs Haywood was in Bath for her health, so apart from a daily visit to the Pump Room, she never ventured from her apartment. A companion and chaperon had been engaged to escort Catherine about, and watch over her. This chaperon favoured Malcolm and so she facilitated his suit by every means at her disposal. I would take Catherine out for a drive, and as soon as I left her, the chaperon would whisk her off to Sydney Gardens where Malcolm was waiting by arrangement. Or if I escorted Catherine to Sydney Gardens, Malcolm would just happen to bump into her later in Milsom Street. And the worst of it was that he believed that Catherine returned his regard."

"And did she?" Louisa said, completely caught up in the story.

"Of course not. It was all in his imagination, as it turned out, although at the time I was terrified that he might be right. Malcolm is everything I am not, you see — tall, handsome, lively and very charming. He is not dull, like I am. For three weeks we played this game, three weeks when I was in utter dread of losing her to Malcolm and terrified to put it to the test in case it went against me. In the end I tired of it and proposed to Catherine, and to my astonishment she accepted me. Malcolm fell into the most appalling rage, after which he stormed off and I have not seen him from that day to this."

"That is a great tragedy, when families are split asunder unnecessarily," she said. "What did Catherine have to say about it? She must have understood what was going on, but did nothing to stop it."

"She was utterly innocent!" he said, bridling. "No doubt she thought all the meetings with Malcolm were accidental."

"No doubt? Did you never speak of it?"

"Never."

"And you had no curiosity? Or perhaps you do not wish to know what she thought, and that is why you never asked her and have not read her diaries."

"I do not need to know," he said quietly. "You persist in believing that everyone has secrets and no one is perfect, but Catherine concealed nothing and to me she was indeed flawless. Like a goddess, an angel come to earth."

"It sounds to me as though you have put her on a pedestal, like a work of art, an object to be admired rather than a real woman," Louisa said, softening her words with a smile and a gentle touch on his hand. "If you were to read her diaries, you might find out that she is less than perfect but perhaps more real to you. And more *alive*, Laurence! You hold an image of her in your memory, but in her diaries she can speak to you, even from the grave. She can tell you about herself, the private Catherine that no one but God ever saw. She lives on in her words, just as the words of Gaius Valerius live on in the *Argonautica* after so many hundreds of years. But I will not tease you about it. Let her be perfect if you wish it. For myself, I am very glad to be imperfect and deeply flawed, for it removes a great deal of constraint. My marriage may not have turned out as I expected, but now I am free to do as I wish and go wherever I please."

"And out of the whole world, you chose Great Maeswood," he said lightly. "Why, Louisa? Why here of all places?"

It was past midnight, and they were both mellow with Cognac and the intimacy of sitting side by side on the floor. It was time.

"It is a long way from Durham," she said at once, making him laugh. "But also no one knows me here. I am a stranger, and may pursue my little project unimpeded."

"Your little project?" His eyes crinkled with amusement. "What are you up to, Louisa?"

"Why, to take a lover, of course." A small pause. "It could be you, if you are so inclined."

And then, because he looked so astonished that she wanted to laugh, she leaned forward and kissed him. Without the slightest hesitation he kissed her back, and oh Lord, what a kiss! There was a deep reservoir of ardour lurking beneath that quiet, unassuming exterior. She had only ever experienced Ned's rather tentative kisses, and this was not like that. This was *nothing* like that. Dear Lord, make it go on for ever, please do not let him stop. Please, please...

He did stop, eventually, gazing at her breathlessly as if he had never seen her before.

"Come upstairs with me," she whispered.

And at that, his face exploded into anguish. "*No!* No, no, no! It is impossible... do not ask me... "

He jumped to his feet and ran from the room. A moment later the front door slammed shut behind him.

14: The Governess

Laurence stumbled home in a swirl of rioting emotions. He was not angry, at least not with Louisa for suggesting such a thing, but at himself for his weakness. He had been tempted. For a few minutes he had seriously been tempted until good sense had reasserted itself. How could he have been so foolish? Such madness to go there so late in the evening, and then sharing Cognac with her, sitting side by side like... like lovers, he realised. No wonder she imagined he would be receptive to the idea, for not only had he told her explicitly that he had no intention of marrying again, but his every action must have conveyed the impression that he was pursuing her. He had supposed they were just friends and she had supposed... something else entirely. Perhaps there could never be pure friendship between two people of the opposite sex.

He was most of the way up the drive before the cold penetrated his cloak of Cognac-fuelled despair. He had left his greatcoat at Louisa's house. Ah well, he could hardly go back for it now.

The night watch boy was fast asleep on his bench, a pair of candles on the console the only light in the hall. The house was silent, the card players long since departed, and the household abed. Holding a candle up to the long-case clock, he discovered it was past one o'clock. He bolted the front door as quietly as he could to avoid waking the boy, then crept upstairs to bed. John attended him in yawning silence, making no comment on the missing greatcoat, but then perhaps he was not aware that Laurence had gone out that evening.

When Laurence was alone again, the same maelstrom of harsh thoughts assailed him, and he lay awake half the night trying to decide what to do next, and wondering how on earth he was to face Louisa again with anything like ease. It was awkward, very awkward.

He woke the next day with the same uncertainties. Of one thing only was he sure — that his present predicament was entirely his own fault. He had been led astray by his own immunity towards Louisa into supposing that she was equally resistant. Right from the start he had sought her out and paid her more attention than was wise in the belief that it was perfectly safe, since neither of them had any thought of marriage, and had never guessed that she might have something less honourable in mind. Viola, for once, had been completely right in her gloomy prognostications.

Yet what a pit he had dug for himself! Louisa's suggestion of a liaison was bad enough, but she could easily have taken his unconcealed pleasure in her company as something much more, as a promise of marriage, in fact. It would not have been an unreasonable assumption, and he would have been bound to honour her expectations. He might at that very moment have been contemplating his forthcoming nuptials, and that would have been a disaster. Surely it would have been a disaster. And yet almost at once his mind conjured up a number of compensations in such a situation, and he could not at all decide whether such compensations might in fact outweigh the disadvantages of re-entering the married state.

Unwilling to meet Louisa accidentally while his thoughts were so disordered, he took the dogs out in a different direction that morning, walking through the park towards Lower Maeswood and then back through the woods, where the dog violets and wood sorrel peeped through last year's leaf litter.

By the time he had reached the boot room again and divested himself of his old greatcoat and boots, he had come to a resolution — since he would have to face Louisa sooner or later, it was as well to get it over with at once and discover how things were to be between them from now on. Could they remain friends, after last night? Yet how could they not be, after the confidences they had shared? It would be uncomfortable for both of them if restrained coolness were to be the order of the day. He needed to know, so he determined to call upon her directly after breakfast, retrieve his greatcoat and learn from her how they were to go forward. He would take his cue from the lady.

He was late to breakfast, so Viola had already gone, but he found Captain Edgerton in the dining room, stolidly working his way through a plate of chops.

"Good morning to you, sir," Edgerton said, politely rising and making a small bow. "And it is indeed a good morning, for we are at last making progress in identifying our mystery lady."

"That is excellent news," Laurence said, sitting down and waiting for Skeates to pour his coffee. "Who is she?"

"As to that, we have no name as yet, and in point of fact we have made more progress in determining who she is *not*. She is not Mary Fielder, a farmer's daughter who vanished twelve years ago, for she has been discovered alive and well and the mother of eight children at the mill at Overbury, having run away to marry the miller's son. She is also not Ann Walmsley, once a scullery maid at Cloverstone Manor, who has been discovered in the work house at Market Clunbury. And she is definitely not John Boyd—"

"*John* Boyd?" Laurence said, half choking on his coffee.

"Indeed. Once elderly retainers start reminiscing, they are apt to wander from the point somewhat. John Boyd ran away to sea twenty five years ago, and is now a Rear Admiral, which his well-wishers were very pleased to hear about, even though it is hardly to our purpose. But yesterday we obtained a more promising lead, and here we hope that you will be able to help us, if you can spare us a little time this morning. Two of your excellent servants remember a governess who left here abruptly some years ago, but as to a name or exact date, they cannot be precise. It may be that you or Miss Gage will have some information that bears on the question. The household records, perhaps?"

"A governess!" Laurence said. "It is a long time since we have had a governess here. The youngest of my sisters is two and forty now. I will check the accounts for you, but I am not optimistic. Neither my grandfather nor my father were terribly good at record-keeping. My sister may remember something, though. She has an excellent memory."

Viola had already breakfasted and gone into the village, so Laurence took Captain Edgerton into his office to look at the accounts while they awaited her return.

"I was ten when we came here," Laurence said, " and the girls would have been twelve, fourteen and sixteen. They had a succession of governesses over the years but I never had much to do with them latterly, for my brother and I were at school by then. They all blended together in my mind. Ah, here we are, this box covers the time when we arrived. Oh, this is very neat work, each year labelled and bound up with string. That was never my father's doing. He must have had a secretary, I suppose, although I cannot remember such a person. Here we are, the first Lady Day after we moved here, the payments of salaries... Miss Eaton. That must have been the governess. Let me check the next year... yes, there she is again. *'To Miss Eaton, fifteen pounds'*. The following year..." He shuffled through the papers. "Ah! A change. No Miss Eaton, instead we have Miss Labett. Ursula would have been... let me see... fourteen by then, so still in need of a governess. And the year after... oh, this is interesting. It is written *'To Miss Labett, fifteen pounds'*, as expected, but crossed through. So perhaps she had left by Lady Day of that year?"

"That is indeed interesting," Edgerton said thoughtfully.

Willerton-Forbes came in at that moment, and had to have everything explained to him, and then Viola returned in a welter of alarmed speculation.

"What has happened? Is there a development?"

Patiently, Captain Edgerton related all that had been discovered, while Laurence rang for tea. Viola was always flustered by any deviation from the usual course of events, and tea was the most efficacious balm for her anxiety.

"Oh, Miss Labett! Yes, I *do* remember her. Mama called her a flighty piece, but all I can recall is that she was quite young — younger than any of our previous governesses — and liked to dress rather well. Not drably, like most governesses, in brown or grey. She always wore bright colours. And lace! She liked lace collars and cuffs, and Mama told her to take them off, for it was not fitting in a governess. But I think she still wore them sometimes, because I saw her once or twice as she was going out, with her hair done up high like Mama's and a big hat. Goodness, I have not thought about her in years!"

"What happened to her, do you remember, Miss Gage?" Captain Edgerton said gently. "Did she disappear, or merely leave in the regular way?"

"I suppose she left," she said uncertainly. "By the time she came here, Selena and I were out, and Ursula was not far off, so— I remember now! She *did* disappear, because Mama was quite cross that she had given no notice, just walked out and left her in the lurch, and there was something... oh, I cannot remember what, but there was some big occasion going on and she had needed Miss Labett to take care of Ursula that day. Now, whatever was it?"

"Do try to recall everything you can about her," Edgerton said. "It is most important."

"Oh, I do not need to recall — I can look at my diary for that year. That will have every detail, you may be sure."

She bustled off to fetch her diaries. The tea came in while she was gone, but Laurence ignored it, pouring Canary for the gentlemen.

"Here we are," Viola said chirpily. "Oh, tea. How lovely! No, no, I will pour, Laurence. No gentlemen ever serves tea correctly. There now, that will set me up beautifully after my walk. The wind is got up again, and there is so much pollen from the catkins all blown about that I sneezed all the way home. There was not a turkey to be had at Birch's, so I had to get a green goose instead, which I know you are not so fond of, Laurence, but you will like it well enough when Rogers has roasted it, and there is a lovely piece of veal. You will enjoy that, I am sure."

"I am sure I shall, Vi, but I suspect Mr Willerton-Forbes and Captain Edgerton are more interested in Miss Labett at this minute."

"Oh yes, Miss Labett. I have brought several diaries from that time, for one of them is sure to have what we want. Let me see... oh, heavens, the outing to Lavery Pond. That was a never-to-be-forgotten day. I had a new bonnet for the occasion — so pretty! Little Lucy Scarrett was stung by bees or it might have been wasps, and then her father fell in the pond trying to scare them away from her. In all the fussing over Lucy, her little brother ate a whole basket of strawberries and was violently sick. Do you remember that, Laurence? Oh... well, perhaps you were at school then. But Miss Labett is still mentioned all that year, right up to Christmas, so let me try the following year." She flicked rapidly through the pages, scanning each one. "Oh, the Easter ball at the Manor! That was the year the Rudd twins from the Grange met the Pawsey sisters, and were married on the same day not two months later. But then they all went to India and died, one after the other. It was very sad. Old Mr Rudd moved away after— Oh! This is it. Lord Saxby's betrothal ball, that was when Miss Labett disappeared. It was to be an all-day affair, with a pavilion built out from the saloon for the dancing, for the library and gallery wings were not built then. That was done with *her* money, you may be sure, for he never spent a farthing if he could help it. Anyway, we were to spend the entire day there, and Miss Labett was the only governess in the village at that time, so of course she was wanted to look after everyone's children, as well as Ursula and Lucy Cokely, for neither of them were out then. And then she vanished and Mama was at her wit's end to know what to do, for no one wanted to miss the occasion, you know. But luckily Mrs Cokely said she did not mind not going — if you ask me, it was because she could not afford a new dress, although she said it was because of the heat. She was never very good in hot weather, so perhaps it truly was that. Anyway, she looked after all the young ones at the parsonage, for Mr Cokely was still alive then, so they were still at the parsonage, and they took baskets of food and sticks and balls and so forth down to the Glebe, and they all had a very good time, seemingly. Better than we did at the Hall, for it was a shabby affair, if you ask me. There! So that is the date precisely — two days before the betrothal."

"Miss Gage, you are a treasure," Edgerton said solemnly, making a note in his pocketbook.

She flushed with pleasure, murmuring a few inarticulate noises that might have been gratitude.

"And do you remember how tall Miss Labett was?"

"Oh yes, quite tall. Taller than I am, certainly, and very tall when she put on her best shoes, with heels as high as Mama's. She certainly dressed very fine for a governess."

"Could you show me how tall she was? Without the shoes?" Edgerton said, and obligingly she stood up and held her hand two or three inches above her own head. Edgerton pulled a measuring string from a pocket and measured the height. "Yes, that fits with our mystery lady. Thank you so much, Miss Gage."

"Yes, indeed, most helpful," Willerton-Forbes said. "So now we have a name. I suppose you do not happen to know where she came from? Her family? Her previous employer?"

Both Viola's diaries and the accounts were silent on the subject. "Mama would have known," Viola said. "There would have been references, letters sent beforehand, interviews, but everything of hers was thrown out after she died, all her correspondence. I should not think there is any way to discover such information now."

"We must see what we can do," Edgerton said. "Now that we have a name, we can begin to ask more direct questions around the village. Someone will be sure to remember something. Were there any other governesses nearby? Anyone she might have been friendly with?"

But Viola knew of no one.

When she had gone to see to some domestic matter, the three men sat on, sipping Canary and pondering this new development.

"A governess who considers herself a bit above her station," Edgerton said thoughtfully. "One who likes to dress like a lady, if she can. Those embroidered shoes with the high heel, which were by no consideration those of a housemaid, were equally unsuitable for a governess."

"She could have been given them by a previous employer," Laurence said. "That is not uncommon."

"True," Edgerton said. "They are still not appropriate wear for a governess, so we can say she was a woman who was not at ease in her rôle as an employee. She wanted to rise in the world, and she was not above using a man for her purposes. She had a lover, she found herself with child, so perhaps she went to him in the expectation of marriage and instead he murdered her."

"That is an extreme response," Laurence said. "I have less experience in the matter of murder than you gentlemen, but I have heard of a great many hasty weddings over the years. If a man compromises his sweetheart, he marries her. If he cannot or will not marry her, he makes sure she is taken care of some other way. Even a farm labourer has a sense of honour in such matters. But murder implies such desperation!"

"Yet what else could it be?" Willerton-Forbes said, setting down his glass and steepling his hands. "There are only four ways in which a woman may die — of some natural cause, such as a physical weakness or disease, of an accident, by her own hand or by some other hand. We may dismiss any natural cause at once, for she was perfectly healthy right up until the day of her disappearance, and if she had suffered a failure of the heart or other sudden illness, she would scarcely have locked herself into the wine cellar to die. Nor could she have taken her own life without some evidence, such as a knife or gun or a poison bottle. An accident, such as a fall, would have been detectable in the skeletal remains, and Dr Beasley found no such evidence. The conclusion is inescapable, gentlemen. Miss Labett was murdered."

Laurence sighed. "Your logic is irrefutable, sir, unfortunately. Is there any possibility after all this time of discovering who her murderer might be?"

"That will be difficult indeed," Edgerton said. "We must identify her lover first, and I am not optimistic."

"But at least the poor girl has a name now, even if we may never know precisely what happened to her," Laurence said.

"We have a name, true," Edgerton said, "but in resolving one mystery, we create another. If our body is Miss Labett, what then became of Dilys Hughes, who vanished two years earlier? We know that she was put onto the stage coach at the inn, and we have discovered that she left the stage at Shrewsbury, exactly as expected. But we can find no sign that she caught another stage to her home, or to anywhere else. She simply vanished."

"It is a puzzle," Willerton-Forbes said, "and we do not like puzzles, do we, Michael? This warrants further investigation."

The two men laughed, not at all cast down by the prospect of uncovering the movements of a former housemaid almost thirty years ago.

For himself, Laurence found it unutterably depressing. Two young women, both inveigled into an affair with a man unwilling or unable to marry, one of them dead and one vanished without trace. To the London gentlemen, these were simply mysteries to be solved but Laurence could not see them as anything other than tragedies.

But the morning's discoveries had been interesting to him in another, quite unexpected, way. Viola kept a diary, had done so for years, in fact, and yet there was nothing in it but scraps of information — who she had seen, where she had gone, bee stings and balls and bonnets, the minutiae of her life. And Louisa's journal was philosophical musings on poems or pamphlets. Perhaps Catherine's diaries had been of that nature, too — not an open door to her soul, but more like a laundry list of domestic trivia, or her thoughts on the vicar's sermon. Perhaps there would be no harm in reading them after all.

15: The Secret Arbour

As soon as he could escape from Edgerton and Willerton-Forbes, Laurence resolved to determine his fate at once, whether he was to be permitted to continue as Louisa's friend or whether he had sunk to the level of mere acquaintance or would be ostracised entirely. He would go directly to the Dower House, but just in case she should refuse to admit him, he summoned the dogs from their resting place by the fire so that he could pretend he was merely out for a walk. If nothing else, he could collect his greatcoat.

William answered his knock and immediately opened the door wide. The dogs bounced inside, but Laurence could not presume so far.

"Tell Mrs Middlehope that Mr Gage is here, and ask her whether she is at home this morning."

William looked puzzled. "She's in the study, sir. Oh! *At home...*"

But before he could ask, the dogs had found the open door to the study, and there was laughter and teasing admonishments, followed by Louisa's head peering out.

"Mr Gage? Do come inside. I am delighted to see the dogs, but they are not your equal where conversation is concerned."

And he found himself ushered inside without the slightest hint of reserve on her part. He had not been fully aware of the leaden lump of fear in his belly until he found it dissolving in relief. They were to be friends again! Only at that moment did he understand just how important that was to him.

There was chatter about the dogs while she dispatched William to see about some cakes and poured Madeira for them both, but when they had taken their usual chairs by the fire, she laughed without a trace of self-consciousness and said, "You are still speaking to me, then? I am so glad. I feared it would be otherwise after I disgraced myself last night." And then, before he could say a word, she went on, "I parcelled up your greatcoat and sent it over to the Grove, with an abject little note describing William's deficiencies as a footman in omitting to return it as you left, and not a word about the time of this dreadful event. I hope I did right, and you did not wish me to burn the evidence."

That made him laugh, too, and he found it easy enough to turn the subject to the new discoveries of the body in the wine cellar, which she heard with a strong degree of interest, although their conversation was somewhat disrupted by the younger dogs snuffling about the room and refusing to settle in front of the fire.

"Do you know, I feel these fellows would be happier in the garden," she said cheerfully. "Shall we take a walk?"

He assented and, rather to his surprise, she led him down the service stairs and out by the side door, taking a cloak and bonnet from a peg. "I have no patience for waiting while my maid runs up and down stairs to fetch this or that," she said. "I hope you do not object to the informality."

"I keep my gamekeeper's outfit in the boot room for convenience," he said. "It is much the same thing."

"There was a garden room at Roseacre for the purpose," she said. "Let us go this way first."

She plunged into dense shrubbery, the overgrown bushes towering above their heads. The dogs raced about eagerly, even Ian showing some liveliness at the unfamiliar surroundings.

"Poor Miss Labett," Louisa said as they walked. "So optimistic, with her fancy clothes and her lover, yet all her dreams ended in my basement. Did she walk in of her own free will or was she reluctant to come here, enticed perhaps by her lover? Did he intend to kill her all along or was he goaded into it? Either way, he must have been utterly heartless."

"Or desperate," he said. They crossed the front drive and entered the orchard, the trees covered in fat, pink buds. A bird shot up from the long grass and the two younger dogs flew off in pursuit.

"What would make a man desperate enough to kill?" she said, frowning. "One must have a reason to kill someone — either to gain something that would be otherwise unattainable, or to prevent something. In this case, I cannot see how the situation would arise. Her lover must have known the likely consequences of his actions, and should have been prepared for them. He could not have been taken by surprise, so what would make him desperate?"

"That is all very reasonable," Laurence said, smiling wryly, "but men — especially young men — do not always follow the dictates of reason. They seldom consider the consequences of their actions and are quite astonished when matters turn out exactly as any sensible person would have predicted. Let us suppose that there was affection between the lovers, but she is a governess and he is... we cannot guess, but he may be married or otherwise not in a position to marry her. His father may disapprove, perhaps, or he cannot afford a wife. What is he to do? He fears discovery so much that murder seems the lesser evil."

"It is still difficult to envisage any situation where murder is a sensible option," she said dubiously.

They had by this time left the orchard behind and passed into the formal gardens that surrounded the house, with the stables and kitchen garden on the other side of them. They looked in on Gaius Valerius, who condescended to have his nose stroked, and after that they walked on in silence for a while, the dogs racing about happily. It was very comfortable, he found, to simply stroll about the garden, past the circular pool with a wide rim just right for sitting and trailing a hand through the water, and then past a statue of some indeterminate goddess and on to a path which meandered along the perimeter wall. Eventually, they came back into the shrubbery again and an elegant little stone arbour hedged about with high shrubs, their heavy buds already tinged pink.

"This is my secret arbour," she said, stopping and turning to him. "There is another one that is visible from the house but this one is secluded. Just right for confessions, do you not agree? Shall we sit for a while?"

He agreed to it, although warily, not knowing quite what sort of confession she had in mind. A repetition of last night's dalliance would undo him completely, so he waited until she had settled herself at one end of the arbour, then sat what he felt was a safe distance away.

"There is something I should like to say, Mr Gage," she said, "and I shall only say it once and then we need never speak of this matter again. I apologise unreservedly for my behaviour last night. I misread you utterly, and am now totally ashamed of myself. You have been so gracious as not to berate me in the slightest, and for your forbearance, my gratitude is heartfelt. Let us pretend it never happened, it will certainly never happen again and thus we may, I sincerely hope, go on as before. And now, we may talk about the weather. It is unseasonably mild for early April, is it not? But I fear we may yet have frost before the month is out."

He smiled, but he was not yet ready to talk about the weather. The two younger dogs were away in the undergrowth somewhere, and there was a lot of undergrowth to explore in this long-neglected garden, but Ian had settled beside Louisa, and was blissfully having his ears rubbed. Dogs understood much more than humankind, in many ways. They certainly knew whom to trust, and the dogs felt comfortable with her, just as Laurence did. She was his good friend, and he wanted no misunderstandings between them.

"I must apologise, too," he began tentatively.

"Whatever for?" she said, turning surprised eyes on him. "*You* did nothing wrong."

"Indeed I did, in running away so intemperately, without a word of explanation."

"There was none needed, I assure you." She looked amused. "Naturally you were very shocked by my wantonness."

"No… well, yes, I was shocked, but not by any action of yours. You were entirely honest and that cannot be wrong, but if there is blame to be attached, then it must be apportioned equally. My behaviour has been such that you must have imagined me to be hoping for exactly what you proposed. My actions seemed harmless to me at the time, for what could be more innocuous than for two friends, a widow and a widower, neither seeking matrimony again, to fall into a comfortable companionship? I see now that I was far too presumptuous. I imagined myself to be too old and dull ever to be propositioned in that way. I also imagined that I was too old and dull ever to be tempted by such a proposition. On both counts I was wrong, and that shocked me to my core, Mrs Middlehope." He scratched his nose thoughtfully. "Not that I would ever succumb to the temptation, for I would not so dishonour my dear wife's memory, and besides, it would destroy all my sister's comfort were she to learn of it, but please do not imagine my refusal to be any reflection on your own…" He scrabbled for a suitable word. "…attractions," he ended lamely.

When he dared to look at her, he saw a face brimming with merriment. "Mr Gage, you are a never-ending source of delight to me! What a pretty speech, considering the unpromising subject matter. I cannot now regret last night in the slightest, when it leads to such agreeable revelations after the event. You were actually flattered by my unladylike suggestion, and tempted, and not in the least angry, by the sound of it."

"Lord, no! Not angry, except with myself for leading you to believe such a thing was possible. But you must see that I could never do anything which would so distress Viola."

"How would she ever know?" Louisa said.

"These things always get about," he said sombrely. "The servants would know, and that means everyone would know, and Vi's position would be intolerable. She is very upright, and would feel obliged to leave at once."

Louisa looked thoughtful. "That is a consideration which, I confess, had not occurred to me. When I planned this—"

"You planned it?" He remembered then that she had mentioned a 'project' as a reason for removing to Great Maeswood. "You came here with just such a scheme in mind, then."

"I did, and it seemed to me that every detail had been thought of, but there! That is my weakness, never to grasp the full implications of my actions. I was always in trouble as a child, you see, for some such start. Like the time when there was some panic in the kitchen over the soufflés — they had been spoilt, somehow, and no one had time to get more eggs, so I thought I would help. I gathered all the eggs I could find, but I had neglected to take a basket and had to try to hold them in my apron. Have you any idea how hard it is to keep hold of an apron full of eggs when one is only six years old? Well, let us merely say that there were no soufflés that day. And another time I set off to pick blackberries and got lost and was out all night, with everyone for miles around out searching for me. I am not very good at anticipating all the consequences of my actions, you see, and so it is here. I thought very carefully about the effects on *myself*, choosing an out-of-the-way village where I am unknown, not venturing beyond the immediate locality and taking on local staff who can be discarded whenever I leave, so that any adverse effects on my reputation will be left behind too. It had not occurred to me until this moment that the other party to my little scheme will be resident here and not able to pack up and leave at the drop of a handkerchief. Even if he has no sister to concern him, he himself must endure some damage to his position in society."

"A man's reputation is less fragile in that regard than a lady's," Laurence said, rather amused. "He will be thought a devil of a fellow, and there are some men who would spread the story themselves in order to bask in the envy of their fellows."

She nodded, her expression serious, but her eyes gleamed with amusement.

"There are other kinds of damage which a man might suffer," he went on. "He might, for instance, fall head over heels in love with you and think of the inconvenience! Your secret lover, whom you expect to show positive indifference towards you in public, mooning about after you like the very worst kind of pathetic fool. How annoying that would be."

"Ah, but that was all considered most carefully," she said triumphantly. "I discounted at once the young, single men who might be supposed to be heart-free and therefore vulnerable to the pangs of unrequited love. I also discounted the married men, for nothing could be more disagreeable than a jealous wife. But this is where my choice was so cunning, for what could be better for my purposes than a widower who is still deep in love with his wife? You were perfect, Mr Gage, quite perfect."

He laughed out loud at that. "But what of you, Mrs Middlehope? Are you not also vulnerable to the pangs of unrequited love?"

"My heart is made of stone, Mr Gage. Cupid's aim is very poor where I am concerned for I have never yet felt the sting of his arrows."

"Is that why you felt the desire to take a lover?" he said, wondering, as he had a dozen times already, whether he stepped too far.

But she answered him readily enough, although the answer was the last he had expected. "No, it was because my husband told me to." He must have looked astonished, for she laughed and went on, "Incredible, is it not? Yet it is so. He urged me to do so even while we were married, for latterly he was ailing and felt the difference in our ages most acutely. For the last few years, he was the wrong side of sixty and I was below thirty, and it preyed on his mind dreadfully. He said that he had kept me locked away at Roseacre and he wanted me to glory in the great joys of life before I was too old to appreciate them. I was not in the least tempted while he was alive, but once he was dead, the idea took hold of me and would not let go. There are advantages to being barren, you see, and I knew I had to leave Roseacre once my mourning was over, so I began to think — why not? Now I am thwarted at the first attempt, and left uncertain how to proceed. There is no other candidate who quite fulfils all my necessary criteria, you see." He was absurdly pleased by this odd sort of compliment, until she went on, "Perhaps Mr Truman might do?"

"Mr Truman?" he said, horrified. "No, no! You must have nothing to do with Truman. He would not do at all." He could only hope she would not enquire as to precisely why he would not do, for he was not sure he could compose any coherent reasons at that moment. He only knew that she must not take Truman as her lover. "Have you considered, Mrs Middlehope, all the difficulties of conducting such a clandestine affair at all? How would you meet, for instance?"

"At night, obviously."

"Then how is he to gain access to your bedchamber? Will he simply walk in through the front door? A back door conveniently left unlocked? Must he climb the drainpipe to reach your window, because I must tell you honestly that such a feat would deter all but the most agile and determined of lovers. Or will you conduct your meetings in broad daylight, instructing your manservant that you are not at home to other callers?"

She frowned. "I confess, I had not thought about the matter quite so... so *practically.* You are entirely right, it is very awkward, and also... somewhat sordid. As for drainpipes — no, I cannot expect that of any man, and I certainly do not see the immaculate Mr Truman soiling his pristine garments in such a way. I can see that my nature is not such that subterfuge comes naturally to me. Now, at Roseacre we had a small fishing shelter beside the lower lake that would have been perfect for an assignation."

"If one could be sure of no interruptions," Laurence said.

"Oh, indeed, how awkward that would be! Also, it was quite five miles from the nearest road and would require a putative lover to leave his horse there — with his groom, no doubt — climb a twelve-foot wall and then walk to the shelter, taking care not to get lost, and to avoid falling in the lake, if it should happen to be dark. Not that I have any structure of the type here, for these little arbours are hardly suitable, especially in winter. One would need a brazier or some such, and fuel for it, and then the servants would be involved. What else is possible? One could not rent a cottage for the purpose without awkward questions, nor could one arrange to meet at an inn, for inn servants are the worst kind of gossips. I begin to wonder if it is possible to overcome these difficulties at all. The whole business sounds most disagreeable, now that I consider it sensibly. Regretfully, I believe my project will have to be abandoned. What a useful friend you are, Mr Gage, to so effectively turn me away from my purpose, and rescue me from sin."

He demurred, of course, protesting that she would have come to the same conclusion by herself, in time, but nevertheless he felt rather smug at his success in deterring her from approaching Truman. He would not have had Laurence's scruples, he was sure, for all he was a clergyman, and probably he would have found some easy way to manage the business, without shinning up drainpipes. He was a resourceful young man who had all the young ladies sighing over him, and Laurence was rather pleased that Louisa was not amongst their number.

She was Laurence's friend, not Truman's, and the thought gave him a warm glow of satisfaction.

16: Of Sermons And Friends

'The Dower House, Great Maeswood, Salop. 4th April. My dear Esther, What a week I have had! Pamela and her father, Mr Pritchard, arrived last Friday with all my things, at least not quite all, for there was only one box of books, and now that I have begun to investigate the box, I discover that half of them are not mine at all, but must go back to Roseacre. Also, Pamela brought the clavichord instead of the pianoforte, for they are both Broadwoods and she could not imagine there was much difference. To my astonishment, she also brought Gaius Valerius, and insists that I must have him, for he was sent on Thomas's explicit instructions. She very generously left his groom here, too, so for this kindness I am very grateful. I have been inclined to fear that Thomas paid too much heed on occasion to his wife's wishes and indulged her beyond what was reasonable, but when he decides on a course of action and deems it proper, he will not be deterred. At such times, I see something of his father's strength of character in him. Pamela left on Tuesday, taking the clavichord with her and also my good, plain cook, Mrs Nokes. Seemingly that lady has a way with gruel that is beneficial to Mr Pritchard's digestive issues, and in return for depriving me of my cook, Pamela is to send me Chambers, the Roseacre man-cook, whose

fancy French sauces are not to her liking. The most delightful part of it is that we both consider that we have the better of the deal, and I am so happy at the prospect of once again enjoying quail in a cockscomb and mushroom sauce and pigeon in crayfish butter that I bear the interlude without a cook of any description with tolerable composure. In other matters, I have had a lengthy and open exchange of views with the neighbour of whom I told you on my project to extend my boundaries, and have reluctantly been forced to abandon it as unworkable. I do not intend to attempt anything so ambitious in future, but shall be content to remain within the regular boundaries. Yours, hungry and much chastened, Louisa.'

~~~~~

Louisa was returning from a ride one morning when she observed a carriage laden with luggage turning into the Dower House drive. She hastened her pace, leaving Spencer on his less powerful mount to follow in her wake. By the time she had reached the top of the drive, she knew exactly who was visiting.

"Esther! How delightful! Do these boxes mean that I am to enjoy your company for more than a few hours? If so, I must advise against it, unless you wish to live on bread and cheese."

"But that is why I am come! Dr Deerham was horrified that you have no cook again, for your travails when you first arrived wrung his heart, I assure you. As soon as I read him your letter, he said, *'My dear, you must go at once, and stay until the man-cook arrives, for Mrs Middlehope will be desolate without a good dinner every night.'* So here I am, and I shall soon get your kitchen ship-shape again, although I wondered a little that your neighbours are not rallying round as they did before. I hope you have not offended them."
~~~~~

"It would not concern me if I had," Louisa said, amused. "They were a trifle over-zealous before. I prefer to be left to my own devices."

"Sometimes you can be *too* independent, Louisa. Oh, careful with that box, Beecham, it has all my spice jars in it."

"Good heavens, Esther, I do not expect you to cook for me," Louisa said.

"Now do not set yourself about, for there is nothing I like better, I assure you. What a splendid horse! I see now why you gave him a Roman name, for he is quite looking down his nose at me, I am certain. Good day to you, Spencer! What a long time since I have seen you! How are you?"

"Very well, madam, thank you," he said, as he helped Louisa to dismount.

"Let us go inside," Louisa said, deftly gathering up the train of her riding habit and ushering her friend up the steps, "and as soon as I have changed, I shall sit down and write a heartfelt letter of gratitude to Dr Deerham. How can he possibly spare you? Do you cook at home? Will he starve while you are here?"

"No, no! I keep a perfectly good cook, but I love to dabble. If a dish is a success, I teach it to my cook, so my dear husband will never starve. He enjoys his food just as you do, so he— that one goes down to the kitchen, Beecham —he completely understands. I have brought a few bits and pieces with me, Louisa, for I am sure that Mrs Nokes never thought of truffles or quails' eggs or rose water. I have turbot and oysters and sole, as well, but there was not much fish to be had at such short notice. Oh, this is going to be such fun! Off you go and change while I dig out my apron."

Within an hour, the kitchen was a hive of orderly activity, with a whole array of tempting dishes in the making, and Louisa had been chased out to *'go and sit upstairs and receive callers, like the lady you are.'*

"Oh no, no callers, for today is Friday and I am only authorised to be at home to callers on Thursdays," Louisa said primly.

Esther burst out laughing. "Gracious, how fusty! But you will be very much in the way here, so go and read a book and drink wine, like a good girl."

That was not an order Louisa found possible to resist, so meekly she went away, poured herself a glass of Laurence's excellent Canary and settled down with a book. Ten minutes later, the crunch of determined booted feet on the gravel heralded a caller, possibly two, undeterred by it being Friday. Miss Gage, she decided, probably with her faithful companion, Miss Beasley, come to find out who her visitor was, in case it should be another member of the peerage.

The door knocker sounded, William answered it and a moment later his head appeared round the door. "Are you at home to Miss Gage and Miss Beasley, madam?"

"I am, William. Please show them in, and then bring in some tea and cakes."

Miss Gage twittered about how she had thought Louisa looked a little peaky last night at the Beasleys' card party and was come to enquire how she was. Miss Beasley clutched her reticule tightly, as always, and said nothing. Louisa wondered what it would take to enable the reticent Miss Beasley to uncurl herself and converse like a sensible woman.

Smiling, Louisa said, "How kind you are, Miss Gage, but I am perfectly well, as you see. There will be tea here in a moment. Do sit down. Would you like a glass of Canary while you wait for the tea?"

The ladies refused the Canary, and sat themselves on the chaise longue, Miss Gage rigidly upright, while Miss Beasley drooped ever so slightly.

Louisa was not unkind enough to deprive them of the information they sought, so she said at once, "You find me just catching my breath after the arrival of my friend, Mrs Deerham, from Shrewsbury. She has visited before for a few hours, but this time I am to have the felicity of her company for several days. She is a great friend from my childhood in Hertfordshire."

"Deerham? Is that any connection to the famous Dr Joseph Deerham?" Miss Beasley said, suddenly taking an interest.

The subject of Dr Deerham occupied them until the tea arrived, and not long after that Esther herself appeared, rather pink from the heat of the kitchen, and with a tiny smudge of flour on her cheek, to describe for herself the perfections of her pious husband. Louisa was very glad of her arrival, for pretending to admire Dr Deerham's sermons was a great test of her acting ability, but she was very glad to have found a subject which animated the timid Miss Beasley.

"Do come for dinner tonight," Miss Beasley said, in a sudden burst of garrulousness. "My brother would be so pleased to meet you. We are such admirers of Dr Deerham, I cannot tell you. He is such a magnificent writer, is he not? We often read his sermons aloud to each other, to admire his splendid way with words, at least, it is usually Roland who reads them, for he makes the words resound about the room, somehow. Gentlemen are much better suited to such oratory, are they not? I should so like to hear Dr Deerham preach, but of course it is out of the question. We never get to Shrewsbury." She sighed melodramatically. "But you will dine with us tonight, I hope?"

Louisa glanced at Esther, but she was in a glow of happiness to hear her husband so praised, and was already smiling and expressing her thanks for the invitation. "We have no other engagement for tonight — do we, Louisa?" she said, her eyes pleading.

"No, indeed, we are quite at leisure," she murmured.

Miss Beasley looked nervously at her friend. Miss Gage had her lips pursed in the manner that Louisa interpreted as disapproval. Was she annoyed because her mousy little friend had dared to speak out for herself? Poor Miss Beasley!

When the two ladies had left, Louisa said, "Your first dinner to be set aside, perforce. The servants' dinner will not stretch you."

"No, and I can leave Tilly and Leah to manage that. They are very good girls, hardworking and sensible," Esther said. "In fact, I might ask Tilly to sweep out the attics, just to get the worst of the cobwebs out. Then we can start investigating those interesting boxes."

"They will be full of hooped gowns and cocked hats and vast amounts of yellowed lace, I daresay."

Esther laughed. "Very likely, but I should like to have a look anyway. Just imagine, they have been here for decades untouched and forgotten. What secrets we may find if we look!"

"But not today, I hope. Shall we walk in the garden while the sun is shining? I do not want to share you with an endless stream of curious callers."

They collected bonnets, gloves and thick cloaks against the morning chill and set off on the same loop around the garden that Louisa had taken with Laurence, and inevitably they came in time to the secret arbour in the shrubbery where, without a word being spoken, they sat companionably. Louisa was very struck that, just as she felt completely at ease with Esther, so she had with Laurence, too. They were both her good friends and that pleased her.

"So tell me about your project," Esther said, leaning forward and lowering her voice, although there was no one to hear. "You were so cryptic in your letter! Did you ask him?"

"I asked him, he fled from me in horror, and then returned the next day to reassure me that he would have liked to, and it was no reflection on my seductive powers but he wished to remain faithful to his dead wife." She gurgled with merriment. "Is that not charming? He is such a kind man, trying to spare my feelings, after I positively threw myself at his head. Such an absurdity!"

"Gracious!" Esther said, eyes wide. "And he has not... cut you, or anything of the sort?"

"Not a bit of it! We had a lovely long chat about it and parted on the best of terms."

"Truly? He must be a remarkable sort of man. I confess, one of the attractions of this visit is that I shall get to meet the interesting Mr Gage, if only at church. But tell me about the Beasleys, so I shall be prepared for this evening's conversation."

"Dr Beasley is the physician who investigated my dead body, so unless you want all the gory details, try to avoid the subject. Otherwise, you will get a middling sort of dinner, with middling conversation and a middling game of whist afterwards."

Esther laughed. "Then I shall be a middling sort of guest."

A snuffling in the shrubbery heralded the arrival of a familiar muzzle, tongue lolling.

"Well, Kenneth, how pleasant to see you again," Louisa said. "Where are your comrades? Ah, good day to you, Julian, and I am sure Ian will not be far behind. I do believe you are about to meet my project, Esther."

And so it proved. They heard his voice calling the dogs from some distance away, and then the man himself appeared on the path, gun in hand and hung about with game bags. He stopped, his face breaking into a grin as he saw Louisa.

"I must apologise for my dogs, Mrs Middlehope. They now regard your grounds quite as their own."

"And they are welcome to do so. Will you come and make the acquaintance of my friend?"

"If I do not intrude..."

"Not in the least. Esther, this is Mr Gage, my neighbour and fellow connoisseur of claret, brandy and port. Mr Gage, Mrs Deerham has come from Shrewsbury to lighten my solitude."

They exchanged greetings, and he carefully set down his gun and game bags and sat beside Esther. His easy manner soon had her speaking freely to him on the subject of Shrewsbury and her husband.

"I have read his sermons, of course," Laurence said. "Who has not? I do not always agree with his points but he makes them very powerfully. I heard him preach once, and regard it as one of the high points of my life."

Esther went pink with pleasure, and encouraged Laurence to talk about Dr Deerham to such good effect that he stayed for more than an hour. When he had finally left them, although with obvious reluctance, she said with shining eyes, "Such a charming man! You will be very happy with him, I am sure."

Louisa froze. "Whatever do you mean?"

"Why, when you are married, my dear. You have an understanding, do you not?"

"Not at all! What gave you that idea?"

"Oh!" Esther's face fell. "I thought... you said... I am sure that you said that after your... your *discussion*, that you parted on the best of terms. Did I mistake you?"

"So we did, but as friends, and nothing more. Neither of us wants to marry again, Esther. He is still in love with his wife, and since he imagines her to be perfect in every way, there is no possibility of her ever relinquishing her hold on his heart. A living wife will grow old and fat and cross, or at least irritating, but a dead wife wraps herself in armour that can never be tarnished."

"And you?" Esther said timidly. "Surely you want to marry again, Louisa?"

She shook her head.

"Not yet, perhaps, but in the future?" Esther said. "Marriage is so fulfilling for a woman, do you not agree?"

"It was not fulfilling for me," Louisa said sombrely. "Oh, I was never discontented, and I accepted that I would never be a mother. One cannot rail at God's will in these matters. I have no complaint to make, and I never regretted my choice, but my marriage left me feeling... incomplete, somehow. Hollow."

"That is surely the lack of children," Esther said gently. "The emptiness of life without a child... I cannot imagine how difficult that must be."

"No, it was not that, for I felt it almost from the start, long before I knew I was barren. Ned was always kind to me, and I never, ever had the slightest cause for complaint, and his parents made me welcome, but... there was something missing. I cannot tell you what it was, some nameless thing, but I was aware of it. Lord, Esther, how maudlin I am getting, and I have not had a drop to drink, either. Shall we move on? The sun has shifted now and it is too cool to sit here in the shade."

They went inside, and had tea and some coconut buns that Leah Timpson had made. Esther wrote to Dr Deerham to tell him that she had arrived safely, and Louisa to thank him for sparing Esther to her, and they walked to the Boar's Head to leave the letters for the mail collection. By the time they returned, it was time to change for dinner. The evening was exactly as Louisa had described — a middling sort of occasion, pleasant enough, apart from an excess of description from Dr Beasley on the subject of dead bodies, but Esther lapped it up, eyes wide.

After dinner, Dr Beasley was inspired to read one of Dr Deerham's sermons — "'*On Friendship*', my favourite," Miss Beasley gushed — and for the first time, Louisa felt all the power of the author's words. Dr Beasley struck an attitude, the book in his hand, and then recited as if it were Shakespeare. Indeed, it might as well have been, for the extent to which he held his audience spellbound. Esther and Miss Beasley listened avidly, speechless with admiration, and even Louisa, the most cynical of observers, could not deny that it was a stirring and uplifting speech. She could well imagine Dr Deerham orating the same words from the pulpit, and began to have some inkling of Esther's admiration for such a man, and how such admiration might be the foundation for marriage.

For herself, she could not marry a man merely because he was a rousing orator. Indeed, she could not think of any reason to marry, except for the most pragmatic of motives, for security and duty and a place to shelter. Now that she was financially independent, she need never marry again. She needed no man to protect her. No husband could fulfil her, and make her whole. Ever since she had left her father's house, she had been aware of the emptiness within her. It had been her constant companion through twelve years of marriage, and the year of mourning. When she had arrived in Shropshire, it had been with her still.

But now it was gone. Somehow, in some mysterious way, the Dower House and this tiny little village had filled the aching void within. How strange. How very, very strange.

17: Luggage

On Saturday, Louisa and Esther visited Miss Cokely, the milliner, to collect a bonnet Louisa had ordered. While Esther exclaimed over it and tried on a number of very fetching confections, entirely unsuitable for the wife of so sober a man as Dr Deerham, Louisa went to talk to Miss Cokely's very elderly mother. Mrs Cokely was the widow of a former parson in the village, and on his death had moved with her daughter from the parsonage into a tiny cottage just across the road. On her first visit to the milliner's shop, Miss Cokely had told her in a whisper that her mother had not been herself since Mr Cokely's death.

"She's never been quite the same, Mrs Middlehope," Miss Cokely had said. "Like a poor lost soul, she is. She sits in that front window all day, watching who goes by and noting every wagon and walker who passes. *'The mail carrier is seven minutes late today,'* she'll say. *'Yesterday it was only two minutes late.'* That is how she goes on, but quite harmless. Wouldn't hurt a fly. Ask her about things that happened forty years ago, and she's perfectly sensible, remembers it all as clear as if it was yesterday, but as to what actually happened yesterday, well... you see how she is. Poor Mama! I keep my display of bonnets in the same room so that she gets a bit of company from time to time. Not that she'll answer to the point if you ask her a question, but it would be a kindness if you were to pass the time of day with her."

Louisa sat on the chair conveniently placed for visitors beside Mrs Cokely. "Good morning, Mrs Cokely. How are you today?"

"Mr Exton went by at seven minutes past noon." At her side was a small table with a clock and a notebook, and she tapped the clock with her pencil as she spoke the time.

"Did he so? I have never met Mr Exton. What is he like?"

"Mags passed here at eight minutes before noon." Another tap.

"Mags… from the Hall?"

"Parson's maid scrubbed the front steps of the parsonage from twenty minutes before noon until two minutes after." Again a tap.

It was very sad, for she seemed lucid enough, just somewhat disconnected from the world.

Three of the Miss Saxbys arrived just at that moment, and in the flurry of greetings, Louisa found her arm being touched gently.

"Miss Agnes?" she said, smiling at the girl's anxious face.

"I wondered… do you know anything very much about… about the gentlemen staying at the Grove? Miss Beasley knows very little about them, but they are friends of yours so—"

"Not friends," Louisa said quickly. "I heard of their exploits through my sister-in-law's family, that is all."

"But you have talked to them... *dined* with them. Do you know if any of the gentlemen is married? I met them at church, but naturally one cannot ask directly."

"Oh." Louisa tried not to smile at such a question. Poor Agnes! And she was not in the least abashed by her own forwardness. "Mr Willerton-Forbes is probably not a marrying man. Captain Edgerton mentioned a wife, I believe. As for Mr Chandry..."

"Yes?" Agnes said eagerly.

"I *think* he is a bachelor, but he is a dreadful flirt, Miss Agnes. If you will take my advice, you will be very wary of such a man. I should hate you to have your heart broken by him."

"Oh no, I am in no danger of that," she said breezily. "I never fall in love. Mr Truman was very attentive for a while, but when he turned his eyes elsewhere, I was perfectly unaffected by it, so Mr Chandry will not break my heart. I know his sort very well, but if he is hanging out for a wife, I should be very willing. There are so few eligible men in the neighbourhood and none who look twice at *me*, and I should so like to be married," she added wistfully.

"Somewhere in the world exists the perfect man for you," Louisa said. "You are young still, and need not despair of one day finding a man who will love and cherish you as a husband should cherish his wife."

"I do not mind about being cherished," Agnes said robustly. "Nor do I care if he is what Mama calls *suitable.* I just want to be a wife, and have my own establishment and some children. It is not much to ask, is it?"

"No, indeed," Louisa murmured, but her heart ached for the girl. She could only hope she would not marry incautiously and suffer for it.

At length, Miss Cokely handed over the new bonnet, and Louisa and Esther made their farewells.

"Such lovely creations!" Esther sighed, as they walked back to the Dower House. "I cannot wear anything but the plainest of bonnets, for Dr Deerham does not approve, but I may still admire pretty things, may I not?"

"I have never seen anything wrong with wearing clothes with a little dash," Louisa said, "especially when it keeps poor Miss Cokely and her mother from starving. There is something wrong with the world if a clergyman's daughter is reduced to making bonnets to put food on her table."

"Do you think so?" Esther said. "Dr Deerham says that the poor are necessary so that those more fortunate may show them compassion. *"Blessed are the poor for theirs is the kingdom of heaven.'"*

Louisa had to choke back the acid response that rose to her lips.

~~~~~

With Esther as cook, Louisa enjoyed her first good dinner in the Dower House. On Sunday, she took her friend to church, and observed with interest the slight wariness with which Mr Truman greeted Esther, remembering her reservations about him. It was nothing much — that he had not been well liked at school, had inherited some money from an elderly churchman and had manoeuvred to obtain the Great Maeswood living. Nothing of substance, mere rumour and hearsay, but she recalled Laurence's opinion of him, that he was oily... he had had reservations about
~~~~~

Mr Truman too. What had he said of him? That he was too puffed up in his own importance, that was it, and seeing him talking to Lady Saxby and her daughters, she conceded the truth of it. Miss Saxby held out her hand to him, and he took it and lifted it to his lips in a most forward way for a clergyman towards his noblest parishioners. When he was using his hands to make a point, he even touched her on the shoulder, in the most improper way. Yet there was no sign of displeasure from them, for they smiled and stood talking to him for some time, parting on the most cordial terms.

She noticed Miss Agnes watching Mr Chandry, but as they had not been formally introduced, she could not approach him. Louisa could not resist a little match-making, for why should not Agnes Saxby, plain as she was, have her chance of happiness too? She deftly detached Agnes from the group clustered around Mr Truman, and strolled about from group to group gathered outside the church until, seemingly by chance, she came across Mr Chandry. Introductions were made, Agnes swiftly engaged him in conversation — she was not shy, that was clear — and Mr Chandry responded as any young man would to such obvious interest. Louisa did not anticipate a betrothal, for she suspected Michael Chandry to be far too experienced to allow himself to be drawn into matrimony, but one never knew.

Monday was such a fine, sunny day that Louisa and Esther ventured out in the gig, and found themselves, almost without realising it, entering Market Clunbury.

"Well, I did not intend to travel so far, but since we are here, shall we do a little shopping?" Louisa said. "Look, there is a respectable-looking inn where we may leave the gig."

They spent a happy two hours acquiring a number of interesting packages, and had begun dawdling back to the Lamb and Pheasant, when a man strode out of a side road in front of them.

"Why, Captain Edgerton, fancy meeting you here," Louisa said. "Judging by your frown, you have not been so agreeably engaged as we have." She waved her armful of packages gaily.

He laughed. "No, nothing so pleasant. But allow me to offer you my escort, and relieve you of some of your burdens."

Gratefully, Louisa agreed to it, for they were rather overladen, and they made their way back to the inn, where the captain joined them for refreshments.

"You caught me in a frustrated mood," he said, after the food had been laid out and the first pangs of hunger had been assuaged. "I am trying to find out more about the mysterious Miss Labett, but I cannot find a single employment agency who knows of her, or an attorney or bank or post office with any knowledge of a Labett family. I have been to both Shrewsbury and Ludlow, without success, and am now engaged in eliminating the last possibilities. I can only conclude that she was not from Shropshire. You are aware of our enigmatic lady of the wine cellar, I take it, Mrs Deerham?"

"Oh, yes! A most intriguing case! And she was a governess at the Grove, as I understand it? She just... vanished, one day, without a word of warning, or anyone knowing anything was amiss. How very curious it all is. How did they account for it, at the house? Did they look for her at all?"

"No one suspected that she had been murdered, ma'am," he said with a slight smile. "They just thought she had left."

"Oh! Then her things were gone, too? I assumed that she went off one day to meet her gentleman friend and ended up dead, so her belongings would have been left at the Grove, but if they had gone too—"

Captain Edgerton gave an exclamation. "What a fool I am! Her belongings! Where are they? Clearly, they were not left at the Grove, or she would have been looked for. I wonder if anyone would remember, after all this time, whether she had a box or just a portmanteau."

"Does it matter?" Louisa said.

"Of course!" Esther said, looking at her in astonishment. "A box would need a man to lift it, whereas she could have managed a portmanteau or two herself. You are not very practical sometimes, Louisa."

She acceded to it rather guiltily, for her plans for Mr Gage had run aground for just such a lack of practical forethought. "So she simply walked out of the house with a portmanteau in her hand, and no one noticed?"

"She would have left at night, of course," Esther said, as if this was obvious. "Either her gentleman friend came to help her with a box, or she carried her own luggage. I cannot imagine she had much to take. But that does mean that she had no intention to return. She was leaving for good, and not seeing out her notice or hoping for a reference for another employer. She was finished with being a governess."

Captain Edgerton chuckled appreciatively. "If ever your husband can spare you, Mrs Deerham, I shall recruit you to the ranks of Edgerton, Chandry and Associates. That is admirable deduction."

She coloured with pleasure. "Oh, but it is obvious, do you not think?"

"It is obvious now, but I confess I had not seen it in that light before," he said. "If I can confirm that she took all her clothing and so on when she left, then yes, we can safely say that she was finished with being a governess. Since it seems unlikely that she had suddenly inherited an independence, or stolen her mistress's jewels, we must assume that she was about to put herself under the protection of a man."

"To marry her gentleman friend," Esther said.

"Or to be his mistress," the captain said.

"No, because he would hardly need to murder her if that were so," she said solemnly. "There had to be a reason for him to kill her, and it could only be because she expected him to marry her and for some reason he could not."

"Perhaps he was married already?" Louisa suggested.

"She would have known that, because he was local," Esther said.

"How can you possibly know that?" Louisa said, rather amused at her friend's confidence.

"Because he had the keys to the Dower House, of course. He either killed her and then secreted the body in the wine cellar, or he lured her into the Dower House somehow and murdered her there. In either case, he must have had the keys."

"Miss Labett herself might have got hold of the keys and opened up the house," Louisa said. "He might have been a stranger to the district."

"Then how did he get to know her, and meet her over a period of months?" Esther said.

"Excellent points," Captain Edgerton said. "We have already investigated the matter of the keys. The Saxbys' steward kept them in a drawer in his office, both sets. But he only checked the Dower House two or three times a year, just as a precaution against leaks and so forth, and the rest of the time anyone could walk into the office and remove the keys whenever they liked. Everyone at the Hall knew where the keys were kept. In fact, half the village knew, because he kept spare keys for all the village cottages that Lord Saxby owned, which is most of them."

"So Miss Labett could easily have found that out and taken the keys herself," Louisa said.

"No, dear," Esther said patiently. "Remember that she was locked into the wine cellar with the key to the inner door in her pocket. Since she was murdered, clearly someone else locked her in with the *other* key. Both sets were used, so someone took both and set off for the Dower House knowing that he was going to kill poor Miss Labett and lock her in the wine cellar."

Louisa pondered that. "Knowing that he was going to kill her… that sounds so cold-blooded. Is it not possible that they met at the Dower House, quarrelled and he killed her in a rage, and then tried to make it look like a suicide by leaving the key in her clothing? Or perhaps he threatened her with violence, she locked herself into the wine cellar for safety, and he then fetched the other set of keys, opened the door and murdered her?" She sighed. "No, there is something cold-blooded about it whichever way one looks at it, and he must have had both sets of keys, for the other key to that door was missing, and only the murderer could have disposed of it. I cannot suppose that we will ever know exactly what happened that day."

Captain Edgerton leaned forward, eyes gleaming. "But we can say one thing with certainty, ladies — if Miss Labett's luggage was not left at the Grove then she must have taken it away somewhere, and where more likely than the same place where her body was found?"

"The Dower House?" Louisa said, surprised.

"The attics!" Esther said. "It is full of old boxes, Captain. Perhaps Miss Labett's is amongst them."

Nothing else would do for Captain Edgerton but to leave at once, immediately and without a second's delay. In vain Louisa protested that Miss Labett had been dead for a quarter of a century and a few more minutes would not hurt her. Shaking her head in amused dismay, she gulped down her glass of wine and grabbed a Bath bun to sustain her while they waited for Goronwy to be hitched to the gig. The captain was mounted on a rangy black horse, and he rode sedately behind them as the gig threaded its way through the thronged streets of Market Clunbury, but once on the open road, he galloped ahead and then was forced to wait impatiently while they caught up. Louisa could not quite see the urgency, but she hurried Goronwy along at a fast clip, slowing only for the villages of Astley Cloverstone and finally Great Maeswood. Esther's sigh of relief was audible, and she finally released the rail to which she had been clinging tightly.

Ahead of them, the captain turned into the Dower House driveway, and Louisa flicked the reins to follow in his wake. Goronwy trotted on, oblivious.

Louisa groaned. "I had forgotten that he likes to return to his old home. Hold tight. I am just going to swing round in front of the house."

She gave the pony a nudge to speed him up, and away he went, racing up the drive, faster and faster. Esther was clinging to the rail again. They approached the turning to the stables but Louisa was firm and by sheer determination held the gig on course. They slowed, trotted round in front of the entrance steps, then set off down the drive again. Once more speed deterred the pony from trying to turn towards the stables and the gig successfully made its way back down the drive and into the Dower House next door.

Captain Edgerton was pacing about in front of the house. "What happened?" he cried.

Louisa explained, and his face creased in laughter. "You need a carriage, Mrs Middlehope, with a respectable coachman on the box and a footman behind. I am sure that is what you are used to."

"True, and I shall buy my carriage in time, I daresay, but just for now the gig suits me well enough, however faulty the pony's homing instincts. Esther, will you take Captain Edgerton inside and let him loose in the attics while I take the gig round to the stables?"

By the time she returned to the house, laden with parcels, there were scraping and banging noises emanating from the attics. Louisa left them to it, and went to change her dusty gown, as Marie fussed with her hair, and pinned a fresh lace cap atop her hair.

"Il y a une lettre pour vous, madame. De la baronne. Là bas." There is a letter for you from the baroness.

"A letter? From Lady Mountsea? Where? Oh, I see it... hmm, trouble with a wheel but they arrived home safely. The children are well... what a relief, I was prostrate with anxiety about *that.* Oh! She wants Chambers to train Mrs Nokes, so I have to wait for my man-cook, I suppose. More bread and cheese, Marie. Still, at least she is two hundred miles away from me again."

"Ce n'est pas assez loin," Marie muttered. *It is not far enough.*

Louisa's French was not up to the task of translation so she merely laughed and patted Marie's cheek. "I am sure that was impolite, but so long as you are impolite about my dear sister-in-law, I do not mind. Be impolite about me and I will turn you off without a reference, you cheeky creature, you."

"Seulement si tu peux me comprendre." Only if you can understand me.

Louisa shook her head in bewilderment. "I shall wear the pale green crêpe tonight."

"Oui, madame."

"Thank God I am out of mourning at last, Marie. I was so tired of black. I bought some very pretty sarcenet, today, such a lovely clear blue colour. I am sure you can make me something charming from it, but no train. I believe trains are quite out of style now. How are you getting on with the new round gown?"

"C'est fini. Voulez-vous le porter demain? You wear tomorrow?"

"Why not? Thank you, Marie. You should speak English more often, then I might understand you better."

"Pfft. Il n'y a pas de plaisir là-dedans." Where would be the fun in that?

"You see? I did not get a word of that."

Marie only laughed, and Louisa went to find Captain Edgerton in the attics. Tilly had done some cleaning already, so the worst of the spiders' webs had gone, but the air was still thick with dust. The whole floor was covered with boxes, old half-broken bits of furniture, several paintings, some rolled up rugs and, rather incongruously, a shrouded shape that could only be a harp. All the boxes were open, their contents jumbled up. Captain Edgerton sat disconsolately on a rickety chair.

"Captain? Have you found anything?"

"Who can say?" he said mournfully. "Tell me what you see here, Mrs Middleton. All these boxes — tell me what you see."

"I see a lot of clothes, all mixed up. You have made a thorough search, I see."

"This is exactly how they were when I opened the lids," he said. "There must be... oh, twenty boxes here. If any one of them belonged to Miss Labett, it is beyond my ability to determine it."

"Well, this did not!" she said, picking up a lamp and holding it high to illumine a very large box. "Solid mahogany, by the look of it. Heavens, how heavy that must be! And this one... see how the inner portion opens to reveal all these little drawers? These big, ornate boxes look as if they were designed for the Grand Tour."

"Very true," he said, brightening. "So we must look for a small, plain box, like that one over there."

She walked round it, holding the lamp close to examine it. "The lid is engraved *'Captain James Saxby'*. But this one is small enough and plain enough to belong to a governess. Oh, but that cannot be right," she said, laughing, pulling out a vast hooped skirt of heavy brocade, encrusted with embroidery in gold thread. "What a monstrosity! No governess ever wore this. In fact, no one at all wore such things even in Miss Labett's day, for such styles were quite out of fashion. Oh but... wait a moment." She pulled out a chemise. "Now this is more of a governess's style. See how thin and cheap the fabric is? And it is almost grey with age. This does not at all belong to the same lady as the sack dress."

"Then everything has become muddled," he said sadly. "The murderer hid Miss Labett's clothes by mingling them with the old clothes already here. It will be impossible to find them all."

"Courage, Captain!" Louisa said. "It will be a painstaking task, but not impossible, I fancy. We need only remove every item from every box and determine those which may have belonged to the governess. That is something you may leave to the ladies."

"You are a treasure, Mrs Middlehope," he said with a smile.

18: Memories And Discoveries

Laurence had much to occupy his mind. Lady Day had come and gone, the rents in and safely stowed in the bank, salaries paid and the tradesmen's bills settled. That meant that the accounts must be worked on and his plans laid for the coming year. There would be long, difficult discussions with his steward to determine what must be done, what would be useful to do and what could wait for another year. There was always too much that had to wait for another year.

At least the house itself was in good shape, for he had had a great deal of work done on it when Catherine was alive. Or rather, when he had been able to draw on Catherine's money. For a few years he had been rich, and so the roof had been fixed, a number of windows and shutters replaced, the kitchens improved and every room redecorated. He had just begun on the estate improvements when Catherine had died and the money had dried up, and now every year was, not a struggle exactly, but a matter of juggling competing requirements.

Catherine… Talking to Louisa about his marriage and having to describe the circumstances of it with unblinking honesty led him inevitably to Malcolm. He had not thought about his brother a great deal lately, but occasionally some incident would remind him, and then all the old feelings would surge up. Not anger, not any more. He had raged at Malcolm at the time, but that had long since faded. He could not be angry, for he was the one who had won Catherine's heart. He had won and Malcolm had lost.

What he mostly felt was bewilderment. How could they have fallen out so spectacularly, two brothers who had been as close as twins when they were boys? With only a couple of years between them, and their sisters all older, they had fallen quite naturally into a unit of two against the world. They had done everything together, and since Malcolm was far cleverer than Laurence, they had marched in step through their education, too. They had never even had a difference of opinion, until they met Catherine and Malcolm had declared implacable war. When he found himself on the losing side, he had left, never to return, not even for Catherine's funeral.

Malcolm had never married, choosing instead to pursue a lowly career as a schoolmaster at Harrow. He was an intellectual, too, who maintained his links with Oxford. There were letters occasionally to mark his steady march through the halls of academia — an award, a paper published or a lecture given to some prestigious society. Not that he ever gave Laurence notice of the latter before the event, so there was never the opportunity to attend. It was merely notification. Look how well your brother is doing, he seemed to be saying, even though you stole the love of his life. Look how he advances in the world while you idle away your life in your country retreat.

Malcolm... his brilliant, imaginative, handsome, amusing brother. Why on earth had Catherine not fallen head over heels in love with him? Every other woman did, and Laurence had never minded, for he admired Malcolm quite as much as they did. It was only natural that women should adore him. Yet

Catherine had not. What had she thought of him, that month in Bath? Seeing the two brothers side by side, watching them compete to win her, what had been her thoughts? He had never considered the question before, for the answer was obvious — she had judged them both and settled her affections on Laurence. It was as simple as that.

But Louisa had somehow made it complicated. *'And you had no curiosity? Or perhaps you do not wish to know what she thought, and that is why you never asked her and have not read her diaries.'*

Now he wondered whether his easy assumptions were valid. What had Catherine thought about Malcolm... about Laurence himself? What had she thought of their feud? She had never, ever mentioned it, but she must have noticed, and therefore she must have had her own opinion of it. Yet he had no idea what that was.

There was now but one possible way to find out, and that was to read her diaries. Of course, they might contain nothing but details of dress fittings, balls attended, travel details. *'Paid morning calls on the Scrutons, the Bannisters and Lady Adlington... My new blue silk gown arrived today, needs some alteration about the shoulders... Outing to Wells, little sun, the company very dull.'* But then again, they might not. They might reveal her true thoughts. *'Mr Malcolm Gage is very handsome, but Mr Gage is far more gentlemanlike and agreeable.'* Surely she must have thought so, or she would not have married him.

He woke one morning determined to find out. He went through to Catherine's bedroom and unlocked the davenport, withdrawing all her diaries, all nine volumes, taking them to his own room and laying them out in two lines on the small writing desk there. So exquisite, the embroidered covers! The earlier ones were a touch less refined, perhaps, but all of them were works of art. Picking up the first volume, he slowly opened the cover, and read the first line.

'Today I am sixteen years old — a woman. My childhood is in the past, and yet my future is shrouded in darkness. I cannot know what my life will be. Will I be happy or merely contented or even miserable? Will I be a wife and mother, or live out my days with a spinster's cap? Will I live a long life or short? Will there be regrets or will I be confident that I made the right choices? None of this is known except to God, but however it may be, I vow that every moment of it will be recorded here, and whether it be good or bad, exciting or dull, memorable or forgettable, every word of it will be true to my nature.'

He closed the book, and set it back with its fellows, then made a minute adjustment so that it was precisely straight. Did he want to read on? Did he dare? With a sigh, he gathered them up and put them into a locked drawer of the desk, then went to walk the dogs.

He had not gone half a mile before he stopped, considered, turned round and walked home again, the dogs whining their displeasure. He had opened the first diary and now the desire to read on gnawed at him, and would not be appeased. Inside, the dogs disappeared to their accustomed spot before the study fire, but Laurence returned to his bedroom, shut the door and sat down at the desk. Unlocking the drawer, he withdrew the first volume and began to read.

It was exactly as he had expected, the musings of a young girl on first stepping out into the world. The morning calls, the gowns, the first evening engagements, the excitement of the first ball, mingled with the mundane, the duty letters, the endless hours practising at the instrument, the quiet evenings at home.

But this was not what he wanted to read about. He skipped quickly over the first two volumes, and went straight on to the third.

'7th February. Today we arrived in Bath, such a busy place! People everywhere, and all fearsomely fashionable. Mr Slythe says that Bath is full of quizzes, and it is true that we are greatly stared at. As we entered the hotel, a man standing outside raised his quizzing glass at me in the rudest manner! The York House Hotel is very elegant, and we are assured of every comfort. Poor Mama was quite knocked up by the journey, although we came only thirty two miles today. Mr Slythe said it was forty, and I do not contradict him, but I could read the mileposts perfectly well. Tomorrow we are to write our names in the Master of Ceremonies' books at the Upper and Lower Assembly Rooms, for everyone must do so, Mr Slythe says, and then we shall visit the Pump Room so that Mama may drink the waters. My room is…'

Laurence was not interested in rooms or hotels or dinners. He flipped straight over the page to the next day's entry.

'We entered the Pump Room, a well-appointed place—' He chuckled at this casual dismissal of one of the wonders of Bath. *'—which was crowded with a multitude of people moving around the room and chatting together in groups. It is horrid to know no one and not be able to exchange greetings with anyone. Again the quizzing glasses were much in evidence, and I was repeatedly scrutinised as I walked through the room. I held my head high, however, knowing my new gown to be very much* à la mode. *Mr Slythe insisted we all try the waters at least once, and I drank all of mine, although it was quite horrid. Mrs Fossett said she liked it, but then she never complains about anything. She is the timidest creature. And then the most amazing thing happened. I turned round and there was the handsomest man I have ever seen and he was staring straight at me, his eyes burning into mine. I have*

read in novels of such moments, and thought it all very fanciful, yet it has happened to me, to him, to us — that instant union of two souls that is impossible to deny. I lowered my eyes at once, but when I dared to look again, he was still there, still watching me, still mesmerised.'

Laurence lowered the volume, his breathing harsh. Not for one second could he doubt that she spoke of Malcolm. Laurence's own features were passable, and he had never been afraid to look into a mirror, but no woman would ever describe him as the handsomest man she had ever seen. He knew he should put the diaries away, should lock them up and throw away the key, but he could not. It was as if he had no will of his own. He must read on, though it pierced him to the heart.

There was no more on that day's entry, so he quickly scanned the succeeding pages. *'The handsome man was there again... he smiled at me. Oh, such a smile! Such warmth, such joy in his expression to see me again!... He was there again today and we spoke for the first time! He has a brother, who made himself known to Mr Slythe and was introduced to Mama and so I was allowed to make a circuit of the room with both of them, with Mrs Fossett in attendance, and could talk to my admirer. He has a strong, clear voice, and talked about the Romans and what Bath was like when they were here, which was far more interesting than the usual how-do-you-like-Bath conversation. The more I see of him, the more I like him, and his admiration for me blazes in his eyes whenever he looks at me, which is a great deal.'*

Laurence closed the book, too overwhelmed with grief to read on. *'He has a brother...'* That was all he was to Catherine, Malcolm's brother. He remembered that day clearly. He was the one who had made the approach, first to the courier to enquire who the ladies were and whether they might be amenable to an introduction, and then to Mrs Haywood and Catherine and the chaperon. Mrs Fossett. He had forgotten her name until he read it.

"Do stroll about the room with Catherine, Mr Gage," Mrs Haywood had said, smiling at him. "I have not the strength for it, so I shall sit here while I drink my medicine, but I would not see Catherine tied to my side all the time."

He had held out his arm and she had rested her hand upon it, and he had felt as grand as a lord with her beside him. Malcolm had walked on her other side, but Laurence had talked to her first, the disparaged how-do-you-like-Bath conversation. She had answered readily enough, her clear blue eyes gazing at him steadily. And then Malcolm had talked to her about the Romans, dull stuff, and she had answered him very freely, too, and in all honesty, looking back on it from sixteen years later, he could detect no difference in her manner towards either of them. There had been no sign then of the union of souls, and not by so much as a blush had she betrayed her stronger feelings for Malcolm.

They had met every day after that, at first just at the Pump Room, and later at the Assembly Rooms for concerts and balls. After ten days, he had asked Mrs Haywood if he might talk to her privately, and he had poured out his heart — that he was in love, deeply in love, but he could not afford to marry without some money. He spoke of the house that would be his, and very soon, for his father could not live much longer, of his income and his position in society. She had smiled and told him the good news — that Catherine had one hundred thousand pounds from her father, and she approved his suit.

"It will be for Catherine to decide," she had said. "I will not force her hand if she dislikes the idea, and she is still young, Mr Gage. She is but eighteen years of age, and an innocent in the world. It may very well be that she will not wish to settle for the first eligible man to offer, but you may try to attach her, with my good will."

He flicked through the pages until he came to that day. Had she known of his visit? She did not mention it but one section jumped out at him.

'Mama called me to her room for a serious talk before bed. I am to marry the brother, it seems. It is all arranged. His father has a fine estate in Shropshire and as the elder, it will all be his, and mine too. She is very pleased with me for succeeding sooner than we had dared to hope.'

Nothing else. She did not even give him his name, he was still just *'the brother'*.

It was time for breakfast, and then there were lessons for the children, and later a parish meeting to attend, which went on longer than expected. Truman was a prosy fellow, always determined to have the last word. Then dinner at the Drinkwaters, which was as tedious as usual. It was almost midnight before John had readied him for bed, and he was free to pick up the diaries again.

This time, he settled down beside the fire with two candelabra, a glass of Cognac at his elbow, and began to read the whole section more carefully, weaving his own memories with Catherine's. There were the outings in the curricle he had hired, the walks in Sydney Gardens, the evening concerts, the times he had danced with her, the two evenings he had been invited to dine with her party at their hotel, the latter especially memorable because Malcolm had not been invited.

But then the diary began to record the secret meetings with Malcolm, seemingly by chance. At least Catherine thought them so — *'We happened upon Malcolm walking along Milsom Street.... I was sketching the Royal Crescent when who should happen by but Malcolm...'* When had she begun to call him by his Christian name? He flicked back through the pages — almost at once, in fact. Within three days they had been on intimate terms, at least within the private confines of her diary.

There were other memories, too, darker moments unknown to Catherine. While she sailed through her days in sunny mood, apparently enjoying the attentions of both brothers, behind the scenes there had been so much bad feeling. The first row was almost at once, on the second day. Malcolm had spelled out his intentions with relentless logic, and Laurence had just as relentlessly pointed out that he was the elder, the one responsible for rescuing the Grove from ruin, the one with the better right to court the heiress. After that, they could scarcely be together without arguing. Or rather, Malcolm had argued. Laurence had doggedly pursued his original strategy, slowly getting to know Catherine, and then gaining approval from her mother.

That was the point at which the rows had exploded into something much worse, and Malcolm had dropped all pretence. From then on, it was war. Laurence had the approval of Mrs Haywood, but Malcolm had the force of his own personality and an arrogant disregard for anyone but himself. "She loves me," he said, over and over. "She is mine."

Yet at the time, Laurence had been aware of no such emotion in Catherine. She met them both with equal pleasure, talked to both, danced with both without the slightest sign that she preferred one over the other, or either above the many other partners who led her onto the floor at a ball. Only now, reading her thoughts at the time could he see how much she had loved Malcolm.

'He is the most splendid man in Christendom... he loves me beyond all reason, he says, and I cannot say that I feel any less for him... if only I could be his, and be so deeply loved for ever.'

Almost every time they met in secret, Malcolm spoke of marriage, of persuading her mother, even of elopement. Laurence had been aware of none of it. While his brother had wooed her in hasty clandestine encounters, Laurence had courted her openly with her mother's blessing and had eventually made his offer. And she had accepted him, with a pretty little speech about obligation and gratitude and regard. He had won.

He turned to the page where she had recorded the events of that fateful day. There was but a single line.

'Mr Gage proposed and I accepted him. Mama is pleased with me.'

Nothing else.

19: Of Happiness

Louisa spent the day in the attic with Esther and Marie, and occasionally Sarah and her feather duster if an item was too coated in dust to be touched, sorting through the contents of the boxes. Every single item was brought out into the open, to be examined and set aside if there was any possibility that it might have belonged to Miss Labett, the dead governess.

There was not much. Some hairbrushes and combs, cheap perfume and rouge, some paste jewellery, half a dozen gowns, a couple of bonnets and a few undergarments of such poor quality that Esther was shocked.

"Why would anyone wear such a nightgown?" she said, holding up an item so thin that candle light was visible through it.

"She saved her pennies for the outer garments," Louisa said. "She was all show, Miss Labett was."

By the middle of the afternoon, she was satisfied that everything was correctly identified and left it to Captain Edgerton to make what he could of it, but she had seen little that would be of help. The set of hairbrushes bore the engraved initials 'DL' but otherwise there was nothing to tell of Miss Labett's history.

Esther disappeared to the kitchen and Marie went off to do whatever a lady's maid did, for Louisa had never enquired. What was she to do for the hour or so before dressing for dinner? After the dusty atmosphere of the attics, she was minded for some fresh air, and as she still wore her oldest clothes, she collected her gardening gloves and pruning shears, and began work on an overgrown bush in the shrubbery.

She had not been working for long when a rustling in the undergrowth was followed by Kenneth's inquisitive muzzle, his tongue lolling.

"Well, boy, how kind of you to visit. Where are Ian and Julian today? Ah, Julian, there you are. And where is your master, eh? He cannot be far behind, I am certain."

The dogs snuffled happily round her feet, then bounded off through the shrubbery again, the sounds of their movement diminishing into the distance. Curious, she laid down her pruning knife and gloves, and set off in pursuit. It was not easy going, for the bushes towered above her head and made it hard to know in which direction she was travelling. She could not get seriously lost in her own garden, however, and once or twice she heard noises ahead which kept her on the right track. So it was that in a few minutes she emerged at the secret arbour, and there they all were, the dogs and their master.

The dogs greeted her happily, but Laurence… her heart turned over in fear at the sight of him. He sat inside the arbour, elbows on knees, his head resting on his hands, the picture of utter dejection. He looked up at her approach and gave her a wan smile.

"My dear Laurence, whatever is the matter? What has happened? Are you ill?"

"No, no. Nothing of that sort. No great disaster, beyond my own stupidity," he said, his tone dispirited.

"Will you come inside? Some brandy?"

The answering smile was a little downcast. "Thank you, but no."

She sat down beside him and took one of his hands. "Goodness, but you are cold! Will you not come inside to warm yourself?" He merely shook his head. "How long have you been sitting here?"

"Oh... I cannot say. What hour is it? I left the house at... noon, I suppose. Or about that."

"Good God, Laurence, the wind is too chilly to sit out for so long."

The smile warmed, and he clasped her hand in both of his. "I have alarmed you, and for that I apologise, but the sun was full on this seat at first and I have been perfectly comfortable, believe me, in body if not in mind. I took your advice, you see. I read Catherine's diaries."

"Oh!" That was not at all what she had expected. "Yet you were so set against it."

"It was Viola who persuaded me, astonishingly. She produced her own diaries to find some information about Miss Labett, and it was all the trivial doings of her days, where she went, who she saw, the minutiae of her life. I assumed that Catherine's would be the same, for surely she could have had no secrets? She was so transparent, or so I misguidedly thought. So I began to read and at first it was just like Viola's — balls, gowns, walks here and there, outings, visitors. But then there was Bath and... oh, Louisa! She loved Malcolm! From the first moment, she was in love with him... called him the handsomest man she had ever met... never noticed me at all. I was just *'the brother'*. It was *'Malcolm did this... Malcolm said such-and-such... Malcolm is so wonderful...'* and then *'the brother took me for a drive... I stood up for the cotillion with the brother...'*.

"That is horrid," Louisa said. "But still, she married you, so—"

"Only because her mother told her to do so! *'I am to marry the brother... it is all arranged.'* That is what she wrote. And then *'Mr Gage proposed to me, and I accepted. Mama is pleased.'* That is all. No expression of pleasure, or anticipation of a happy future, just *'Mr Gage proposed. I accepted.'* I closed the book at that point. I had not the heart to read on."

"I can imagine," Louisa said, stroking his hand gently, as she tried to tamp down her anger. To write of her future husband in such a manner! How she wished she could say what she truly thought of Catherine Haywood.

"This makes me feel such a fool," he said. "She never showed the least outward sign of such feelings, indeed it always seemed to me that she was such a calm and composed person that violent emotion was not in her nature. If only I had known! I would willingly have stood aside if there had been the least indication."

"Then you would have been wrong to do so," she said crisply. "You knew that Mrs Haywood approved your suit, but there is no guarantee that she would have approved of your brother just as readily. Indeed, she would have been negligent in her duty if she had done so. It is not my place to say so, but his behaviour was not at all proper. As your brother, he owed you his absolute loyalty, and his assistance in securing the future of the estate. To be meeting the lady in secret and attempting to attach her himself is entirely reprehensible. Forgive me if my words offend you," she added, seeing the surprise on his face. "I feel we know each other well enough for me to express my honest opinion."

"And I value it greatly, although it astonishes me to hear you say so. Do you truly believe he was wrong?"

"Absolutely wrong, and surely anyone would say as much," she said firmly.

"My sisters did not," he said ruefully. "They all sided with Malcolm. He was young and in love, and it was natural to follow his heart in such a matter. That was their opinion, and they thought I should have stood aside for him. I was the heir and would have no trouble securing another connection, they said, but such a match would have been wonderful for Malcolm. He could have been independent. Oh, they were happy for me, but they hated the rift between us and blamed me for the whole of it."

"Again, it is not gentlemanly behaviour to storm away in a huff — and stay away for years!" she cried. "Do your sisters ever see him? Or receive letters from him?"

"Only the occasional letter to let us know that he is still alive. They write to him, but he rarely responds. He severed virtually all connection with the family."

"How childish!" she said sharply. "But as for standing aside for him to marry Catherine, you must always remember that she chose *you*. It was you she wanted."

"She wanted the estate, I suppose, and the combined power of two good incomes. That was certainly what her mother wanted. There was no question of marrying for love."

"Such matters are not necessarily so simple," Louisa said. "The decision to marry is a combination of many factors, and money is only one among many. One must have enough to live upon, naturally, but money is not enough to sustain a lifetime together. Nor is love, very often. Irrational emotion is a poor foundation for such an important choice. Character is of far greater import, to my mind. Catherine and her mother would have looked carefully at the two of you, and seen that one of you was restrained, gentlemanly, very correct, and the other was more volatile, perhaps, and not at all correct."

"I was dull and boring, in other words." But his eyes crinkled as he smiled, the first sign of amusement she had seen in him.

"You are neither dull nor boring, far from it," she said crisply. "You are steady, that is all, and believe me, steadiness is a quality much valued in a prospective husband."

"Good heavens, if you truly think that way, then we should get married at once. Can there be another woman in the world who values my plodding dullness?"

She burst out laughing. "You see? Never boring! Now stop being silly, Laurence. To answer your question — your *real* question — yes, there is, or was, another woman who did not think you boring, and you married her. Did she ever give you the least indication of dissatisfaction with her situation? Was she in the slightest discontented?"

"No, she did not appear to be," he said slowly. "She never complained about anything, and we never quarrelled. She was a very serene person, who never raised her voice, never contradicted anyone, never put herself forward."

"Will you be angry with me if I say that *she* is the one who sounds dull?" Louisa said mischievously, and was relieved when he laughed.

"It must appear that way, but I never found her so. Restful, perhaps. She made me feel very protective and solicitous of her, very grateful for my good fortune. And happy... at least I thought I was happy. It was all an illusion, I suppose."

"You cannot change the past, Laurence," she said quietly. "You were happy at the time, and knowing more of your wife's feelings does not change that. Besides, if you read on through the diaries, you may well find that she writes of her happiness with you, the fulfilment of her children and the pleasures of her new life. However she entered matrimony, she may well have developed a genuine affection for you as the years passed. That is not at all uncommon. A girl of eighteen does not have the perspective on the world that she acquires later."

"Ah, Louisa, you are a kindly woman. You are trying to make me feel better."

"That is what a friend is for, is it not? But I give you no Spanish coin, Laurence. I speak only the truth. Something of the sort happened to me when I was but fifteen, and just taking my first tentative steps into society, amongst friendly neighbours. One family had a cousin staying with them, a major in some regiment or other, and a more outrageous flirt never walked the earth. Of course, I swallowed his Canterbury tales whole, and imagined myself lost in love for... oh, all of ten days, I believe. Whereupon I realised he was a rogue and a charlatan, and returned promptly to the real world of steady gentlemen. So it is very possible that if you read more of Catherine's diaries, you will find out that she was just as happy as you were."

He considered that for a long while, as Louisa bent over Ian, who had rested his head on her lap. Then, just when she thought he had wandered off irretrievably into some private reverie, he said, "Were you happy in your marriage, Louisa?"

She never considered turning the question aside. The friendship between them demanded openness, so she said slowly, "I was not *un*happy."

"Hmm. That is not the same thing."

"True. I was contented, that is the best way to describe it. I went into it full willing, and I never regretted it, not for a moment, but..." She paused, but he said nothing, watching her quietly as she composed her thoughts. After a moment, she went on, "I think I felt excluded. Ned and his parents had lived together for over fifty years in perfect harmony. They were complete unto themselves, needing no other person, so although they made me very welcome and were never less than perfectly kind and thoughtful towards me, it was as if there was no space there for me to fill. Sometimes, if I entered the house after a visit or a walk in the garden and came upon them unexpectedly, they would look round at me in surprise, almost as if they had forgotten I existed."

"If there had been a child, perhaps that would have made a difference."

"Perhaps, but I wondered sometimes if they would have simply absorbed the child into their little circle and I would still have been on the outside."

He reached one hand to stroke her face, and then took hold of her hand again. "Poor Louisa. Poor me, too, for we have both had marriages that were... less than satisfactory."

"But yours was perfect at the time," she protested. "It is only now that you know more about your wife that you see it as less than satisfactory."

"No," he said in a low voice. "It is clear now that it was not perfect at all. I could never talk to Catherine as I talk to you, or sit on the floor with her drinking Cognac until the small hours. The dogs were not permitted in most of the rooms. *I* was not permitted in some of them, and she disliked any open show of affection from me. I could never have sat here like this, holding hands, talking about... well, about anything. It is only since I met you that I have seen how deficient my marriage was."

Louisa's breath caught. Jumping to her feet, she cried, "You must not do this, Laurence! It is unfair to your wife to look back and make comparisons. You were happy then — she made you happy, so let the past alone. Do not pick at it like a scab. Whatever is the time? I must go and change for dinner. I have been scuffling about in the attics all day and I am filthy."

He stood too, his face abject. "You are right... you are always right. I beg your pardon. I shall leave you now, but perhaps I shall see you and Mrs Deerham at our card party tonight?"

"We are looking forward to it."

His face softened into a smile. "Excellent. Do you have plans for tomorrow? If not, it might be a good time for us to go over to Woollercott and collect those pups. We will go in the carriage, if Mrs Deerham will come with us. If not, it will have to be the phaeton."

She agreed to it enthusiastically. Her own dogs! How she would enjoy that.

That evening was as pleasant as any she could remember. Esther again provided a good dinner, and there were eighteen at the card party, so there were three whist tables and one of vingt-et-un, where Louisa and Esther found themselves playing a lively game against Laurence, Mr Truman, Mr Winslade and Miss Winslade. Mr Truman flirted in the most delicate way imaginable with Louisa, and Mr Winslade entertained Esther so well that she roared with laughter, and dared to tease him in return. Louisa had forgotten how vivacious Esther used to be, before Dr Deerham came along. As for Laurence, he seemed far more relaxed than he had that afternoon, and made an effort to talk to Miss Winslade.

The morning saw Laurence's carriage at the door at eleven o'clock sharp. That was the advantage of a man distinguished by steadiness of character — he was utterly reliable. Woollercott was not many miles away, so there was little time to grow bored with the journey, and then there was the joy of choosing two pups to bring home. They were a little older than she had expected, but the breeder explained that he did not like them to leave him until they were mature enough to settle contentedly.

Louisa chose by the simple expedient of sitting in the straw and allowing the pups, and their mother, to sniff around her. After half an hour, it seemed that two of them had chosen her, one almost all black, and one liver and white.

"I should have liked one in Kenneth's colours," she said, stroking the head of the black pup, "but the only one in that colour does not seem to like me. But these two like me very well, and I like them, too. Well, Mr Chapman, are you content to let these splendid fellows come to me?"

"Aye, I am that, mum. Don't like 'em goin' to ladies, as a rule, but you'll do."

"What will you call them?" Esther said, as they lifted the pups into the carriage.

"I shall follow Ned's policy of naming them after planets. Mercury and Mars, I think. The black fellow shall be Mercury and the liver and white shall be Mars."

They drove the short distance back to Great Maeswood in the greatest good humour, in perfect charity with each other and the world. But when they turned into the Dower House drive, there was a carriage drawn up in front of the entrance, and luggage being unloaded.

Esther gave a squeak that might have been either pleasure or alarm. “It is Dr Deerham,” she said. “He has come to stay.”

“Oh,” Louisa said. “What a surprise. And just before Easter, too. How unexpected.”

And how unwelcome. Her heart sank like a stone.

20: Windows Into The Past

Laurence watched the two ladies' faces with interest. Louisa's momentary dismay was quickly masked. Mrs Deerham's expression was more complex — excitement, certainly, but also something else. Was it fear? And perhaps with reason, for Dr Deerham looked a stern sort of man, tall, bewigged and dressed from head to foot in black, with an old-fashioned full-skirted coat and Geneva bands at his throat, every inch the disapproving clergyman.

The introductions were awkward, with the two pups straining at their leashes and yapping excitedly. Dr Deerham's frown deepened rather.

"I had better get these fellows settled in their new home," Louisa said.

"Let me take them while you attend to your guest," Laurence said firmly. "To the side of the stables, I think you said?"

She nodded, then turned to the groom, who was conferring with the Deerhams' coachman. "Spencer, will you show Mr Gage where the dogs are to go?" Then, with a quick smile to Laurence, she said, "Thank you."

He sent his own carriage home, then followed the groom round the side of the house to the stable block.

"Lord, what a to-do!" the groom said, pulling a face. "He looks a strange one. I'd keep clear till he's gone if I were you."

Laurence only laughed. He spent a little while settling the pups into the loose box that had been prepared for their use, and listening covertly to the chatter between the groom and the Deerhams' men as the carriage was brought round and the horses unhitched. Dr Deerham did indeed sound like a strange one. He was not much above thirty, he guessed, but with all the haughtiness of a much older man. Not someone who would put himself out to please the ladies, that much was certain, and most likely they would have a miserable time of it.

Spencer left the Deerham men to settle their own horses, and brought some food for the pups. "Bonnie pair, they are," he said, watching them with a smile. "Be good to have dogs again. I'll walk 'em later if th'mistress is too busy."

"Thank you, Spencer," Laurence said. "How are you settling in here? A bit different from Roseacre."

"Aye, it is that. It's well enough here but th'mistress won't be stopping long."

There was a chill in Laurence's stomach. No Louisa? No friend to share his Cognac? No one to talk to? "What makes you say that?"

"This was always s'posed to be temp'ry. Just till she decides where she wants to live. As far as possible from her ladyship, I 'spect! Cornwall, maybe."

Cornwall! Would even that be far enough away from Lady Mountsea? He doubted it.

When he returned to the Grove, he discovered that Captain Edgerton, Mr Willerton-Forbes and Mr Chandry had commandeered the saloon, which was now covered with trestle tables laden with items of female apparel. The three were bent over one of the tables, examining some object with intense interest.

"Whatever is going on?" Laurence said, more amused than alarmed.

"Ah, Mr Gage," Willerton-Forbes said. "I must apologise for the disruption to the household, but we needed a great deal of space to work and Miss Gage most kindly permitted us to use this room. I trust the inconvenience will be short-lived."

"Oh, we hardly ever use this room anyway," Laurence said easily. "It is far too big and draughty for comfort. On the rare occasions when we plan to entertain half the county, we have fires burning for a week beforehand. But what precisely are you doing?"

"Examining poor Miss Labett's clothing and other personal items. And we have found something most interesting. Michael, where is the box?"

Captain Edgerton produced a small writing box. "The murderer appears to have gone through Miss Labett's possessions to remove anything which might identify her, for we found no letters of any sort, and several of her books had the first page torn out, where there might have been an inscription. However, he was in haste for he missed this." He lifted up an inner flap of the box to reveal a hidden compartment, and nestled within, three letters, all inscribed *'To whom it may concern'*. "References, you see," he said triumphantly. "Her three previous employers, although she never seems to have stayed long at any of them. Two years... three... only eighteen months at the last one. One does not quite like to draw conclusions about that."

"That would concern me, too, if I were engaging her," Laurence said thoughtfully. "It would be a question that one would want to ask her during an interview. Presumably she returned convincing answers, or my mother would not have employed her. What is your opinion?"

"That she was a flighty piece who set out to entrap a son of the house into matrimony," Edgerton said promptly. "Being found out, she was hastily bundled off to another job with a glowing reference, to avoid any scandal. These references are uniformly effusive. She was a paragon of a governess, one would suppose, to read these."

"They are rather colourful," Laurence said, scanning them quickly. "*'The most effective governess we have ever employed... very sorry to lose her... well versed in all the subjects necessary for the most refined education... one has the utmost confidence in her...'* And so on and so on, and nothing about why she left after so short a time. Definitely suspicious. I assume that the next step is to locate the originators of these letters and see what may be discovered about Miss Labett."

"Exactly!" Captain Edgerton said, enthusiastically. "Who knows what interesting tidbits may come to light? We are gradually gaining a clearer picture of our long-dead governess. We will uncover her murderer yet."

Dinner that evening was enlivened by Captain Edgerton and Edward planning a complex campaign to visit the writers of the three notes. When Laurence asked mildly if it was necessary to travel all the way to Kent, Hertfordshire and Norfolk, when there was a perfectly good mail service, Edgerton told him that it was necessary to look someone in the eye to determine whether he or she might be lying.

"I am not sure why these ladies would bother to lie about so trivial a matter," Laurence said. "It is more likely they would remember nothing at all and your journey would be wasted."

"True, and they may have moved away or even have died by now," Edgerton said. "But these houses always have servants who were raised on the estate and know everyone who passed through the servants' hall, so someone will remember Miss Labett, even after a quarter century."

Laurence said no more, and the conversation moved on. Viola and the children left the table and the men lingered over their port, talking about the latest news from London but also, to Laurence's surprise, deeply interested in village news and the prospects for locating the late Lord Saxby's heir. Willerton-Forbes' uncle was involved in the search and was presently in Suffolk tracking down some long-lost descendant of the Third Baron, although he was not optimistic.

"What happens if no living heir can be found?" Chandry asked.

"The title would become extinct, but the property would be divided amongst the female descendants," Willerton-Forbes said. "However, there is hope yet. If the Third Baron's line peters out, there is still the Second Baron or even the First Baron. One of them is sure to have a male descendant yet living."

When the port had been passed around sufficient times and the captain and Chandry were clearly growing restless to return to the drawing room, Willerton-Forbes said, "Yes, go, both of you, but if you would be so good as to stay a moment longer, Mr Gage, I should like a word with you."

Laurence assented, rather curious to know what private matter concerned the lawyer. Was it something to do with Louisa? Surely not. But if not that, he could not guess.

"Mr Gage, I shall not try your patience by speaking as a lawyer, in roundaboutation," Willerton-Forbes said. "Let me speak plainly, therefore. You have most generously offered to underwrite the expenses of our little investigative band, and for that we are grateful. However, so far, we have lived under your roof at very little additional cost to you — except in port," he added, swirling his glass, "which we very much appreciate. However, if the good captain is permitted to go galloping all over the country to trace someone who might remember Miss Labett from twenty-seven years ago, well, I must be honest, the costs will increase enormously."

"And you think I cannot afford it, is that it?" Laurence said, amused. "You want to be sure that I am good for it."

"Oh, indeed, no! Nothing of the sort! Naturally the bill will be met, no one doubts it for a moment, but one does not wish to put you to excessive expenditure, Mr Gage. As you so correctly point out, everything that Michael wishes to do may be achieved just as readily by way of the written word, and... one hears rumours, you understand. Hints... gossip, perhaps, and not necessarily reliable. One never knows, does one? However, it is said that your financial affairs are not as robust as they once were. But forgive me, it is not my intention to pry, only to point out that there is no need to undertake additional costs if you do not wish to. Our activities are entirely yours to command."

"You are very thoughtful, sir," Laurence said. "In this case, rumour is quite accurate. The estate fell into financial difficulties in my grandfather's day, and my father was unable to improve the situation. I was so fortunate as to marry a wealthy woman, and so for a while there was plenty of money. We made extensive improvements to the house — redecoration and new furnishings within, repairs without, the shrubbery replanted, that sort of thing. Many such improvements were done to please my wife, who was particular in her notions of beauty. With that accomplished, I had just begun to recover some portions of land lost from the estate in earlier times, which would have improved my income substantially, when my wife died. Her fortune was settled in such a way that the income from it was lost to me, and so I am reduced to... not poverty, certainly not that, but I must once again be careful with my expenditure. Even so, Captain Edgerton may travel the length of the country with my blessing, if it will help to bring a killer to justice."

Willerton-Forbes nodded thoughtfully. "That is generous, sir, but, I must say that it is unusual for a lady's dowry to revert to the family after her death, especially when there are children."

"The capital is held in trust for my daughter, but the income goes to my wife's mother until Henrietta comes of age or marries."

"Indeed!" Willerton-Forbes' eyebrows shot up. "I have never heard of such an arrangement before. That is most singular, Mr Gage. You had the interest while your wife lived, but after her death it all went to her mother?"

"Not quite. To be precise, Catherine's fortune produced about four thousand a year. When we married, it was agreed that her mother would have one thousand of it, Catherine would have one thousand as pin money and I would have the remaining two thousand. Combined with my own two and a half thousand, that was a very good income. But then she died..." He stopped, grief welling up inside. Surely he should be in better command of himself by now, especially knowing that Catherine had not married him for love.

"May I ask... who drew up the settlements?" Willerton-Forbes said gently. "You had your own lawyers involved, I take it?"

Laurence frowned. "Not the usual family attorney, for this all happened in Bath. I hired a man there, but it all seemed very straightforward to me. I read it, naturally, before I signed, but perhaps I did not read it carefully enough, for I have no memory of the section determining what would happen after Catherine's death. It was a great shock when the will was read. But then I do not understand these things."

"Of course you do not, Mr Gage," Willerton-Forbes said, beaming at him. "That is lawyer's work, to make sense of the intricacies of a legal contract. I wonder... it is impertinent of me, I know, so do not hesitate to refuse if I step too far, but might I be permitted to examine the settlement document? It would be fascinating to read such unusual clauses."

"By all means, if it would interest you," Laurence said, amused.

He retrieved the papers from the safe, and Willerton-Forbes settled down to peruse them, a brandy glass at his elbow. Apart from a request to see Catherine's will also, he spoke not a word for the entire evening, ignoring even the temptations of the card table. It was past midnight, Viola had long since retired to bed and even Edgerton and Chandry were yawning over their cards, but still Willerton-Forbes read on.

"Is it so fascinating, sir?" Laurence said.

"Hmm? Oh, indeed, most interesting. Tell me, is Mrs Haywood still alive?"

"Certainly. She is still in Bath. The children write to her periodically, and she sometimes writes back. She recovered remarkably well."

"Recovered?" Willerton-Forbes said.

"From whatever illness drew her to Bath sixteen years ago. She was there to take the waters and was so ill she went nowhere except to the Pump Room every day. She looked robust enough to me, but there are unseen weaknesses that do not manifest themselves visibly, are there not?"

"Very likely," Willerton-Forbes said, but his eyes gleamed.

Laurence laughed. "You have something in mind, Willerton-Forbes, I can tell."

"Pettigrew always has something in mind," Edgerton said, looking up from his task of gathering together the cards. "It comes from being a lawyer, and is quite incurable, unfortunately."

Willerton-Forbes chuckled gently. "Let us say merely that my interest is piqued, Mr Gage. Some men are excited by business transactions or politics or financial affairs, but I find personal contracts far more intriguing. Wills, marriage settlements, trust funds... such documents are windows into the past, you see. I suppose you do not have a copy of your wife's father's will here? No, I did not expect it. May I ask where his residence was?"

"Myrtle House, near Hereford."

"Hereford," he murmured. "Perhaps I may make a journey to Hereford, just for my own amusement, you understand, Mr Gage. Nothing at all to do with our present enquiries into Miss Labett. I confess I am very curious."

"By all means go and ferret about Herefordshire if it interests you," Laurence said. "I will write you letters of introduction, if you wish. Let me know what excuse you want to give for your visit, and I will write first thing tomorrow."

~~~~~

Louisa's reserves of civility were sorely tested by Dr Deerham. She had nothing against clergymen in general, and most of them were too lax by half, in her opinion, living indolent lives on their rich tithes while a harassed curate did the work of the parish, so a little devoutness was to be respected. Still, Mr Truman was more her style, for he combined the air of a gentleman with a reasonable degree of attention to his duties and admirably short sermons. Dr Deerham never seemed to set aside his piety to enjoy a pleasant evening of conversation, he must always be preaching, and a more tedious, prosy and sanctimonious bore she had never met.

Nevertheless, she could tolerate his company if necessary, and even smile occasionally, if only she had not lost her friend to him. For a few days Esther had been her old self, enjoying sherry in the mornings and long, gossipy chats about anything and everything. With Dr Deerham's arrival, that Esther had vanished, to be replaced by a strangely timid creature whose whole life revolved around her husband. Wifely devotion was laudable, but not when it turned to foolishness. Esther could not sit at breakfast without constantly checking that her husband's coffee was the right temperature, or the eggs were cooked to his satisfaction, or that his preferred type of preserve was within his reach. If she had buttered his toast for him, Louisa would not have been surprised. After that, the whole day would be given over to the man's wishes. Would he like some tea? A walk in the garden? Might he wish to go for a drive later? Was his cushion comfortable? He, of course, basked in such attention and took
~~~~~

advantage of it to send her here and there for a book or his spectacles or to adjust the curtains to admit or exclude the sun, as if there were not servants enough for such tasks.

Dr Deerham had arrived on Wednesday and by Friday Louisa was heartily tired of him, especially as she had felt obliged to miss the Beasleys' card party on Thursday evening to entertain her guest, since Esther could not possibly go. "*Cards*, Mrs Deerham?" her husband had said in shocked tones when the subject was tentatively raised. "Games of chance are the devil's work." And so they sat around decorously in the drawing room, Louisa trying to read while Esther sewed and Dr Deerham wrote one of his sermons. This would have been peaceful if the good doctor had not felt obliged to submit the most felicitous phrases to his wife's raptures. Since this happened every few minutes, whereupon she then repeated each one, saying, "Is that not most happily worded, Louisa? Do you not agree?", Louisa quickly abandoned her book altogether. Oh, for Laurence's easy company, with a glass of brandy and the dogs at their feet!

Had it not been for her two pups, Louisa might have gone quietly mad. Twice a day she was able to escape the house and take them for long, energetic walks, and it was hard to say which of the three of them enjoyed themselves the most. Possibly Louisa, for she had the pleasure of meeting Laurence more often than not on these outings, and they would stop and chat for twenty minutes or half an hour while the five dogs raced about the Glebe or snuffled happily through the woods.

Laurence was one of several of the local gentlemen who came in a steady procession to pay their respects to the great orator now residing at the Dower House. Squire Winslade and his son, the Rycroft brothers from the Hall, Dr Beasley, Mr Truman and many others came to receive the doctor's words of wisdom, and, at least in Laurence's case, to suppress their yawns as best they might.

"Is he always like that?" Laurence said to Louisa, as the dogs ran about on the Glebe one morning.

"Invariably."

"How on earth do you stand it?"

That made her laugh. "I stand it because I know he will go away again soon. It is the question of how Esther stands it that exercises my mind."

"Yes, poor Mrs Deerham. Why ever did she marry the man?"

But Louisa could find no rational explanation. "She seems contented enough, I suppose," was all she could find to say on the subject.

Easter Sunday arrived, and Dr Deerham was gratified by the ecstatic response to his appearance at St Ann's church, where he accorded some slight praise to the rather fine Norman tower, and thanked Mr Truman graciously for his sermon. There was some wonderment at his presence in such humble surroundings, for the villagers were united in feeling that his stature required the backdrop of a cathedral or at least an imposing town church, but Louisa suspected that he had left home in a huff after not receiving an invitation to preach at any Easter service worthy of his talents. Nor would he condescend to minister to any of his own parishes, leaving them to the care of his curates.

By Tuesday, Louisa had decided that she would go to the Grove that evening for cards and conversation and two or three hours free of sanctimony. Her spirits lifted greatly at this decision, even though she knew Dr Deerham would wear his most disapproving expression. She was even cheerful as she walked down to the Boar's Head that afternoon to leave her letters for the mail carrier and collect the arriving mail.

"Franked one for you today, Mrs Middlehope," John Brownsmith, the innkeeper said, handing it to her personally. "That'll be from her ladyship up north, I 'spect."

"I expect it will," Louisa said, taking it eagerly. At last there would be news of Chambers' arrival!

She was right about that, but there was just a small snag — Pamela planned to convey Chambers personally.

'We are on our way and expect to be with you on Thursday. So looking forward to the ball at the Manor!'

Louisa's spirits plummeted.

21: Settlements

The Grove seemed empty. Laurence had become so used to having Mr Willerton-Forbes, Captain Edgerton and Mr Chandry around that he was rather sorry when they left. There was no longer a guaranteed four for whist in the evenings, or adult male conversation over the port, or any counterweight to Viola's incessant chatter. He loved his sister, but sometimes he wished that she were a little less feather-headed. Now his guests were scattered, Edgerton and Chandry to trace the writers of the references for Miss Labett, and Willerton-Forbes to Hereford, to investigate the background to Catherine's will and the marriage settlements.

The will! Laurence could hardly remember that day when the will was read out. Such a terrible time, with all the arrangements to bring her back from Bristol, and then the burial. His only memory was of Crossley, the attorney, saying to him over and over, "Do you understand, Mr Gage? Do you understand?"

But he had not, of course. It was not until several months later, when he had requested some money from the bank for a land transaction, and been told, calmly but firmly, that they would advance the amount as an unsecured loan this time, but in future they would require collateral, that he had realised something was amiss. Crossley had patiently explained it all — that all the income from Catherine's fortune now went to her mother, and Laurence had only the income from his own holdings to live on. He had cancelled the purchase of land, and set about revising his budget.

Now that he looked back on it, everything about the business had been odd. The marriage settlements with their unusual clauses... he had known nothing of such matters at the time, and was too dazzled by the prospect of marrying Catherine to take notice, but he was a little more cognisant now of how such things customarily worked. No matter how tightly Catherine's fortune had been bound up for the future generation, the income from it should have been in his own hands, both before and after her death. That was the usual way. Willerton-Forbes' interest in it set him wondering for the first time.

With his thoughts thus turned back to Catherine, he began to read the diaries again. Each night when he retired, and sometimes when he had an hour free during the day, he would retreat to his room and read on. Would there be any mention of the marriage settlements in the weeks before the marriage? There was not. Catherine's thoughts were entirely occupied with spending the newly-released tranche of funds from her fortune to allow her to buy wedding clothes. Each day's entries were a catalogue of fabrics and shops and milliners and seamstresses and the difficulties of finding a button of the exact style to match a particular gown. Neither Malcolm nor Laurence himself rated a mention. The wedding itself, the most glorious day of Laurence's life, drew only two words — *'Was married.'*

Their brief honeymoon in Cheltenham, accompanied at Catherine's request by Mrs Haywood, Mrs Fossett and Mr Slythe, merited an outbreak of descriptive prose in the diary, and again when the couple, finally free of her family, reached Shropshire and Catherine saw her new home. She was not effusive, merely describing everything she found dispassionately. *'The saloon is large and elegant, a forty foot cube, with a balcony around the upper level. A few good pictures, but many gaps. The upper floor would overlook a fine prospect were it not for a much overgrown shrubbery. I shall have the dining room here... The kitchens are spacious enough but will need much improvement... The library is smaller than expected, but I do not intend to use it.'*

She detailed every small change she made to the house — the colours chosen, the wallpapers and which supplier had the best quality, the furniture ordered, the work on the gardens. Then there were the calls made and received, the dinner engagements, the balls, routs and parties, the summer outings and the Christmas feasts. She enjoyed these, seemingly, noting the gown she wore for each one, and the way her hair was arranged. *'My new pale blue silk with the demi-train much admired. Mr A stared at me all through dinner, and whispered in my ear that he thought the colour matched my eyes and that I looked like a cornflower he would like to pluck. Was asked to play three pieces after dinner.'*

The months passed by and turned into years, and the relentless chronicle of Catherine's life continued. Henrietta's birth was a mere footnote — *'A girl, healthy. The wet nurse is sent for.'* Laurence's three week battle with a particularly virulent putrid fever, where even Dr Beasley had despaired, was ignored, noticeable only by the purely domestic nature of the diary entries. After his recovery, there was a return to visits and dinners and balls, but no mention of her family.

Gradually the awful truth dawned on him. There had been no growing love for him in Catherine's breast. Her husband drew neither admiration nor respect from her. There was not even a sign of affection for her children. None of them were even worthy of mention.

Anguish gnawed at him with unbearable pain. How could he have been so deluded? Catherine had been the centre of his life, his beautiful, perfect wife, but to her, it was as if he did not even exist. None of them existed. She cared nothing for her husband or children.

He closed the book, curled into a ball on his bed and lay as if dead.

~~~~~

Mr Willerton-Forbes returned from Hereford with a satisfied twinkle in his eye.

"A most interesting expedition, Mr Gage," he said, as Laurence greeted him in the hall. "*Most* interesting."

Laurence swept him into his study, shooed a grumbling Edward out to get some fresh air, and put two glasses of Madeira on a small table set between two chairs. "Tell me all, Willerton-Forbes. I am minded for some interesting news."

For answer, the lawyer produced a folded paper from an inner pocket. "This is a true copy of an entry in the Harstock parish register of burials."

'Elizabeth Anne Haywood, wife of John Haywood', he read. "Mrs Haywood is dead? Oh, but— The date! This is years before I met Catherine. So the Mrs Haywood I met is a second wife?"

"Not quite." Mr Willerton-Forbes' smile widened. "The attorney you deal with there, Mr Turnbull, was unwell and could not see me, but I have talked to the parish clergyman and his sister. What I learnt was *most* interesting, Mr Gage." He took a
~~~~~

small sip of Madeira, then linked his hands across his ample stomach. "Mrs Haywood died when her daughter was eight years of age, but there was a governess, a Miss Fossett."

"*Miss* Fossett? Catherine's chaperon in Bath was a Mrs Fossett."

"Indeed. The chaperon is Miss Fossett's sister-in-law, who joined her at Myrtle House to assist with the child's education. The father left the matter entirely to them, for he travelled about a great deal. He was a wool merchant — wool, and many other things. A bit of a dabbler, as one might say. Did you know that?"

"That he was in trade? Certainly. There was no secret about it, and it was of no consequence to me. It was always likely that I would be forced to accept a wife of that ilk."

Another sip of Madeira, the glass set down with a sigh of satisfaction. "The two governesses seem to have been well-regarded locally, and the parson said that Miss Haywood grew up to be a very pretty-behaved girl, rather quiet, but docile. That was her father's influence, for he believed women should be submissive. Despite her background, he wanted her to be ladylike in every way, beyond reproach."

"She was certainly that," Laurence said pensively. "It was her elegance and demureness that first drew me... after her great beauty, of course."

Willerton-Forbes smiled. "Ah, yes, a diamond of the first water indeed. That was much mentioned. But misfortune struck Miss Haywood at the age of fifteen, when her father died. The will was read, everything was left to Miss Haywood, with the attorney and a banker as trustees, and the clergyman and his sister as guardians. There was nothing unusual about the will. Miss Haywood had no other relatives, and so the guardians and trustees agreed that Mrs and Miss Fossett should stay on to look after her until such time as she married. An attorney called Slythe joined the ladies at Myrtle House. He was some kind of relation, at least they called him a cousin, and they felt they needed a man in the house." He raised his glass again. "And now the tale becomes rather… peculiar. Miss Fossett began to call herself Mrs Haywood."

"What!" Laurence said, dumbfounded. "And had she married Haywood?"

"Almost certainly not. The late Mr Haywood would have included her in his will if it had been so."

"Can she do that? Just call herself Mrs Haywood?"

The lawyer pulled a rueful face. "A lady may call herself whatever she wishes, so long as there is no underhand motive. She made no claim on the estate, which would have aroused great concern, and never herself mentioned a marriage. She simply called herself Mrs Haywood. And the oddest part of all was that Miss Haywood called her Mama, and spoke of her as her mother."

"That is true, and I never suspected anything untoward when I met them all in Bath," Laurence said. "This is quite beyond belief."

"Oh, not that, Mr Gage," Willerton-Forbes said sadly. "Never underestimate the human capacity for outrageous behaviour."

"You are cynical, but perhaps as a lawyer you have seen the worst of humanity," Laurence said. "What I cannot understand is why Mrs Haywood… I mean Miss Fossett would do such a thing. Was she deranged?"

"Far from it," Willerton-Forbes said. "It was a very clever scheme. The two governesses had in their hands a very valuable property, an heiress with a fortune of one hundred thousand pounds, as well as the house. However, she had trustees who guarded that fortune assiduously, and once Miss Haywood married, it would be gone for good, and their comfortable lives likewise. So they hatched their scheme. The first priority was to get Miss Haywood away from her protective guardians and trustees."

"So they went to Bath," Laurence said.

"Indeed. It was not unreasonable, for the local gentry would have nothing to do with the daughter of a wool merchant, fortune or no, and Miss Haywood had to be found a husband. The guardians agreed, and the trustees advanced a sum for the project."

"Then it was nothing to do with Mrs Haywood's health. They went to Bath to snare a husband for Catherine and tie up the settlements to their benefit." He recalled the words of Catherine's diary on her betrothal — *'She is very pleased with me for succeeding sooner than we had dared to hope.'* It had all been carefully planned. "I was very stupid," he said in a low voice. "I suppose that is why I was chosen."

"Not stupid, but naive, perhaps. Inexperienced in the world, and with no father to guide you. I have no doubt that Slythe was very persuasive where the marriage settlements were concerned. Probably he recommended a local attorney to advise you?"

"He did! An accomplice of his, no doubt. And insisting that the money be managed by a bank in Bath... to get it away from the oversight of the trustee, no doubt."

"Most assuredly. I do not wish to alarm you but can you be sure the capital is safe?"

Laurence laughed. "You are cynical indeed! Most of it is perfectly safe in the funds, and the bank writes to me once a year to advise of the interest earned, and of the investments they have made. I have no reason to doubt the bank. But give me your honest opinion, Willerton-Forbes — is there anything that can be done about this?"

"Possibly. The settlement papers and your wife's will refer to Mrs Eugenia Haywood, but there was no such person, and Miss Fossett has no claim whatsoever on you, none at all. You could make a case for setting aside the terms of the will, on the grounds of false pretences. The English judiciary are very nice in their notions of what is due to the husband of an heiress, and most strongly disapprove of governesses who inveigle a share of their charge's fortune. There is a more straightforward method, however. According to the will, you are the sole trustee for your daughter's inheritance. You have the right to instruct the bank to make all future interest payments directly to you. That would leave Mrs Haywood to sue for the restitution of her income, if she dares. My principal concern just now is to ensure that the capital is secure, and that Slythe and the Fossett ladies cannot abscond with it. What do you say to a trip to Bath, Mr Gage?"

"Excellent idea. I am engaged to this affair at the Manor, but I can leave after that. What those three did was reprehensible, and must be stopped."

"Those *four*, Mr Gage," Willerton-Forbes said heavily. "Your wife must have been party to the deception, for it could not have been accomplished otherwise. I am afraid she must take her share of the blame."

It was another chip in the pedestal upon which his perfect wife had stood for so many years. He had not known his wife at all. Such thoughts drove him back to the diaries, for he felt that surely there could be nothing more to distress him. More gloomily, if there were further miseries to be unleashed upon him, it was as well to get them over with. After dinner that night, therefore, he retired early to his bedroom and settled down to read, determined this time to reach the end and know the worst.

He had stopped reading some two years after Henrietta's birth, the third anniversary of his marriage to Catherine. To celebrate, he had taken her to Bath for a week to see her supposed mother. The diaries mentioned the trip, but there was no reason given, and the descriptions of the joyful reunions did not quite match his memory of the event. Catherine had seemed pleased to see her friends again, but had greeted them with her usual serenity, he had thought. Yet the diary spoke of *'...the greatest delight... such ecstasy to be together again... they make so much fuss of me that I feel greatly cherished... how shall I bear their loss when I leave this dear place?'* Even when they made their farewells, there was no sign on the surface of the turmoil within, and she had never invited them to Great Maeswood. The disparity was unsettling.

'Malcolm has written to me. He still loves me and wants us to be together.'

The words jumped off the page at him, so that he almost stopped breathing in shock. He had written? They had been in touch? Quickly he read on, but she continued calmly, *'It is impossible and so I shall tell him.'*

Nothing else. He breathed again, aware of his rapid heartbeat, a sudden shaky feeling like a fever. Dear God, they had written to each other! Malcolm was estranged from the family, yet he had written to Catherine. He scanned the rest of the page, then the next and the next, flipping the leaves with trembling fingers, but there was no further mention. Gradually his racing heart slowed.

Then another mention. *'I have seen him! He was in Market Clunbury, just across the street as I came out of Parker's. He made no attempt to speak to me, merely watching me. I lowered my head and hurried away.'*

A few weeks later there was another letter, which she copied out in all its anguished, lovelorn glory. Then another sighting, in a village as she drove through in the barouche. Twice more he was in Market Clunbury, and once in Shrewsbury, in the abbey, bizarrely, for Malcolm had always had to be dragged to church by main force. Love, it seemed, was even enough to overcome his aversion to the Christian faith.

Edward's birth was marked with the same brevity as his sister's — *'A son, very skinny but noisy.'* Almost at once there was a flurry of letters from Malcolm, lovingly transcribed by Catherine. *'I burned it, as usual'*, she said of one such. But then she had replied. *'Three pages, closely written, and even that was insufficient to express all that I feel for him, my life's true love, my one sweet darling. If only we could be together! If only there was a way!'*

Almost a year before she died, it seemed that she had found a way after all. Malcolm began to appear in the woods, and Catherine stole out to meet him. Every page of the diary was filled with her ecstasies over meeting him again, with his words of love, the way he looked at her, the tender way he held her hand or stroked her cheek. There were stolen kisses, passionate embraces and tears of despair. Laurence could hardly believe that this ardent woman was the demure wife who never raised her voice and never showed the least emotion to him or the rest of the world. Presumably everyone must have some inner turbulence from time to time, well hidden by outward restraint, but the disparity here was overwhelming.

Eventually the inevitable happened. *'We are united. I am his at last!'* she crowed.

Laurence was scarcely aware of the tears on his cheeks. But after the tears came anger, as the pedestal upon which his angelic wife had stood finally came crashing to the ground. Catherine could not have been further from an angel. She had betrayed her husband, her children and her marriage vows, spoken before God, and *Malcolm* had been her seducer. His own brother! They had quarrelled over her, as they had quarrelled fleetingly over many things in their boyhood, but to discover that Malcolm had betrayed him so utterly was unbearable. He was unspeakably wicked. They were both wicked.

And the worst of it was that the child, the third child whose birth had killed her, might not have been his at all, but Malcolm's. The pain of it lanced through him, leaving him groaning in anguish.

Laurence hurled the diary against the wall, buried his face in his hands and uttered a growl of pure rage.

22: A Ball At The Manor

The next morning was Saturday, and the carriage was ordered for ten o'clock sharp to convey them all to Cloverstone Manor for the annual ball, that is, Laurence, Viola and Mr Willerton-Forbes. Henrietta and Edward had already left, together with the servants and luggage, for there were special events for the children, as well.

Laurence was in no mood at all for company, and might well have cried off had it not been for the prospect of seeing Louisa there and perhaps having an opportunity for some private conversation with her. She, he knew, would listen to him uncritically and perhaps bring some balm to his troubled mind. He had not seen her for some days, not even walking the pups, for the groom seemed to have taken on that task, and he was growing anxious for her. The Deerhams had at last gone home to Shrewsbury, only to be replaced by an even worse guest, Lady Mountsea. Viola had contrived to call on the baroness within two hours of her arrival, but when Laurence had asked how Louisa was bearing up under her deluge of visitors, she had looked at him in amazement.

"Bearing up? Why, she is perfectly delighted to be so honoured, naturally. Dr Deerham is such a distinguished gentleman, and Lady Mountsea is so gracious and affable, I never saw anything like it. One would never suspect her humble origins. Mrs Middlehope must be so happy to have her sister-in-law with her again."

Laurence saw that he would not know the truth until he could see Louisa for himself.

Squire Winslade was his usual genial self, and received them in the Great Hall, where all the guests were gathering. Cloverstone Manor was a fine house, and the Great Hall was magnificent, but it had a somewhat neglected air about it. The marble floor tiles were stained in places, the beautiful painted ceiling faded and the flags and shields that adorned the walls were grey with dust. Still, there was a good fire blazing and bowls of arrack and rum punch, which was, not surprisingly, where Laurence encountered Louisa. His first lift of the spirits at the sight of her was immediately banished by shock. So pale and strained! She had a haunted look, and the reason was standing beside the fire, loudly relating some detail of her journey from Durham to a glassy-eyed Susannah Winslade.

"How are you?" Laurence whispered to Louisa over the punch bowl.

Her face lit up at the sight of him. "Oh, I am so glad you are here! Shall we hide behind the suit of armour and get quietly foxed?"

"That sounds like a splendid plan. Did everything arrive safely from Durham?"

She pulled a rueful face. "Not quite. I have my pianoforte at last, but the books—! No one seemed able to work out which were mine and which belonged to Roseacre. I left a detailed list of which shelves were mine, but there has been some reorganisation, seemingly, and everything has got muddled up." She sighed. "I shall get them all eventually, I am sure."

"But you have your man-cook, I trust?"

"Yes! Last night we had sautéed pullet with a foie gras sauce and apricot soufflé. It was wonderful! Oh, good day to you, Miss Gage. I am so sorry that my visitors kept me away from your card party this week, but it was their last evening with me. I shall certainly be there next Tuesday."

"Oh... oh, yes. You will not mind if I whisk my brother away for a moment, I am sure? Laurence, will you come and translate the Latin inscription over the fireplace for Lady Mountsea?"

Louisa smiled and said all that was proper, but the strained expression was back on her face, and Laurence himself was irritated by the interruption. A whole week since he had seen Louisa, and she was as pleased to see him as he to see her, yet Viola was set on ripping him away from her side.

"Must it be this very minute, Vi?" he said, a little more sharply than he had intended.

Viola looked startled and then dismayed. "Oh, well... but *Lady Mountsea*, Laurence... Surely...?"

"Yes, do go, Mr Gage," Louisa said, her tone level but her smile somewhat forced. "You will find me behind the suit of armour whenever Pamela has finished with you."

He laughed a little, as she no doubt expected, but Viola said in bewildered tones, "Behind the suit of armour, Mrs Middlehope?"

"Just my little joke, Miss Gage."

Seething, Laurence allowed himself to be led to Lady Mountsea where he wasted twenty minutes translating the Latin and then explaining the meaning of it to her ladyship, who looked thoroughly bemused. When he at last had an opportunity to look around, he could not see Louisa at all.

The day proceeded in the usual fashion. There was an archery competition on the lawn, a wooden boat sailing competition on the lake for the children, and the usual fencing display on the terrace. He had seen it all before and could not summon interest in any of it. Occasionally he caught glimpses of Louisa, once with the children down by the lake, and later in a corner of the terrace, her shawl clutched around her, looking lost and miserable in the crowd watching the fencing, but he could not squeeze through the throng to reach her. It was almost a relief when the dressing bell sounded and he could stop pretending to enjoy himself and retreat to his room for a brief reprieve before dinner.

The Manor was a vast building with a central block and two large wings, spread over three main floors, but he knew his way around it, the back stairs and secret ways that may be found in any house of such a size and antiquity. There was a servants' ante-room where boards were set up listing the rooms where each guest was accommodated. He checked, as he always did, where the children were, and Viola, in case of an emergency. Somehow, he could not resist looking for Louisa's name on the list, and smiling when he found it. He might not be able to spend as much time with her as he would like, but it was still a comfort to know that she was under the same roof as he was, and imagine her looking out over the lawns towards the sunken garden and the shrubbery beyond. He had no need to question why it was a comfort. She was his friend, and he was happy in that friendship, and if he sometimes thought wistfully of that long, warm kiss before the fire in her study, it meant nothing at all. Louisa was no more than a friend.

Everyone gathered in the Armoury before dinner, a long, echoing room not conducive to quiet conversation. Only half the guests were gathered there when he arrived but already the noise was enough to give anyone the headache. A slow cruise around the room told him that she was not there, so he stationed himself near the door where she was most likely to enter. The squire sank this promising scheme by drawing him into a circle of other landowners to discuss the question of pheasant. Laurence was as happy as anyone to shoot pheasant, and to eat it, too, but he really wanted to talk to Louisa and it was hard to hide his impatience.

At last she came, and he could not help smiling as he saw the stunning gown she wore. She was not an ostentatious dresser, but so elegant and always stylish. He knew nothing about fashion, but to him she was the most modish woman in the room. He made his excuses to the gentlemen and set off determinedly towards her, only to find Viola in his way.

"Laurence!" she said brightly. "Do come and talk to Mr Pritchard. He is very keen to renew his acquaintance with you."

It was too much. "Not now, Vi," he snapped, only to be taken aback by the hurt in her eyes. "Oh... well... of course."

When he looked again, Louisa had disappeared.

Dinner was as fraught as any he could remember. Everyone else seemed to be relaxed and merry, but he felt as tightly wound as a clock spring. Louisa was across the table from him, near enough for him to see every slight change of expression on her face, but not near enough to talk to her. And both of them were well within earshot of Lady Mountsea, who was talking volubly about her husband's unexpected elevation to the peerage.

"Such a fraud I feel to be a Lady, for the title should never have come to Thomas at all. It should have been his brother of course, and then dear Louisa would have been Lady Mountsea. But there, it was not to be. Such a tragedy for them both, not to have a son and I feel for Louisa deeply, I assure you. I have seen how much it distresses her to be around children, which is why she ran away from Roseacre, despite all my attempts to make her stay, but she bears her grief nobly and makes no complaint. Not that I wish her to suffer in silence, for that is what family is for, do you not agree, Squire? We should comfort each other in our darkest hours, but there, Louisa likes to keep her feelings inside and you would not know, no one would guess, just how much she has had to bear."

It was as much as Laurence could do to keep a still tongue in his head and not slap the silly woman into silence. Poor Louisa could only sit and suffer, but he saw the distress in her face, and she ate nothing at all. As soon as the dinner was over and the guests began to drift out of the Great Hall, he watched her slip silently away.

It was too much to hope that her disappearance would pass unnoticed.

"Where's Louisa?" Pamela said, her shrill voice cutting across the chatter. "Where is she hiding? She's always running away, the naughty creature."

Laurence held his breath, willing her to let it go.

"I daresay she will be back before long," Susannah said evenly. "Shall we go through to the gallery? The musicians will be starting up very soon."

"She slipped out a few minutes ago and she is not in the retiring room," Viola said worriedly. "She looked very peaky, I thought. Quite pale."

Laurence closed his eyes in dismay. Now they were in the suds!

"I must go and find her," Pamela said. "She often gets like this in company, and I have to jolly her back into spirits. I know where her room is."

Impossible to stand idly by! "I think the noise may have been too much for her," he said. "She is used to a quiet life, after all. A few minutes of solitude will set her to rights, I am sure."

"Solitude?" Pamela said, in disbelieving tones. "That's the last thing she needs. She has too much liking for solitude altogether. It's positively unhealthy. Company is the very best cure for melancholia."

"But it need not be your company, Lady Mountsea," he said, his temper holding by the merest thread. "Anyone may attend Mrs Middlehope, but as the principal lady here tonight, I believe your duty is to the dance."

"I shall send someone to enquire if there is anything she needs," Susannah said soothingly. "Do go up to the gallery, Lady Mountsea, then everyone will follow your lead."

"Oh, very well," she said, inching towards the stairs, "but I do think it too bad of Louisa, to be causing us worry like this. Slipping away without a word, as well. It is all of a piece with her entire manner since her husband died, and I do sincerely pity her, for she must feel it so desperately, having no children of her own, but she has become quite wild and erratic. Positively eccentric, if you ask me. Settling so far from her family, too. Two hundred miles away! It is too far."

"Apparently not far enough," Laurence snapped.

She stopped, looking at him in puzzlement. "Whatever can you mean, Mr Gage?"

He could not stop himself as the words poured out. "I mean that perhaps being two hundred miles from Roseacre was one of the advantages of Shropshire. She came here because she wanted to leave her family behind, and who can blame her? Not I!"

With that, he spun on his heel and pushed through the mass of astonished onlookers, past the grand staircase and down the dimly lit corridor. There was a set of smaller stairs further on, so he went up and then up again. He knew where her room was, and if she was not there... well, he would go and get drunk alone.

He tapped on the door.

"Who is it?" she called out sharply.

"Chambermaid," he called back.

The door opened to her laughing face. "Thank God! I was terrified it might be Pamela. Do you know anywhere else I can hide, where she cannot find me?"

"I can find a secluded room with a supply of brandy."

"That sounds perfect."

"Not quite, for it will have me in it, bent on getting as drunk as a wheelbarrow."

"Then let us get drunk together," she said smiling so warmly that he could feel the knot of anger in his belly loosening just a fraction.

He took her back down two floors again, and into a small, untidy room used by the squire and his steward to conduct business. It was neglected and dusty, the furniture dilapidated cast-offs from smarter rooms, but there were candles and a fire ready to be lit, and a sideboard bearing an array of interesting decanters. He identified the brandy and poured them each a generous measure, then sat beside her on the worn sofa.

"I would have murdered her, you know," Louisa said conversationally. "If I had stayed a moment longer in that room, with Pamela droning on and on and on about how I bore my grief so well, and the other ladies looking pityingly at me, I should certainly have strangled her with my bare hands."

"You would not have needed to," he said curtly. "I should have done it for you. Insufferable woman! The only reason to pity you is because you have such a damnable bird-witted imbecile of a sister-in-law." He was too angry to sit still, so he got up and paced about the small room, back and forth, back and forth, like some kind of caged beast. "I was abominably rude to her, you know. After you left, when she started wondering where you were and was all set to go haring after you, I told her that you came here to get away from her and her miserable family, and that two hundred miles of distance between you was not nearly enough."

She stared at him, horrified. "You did not! Tell me you are joking, Laurence."

"Utterly serious and I meant every word of it, too."

"Good God! What did she say?"

"I have no idea, and have not the least interest in knowing. I came to find you… and the brandy."

"Well! I daresay she will not understand the insult, and if she does, she will assume you were speaking in jest. She is remarkably thick-skinned, you know, and cannot imagine that she is not wanted. We must hope she did not understand it, anyway."

"Why should you care? If she takes umbrage and goes off in a huff, then good riddance."

"Heavens, Laurence, whatever has got into you? You have been as cross as a bear all day, but this is beyond anything. You are the kindest of men at heart. This is not like you."

"I am tired of being kind," he said, refilling his brandy glass. "I am utterly sick of being thoughtful and unselfish and never saying what I truly think, never doing what *I* want to do. It feels like being caught up in a spider's web, all wrapped up so tightly that I can barely breathe and I want to be free of it, to be myself and not this façade of a gentleman."

She put down her glass and crossed the room until she was close enough to lay a hand on his brow. "Are you feverish? You are not at all yourself."

"There is nothing wrong with me," he said shortly.

"But *something* has put you into this strange mood. Will you not tell me what it is? Perhaps talking about it will help a little, for I hate to see you so out of frame."

He hesitated, but why should she not know the worst? "I read the rest of Catherine's diaries."

"Oh! Something bad?"

"She betrayed me!" he said, aware that he was on the verge of hysteria, yet quite unable to moderate his tone. "I thought she was perfect, fool that I was, but she betrayed me. She had a lover, Louisa, my own brother, and I never had the slightest idea. I cannot even be sure if that last child was truly mine. God, how I hate her! I wish I had never met her. All those years of tiptoeing around her, considering her delicate feelings, never telling her what *I* felt, what *I* wanted. Well, no more. I shall do whatever I want from now on."

And he knew exactly what he wanted at that moment. He drank the last drops of brandy, set down the glass and swept her into his arms. "What I want is to be your lover, Louisa. Let me come to your room tonight. That is what you want, too, is it not? I know it is. Let us be together and damnation to the world."

Pulling her even tighter into his arms, he kissed her hungrily. Probably he was bruising her lips but he did not care. He kissed her and kissed her until very gradually it dawned on him that she was less than receptive. A great deal less than the last time they had kissed.

He released her abruptly, and to his astonishment, she pushed him so hard that he staggered and almost fell.

"How dare you!" she hissed, her eyes shooting fire at him. "How dare you try to use me as some kind of *revenge* against your dead wife."

"You *wanted* this!" he said, astonished. "It was your idea, Louisa, so why are you coy all of a sudden?"

"Yes, I wanted it, but not like this, in anger and pain and grief, as some way of assuaging your own misery. Besides, you talked me out of it, remember? All that business with drainpipes and how it would hurt your sister, and you were right, absolutely right. So you cannot now decide that, yes, you would like us to be lovers, thank you very much, just because *you* want it. It has to be mutual, Laurence. We *both* have to want it, and I do not, not any more. I thought you were my *friend*, and now I see that you are no friend at all."

And so saying, she turned and ran from the room.

23: The Sunken Garden

Louisa ran blindly, hardly knowing where she was. She came to a wide staircase leading up, but as soon as she reached the turn she realised her mistake, for the sounds of music and laughter drifted down to her. She must be close to the long gallery where the dancing was going on.

Irresolute, she paused.

"Hoy, there!" a man's voice called down from above. "Why are you not dancing, Mrs Middlehope? Come along, it is a reel, my favourite. You must dance with me, I insist."

A reel! How could she smile and jig about and make any pretence of enjoying herself after that altercation with Laurence? Her friend, her *true* friend, or so she had thought, to turn on her in that way! All she wanted was to run away and hide until her anger had simmered down.

Before she could move, the man flew down to the half-landing and grabbed her hand. "Do come! You must!"

"No... I cannot..."

She could not even remember his name. But he began to tug her along, up the last few steps and through an ante-room into the gallery. The light was dazzling, so many candles flickering, jewelled aigrettes and bracelets sparkling and the ladies' skirts swirling in a maelstrom of shimmering silk. The air was heavy with perfume and sweat, and loud voices brayed in her ear as her companion led her inexorably through the crowds and onto the floor.

And she danced. At first, her feet and arms moved instinctively, driven by the hypnotic pace of the music, but gradually her anger fell away and she began to enjoy herself. Perhaps it is impossible to feel anything but pleasure in a Scotch reel, or perhaps the physical exertion drove out any other consideration, but by the end of the set she could smile with genuine feeling and agree with her partner — Mr Jeffrey Rycroft, she remembered — that the exercise had been refreshing.

She danced one more set, but by then she had had enough. Creeping into the supper room, she filled a plate and a glass, and slipped behind the screen to the service stairs. Having got her bearings now, she made her way swiftly to her own room and closed the door behind her with relief. The dreadful day was over.

~~~~~

Louisa slept late, but she was still up before Marie arrived with her washing water and morning chocolate. No doubt there was turmoil below stairs with a house full of guests, the servants jockeying for supplies for their masters and mistresses, and the kitchen unable to cope. There was no rush, however, for it was Sunday, a day of leisure for the adult guests. Breakfast at ten, followed by divine service in the chapel at noon. In the afternoon, the children were to perform tableaux of religious scenes in the armoury, which conveniently provided everyone with
~~~~~

entertainment, yet of a nature fitted to the Sabbath. Then another grand dinner, followed by readings from the Bible by those of a dramatic bent.

As she lay in bed, mulling over the day's events and wondering whether she could yet manage to leave her warm blankets, there was a slight scratching noise by the door. When she went to look, there was a note pushed under the door from outside. Smiling, knowing who it must be from, she unfolded it.

'My dear friend, for such it is my fervent hope that I may once again call you in the future, may I offer you my deepest and most heartfelt apologies for my despicable behaviour towards you last night? I am the lowest worm crawling on the face of the earth, and if you should choose to shun me hereafter, it will be no more than I deserve. I know myself to be unworthy of your friendship, yet it is most precious to me, and to lose it for ever would grieve me beyond telling. This paper is an inadequate vehicle to convey the depths of my remorse. Forgiveness is too much to hope for, but if you would be so gracious as to hear my regrets in person, I shall be in the sunken garden at nine. Yours in desolation, Laurence Gage.'

Poor Laurence! So much abject despair, when her anger had long since abated. When Marie arrived, therefore, she drank her chocolate quickly and hastened into her outdoor clothes.

'Sortez-vous, madame? Il fait froid aujourd'hui.' Are you going out? It is cold today.

Louisa frowned, grasping at a word she understood. "Cold? You have a cold?"

Marie giggled. *'Non, madame. Dehors.'* She pointed through the window. *'Froid.'*

"Ah! Cold *outside*. I am well wrapped up against the chill."

'Il faud marcher vite.' She pretended to run on the spot. *'Comprenez vous?' You must walk quickly. You understand?*

'Oui. Je comprenez... comprends... I think," Louisa said. "I shall try not to get too cold."

She used the service stairs again, just in case any other guests were also up early. She had to ask a housemaid to direct her to an outside door, and from there to the sunken garden, which was in a part of the grounds she had not previously seen. After one wrong turn, she soon found the avenue of pleached limes which led her to a gap in a high yew hedge. There beyond it was the sunken garden, with a round courtyard in the centre boasting a sundial, surrounded by several levels of terraced flowerbeds. It was a little oasis of colour in the unrelieved green of this part of the garden. Clusters of crocus, daffodils, tulips and anemones jostled each other in a riot of colours and shapes and sizes, with no regard to order or harmony. It was delightful.

Laurence sat on one of the stone benches surrounding the sundial, hat in hands, looking miserable. When he saw her he jumped up, his face an endearing mixture of hope and anxiety. Louisa went slowly down the steps as he bounded up halfway to meet her.

"Mrs Middlehope, I cannot tell you how—"

"Stop at once," she said, holding her hands up in appeal, but smiling to show she was not angry. "If you are going to call me *'Mrs Middlehope'* in that horridly formal way, I shall be obliged to turn around and return to the house immediately."

He laughed, the tension dropping from his face instantly. "You are all generosity, as always. Thank you for meeting me, Louisa. I had no right to expect it, after the way I behaved. It was despicable, quite despicable. Permit me to say—"

Again she held up her hands. "Do you know, I feel we could dispense with the grovelling apology altogether. Shall we just assume that you have made it and I have accepted it, and go back to being friends again at once? After all, I am not blameless myself in the matter of inappropriate advances, and I do feel that the less said the better."

He looked at her uncertainly. "But *something* needs to be said!"

"You said all that was necessary in your letter."

"Even so..."

"Very well," she said. "You may have ten words, and not a word more, mind, to make your apology."

"Hmm... ten words. I am very sorry. Please forgive me. No, that is only seven words. I am very sorry for the unspeakable insult— No, that will not work. Ah, I have it! I am very sorry for the insult. Please forgive me."

She laughed. "That will do very well. You are forgiven. Let us shake hands on it, and be friends again." He bowed in assent, and took her hand with a smile. She went on, "Shall we sit down? This is such a lovely spot, and sheltered from the wind. I should like to enjoy the flowers for a while. I miss my garden more than I had imagined when I left Roseacre."

"Have you settled the question of improvements to the Dower House garden?" he said, and she thought there was a trace of anxiety in his eyes.

"Perhaps."

"I did hear," he said tentatively, his gloved finger tracing a pattern on the bench, "that you might not stay here long. Your groom thought so, anyway. Is that true?"

"Ah, well, that was the original plan," she said, chuckling. "I was going to loosen the bonds of propriety for a while, and when I tired of that, I should move on somewhere, become respectable and lead a blameless existence thenceforth. Bath, I thought."

"Bath! A dull place for someone as lively as you, Louisa."

She stretched her legs out, leaning back on her hands. "I am not as lively as all that, you know. You have seen the absolute worst of me so you think me every kind of decadent, but I am quite a restrained person normally. A small house in Bath with a proper garden would suit me very well. Shops, a library, weekly concerts and everywhere within walking distance, and when I grow old and decrepit, I would be carried to the Pump Room every day in a chair. I feel I would make an admirable Bath quiz. Can you not picture it?"

"No, and you would be so lonely. You need friends about you."

"Friends can be made more readily in the town than the country, and I could always find myself a companion."

He looked at her with clear distress in his face. "I should miss you abominably! You are the first person I have been able to talk to — *truly* talk to — since Malcolm left. I should be lost without you."

She put one hand on his. "My dear friend, it is so for me, too, but nothing is decided. That was my original plan, but now that I am settled here and have given up all plans for debauchery, perhaps I will stay for a while after all."

He was silent for a while, frowning and chewing his lip. She did not press him on why the prospect of her leaving so upset him. It was surprising, but then he was not his usual calm self just now. The diaries had knocked him out of his settled state and disrupted the even tenor of his life. He was bound to feel everything more acutely. It would be dangerous, however, for him to come to depend on her. She must be very cautious.

With a sudden heave of breath, he said, "Do you think we should get married?"

Louisa almost groaned. Sorrowfully, she said, "No, Laurence, I do not. It is not what you want, I thought, and it is certainly not what I want."

"But we get on so well and—"

"That is hardly a reason to marry."

"But I could protect you from that horrible sister-in-law of yours, since you are too polite to do it. Mostly I do not want you to disappear to Bath, or anywhere else. Louisa, I feel as if everything that was once so certain has been swept away, the very ground beneath my feet has become shifting sand that may slide away from me at any moment. *You* are the one person who will listen and understand and not tell me I am being foolish, as Vi would."

She sighed. "And you feel guilty because of last night. These are the worst reasons in the world for an undertaking as serious as matrimony. You are very muddled, Laurence — not your usual sensible self at all, and I am afraid it is my fault. I have unthinkingly intruded into your peaceful existence and upended it entirely, for which I am deeply sorry. I should never have encouraged you to read those diaries, for you were perfectly contented before that."

"Do you know, I am not certain that being upended, as you put it, is such a bad thing. What you call contentment was a kind of suspended animation, I think, not fully alive. I was a wasp caught in the jam, unable to move forwards or backwards. But now... I may be muddled but at least I am *feeling* something again. It was good for me to read those diaries. You said it would make Catherine real to me, and that was true. I now know exactly what sort of a wife I had, and I cannot regret being undeceived, only that I turned my rage against you and offered you insult."

"Well, as to that, it was my own stupidity that put the idea of an affair into your head in the first place."

"Are you sure that is not a solution to our difficulties?" he said with suddenly twinkling eyes. "It avoids the permanence of marriage but it brings us something of the closeness of marriage."

"It would also bring us scandal and shame," she said soberly. "I cannot see that either of us is of a nature to shrug off the disapprobation of the world, and you were the one to convince me of that, not to mention the inconvenience of drainpipes. Laurence, there is no solution unless we are of one mind. We can be friends or lovers or spouses, but there will only be lasting harmony if we both want the same thing. Since I do not want marriage and neither of us truly wants a clandestine liaison, we are left with only one option, I believe."

"Friendship," he said softly, with the lightest release of breath, like a sigh.

"Is it enough?" she said. "I promise not to decamp to Bath at a moment's notice... or at all, possibly. I rather like Great Maeswood, as it happens. I have a good vintner, my horse, my man-cook, my pianoforte and two gorgeous little pups. I daresay I shall have my books eventually. And I have good company — two evenings a week of cards, and a friend to drink Cognac with. I am content with that, but will it content you?"

The tension dropped away from him, so that his face softened. "That would content me," he said quietly. Then, with a mischievous smile, "For the moment, at least. I accept that an affair would not suit us, considering the drainpipes and so forth, but I have not yet conceded the point on marriage."

"Stop it!" she said, laughing and playfully tapping his hand. "Do not tease me on the subject, for I am quite implacable, and any further discussion might annoy me sufficiently to drive me in all haste to Bath."

He laughed too. "Your wishes are noted. And now, if you will forgive me, it is time for me to prostrate myself before Lady Mountsea and beg her forgiveness."

"It seems to be your day for apologies," Louisa said.

"Yes, and this one is likely to need more than ten words," he said with a grimace. "Are you ready to return to the house? May I offer you my arm?"

She accepted, and they walked back through the gardens in perfect harmony.

~~~~~

Laurence had planned to depart for Bath at once to investigate the false Mrs Haywood, but he found himself finding excuses to put it off. He was delayed in part by Viola's dismay at hosting the Tuesday card evening alone, and partly by his own desire to wait until Lady Mountsea had departed for the north once more. He could not be easy in his mind until he knew that Louisa was free of her unwelcome guest.

His proffered apology had been turned aside with a wave of her ladyship's hand. "But of *course* I understand, Mr Gage," she had trilled. "I understand only too well how dear Louisa feels, and naturally I've never been offended that she chose to settle so far from Roseacre. So many sad memories for her! Poor, poor Louisa, and you're quite right to say that two hundred miles is not far
~~~~~

enough, but then two thousand isn't enough when she carries her sorrow with her. But there, she bears it wonderfully, doesn't she? No one would guess how she suffers."

He gave it up. Clearly no power on earth could convince Lady Mountsea that she, and she alone, was the cause of Louisa's departure.

Viola brought news on Tuesday that her ladyship's carriage had been seen passing through the village, laden with luggage, although she took it as a personal affront that she had not observed it herself. "I had not the least notion of it, for there was no sign of activity at the Dower House when I went into the village, and unluckily I had called on Jane Anderson, quite out of sight of the road. And then when I got to Timpson's, I had to hear it from Mrs Timpson, and perhaps I should not have believed it, for she is shockingly untruthful, you know, except that Kitty Preece was in there buying oranges — oranges! What should they want with oranges at the smithy, I should like to know? It is excessively extravagant, if you want my opinion. But she said it was quite true, she had seen it go by herself as she was just coming out of Birch's, and Mr Birch confirmed it. Can you imagine it, that man-cook of Mrs Middlehope's has ordered duck twice weekly, and a turkey and a green goose every week from him. And chicken! So much chicken! Well, they have none of their own, I suppose. And any game birds in season, Mr Birch said. All for one widow. She cannot possibly eat so much, and no one feeds game to the servants. It is quite excessive, if you want my opinion."

"Perhaps she plans to entertain," Laurence said, suddenly hopeful. Dinner with Louisa at the Dower House! That would be fun.

"Oh... perhaps she does. Well, that would be very proper, to return our hospitality. I wish Mr Truman would hurry up and get married, so that he might have dinners, too."

"He entertains the gentlemen," Laurence said. "A very good table he keeps, too. His cook is excellent."

"That is neither here nor there," Viola said. "A single man with an income above two thousand! He should marry, and provide the neighbourhood with an extra family to dine with — that the ladies may dine with, that is to say. It is his duty. Although if he is angling for one of the Saxby girls, they will be in mourning for some time yet."

Laurence never attempted to dissuade Viola from this line of thought, even when he disagreed with her, but in this case they were of one mind. He had his own reasons for wishing that Truman would marry that had nothing to do with the excellence of his cook. Louisa seemed to have given up the idea of taking a lover, but Truman was a slippery character and a decided flirt who might yet succeed in enticing her, and then Laurence would lose her friendship.

That evening, he was relieved to see Louisa back at the card table, and looking in decidedly better spirits, but he made very sure to keep Truman at a different table. Viola, for her part, made very sure to keep Laurence from her table, too, which amused him. Considering how often she had told him that he ought to remarry, she was very determined that he should not take Louisa as his wife... or anything else. But he went unresisting where Viola directed him. There was pleasure enough in knowing that his good friend was in the room and sitting not ten feet from him, even if he could not be any closer to her.

24: A Visit To Bath

It was Wednesday morning before Laurence set off for Bath, together with Mr Willerton-Forbes and his valet. The lawyer had insisted on coming along, and using his own very commodious carriage.

"There is nothing for me to do until Captain Edgerton returns from his travels, and I feel some responsibility, having set this particular hare running," he told Laurence. "Besides, it is always helpful to have a lawyer by your side, and my man can do for you as well, so you need not deprive Miss Gage of her footman."

It was certainly helpful to Laurence's state of mind to have company on the journey. Willerton-Forbes was an entertaining companion, who dropped the names of dukes and marquesses into the conversation with casual aplomb. The valet, a slender, black-clad man called Neate, attended to Laurence with unobtrusive efficiency and turned him out looking somewhat less rustic than usual, so that he almost wondered if it might be time to leave John to be a footman and get himself a proper valet.

They arrived in Bath late on Thursday, and were outside the bank at nine o'clock sharp the following day.

"First, the money," Willerton-Forbes had said. "Then the attorney you employed. Only then, fully armed, as it were, shall we approach the lady."

The banker was a serious man of no more than thirty-five, but he had been overseeing the account for several years and knew all about it. He received them civilly but with a cautious eye towards the lawyer.

"My uncle was the one who first set up the account for you, Mr Gage," he said. "He is the senior partner now, and will be in a little later if you wish to speak to him in person, but he apprised me of all the circumstances. I trust there is no difficulty with our handling of your daughter's inheritance?"

"Not at all. May I see the present balance?" Laurence said.

"Of course. You will find everything in order, the principal sum is here, you see, with the various dispositions that we have made. The interest is added here, you see, and the payments made to Mrs Haywood, here and here, and again here, exactly as specified in your instructions."

Laurence was aware of a slight release of tension in Willerton-Forbes. He had truly feared some embezzlement of the capital by Mrs Haywood, or whatever her name was.

"Do you wish to make any changes?" the banker said, when they had examined the documents. "I assure you that this bank is completely sound, and I can provide all our accounts if—"

"No, no," Laurence said. "It is not your bank that is in question, but Mrs Haywood."

He left Willerton-Forbes to explain, admiring the lawyer's dry but precise phrasing as he summarised his discoveries succinctly.

The banker nodded thoughtfully. "We have always considered it an odd arrangement, but it is not for a bank to question its clients' dispositions," he said. "Since you hold the account in trust for your daughter, Mr Gage, you may, if you wish, order us to suspend all payments to Mrs Haywood until this matter has been resolved in law. We act only on your instructions."

"That would be most helpful," Willerton-Forbes murmured. "Does Mrs Haywood come in person to draw money from the account?"

"No, she has requested us to transfer the payments to an account at another bank."

"Then she would have no reason to withdraw any sums from this account?"

"None at all, sir, and we should naturally refuse any such request."

As they left the bank, Willerton-Forbes said, "It is a great weight off my mind, Mr Gage, to know that your daughter's inheritance is secure and Miss Gage will not be disadvantaged. And now for Mr Guddle."

The callow young attorney that Laurence remembered had grown sleek and fat in the sixteen years since he had last seen him. Gone were the threadbare coat, scuffed shoes and moth-eaten wig, replaced by the products of the finest artisans of the clothing trade. Clearly the legal profession had been kind to him. Passing through an outer office filled with silently scratching clerks to an inner sanctorum awash with dazzlingly polished mahogany, Laurence and Willerton-Forbes beheld the attorney rising from behind a vast desk, a row of gold fobs dangling from a waistcoat stretched over an ample stomach.

"Good day to you, Mr... erm, Gage and Mr Forbes," the attorney said, reading their cards. "How may I be of assistance?"

"We should like to talk to you about a marriage settlement that you helped to draw up sixteen years ago," Laurence said.

"Certainly, certainly. I had not been in practice long then, but I will have all the documents safe, naturally. What were the names of the parties concerned?"

"Myself and Miss Catherine Haywood."

The attorney started. "Miss... Miss *Haywood.*" He picked up Laurence's card again. "Oh... Gage." The colour visibly drained from his face, and he licked his lips. "I... yes, of course. I remember the case well. My first marriage settlement, although I have drawn up a great many since that day. A great many. What... what did you wish to ask about, Mr Gage?"

Willerton-Forbes cleared his throat. "About the fact that one of the beneficiaries named in that settlement, Mrs Eugenia Haywood, masqueraded under a false name," he said smoothly. "About the unusual and injurious clauses contained within that settlement. About the concerted effort to deprive an innocent young man of monies to which he was fully entitled."

There was a prolonged silence, as Guddle paled even more. A sheen of sweat marred his forehead. "False name..." he croaked. "I... I had no idea. But... but... Mr Gage signed the document. He signed it freely... didn't you, sir? You signed it freely."

Willerton-Forbes shook his head slowly, as if disappointed in him. "Your duty, Mr Guddle, was to advise your client of any provisions within the settlement which would be injurious to him. Did you do so?"

"I did!" he cried, seizing on this idea. "Certainly I did. At least, it was a long time ago and which of us can remember precisely what was said, eh? But I would have done so. Definitely I would have done so."

"Might I examine your records on the case?" Willerton-Forbes said blandly.

"Erm... those records are private, sir. Private. I cannot divulge—"

"Of course you can," Willerton-Forbes said. "The client is here now, and gives his permission, so there can be no possible objection."

"I... may have... lost the records. There was a fire in my previous office, yes, a fire. Everything from that time was destroyed."

Willerton-Forbes produced a notebook and pencil. "And the date of this fire? I am sure the local newspapers will have reported on such a tragic matter."

Guddle leapt to his feet, his expression harassed. "Look, it wasn't me! I had nothing to do with it, it was Slythe who arranged everything. I was just there to represent Mr Gage. You need to talk to Mr Slythe."

"You may be sure that we will," Willerton-Forbes said. "Do not leave Bath, Mr Guddle. You may be needed as a material witness when this comes to court. Or you may be in the dock yourself, who can say? That will be for the magistrates to decide."

So saying, he rose to his feet and swept out of the room, Laurence in his wake, leaving the hapless attorney quaking.

"Breakfast next, I think," Willerton-Forbes said, patting his stomach in anticipation, as they emerged onto the street. "There are usually some chairmen just around the corner who will convey us back to the hotel."

"Should we not go directly to Mrs Haywood's house?" Laurence said. "Catch them unawares... or something?"

"Oh no, I think not. Best if they are forewarned. I am reasonably confident that they will be forewarned."

Laurence nibbled some toast and drank coffee while Willerton-Forbes worked his way steadily through eggs, devilled kidneys, a mutton chop and an array of pastries. He had just pushed aside his plate with a sigh of satisfaction, when an almost inaudible scratching at the door heralded the arrival of Neate, the valet.

"Ah, James!" Willerton-Forbes said. "What do you have for us?"

"Guddle left by the back door just as you were leaving by the front," Neate said, grinning. "Straight down to the Haywood woman's house, inside for a bit above half an hour, then scuttled off again. They will be ready for you. I left Fenton watching the house in case they make a bolt. Rather a grand house for a former governess, if you ask me."

"Fenton?" Laurence said. "The coachman? You set your valet and coachman to act as spies?"

Willerton-Forbes chuckled. "Indeed. I should explain, Mr Gage, that Neate is a lawyer too, but his greatest talent lies in moving unobtrusively through the lower ranks of society. If one wishes to know what the grooms and footmen and innkeepers know or have seen, then Neate is your man. Fenton is less versatile, perhaps, but they are both very useful when one is investigating miscreants. Now, James, sit down and tuck in, for Mr Gage is going to tell us in minute detail all that occurred when the settlement document was drawn up. Who drafted it? Slythe, presumably."

"No, it was Turnbull, the Haywood family lawyer in Hereford," Laurence said. "He suffered from dyspepsia and greatly disliked travelling, so he did not come to Bath himself, but sent a clerk with the draft document. The changes were agreed with him by letter, and when all was signed and sealed, the clerk took a copy back to Hereford."

"What were the changes?"

"Some minor details of names and directions, mainly. In addition, Catherine's pin money was increased from five hundred to one thousand pounds, and Mrs Haywood's allowance was written into the settlement. Previously it had been agreed between us that I would make her an annuity of five hundred pounds a year, but that was increased to one thousand and became part of the settlement. It seemed reasonable at the time, since she was not expected to live long."

Neate chuckled. "Made a miraculous recovery, did she?"

"And Turnbull agreed to these changes?" Willerton-Forbes said.

"He did."

"Who communicated with him? Was it you?"

"No, Slythe wrote to him."

"Ah. And the clause about Mrs Haywood receiving the full interest in the event of the death of either you or your wife?"

Laurence frowned. "Do you know, I cannot remember that at all. I remember reading the whole thing through very carefully, and Guddle explaining every clause, and I have to tell you that all that legal verbiage is impossible for a plain man to understand. There *were* clauses about my death or Catherine's death, and a lot of complicated business about the children, but the only part that mentioned Mrs Haywood was the thousand pounds. So far as I can recall, in any event, but it was a long time ago."

"Hmm." Willerton-Forbes' eyes gleamed. "And she always called herself Mrs Haywood? Her friends all called her that?"

"They did, and Catherine called her *'Mama'*."

"To her face?"

"Why, yes."

"And she never denied it?"

"Not at all."

"Ha!" Neate said, looking up from his plate. "Got her!"

Willerton-Forbes chuckled. "Possibly, James, possibly, but let us not get too excited. There is a long way to go yet, but it is promising. Tell me, Mr Gage, did you ever meet Mr Turnbull?"

"I never did. There was no occasion for it. Slythe wanted me to sell Catherine's house, since she would not need it, but I thought it might be useful for my son when he married, to have a place of his own, so it was leased to tenants. Turnbull and Crossley, my own attorney, managed the business between them."

"He must have been in on it," Neate said, with a mischievous grin that made him look quite different from his lugubrious performance as a valet.

Willerton-Forbes looked unconvinced. "Possibly. We shall certainly need to talk to him and the other trustee as to why they agreed to wind up the trust on such injurious terms. Turnbull must have known perfectly well that Mrs Haywood was merely the governess, for it was common knowledge in Hereford. We will make a detour there on our return journey. Well, Mr Gage, shall we sally forth to meet the interesting Mrs Haywood? But you must let me do all the talking."

"By all means, for if I say anything to her it will not be very gentlemanlike."

Mrs Haywood lived in rather a smart house not far from the Royal Crescent. A superior butler showed them into the drawing room, furnished with somewhat more money than taste, where Mrs Haywood rose to greet them. Laurence had not seen her since the day of Catherine's funeral when the will had been read, but she looked little different from that day nine years before. A little older, a little scrawnier, a lace ruff hiding signs of age about her neck, but greeting him with what could only be the insincere appearance of pleasure. Slythe stood beside her, bowing with a smugly self-satisfied smirk. Mrs Fossett was there, too, even thinner than Laurence remembered, the only one of the three who looked nervous.

When Laurence introduced Willerton-Forbes as a lawyer, there was a hint of wariness from Mrs Haywood, but Slythe's oily expression never faltered.

"What a pleasure to see you again, Gage," Slythe said, beaming at him. "Are you making a long stay in Bath?"

"Oh, I hope not," Laurence murmured.

Willerton-Forbes intervened smoothly. "That rather depends on Mrs Haywood... or perhaps I should say Miss Fossett? That is your name, is it not, madam?"

She began to reply, but Slythe laid a hand on her arm. "There is no reason why a lady may not change her name if she wishes, you know. As a man of the law yourself, you will understand that it is perfectly legal."

"Was the change of name made officially?"

"That is not necessary," Slythe said, still smiling. "An informal matter, by the lady's choice. It is not against the law."

"Only if there is no underhand purpose, Mr Slythe," Willerton-Forbes said calmly. "It is my belief that Miss Fossett assumed a false name in order to defraud Mr Gage of property that was rightfully his, to whit, the income from his wife's portion, by means of clauses in a marriage settlement inserted by deceit, money to which she had not a shred of entitlement as Miss Haywood's governess."

The ladies were now definitely alarmed, but Slythe laughed genially. "Nonsense, nonsense! There was no deceit, and Gage had legal advice. He agreed to every clause and signed the settlement perfectly willingly. Is it not so, Gage?"

Laurence knew better than to answer to such provocation, but he could barely contain his anger at being addressed by an attorney as if he were an intimate.

"The legal advice came from a man barely qualified to offer it, who was in fact in your employ," Willerton-Forbes said quietly. "Miss Fossett led Mr Gage to believe that she was Miss Haywood's mother, a deception to which you, Mr Guddle, Mrs Fossett and Miss Haywood herself were all party."

"Now, she never said so," Slythe said, his voice growing louder, in marked contrast to Willerton-Forbes' calmly precise tones. "No one ever said so, and Gage never asked. There was no deception by anyone, everything was done legally and Gage agreed to every proposal that was put to him. Eugenia never took anything, it was all given freely. This won't fly, I'm afraid. You'll find it's all right and tight, Forbes. Not a thing illegal about it."

"Do you think so?" Willerton-Forbes said, his voice benign. "How interesting. By my reckoning, there are at least five charges that may be brought — fraud, false pretences, false personation, conspiracy to defraud and either falsifying a legal document or forgery, I cannot quite be sure which. But you may well be right. I am sure the courts will give us a definitive ruling. Come, Mr Gage, let us go and find a magistrate."

"Wait a minute!" Mrs Haywood cried, grabbing hold of Laurence's arm. "You can't take us to court! It was Catherine's money and she *wanted* me to have a little bit of it. It was her wish to see me comfortable after I looked after her all those years. She asked for it and you agreed to it and signed all the forms, and you can't come along now and talk about charges and courts as if we committed a crime. There was no crime! I never said I was Catherine's mother, not once! I never, ever pretended to be her mother, not once! I never lied about anything!"

"Except being ill," Laurence snapped. "That was part of it, was it not? You wanted me to believe you were at death's door, so I would agree to everything without fuss."

"An excellent point," Willerton-Forbes said, with a pleased expression. "We will add that to the list. But yes, Miss Fossett, you lied by not correcting an erroneous assumption. That is false pretences, which is illegal."

She squeaked in alarm, and now Mrs Fossett grabbed his other arm, her face riddled with distress. "Please, please have mercy!"

"Amelia, Eugenia, enough!" Slythe said sharply. "They cannot touch us. It is all bluff. We have done nothing wrong, remember? Nothing at all."

"That's true," Mrs Haywood said. "Nothing wrong. I told no lies."

"What I do not understand," Laurence said, turning to Mrs Fossett in puzzlement, "is why you encouraged Malcolm to dangle after Catherine. All those secret meetings must have threatened the whole of your little enterprise. Why did you do it?"

"Secret meetings?" Slythe said abruptly. "What is this, Amelia?"

"Oh, but it was so romantic! They were so in love, the two of them, I had not the heart to deny them. It was so cruel the way they were torn from each other, just so she could marry *him*."

"Nonsense!" Mrs Haywood said. "If you think that, you're even more of a fool than I'd thought, Amelia. Catherine never intended to have anyone but the elder brother — the *heir*. She knew which side her bread was buttered." She caught sight of Laurence and her face hardened. "Oh, go away! And do not come back here, for I will make sure you are forbidden entry. I never want to see you again."

"I am afraid another meeting is quite unavoidable, Miss Fossett," Willerton-Forbes said gently. "You will encounter him in court, after all."

She shrieked in rage, and if she had had a heavy object in her hands at that moment, she would undoubtedly have thrown it at him.

Laurence and Willerton-Forbes beat a hasty retreat.

25: Dinner At The Dower House

Louisa was beginning to feel dangerously settled. Every day she told herself that her original plan had been washed away by the application of Laurence's good sense, and that therefore she ought to start her new, more permanent, life in Bath as soon as may be, but somehow it never quite reached a point of urgency. She had a full complement of servants now, not the least of whom was her wonderful man-cook, the garden was beginning to emerge from decades of neglect and there were even vegetables growing in the now immaculate kitchen garden. She had her dogs to accompany her on long walks and to sit at her feet in the evenings, and Gaius Valerius to take her further afield, exploring the lanes and woods and meadows that surrounded Great Maeswood. The helpful Mr Jeffrey Rycroft had found a key to the gate in the garden wall, and she had permission from Lady Saxby to use it to enter the grounds of Maeswood Hall whenever she wished. She rode and walked energetically every day, once or twice a week she took the gig to Market Clunbury to shop, and most of the time she managed to persuade the pony to return to the Dower House.

She lacked for nothing, except good company. The two card parties every week were delightful, but all too often, her evenings were spent alone with her books, the dogs and a glass of something. Much as she enjoyed the tranquillity of her present life, she was not willing to spend so much time in solitude. She had received a great deal of hospitality from local society, so now she determined to return it in full measure. It was time to hold her first dinner for guests.

Squire Winslade and his family were first on the list, and it would be unexceptionable to invite the clergyman, the handsome Mr Truman, who flirted with her with such finesse at the card parties. He had made somewhat enigmatic overtures towards her when she had first arrived, and there was still a corner of her mind that wondered whether the seemingly upright parson would be amenable to a liaison, if she had not herself abandoned the idea.

The Saxby ladies from the Hall were more problematic, for she was not sure whether they were yet entering company. However, it was almost four months since Lord Saxby had gone to meet his Maker, so she sent William with her invitation and hoped. To her surprise, he returned with an immediate response asking who else might be attending. She replied and Lady Saxby accepted immediately on behalf of all her family. If everyone else accepted, that would be twelve people! Chambers would be delighted to display his culinary talents for such an audience.

She chose her gown with more care than usual. There was some suspicion of her amongst the wives of the village, partly because all widows were viewed as potential threats to the equanimity of their marriages, and partly, Louisa admitted reluctantly, because she had made little effort to blend into the neighbourhood. She had set out with seduction in mind and had dressed accordingly, but now that she wished to entertain, it would suit her purpose to exude an aura of matronly respectability. So it was that, despite Marie's head-shaking and rattle of disapproving French, she had chosen a more modest outfit for the occasion, not precisely demure, but certainly more restrained.

The ladies from the Hall were the first to arrive, the Miss Saxbys' eyes shining with excitement, and even Lady Saxby smiling benignly, although her assessing gaze swept the drawing room from floor to ceiling. The squire and his son and daughter were not far behind, and then the Rycroft brothers, who had walked down from the Hall by way of the gate into Louisa's garden. Some of the guests were old friends from the card parties, but she was curious to see the Saxby ladies out of their home environment.

The last to arrive was Mr Truman, and again Louisa was intrigued. Would he continue his mild flirtation with her, or would he devote his attentions to the other ladies, and in particular was Miss Saxby still responsive to his smooth charm? Before dinner, there was a general mingling and Mr Truman moved about the room freely, and seemed to favour no one in particular. When they moved through to the dining room, Louisa invited the squire and Lady Saxby to sit either side of her, but otherwise left the guests to sit where they pleased. Mr Truman was very quick to take the seat beside Miss Saxby, and there was that little blush on her cheeks again. Yes, she definitely had a *tendre* for him, but although he was most attentive, speaking to her in a low voice, his gaze intense, that was his habitual manner with all ladies. He was certainly so with Louisa, and while she saw no harm in a man engaging in a flirtation with a widow older than he was, it was cruel to do so with Cass Saxby, who was not only susceptible, but might come to have expectations of marriage. Louisa rather liked Cass, who made light of her limp, the result of a childhood illness, and was invariably cheerful and friendly.

There was another couple who drew Louisa's attention, too. The elder of Lady Saxby's two sons, Mr Jeffrey Rycroft, had slipped into the seat beside the squire's daughter with unusual eagerness. Having no one on his other side, he directed all his conversation towards Miss Winslade, but she received his attentions in a cool manner. Was he in love? There was a gleam in his eye that suggested it, but the lady was distinctly unencouraging.

Then there was Agnes Saxby, who was desperate for a husband and seemingly surrounded by eligible young men, yet conducted herself without a sign of interest in any of them. Perhaps they were too familiar to be interesting, or perhaps they fell outside Lady Saxby's parameters as to suitability. She seemed unaffected by Mr Truman's attentions to her sister, however, and showed no consciousness when Mr Chandry's name was mentioned, even laughing when one of the Rycrofts teased her in brotherly fashion about him.

"He is not at all minded for marriage, he told me so," she said cheerfully. "I shall just have to look elsewhere."

Louisa liked her easy-going attitude, and hoped she would find a congenial man before too long. How interesting these little romances were!

The meal was a triumph of Chambers' culinary art, and although some of the guests cheerfully ate everything without comment and would probably have done the same for boiled mutton and potatoes, the more discriminating of the party were effusive in their praise. William and Spencer were quietly efficient in their duties, too, and altogether Louisa was rather pleased with the success of the meal.

When the ladies withdrew, most of the party gathered around the pianoforte at one end of the room. All the ladies from the Hall still wore full black, but it was clear from the light-hearted chatter that their deepest mourning was behind them.

Louisa sat beside Lady Saxby. "How delightful to see your daughters out in society at last," she began. "They were much missed at the Manor last week, but of course it is still too soon after their bereavement for a ball. A quiet dinner is very different and it will surely lift their spirits to mingle more freely with their friends."

"Yes indeed, and they must enjoy such snatched moments of happiness while they can, for their future is most uncertain."

That was an unpromising opening. "You refer, I presume, to the arrival of the new Lord Saxby? Is there any news?"

"None. The lawyers are trailing all over the country to find an heir to the Third Baron, but so far without success. So here we sit in limbo, awaiting the moment when we are turned out of our home."

"It has been fortunate for me, however," Louisa said. "I am able to enjoy your lovely Dower House until you need it."

Lady Saxby turned her languid gaze on her. "Do not concern yourself on that account, Mrs Middlehope. The Dower House is far too small for my needs."

"At the moment, certainly, but when your daughters marry—"

The gaze sharpened. "But who knows when that will be? It will be difficult to find husbands for all of them, for I cannot go much into society myself, not when I am so frequently unwell. My constitution has never been robust, and I am not strong enough to be trailing to assemblies all the time. They will just have to take their chances with the more restricted society that Great Maeswood affords."

"I have always held to the opinion that it is better for a young woman to marry a man she knows well," Louisa said. "If he is from her own neighbourhood, so much the better. So many go off to town to do the season, and find themselves tied to a man they hardly know, and confined to an estate far from home. It is not comfortable to be bereft of every familiar face."

Lady Saxby raised elegantly arched eyebrows. "Perhaps, but the possibilities are wider in town, without doubt. That is how I met Lord Saxby, after all. One meets with a far superior sort of man in the metropolis. There are few men in our corner of Shropshire that I would regard as suitable matches for my girls."

Was the handsome Mr Truman one of those few men? Cass Saxby was already half in love with him, if not more, and Louisa was uneasy about it. Impulsively, she said, "I hope you regard Mr Truman as suitable, for I am very much afraid that Miss Saxby has formed an attachment in that direction."

There was a delicate ripple of something that might have been laughter from Lady Saxby. "You sound as if you disapprove, Mrs Middlehope."

"It is not for me to approve or disapprove, but he is a very charming man who is attentive to many young ladies. He does not show signs of wishing to fix his interest with Miss Saxby. It would distress all her friends to see her hurt."

Lady Saxby's smile widened. "There is no need to feel any concern on that account, I assure you. Mr Truman is very discreet, for Cass is still in mourning, but he has made his intentions perfectly plain."

That was intriguing. A man who had made his intentions plain to one young lady yet felt himself at liberty to flirt with another, or even several others, was not steady enough to be a suitable match, and such behaviour was especially deplorable in a clergyman. He was certainly not as steady as Laurence, who epitomised that quality. How had Laurence described Mr Truman? Oily, that was it, and she could only agree with him.

"It is very agreeable to have Cass settled, I can tell you, Mrs Middlehope. Perhaps a little of her good fortune will fall on Agnes, poor child. Of Flora and Honora I have not the least concern, but poor Agnes sets her cap at the most unsuitable men. She would have married the apothecary if her father had not intervened, and now she has hopes of Michael Chandry. She looked to the captain first, but he is married, seemingly, so now her thoughts are fixed on Mr Chandry and nothing I say will deter her. Although it would be a good catch for her if she can get him, for his sister is a duchess, but I think he is just amusing himself with a flirtation."

"He is certainly a charming young man," Louisa said. "I can quite see why Miss Agnes should admire him."

Lady Saxby laughed mirthlessly. "Admire him? She would admire any single man just as much. Poor Agnes! All she wants is someone — anyone — to marry her, but such desperation is too pathetic for words. I doubt I shall ever see her in her own establishment."

Poor Agnes indeed, when her own mother made not the least push to provide her with more fertile society for her modest ambitions.

Since Lady Saxby was in a confiding mood, Louisa lowered her voice even more. "Your eldest son is another who seems to have formed an attachment, although the lady seems less keen."

Her expression clouded instantly. "Jeffrey is a fool! He has been mooning about after Susannah Winslade for years, but happily she has more sense than to encourage him when neither of them has two pennies to rub together."

"I am sorry for it, if so. Has she no dowry at all?"

"None. The squire's first marriage was... somewhat imprudent, by all accounts. His second brought a little money but his third! An apothecary's daughter," she sniffed. "No money and then a string of children to be provided for. Now that she is so ill, Susannah is needed to run the household. I quite believe she is destined to remain a spinster."

When the gentlemen came through and the card tables were brought out, Louisa found herself partnering the lovelorn Jeffrey Rycroft against Lady Saxby and Mr Truman, while the rest of the gathering played a noisy game of speculation.

"I see the Timpson boys have done a splendid job hacking back the wilderness in your grounds, Mrs Middlehope," Mr Rycroft said in one of the breaks between rubbers. "It must have been a fine garden at one time, and it pleases me to see the bones of it emerge from so many years of neglect. Do you have any plans to make improvements?"

"I have not yet thought so far ahead," she said cautiously.

"Perhaps Mrs Middlehope does not intend to stay in Great Maeswood for long," Lady Saxby said.

"Oh?" Mr Truman said. "You are not planning to leave us so soon, I hope? You have been such a welcome addition to our weekly card parties, and in your own home you are a hostess *par excellence.* You would be very much missed if you were to take your *many* talents elsewhere." He smiled at her with a warmth that felt a shade too intimate for the setting. Yes, he was definitely oily.

"It is less than two months since I arrived," Louisa said with a smile. "Pray allow me to fully unpack before I consider moving on."

Mr Rycroft leaned forward eagerly. "I hope you will not do so. If you decide to stay, and you wish to undertake some enhancements to the garden, I should be very happy to help you with designs, commissioning builders, obtaining materials and so forth. Perhaps I might call to discuss the possibilities?"

"The Dower House is not mine," Louisa said firmly. "I cannot consider any substantive work on the grounds."

"Oh, no one would mind," Lady Saxby said airily. "I certainly should not, and the house is mine for life, you know. Do as you wish with it."

"There you are," Mr Rycroft said in pleased tones. "Mama has no objection. What do you say, Mrs Middlehope?"

Did she truly want to leave? Somehow Bath now held little attraction for her. In just a few short weeks, she had put down surprisingly deep roots. If she left Great Maeswood, she would never see if Jeffrey Rycroft could secure Susannah Winslade's affections. She would never know whether Cass Saxby could tame Mr Truman's flirtatious tendencies, or her sister Agnes have her own establishment. She would never watch Henrietta and Edward Gage grow up. And always at the back of her mind was Laurence, her wonderful friend, with whom she could be utterly herself.

"Come and see me tomorrow, Mr Rycroft," she said. "You may tell me what you have in mind for the gardens."

~~~~~

For some reason, Laurence had never been to Hereford before. He found it a fine town, smaller than Shrewsbury but with several magnificent edifices, many interesting older properties and wide, well-paved streets. It was not difficult to find Mr Turnbull's office but he was not there. He was at home, the clerk told them, owing to an indisposition. A flurry of messages back and forth elicited an invitation to visit him at his house, no more than five minutes away.

A very elderly manservant admitted them, and led them to a small room filled with books, or so it seemed to Laurence at first sight. Every spare inch of wall space was taken up with bookcases, and every surface was covered with orderly piles of them. Beside a low-burning fire, Mr Turnbull sat in a comfortable chair, swathed in shawls, one foot resting on a stool. On a table at his side was a glass of Canary, and yet another book.

"Pray forgive me for not rising, gentlemen," he said as Laurence and Willerton-Forbes were announced. "My gout is troublesome today."

While the manservant brought chairs for them and poured Canary, Laurence assessed the attorney. He was elderly, certainly, and a large man who clearly enjoyed both his food and drink in a manner which would have been approved by the Prince of Wales, but his eyes were clear and filled with a sharp intelligence. He looked benign enough, but he had been party to the deception played on Laurence sixteen years ago, and must therefore be viewed with suspicion.

"What a pleasure to meet you at last, Mr Gage," Turnbull said when the manservant had withdrawn. "All these years I have
~~~~~

acted for you regarding Myrtle House, yet we have never met. And the famous Mr Pettigrew Willerton-Forbes, who acted so efficiently in the matter of the Benefactor after the tragedy of the *Brig Minerva*. I am very honoured to make your acquaintance, sir. But how may I be of service to you gentlemen?"

It was Willerton-Forbes who answered. "We wish to speak to you about Mr Gage's marriage settlement, which you helped to draw up, although it was some years ago, and—"

"Sixteen years," Turnbull said at once. "Miss Catherine Haywood. I was a trustee for her fortune of approximately one hundred thousand pounds, so I was necessarily involved in drawing up the settlement and approving it before the funds could be made over to you, Mr Gage. You met Miss Haywood in Bath, although your home is in Shropshire. Both of you had left your homes with matrimony in mind, and it was all settled in a very short time. A most pleasing outcome. I remember it very well, although I was saddened to hear of the demise of your wife nine years ago, Mr Gage. But you have a daughter who now inherits her mother's portion, I believe."

"You know a great deal about it, considering it was so long ago," Laurence said, puzzled. "Have you had occasion to review the papers recently?"

"I have perfect recall, Mr Gage," Turnbull said placidly. "I remember every case."

"Do you remember Mrs Haywood?" Willerton-Forbes said.

At once Turnbull's face grew wary. "I remember the lady, yes."

"She was formerly known as Miss Fossett," Willerton-Forbes said.

Instantly, the attorney's expression relaxed. "Oh, so you know! That is very good. Yes, she was Miss Haywood's governess, but after Mr Haywood died, she began to call herself Mrs Haywood. It was most concerning, and I feared that there was some mischief afoot, but it seems not to have been so, and the lady settled in Bath, I believe, well away from Miss Haywood... Mrs Gage, I should say. I always supposed it to be a way of elevating herself in society, by claiming to be a widow, but harmless, quite harmless."

"You call it harmless to appropriate the interest from Miss Haywood's fortune to herself?" Willerton-Forbes said.

"Appropriate the interest? But how could she possibly do that?"

"Through the marriage settlements, Mr Turnbull. Mrs Haywood, or Miss Fossett, received one thousand pounds a year through the terms of the marriage settlement, and when Mrs Gage died, she received the full interest amount. Four thousand pounds a year."

"Mrs Haywood? Through the settlement? No, you have been misinformed, Mr Willerton-Forbes. There was no mention of Mrs Haywood or Miss Fossett in the settlement."

In answer, Willerton-Forbes produced the settlement document, and silently handed it to Turnbull.

"No... this is not right. This is not the settlement that was agreed. Not at *all* the settlement that was agreed." He picked up a small brass bell sitting on the table at his elbow, ringing it furiously. When the manservant did not appear instantly, he rang it again, with even greater violence.

The manservant appeared at a run, eyes wide with alarm.

"Send the boy down to the office to fetch the Haywood file. *At once!*"

He must have run all the way there and back, for it was no more than five minutes before a harassed clerk rushed into the room with a box of papers. From it, Turnbull extracted a document.

"*This* is what I received, exactly as I agreed with Mr Guddle and Mr Slythe in Bath, and signed by all parties — signed by *you*, Mr Gage, and properly witnessed and sealed. Yet this one that you brought with you is also signed and sealed, yet it is *different.* How can this be? There is serious malfeasance afoot here."

Willerton-Forbes examined both documents carefully, before passing them to Laurence. "Did you sign both of these, Mr Gage?"

"I only signed one document... at least, there were four copies of it, one each for Slythe, Guddle, myself and you, Mr Turnbull. Is it possible that they were different? They all looked the same to me. I read the first one through carefully, and then glanced at the others... but this one of yours is clearly different, Turnbull. I should have noticed the difference... and this signature... the initial letters are very like the way I write them, but the 'a' in Laurence... here, you see? And again in Gage... that is not my hand."

"Aha!" the two lawyers said in unison.

"Forgery," Turnbull said.

"A felony," Willerton-Forbes said with satisfaction. "Now we have them."

26: Of Wives And Bachelors

MAY

Nothing else would do for Mr Willerton-Forbes but to get straight back in the carriage and drive immediately to Bath.

"It is Saturday," Laurence said plaintively. "I thought we might rest here and attend divine service in the Cathedral, then go to Bath on Monday."

"You are welcome to do so, Mr Gage, if you wish," Willerton-Forbes said, "or you may even return home, if you choose, for all I need is a letter from you authorising me to inform the magistrates on your behalf of the crime that has been committed against you. However, I should like to be sure that Miss Fossett and her accomplices do not evade justice. The sooner an arrest is made the better."

Return home... was he ready for that? His turbulent feelings were no more settled than they had been when he had talked to Louisa in the sunken garden after that dreadful evening. What had got into him, to snap at everyone, even Viola, and to be so appallingly rude to Lady Mountsea? And then he had proposed to Louisa! *'You are very muddled, Laurence — not your usual sensible self at all,'* she had said to him, and it was true — he felt very muddled.

No, he could not go home yet. "Would you be so good as to take me as far as Gloucester? I shall pay a visit to my sister, I think."

They were packed and on the road within an hour, and by the middle of the afternoon, Laurence was directing the coachman through leafy lanes to the small village where Ursula lived. It would serve him right, he supposed, if he arrived unannounced to find the shutters closed and the knocker off the door, but happily it was not so. However surprised the Malling family were to see him, they expressed great pleasure in his visit and asked no awkward questions. After unsuccessfully pressing Mr Willerton-Forbes to stay with them over the Sabbath, they listened with all the proper exclamations of shock and alarm to Laurence's recitation of his recent discoveries.

"I always felt there was something havey-cavey about the whole settlement," John Malling said smugly.

"You never said so," Laurence said mildly.

"One always assumes that the attorneys know their business," Malling said. "Still, I felt it was odd. Did I not say so, Ursula? You will remember that I said so at the time."

"I am sure you did," she said equably.

Ursula was only two years older than Laurence, but she had married early and settled with an almost audible sigh of relief into her matronly years, so that in many ways she felt much older than she truly was. Or perhaps it was the way she mothered Laurence that made him feel so much younger. Whatever the reason, it was always a comfort to stay with her. Despite arriving unannounced in the middle of the afternoon, within a very short time a room was prepared, bathwater and a decanter of Madeira sent up, and a junior footman appointed to serve as valet. Without fuss, an extra place was set at table for dinner and Laurence was absorbed effortlessly into the family.

It was Sunday afternoon, a full week since his meeting with Louisa in the sunken garden, before Ursula discreetly drew him away from the family and took him to her boudoir.

"I am not going to ask," she said, pointing him to a chair with the Madeira and a glass conveniently within reach. "However, if you wish to talk about her, I am perfectly willing to listen, if it will help. I promise not to offer you pointless advice."

"Her?"

"Louisa Middlehope," she said, with the sort of patient tone one might employ with a child. "Do you imagine we know nothing about it? Vi has been writing agonised letters for weeks now, but Vi is… well, she is Vi, and I do not regard her word as totally reliable in such a matter. I should love to hear all about it from your own lips, but that is up to you. I shall work on my tapestry and you may drink your Madeira, and we can just as easily talk about the weather, if you wish."

Laurence laughed. "Whatever has Vi said about Louisa?"

"Only that she is a widow and she fears of the more predatory kind, but I cannot tell whether she most fears that you will marry her or that you will not."

"Vi has been telling me to marry again for years, yet now when a woman comes along whose company I enjoy, she is set against it. I cannot make her out at all."

"Oh, Laurence! She is terrified of being displaced, of course. If you marry, she will have to leave, and where does she have to go now except here, or with Selena? She wants you to be happy, as we all do, but she is a spinster of six and forty and her options are limited. Do you truly enjoy Mrs Middlehope's company? She does not sound at all like the sort of woman you would like. She is nothing like Catherine, from Vi's account."

"She is *nothing* like Catherine," he said, with sudden vehemence. Then, seeing the surprise in Ursula's eyes, he went on, "Did you like Catherine, sister? Answer me honestly."

Ursula laid down her tapestry frame and removed her spectacles. When had she started wearing those? Lord, how old they were all getting!

For a moment she looked at him, her expression clouded. "She was... very lovely, very calm. A restful person to be with," she said eventually.

"But?"

"She was cold, Laurence. I always thought her cold. With you, with the children... there was no true warmth. That was how I felt, anyway. No doubt she was different in private but—"

"No," he said quickly. "She was always cold. Even in our most private moments, there was no warmth in her... no affection. I..." He stopped. How much should he say? Even now, with all that he knew of Catherine, it felt like a betrayal to speak so openly of her. Yet he needed to say it, to tell someone of his grief. "I read her diaries, and she never loved me, not when we married, nor later, when we knew each other better. She never even loved her own children. What kind of mother feels nothing for the child she carried inside her, Ursula?"

She reached across and laid her hand on his. "Oh Laurence, I am so sorry, so very sorry. We often wondered... but you always seemed so happy with her, and you grieved so much after she died that naturally we said nothing. And is this widow warmer?"

He smiled just thinking of Louisa. Warmer? Yes, she was all warmth, all humanity, her nature all generosity. And her kisses... Lord, her kisses! "Yes, she is warmer."

"Oh, Laurence! You are in love with her! I can see it in your face. Oh, how wonderful!"

"Am I? How does one know? That is to say, with Catherine, I felt something instantly and I was in no doubt that I wanted to marry her, but with Louisa... it feels just like friendship. I feel comfortable with her."

Ursula chuckled. "There is no better start for a marriage than friendship, my dear. Better than falling head over heels for a beautiful face and an empty head. Is she beautiful, your Louisa?"

He pondered that, recalling that he had described her to Viola as neither beautiful nor plain, merely ordinary. How long ago that seemed, and how much his view of her had changed. "I think her beautiful," he answered cautiously.

"Ah. And does your heart beat faster when you see her?"

That was a difficult question. "I am always glad to see her."

"Do you dream of spending your life with her? Does she fill your thoughts?"

More difficult questions. He frowned as he considered. "I *do* think about her, but... spending my life with her? Marriage? I enjoy her friendship, very much so, but do I want to go beyond friendship? That is precisely what I cannot decide."

"Well, then, think of it another way, Laurence. If she disappeared from your life, if you could never see her again, how would you feel about that?"

The cold chill that assailed him was like a blow, sudden and acutely painful. Bath! If she were to go to Bath— "I should *hate* it!" he said fiercely. "More than anyone else, I can *talk* to her. No matter how low I feel or how stupidly I behave, she always makes me feel better. I should be wretched without her company... her understanding... her unquestioning fellowship. Good God, I should be so miserable if she were to go away. I could not imagine my life without her." He gave a shaky laugh. "I suppose I have my answer, do I not?"

"I suppose you do, brother dear. May I be the first to wish you joy?"

"Ah, well, do not be too hasty, for there is just a tiny difficulty. Even if my mind is made up, I have yet to convince the lady. She relishes her freedom and is in no hurry to surrender herself to another man. The first time I mentioned the subject, in the most roundabout way, she told me not to be so silly."

"Then you will just have to change her mind about it," Ursula said with a throaty laugh.

"How on earth am I to do that?"

"By convincing her that *she* cannot live without *you*, of course," she said triumphantly. "When you go home, you will discover just how much she has missed you, and I daresay she will fall into your arms."

If only it could be so simple!

~~~~~

Louisa had so much enjoyed her first dinner at the Dower House that she immediately sat down to plan the second. Laurence must come, of course, and Miss Gage, and she would invite Henrietta, too. It would be good for her to enjoy an evening out amongst good friends. She would include Mr Willerton-Forbes, Captain Edgerton and Mr Chandry if they had returned by then, and the Beasleys. The Drinkwaters and the Andersons? She
~~~~~

supposed she owed them the courtesy, although they were dull company. That would be thirteen, so she would add Miss Cokely to the list. That should do it. She would tell Chambers to start preparing a menu. He could go to Shrewsbury, if need be, to obtain the ingredients, and as soon as Laurence returned, she would send out her cards.

Jeffrey Rycroft called promptly to discuss plans for the garden, which seemed to involve tearing up the orchard and most of the shrubbery, and a vast amount of earthmoving to create what he grandly described as topography. He walked about with her, the dogs bouncing excitedly around them, his arms windmilling as he tried to explain the splendour of his vision.

"This is a garden of modest proportions, not a great estate, Mr Rycroft," Louisa said in amusement. "This all seems a little ambitious."

"Oh." He deflated at once. "Is it too dramatic? Something a little more restrained, perhaps? More formal, like the house or—Oh. Is it too expensive? I should have enquired as to your budget."

"It is not a question of money," she said firmly, "although I should want everything properly priced up before I agree to anything. Why do you not draw up two different plans, one dramatic and one restrained, with a rough estimate of costs, and then we will discuss it further."

He nodded but his face was troubled.

"What is it?" she said. "You cannot expect me to agree to anything after an hour of walking round the garden and coming up with ideas on the spot."

"No, no, but… may I be frank with you, Mrs Middlehope? When Lord Saxby died in January, he left my brother and me with a dilemma. We were only his step-sons and had no claim on him, but when he married our mother he agreed to pay for our education and raise us as gentlemen. However, that was *all* he promised. We have had no help to find a career, or do anything useful and now… now we must. This would be a useful start for me, if… if…"

"If you are paid? And you will be, Mr Rycroft. When I had work done on a new shrubbery and dell at Roseacre, the garden designer produced a series of drawings of his proposals from different angles, showing how the finished work would look. He would bill me for the hours spent on the designs plus his materials and other expenses. Sometimes I would ask for changes, and he would make fresh drawings, again charging me for the work. If I liked the design, I could either commission him to execute it or engage local labour to work from the drawings. That would be paid for separately, but everything he did, he charged me for. I will let you have his direction and you may write to him for his advice, or go to see him in London, if you wish. That would be a legitimate expense for which you could bill me."

"Oh." His eyes were wide at this glimpse of another world. Then he laughed. "Go to London at your expense? That would be beyond the pale!"

"Research, Mr Rycroft, research," she said, smiling. "A perfectly reasonable expense."

Later that day, when she was just returning from a long walk with the dogs, she met Captain Edgerton walking up her drive.

"I was just coming to call upon you to report on our successful mission," the captain said, according her one of his flamboyant bows.

"You found the three ladies who wrote the references for Miss Labett?"

"Well… not all of them admittedly, and the servants were less helpful than I had supposed. It is astonishing how often some people contrive to lose all their servants. As for their mistresses, one lady had died and all her papers had been burned, so there was nothing to be discovered there. Another was still alive, but her house had burnt down, so all her records had gone up in smoke, too. But the third… ah, the third was a great deal more successful." He grinned at her happily.

"Come inside and tell me all about it," Louisa said, smiling at his excitement.

William poured Madeira without being asked, and then the captain, practically bouncing with enthusiasm in his chair, told her the story.

"Mrs Harker is a very old lady now, but her memory is as clear as a bell. She remembers Miss Labett perfectly, and even sketched us a drawing of her. There now, what do you think of that?"

She gazed at the paper he gave her, the face of a woman dead for a quarter of a century. She was not a beauty, and not even pretty, if she were being honest, despite the curls carefully massed around her face and the feminine froth of lace at her throat. It was a hard face, filled with determination. Or was that ambition?

"What did Mrs Harker say about her?" Louisa said.

"That she was no better than she should be," he said at once. "She was not in the least surprised to hear that she was with child when she died. She seduced the Harker son and heir, a boy of only seventeen, and had him on the point of a proposal before his parents got wind of the affair. Very persistent about it she was too, and had to be paid quite a substantial sum to go away."

Louisa sipped her Madeira thoughtfully. "She was an ambitious little madam, by the sound of it. And so she has moved from one post to another, looking for an opportunity... or a man too honourable or stupid to see what she is about. But the man she met here was neither stupid nor honourable. Have you made any progress towards finding her lover, Captain?"

"Not yet. So far, we have been more concerned with tracing Miss Labett's history. She came from Chester, the daughter of some kind of clerk, although she claimed her mother's family was gentry. It is probably a wild goose chase, but we must try to find anyone there who remembers her before we start stirring the ants' nest to find a murderer."

"Lord, yes! What a to-do, once you start interviewing likely suspects! But you must have a list, surely?"

"Not yet. It is rather a difficult undertaking. One would need to know everyone who was in the village at the time."

Louisa pondered that. "You are the expert, Captain, but I should have thought there would not be terribly many single men about."

"You would exclude the married men? And the jealous wives?"

"Miss Labett— What was her Christian name?"

"Dorothea."

"Oh. Such a pretty name. She does not look a bit like a Dorothea. That is nothing to the point, however. Dorothea wanted a husband, so she would not waste her efforts on a married man. By the same token, there would be no jealous wife in the case, even if one supposed one could be found with the strength or ingenuity to kill the poor girl and drag her into the wine cellar. That seems like a job for a man, do you not think?"

The captain smiled, and said, "I agree with you, but one does not quite like to eliminate all but the most obvious possibility. But let us suppose we restrict ourselves to single men. How would one find them all out after all this time?"

"Oh, that is easy," Louisa said, laughing. "One asks the single women, of course. Miss Gage and Miss Beasley would have been here at the time and would have known all the eligible young men. Should you like me to ask them?"

"That would be most helpful, Mrs Middlehope. Such an enquiry would be much better coming from another lady. Then, when we return from Chester, we shall have our list of possible murderers ready and waiting."

Louisa sent notes to Miss Gage and Miss Beasley at once, and they entered into the spirit of the exercise with enthusiasm. Sitting either side of Louisa's davenport with cups of tea and plates of delicate strawberry tarts and almond biscuits, they rattled off names while Louisa copied them down.

"Thomas Saxby was the most eligible young man in those days," Miss Gage said. "Not that he was handsome or particularly good-natured — he had *such* a temper when he was thwarted. Do you remember the time he smashed that beautiful ormolu clock because it had stopped again and he said what was the point of a clock that never worked? And he broke a window in one of his own glass houses when the gardener did something to upset him *and* he made the fellow pay for it, too. He was always careful with his money. Oh, but wait… what year was this? No, he was firmly betrothed by then, so that is no good. John Winslade… he was not married until the following year. He was *much* handsomer, and had prettier manners, too. His father was squire in those days, of course. Who else? Oh, Luke Winslade. Now *there* is a likely murderer, if you want. Always in trouble, always."

"He was in India, Viola," Miss Beasley whispered.

"Was he? No, that was later… no, I do believe you are right, Phyllida, so cross him off, Mrs Middlehope. Roland, of course."

Miss Beasley started violently, and made inarticulate noises of protest.

"Well, naturally he is not a murderer, but his name must go on the list. Write down *'Roland Beasley'*, Mrs Middlehope. There was no one else from our class that I can recall. Can you think of anyone, Phyllida? No, I am sure there is no one."

"Great-uncle Zachariah," Miss Beasley said, almost under her breath.

"Oh, good grief, Phyllida! He could not possibly— No, you are right, we must have every one who was unmarried at the time. Zachariah Gage, Mrs Middlehope, who must have been sixty or more at the time. He has only just died, if you can believe it. Eighty-seven, and not stirred from his house for twenty years, but he was living at the Grove when Miss Labett was here. Oh, and his son! Illegitimate, you know," she added in a semi-whisper, her lips pursed in distaste. "Kenneth Gage, another ne'er-do-well if ever there was one. He was here."

Miss Beasley shook her head. "In prison."

"Was that then? Yes, it must have been. Oh, well, take him off the list, Mrs Middlehope. Who else? John Brownsmith from the Boar's Head. He would have been about one and twenty then. Several of the Vale boys from the Home Farm. Oh, and the smith... *such* a well-looking man, so tall and all that black hair. Do you remember him, Phyllida?" Miss Beasley nodded, a little smile on her lips. "This was before those no-good Preeces came, of course. What was his name?"

"Harry Smallwood," Miss Beasley whispered, with a tiny sigh.

"And that is all, I believe. Can you think of anyone else, Phyllida? No? It is not a very long list, is it, Mrs Middlehope?"

It was depressingly short, and the worst of it was that the most likely candidate, the most obvious target for an ambitious governess looking to trick her way to a husband, was John Winslade. The squire.

27: Considerations Of Matrimony

When Louisa entered the Grove on Tuesday evening, she was pleased to find that Laurence had returned and was beaming at her from the far side of the drawing room.

"Was your journey successful?" she said, when he came to greet her.

He bowed over her hand with unusual formality. "Very. I have left Mr Willerton-Forbes busy on my behalf in Bath. You will also be pleased to hear that I am less muddled than I was when we last met. I visited my sister in Gloucester and have got a great deal straightened out in my mind. I should like to talk to you about it, if I may? Tomorrow, perhaps?"

There was an eagerness in him that she had not seen before. But how sweet that he wished to tell her of all his thoughts! "I shall be at leisure all day," she said, immediately cancelling her plans to drive to Astley Cloverstone.

She was still at breakfast the next morning when the door knocker sounded. William returned with a note on the silver salver.

'I shall await you in the little arbour in the shrubbery. Laurence.'

Abandoning her breakfast with a laugh, she gathered the dogs and went out through the drawing room door. Crossing the lawn to the shrubbery, she made her way to the secret arbour hidden amidst the greenery. He was there, sitting with his arms folded and legs stretched out in front of him, neatly crossed at the ankles, looking as if he belonged there. He jumped up and bowed as she approached, and there was that eagerness again that made her smile.

"What is it you wanted to say to me?" she said, positioning a cushion on the stone bench and sitting down.

His lips quirked ruefully as he sat beside her. "I am afraid I am going to annoy you by asking you to marry me. I am sorry for it, but it cannot be helped. And now you will give me a score of reasons why you should not."

"Perhaps you should start by giving me a score of reasons why I should," she said, not at all sure whether he was serious or not. Was he drunk? He seemed sober enough.

"There is only one reason," he said. "It is a very selfish one, but I have discovered that you are quite indispensable to my happiness. It is unaccountable, but somehow I seem to have fallen in love with you. I do not know how it happened, but there it is."

Her breath caught. This was a declaration indeed! "But... what about your wife?" The words were difficult to say. In love with her! Heavens above, how had they come to this?

"Ah, yes, Catherine... my perfect wife, who was very far from perfect. You were quite right about that, as about so many things, my dear Louisa. But she is dead and I am alive, and must look to the future now, and I hope... I very much hope that will be with you. What do you say? Can you set your past behind you too, and go forward side by side with me?"

How to answer him? She had never seriously considered marrying him. "Marriage is... so *final,"* she said eventually. "I spent twelve long, very dull years with Ned and another year counting the days until I could escape. I am not sure I want to hurtle into another marriage so soon, especially when—" She chuckled. "You will forgive me for being practical, I trust, but you are still young and healthy, so—"

He gave a bark of laughter. "I am flattered that you consider a man of forty as young."

"Young enough to live for another forty years," she said. "Despite all your charms — your *many* charms — I am not at all convinced that I want another husband. I came here in search of a lover, and that idea still appeals to me more than marriage."

"Do you wish to elaborate on my many charms?" he said interestedly. "You may take as long as you wish. I am a very good listener, when the subject is such a pleasing one."

She laughed but said, "Conceited man! Some other time, perhaps."

"Ah, well," he said, with an exaggerated sigh. "Louisa, are you truly so set against marriage?"

She let out a long breath. "I felt as if I were being suffocated, as if the walls were closing in and there was no air. You cannot understand it, I daresay, because it is different for a man, but I have been subservient to a man for virtually my entire life. First my father, and then Ned, and do not mistake me, neither of them ever showed me anything but kindness and generosity. The settlement my father agreed for me was already generous, but Ned's will doubled my jointure. They both let me spend as much as I wished, to fill my days with whatever occupation seemed good to me. Ned let me travel, even when he no longer cared to, and I took one or two trips, but..." She sighed again. "He looked so sad when I went away and was so happy to see me again that I never liked to do it, and that is how it works, you see. If our circumstances had been reversed, he would never have thought twice about going away if he wished to, whereas I felt obliged to stay. It was my duty to please him, and I did it whole-heartedly, but still it was *his* wishes that prevailed, and not mine."

"Perhaps that was because he was of an age with your father," Laurence said gently. "If you were married to a man nearer to your own age, a marriage of equals—"

"There is no such thing!" she cried. "A woman is *always* less than a man in the eyes of the world, and nothing at all in the eyes of the law and the church. A wife does not exist in her own stead, she is the property of her husband, her only purpose to provide him with children, if she can, and to ensure his comfort. To be subsumed like that... it is horrible, Laurence."

Laurence nodded, frowning. "You know, of course, that Ned would never have wanted you to do only what you thought he wanted? He would have wanted you to be happy. Of course he would have been sad when you went away, for who would not be? But he would never have wanted you to feel tied like that — *suffocated!* No one who cared anything for you would wish it, and nor would I. You said once that we could be friends, or we could be lovers, or we could be husband and wife, and whichever one we settled on, we both had to want the same thing... do you remember that?" She nodded mutely. "Well, I should like us to be all of those."

"All at once?" she said, chuckling. "That sounds... complicated."

"Very well, then we shall be friends on Mondays and Thursdays, lovers on Tuesdays and Fridays, and respectably married on Wednesdays and Saturdays. How does that sound?"

"How absurd you are! What about Sundays?"

"We shall be excessively pious, and pretend we have never met before." When she laughed and shook her head at him, he went on earnestly, "Do you not see, we can make of marriage whatever we wish... mould it to our own needs. You are not the only one who spent years tiptoeing around another person, Louisa, bending your wishes to those of someone else. I no more want another marriage like that than you do. But you are so different from Catherine, and I, I trust, am not like your Ned, so together we can forge something new, something better suited to our temperaments. I could not bear you to feel *tied* to me, forever walking in my shadow like some kind of timid mouse... like your friend Esther. I want us to stand side by side in the sunshine, to walk hand in hand into the future, facing whatever life throws at us, but *together*. Would that be so terrible?"

"No, not terrible," she said softly. Oh, if only it could be so! A marriage of equals... was it possible? Or would they start in great optimism, only to see all their hopes trickle into dust? "But *marriage!* Even with affection, it is a prison, Laurence. I had a much better marriage than many women, but I still wished to be free. Now I am, and I cannot willingly surrender that freedom. That is why I considered taking a lover, for at least I could forge my own path."

He nodded, his face serious. Dear Laurence! So earnest, and yet he was so much fun to be with. No, marriage to him would not be terrible, but it would still be a cage, the bars solid and immovable.

He leaned back against the wall of the arbour, folding his arms and stretching out his legs again. "Let us talk, then, about lovers. We have discussed it before, and agreed that it would be too inconvenient, what with all that creeping about at night and climbing up drainpipes to reach your bedchamber, and so forth. I cannot help but feel, despite my youthfulness, that my days of climbing drainpipes are over. Yet still the idea has taken root in my mind, and will not quite relinquish its hold. When we kiss..." He stopped with another sigh, then went on more firmly, "When we kiss, the desire to be your lover is... almost overwhelming. But how could it be managed without drainpipes? To walk into your house in broad daylight and whisk you up to your bedroom, however delightful it would be, would inevitably give rise to just the sort of gossip we would both abhor."

"Not merely gossip," she said soberly. "The scandal would damage both our reputations, and adversely affect your family. Any such affair would have to be conducted in the utmost secrecy."

"Exactly so!" he cried. "And I believe I have hit upon the very manner of it — utterly secret, and yet giving rise to no comment at all."

"If that is so, I should be interested to hear of it," she said, although cautiously, for the conversation was a strange one. He had begun by talking of marriage, but now that seemed to have been set aside.

"There are two sets of rooms at the Grove that are connected by a balcony," he said. "Do you see how fortuitous this is? You could have one suite of rooms, and I the other, and when we wish to conduct our secret liaison, I need only climb out of my window onto the balcony, walk along it and climb in through your window. I believe my limbs to be capable of such a feat. We should need to arrange some sort of signal, of course, with lamps or a certain colour of cloth hung in the window, the particular details do not matter. But just think how convenient! And no one any the wiser."

She looked askance at him, not at all sure if he was merely teasing her.

"Of course, there is a small catch," he said ruefully. "No scheme is ever quite perfect, and this one has a tiny flaw as well. Naturally you cannot live at the Grove openly unless we are married, but it is a small technicality and we need not regard it. You could remove your wedding ring whenever we conduct our liaison."

She burst out laughing. "Oh Laurence, what an idiotic man you are!"

"Is that one of my many charms?" he said hopefully.

"Surprisingly, I believe it is," she said. "Are you in earnest? You want us to marry, but pretend we are merely lovers?"

"I am very much in earnest about wanting to marry you," he said, suddenly serious. "I want to be your lover, but it cannot be done without marriage, it seems to me. My conscience would not permit it. Once that became clear to me, everything fell into place and I knew that I wanted to spend the rest of my life with you. I will not press you, however. For me, there have been nine years alone and more than enough time to make me ready for a new venture. For you it is different, I understand that. Take as long as you need, my precious love, and if ever you find you want me as much as I want you, then just say the word."

My precious love… such an endearment made her want to cry. In twelve years of marriage, Ned had never once spoken of love. He had called her *my dear* and he had felt some affection for her, as she had for him, but this… this was different.

"I want…" she began.

"Yes?" he said, leaning forward eagerly.

"I want you to kiss me."

A slow smile spread across his face. "Happy to oblige."

Then she was in his arms, the warmth of his lips on hers, and abruptly all the jagged disconnected worries in her mind slid away into clear certainty. *This* was what she wanted, *this* was where she belonged.

When eventually they parted, she rested her head on his shoulder, his arm still wrapped tightly around her waist. "When we kiss, I feel as if everything in the world is right. All my uncertainties fade away, and I truly want this… to make you happy—"

"No!" he said sharply, jerking away from her. "You are too good, too unselfish, my dearest Louisa, but you must think for once about what would make *you* happy. I want you as my wife, but not as some kind of sacrifice, however willing. There must be more than friendship and affection, there has to be love and passion and longing and great need and desperate yearning. You must not marry me because you feel that you could live with me, but because you find that you cannot live without me. When you feel that life would be unendurable without me, that will be the time for us to marry."

"But what if I never reach that point?"

"Then we will stay as friends. We will *always* be friends," he said, but his voice wavered as he spoke. "Louisa, it seems that I have taken you by surprise. Will you think about all that I have said?"

She nodded, seeing the bleakness in his eyes. Dearest Laurence! So generous, so amazingly generous, and she wanted more than anything in the world to see him happy, but he was right — she had to be true to her own nature and find the life that would make her happy, too. If only she knew what that was.

~~~~~

"Laurence, you go nowhere for years, and now suddenly you are dashing off here there and everywhere," Viola said, a sharp edge to her voice. "Bath and Hereford and then Gloucester... Ursula was quite shocked when you just appeared without warning. And now you are off to Chester, and I am sure there is not the least need for it, none at all. Whatever has got into you?"

They both knew exactly what had got into him, but neither of them mentioned Louisa, perhaps because neither of them could be rational about her. Laurence was both exhilarated that she had not refused him outright and yet disappointed that she had not fallen into his arms. Somehow, now that he had settled in his own mind that they should marry, he had supposed that her views had changed just as much and he was rather downcast to find her just as implacable as ever on the subject.

As for Viola, he saw the strained expression on her face whenever she met Louisa, or even when her name was mentioned. Perhaps Ursula had written to reveal something of her conversation with Laurence. There were no secrets between sisters.
~~~~~

They were in Laurence's bedroom, while John packed the box for the journey. Impulsively, Laurence said, "Vi, come through to Catherine's room for a moment."

He led the way, unlocking Catherine's davenport, and lifting out all her diaries with their so exquisite covers and their shocking interiors.

"Oh... how beautiful!" Viola murmured, gently stroking the covers. "Such delicate stitchwork. Poor, dear Catherine... so accomplished."

"I read them," Laurence said abruptly, for there was no gentle way to say it. "I read every word of them, from the day of her sixteenth birthday, until the day she died."

"Oh, Laurence!" Viola's voice trembled. "You read her *diaries?"*

"She is dead, Vi, and nothing I do can change that. At least now I know what she was like beneath that serene façade. I know that she never cared in the slightest for me or the children. I know that she was in love with—" Should he name him? Could he destroy her good opinion of Malcolm for ever? He could not do it. "She was in love with another man and—"

"No..." Viola whispered.

"—she conducted an adulterous liaison with him."

Viola moaned gently.

"It pains me greatly to tell you this, but it is very necessary. For all these years I have been frozen, unable to move forwards, because I believed that Catherine was perfect and no other woman could possibly compare. But it was not so. She fooled all of us, for she was very far from perfect. And as for *him—!"*

He stopped, his breathing ragged. It was just as well that Malcolm was far away for the urge to rain violence upon him was almost overwhelming. That his own brother should serve him such a trick! But he could not destroy all Viola's illusions at once. It was enough to tell her of Catherine's perfidy, without including Malcolm's name. It was for the best that she should not know of their brother's unforgivable betrayal.

His sister buried her face in her hands, sobbing convulsively.

"Oh Vi, I am so sorry that you should know this, but it is important that you appreciate how it is that I have changed. Knowing all this sets me free at last, free to look elsewhere for happiness. Do you understand?"

She nodded. "You are going to marry her," she said, her voice cracking with emotion.

"I have asked her, but she has not yet given me an answer."

Viola looked up with sudden hope. "Then she may refuse?"

"She may, but that would grieve me very much. Vi, you have been telling me to marry again for years."

"Oh yes, but I never thought you would!" she cried. "I thought I was quite safe."

"Vi, you *are* quite safe. This is your home for as long as you want it, you know that. If I marry Louisa, nothing will change."

"Only a man could say so," she said sadly. "If you marry her, *everything* will change, you mark my words."

He took her hand and raised it to his lips. "Dear Vi! It may be that Louisa will not wish to entrust herself to the care of a man again, so you may yet be safe, but if it should happen... if I should be so fortunate as to secure her, will you be happy for me? And make her welcome here?"

"I shall wish you joy with the greatest of pleasure, my dear brother," she said with dignity. "However, it will be impossible for me to welcome her to this house, for the day she enters it will be the day I leave."

28: *Reunion*

Captain Edgerton had no carriage of his own, so they took Laurence's travelling coach, a great, ponderous contraption with a most luxurious interior, but nothing in its construction to cushion the hapless passengers from every rut and dip and unevenness in the road. Although the weather and the road were dry, Laurence felt as if he had been wallowing aboard a ship in rough seas. Even the stalwart captain looked a little pale when they disembarked at the Albion Hotel in Chester.

Laurence had no expectation of a successful outcome to their journey, for who would remember a young woman who left home more than thirty years ago? All they had was the address of her parents, but at once they struck lucky, for Mr and Mrs Labett were not only still alive, but still in residence at the same house, together with two sons and their families. Laurence, Captain Edgerton and Mr Chandry were shown into a tiny parlour where the elderly couple sat either side of a low fire, swathed in shawls despite the warmth of the day.

"You'll have to shout," said the daughter-in-law who showed them in. "They're both terribly deaf now." Raising her voice, she said to the old people, "Here are some gentlemen from Shropshire to see you. They want to talk to you about Dorothea."

"Dorothea?" said the old lady, brightening. "Have you word of her? Is she found?"

"We have news of her, Mrs Labett," Captain Edgerton said loudly. "I am afraid it is not good news."

"Ah, then she's dead," said the daughter-in-law. "I was afraid of that."

Edgerton told them the story succinctly, while they listened in dignified silence.

"Did she suffer?" Mr Labett said.

"No," Edgerton said at once, although he could not have known it. "No, she did not suffer at all. Did she tell you anything about her life? Did she write to you at all?"

"Oh, yes," Mrs Labett said. "She wrote to us every week, without fail."

"I suppose you do not remember what she said... whether she mentioned the man she was in love with?"

"We practically have all her letters off by heart," the old man said, smiling. "Such a lovely way she had with words. She was always the cleverest of the girls, working so hard as a child to learn her letters and numbers. She was the only one of them who went to school, of the girls, that is. The boys went, of course, but the other girls were content to stay at home with their mother and learn the domestic skills. Not Dorothea, though! She was determined to make something of her life, and she almost did. She was so close to achieving her ambition."

"What was her ambition, Mr Labett?" Edgerton said.

"Why, to marry, of course, but not just anyone. A clerk like her father wasn't good enough for Dorothea. She was going to marry a gentleman, and so she learnt how to be a governess so that she'd have a way to meet such men. Such a clever girl, Dorothea! Why would anyone want to kill her, Captain Edgerton?"

"Until we know who it was, it is impossible to say," Edgerton said. "Did she mention a name? Or tell you anything about him? If you can remember her last words—"

"You can read them," Mrs Labett said. "We have kept all her letters."

And so they had. In a special box for the purpose was every single letter written by Dorothea Labett to her parents, and the very last one laid out all her hopes very clearly.

'My dear Mother and Father, I write to you in the greatest excitement, for all I have ever wished for is about to come to fruition. Can you believe that your humble daughter will shortly become a great lady, with wealth unimaginable and a fine house of my own at last. No longer will I be at the beck and call of insolent children and their haughty parents. No one will despise me ever again, for my future is about to change beyond all recognition. How happy I shall be, and how rich! Tell Jack he may have his apprenticeship after all, for I shall be well able to pay for it. I shall have so much money I shall hardly know what to do with it! I shall write more as soon as all is settled. Your loving daughter, Dorothea.'

"No name," Edgerton said, disappointedly, flicking through several more letters. "She never says his name."

"There is enough here to identify him, surely," Chandry said. "She says she will be a great lady with a fine house, and there cannot be many such around Great Maeswood. We will find him out soon enough."

~~~~~

Louisa found herself greatly troubled in mind, and it was all Laurence's fault. How perfectly hare-brained of him to fall in love with her and start talking about marriage in that ridiculous way! And just as she had settled her future to her own satisfaction, too. She had given up all thought of taking a lover — what a foolish scheme that had been, she quite accepted that now. She had even abandoned her plan to move to Bath. Great Maeswood was clearly not sufficiently far away from Pamela, but somehow, with her friends around her, she felt she could withstand even Pamela's visitations. She would stay in the Dower House and improve the garden and be boringly respectable.

And now Laurence wanted to marry her. What would it be like, such a marriage? She did not have to struggle to imagine it. There would be smiles over the breakfast table. There would be long, long walks with all the dogs. There would be rainy afternoons beside the fire with their books, partly reading and partly discussing this point or that. The evenings would be filled with leisurely dinners and cards and conversation — endless conversations over the Cognac. And at the end of the day, she would have her lover, too.

Of course, it would not be just the two of them. Henrietta and Edward would be a part of their lives for many years to come, and Miss Gage, too. There would be friends and evening engagements and morning calls and perhaps stays in London or Bath. But always at the heart of it would be Laurence, the sun around whom her world orbited.

Which was exactly the trap he had pointed out to her. Naturally she would accede to his wishes and then... she would
~~~~~

suffocate. It was madness. Barely a year since Ned had died and already she was contemplating surrendering her longed-for freedom. No, she could not do it. And yet somehow, the thought of it filled her head.

Worse, she missed him abominably. Why did he have to keep going away, depriving her of his friendship? The emptiness that had haunted her marriage and her year of mourning had disappeared when she had moved into the Dower House... when she had met Laurence. That day when he had brought her a whole box of wine, and they had sat drinking together in the butler's room as if they had known each other for ever... that was when the emptiness had vanished. When he went to Bath, it had gnawed at her again, but then he came home. And now he had gone again.

Was it love, this strange feeling? Was that what she had lacked, all those years with Ned? She could not tell, and somehow it evaded all her efforts to analyse it. If she attempted to examine her own heart rationally, the feeling slithered away from her, like the tiny speck in one's eye that moves whenever one tries to look at it. She could not trust to so flimsy a sentiment, so seemingly ephemeral that she felt it might fly away at any moment. It was hardly a firm enough foundation for marriage. There needed to be solid, reasoned arguments in favour before one made such a serious commitment, and there was no reason to marry Laurence, none at all. She had ample money to live upon, her own home, her friends and her reputation was intact. She could still enjoy Laurence's company as his friend, so what need was there to marry? And he had told her very clearly not to marry just because she could contemplate living with him, but only if she found she could not live without him. And she could, perfectly well, so that was an end to it.

So she went about her daily round, telling herself sternly that she had no desire whatsoever to marry Laurence, and yet thinking about him every moment. He was her first thought when she woke, her last before she slept and he haunted every waking moment. He so distracted her that she twice walked to the village and forgot why she was there, she received an agonised letter from Esther asking why she had not written for an age, and she was so wrapped in her thoughts one day as she drove the gig that the pony turned out of the Dower House drive and straight in through the gates of the Hall. Louisa arrived at the stables almost before she knew what was happening.

"Good day again, Mrs Middlehope!" the head groom called out cheerfully, looking up from the coach wheel he was inspecting. "We haven't seen you for a while. Thought Goronwy was getting the hang of it."

"So did I," she said. "The little fellow is determined not to change his ways. Do you know, I think he will be happier here. You may keep him, and the gig, too. "

Nimbly she jumped down from the gig, and set off to walk back through the park to the Dower House, collecting the dogs from the stables where she had left them not ten minutes earlier.

"Come along, you two. It seems I am not going to Market Clunbury after all, so we can go for a very long walk instead."

They entered into the project with enthusiasm, bounding away down the drive and across the road into the lane that ran between the Grove and the Glebe. Louisa followed them, not really caring where she went, head down, lost in her own thoughts. So it was that she found herself emerging from the lane into a hamlet, no more than a dozen or so cottages, sleeping peacefully in the sun. This must be Lower Maeswood. An old woman sitting outside peeling vegetables waved cheerfully to her, and two small children ran to see the dogs, who promptly rolled over to be tickled. They tired of the game even before Louisa reached them and streaked away again, this time through a pair of ivy-clad wrought iron gates enticingly left ajar.

"Mercury! Mars!" she called, but without much hope of being attended to. Mercury's nose appeared momentarily inside the gate, then off he went again. Laughing, Louisa squeezed through the gap between the gates and followed him. As she brushed the ivy aside to pass through, a metal sign became visible — *'Lower Maeswood Grove'*. This, then, must be another, long disused, entrance to the Grove. On the other side of the gates, the drive was almost invisible beneath burgeoning weeds, and the towering trees of an avenue cast the way into deep gloom. The dogs were invisible in the undergrowth to one side of the drive, but their progress was marked by snapping twigs and rustling leaves and every so often they bounded back to her for reassurance, then off again.

After about a half hour of walking, long after the drive had dwindled to a mere track, the gloomy overgrown avenue gave way to more orderly parts of the garden, and above the highest shrubs, she could see the smoke rising from the chimneys of the house. There was a dried-out fountain not far away with a rusty metal bench nearby, and here she sat, watching a blackbird rummaging for grubs and beetles in the cracked and debris-laden bowl of the pool. The dogs, tiring by now, came and sat at her feet, and absently she stroked their heads and ran her hands over their soft fur.

This, she supposed, was the way her life would be from now on. Long walks with the dogs, long evenings with her books, two card parties a week and the occasional dinner invitation. Most of the time, the dogs would be her only companions. Laurence would be there sometimes, but there would be so many hours alone. Months, years, decades alone. She was thirty years old, and she might, if she were very fortunate, live for another fifty. Five decades of being alone. These dogs would grow up and mature and die, and others would take their place, and yet others, and still Louisa would be alone. Her longed-for freedom from the tyranny of matrimony merely set her free to be lonely.

She cried. There was no comfort to be found in such thoughts. No friendship, not even Laurence's, could protect her from such a future. The only answer was family... marriage...

The dogs' heads lifted in unison, then abruptly they bounded off again towards the house. Wiping her tears away with her sleeve, she followed them.

Could she do it? Could she submit to marriage again? Perhaps in a year or two...

Three dogs raced back towards her, then a fourth.

"Kenneth! Julian! Hail and well met, my friends. How lovely to see you again." She bent to stroke Kenneth's head as he nuzzled against her. "So who is with you today?" She caught a glimpse in the distance of a man following them with the look of a gamekeeper about him. "Is it—?"

Laurence!

Her heart leapt with joy and she let out a little cry of delight. She turned towards him with eager steps, faster and then faster until she was running in good earnest, the sooner to be with him. He was rushing towards her with just as much urgency, his face alight with happiness, his arms held out to her and then she was there, swept into his embrace so firmly that she was lifted clean off her feet and swung round in a circle, as her lips found his. They kissed, laughed, kissed again and again, laughed some more.

When the wave of elation which had swept them together had ebbed a little, he held her tight in his arms and she closed her eyes and rested her cheek on the rough wool of his coat with a sigh of contentment.

"Louisa?" he murmured, his voice very close.

"Mmm?"

"Does this mean... dare I hope that... have you... changed your mind?"

"Oh yes."

"You will marry me?"

She lifted her face to see his incredulous expression. "I will. I looked into my future without you and realised that it would be bleak and desolate and unbearably lonely. I cannot imagine what took me so long to see that."

"Nor can I," he said innocently. "It is quite unaccountable, so charmingly irresistible as I am."

"Idiotic man! But Laurence, you know I can never have children?"

"Then you will just have to share mine," he said equably. "Shall you mind having Viola living with us? She has some absurd notion of leaving if we marry, and—"

"I sincerely hope she *will* stay," Louisa said at once. "I am hopeless at managing a house, and depended utterly on my mother-in-law and the servants at Roseacre. I am perfectly willing to depend utterly on your sister instead. However, there may be one point of conflict and I have to tell you, Laurence, that I am implacable on the matter. I cannot marry you unless Chambers can have free rein in the kitchen."

He laughed out loud. “You will find no objection from me on that score. Mrs Rogers is competent enough in her way and has an excellent hand with a sponge, and her rabbit pie is incomparable, but to my regret she cannot make a good soufflé. We will find a way to arrange matters to accommodate Chambers, and all your servants. Viola is always saying she would like another footman and a housemaid or two. Do you wish to have the bedroom at the other end of the balcony? I will climb in and out of windows if it is what you truly want, but I cannot help thinking we would be more comfortable in adjoining bedrooms.”

“Or the same bedroom,” she said softly. “My parents always shared a room and their marriage seemed to thrive on it.”

He went very still. “Do you know, that seems like a *wonderful* idea,” he said huskily. “This is going to be a very different kind of marriage from my last.”

“For me also,” she said. “We shall make a life that suits us both, Laurence.”

29: A Bonnet For Miss Gage

Louisa had rather hoped they could have a quiet hour together before facing the world again, but Laurence was impatient.

"Let us tell everyone at once!" he cried, his face alight with enthusiasm. "They must share our happy news. I cannot wait to see their faces."

Louisa felt she could wait quite easily. The children... well, children were adaptable, but Miss Gage was another matter. She had never taken to Louisa and would have her view of her as a predatory widow fully confirmed. Still, there was no use in putting it off. Depositing the dogs at the stables, Laurence marched into the house with Louisa firmly on his arm and sent Skeates to summon the family to the Roman Saloon, which he deemed suitable for an announcement of such import. They came scurrying in, and sat in a line on the sofa, Miss Gage anguished, Henrietta excited, Edward frowning, still clutching his Latin book.

"You will be delighted to hear that Mrs Middlehope has consented to become my wife," Laurence said, resting his hand on hers where it lay on his arm. "I need not tell you that this makes me very happy, and grateful for my good fortune. You may be assured that this need not cause any disruption to our settled way of life. We shall go on just as before except that Louisa will be added to our little family."

"Will you still give me lessons?" Edward said.

"Of course. Nothing will change."

His face lifted, and Louisa could only marvel at the confidence of a man who could inflict a new wife on his family, not to mention her entire household, and say without the slightest hesitation that nothing would change. Perhaps that truly was the way he saw it, that Louisa would simply fill an empty corner of his life and everything else would go on exactly as before. She knew otherwise.

"Oh, I am so, so happy for you!" Henrietta cried, bursting out of her seat to try to wrap her arms around both of them. "I knew it would happen, I knew it! Honora said you would never marry again, Papa, but I could see how much happier you have been since Mrs Middlehope came to the village. May I be a bridesmaid? Please?"

"Naturally," Louisa said, laughing, but she was scarcely heard over Henrietta's effusions.

After a while, Laurence said, "Enough, child. Louisa will come to dinner and we can discuss it further then, but for the moment you and Edward should return to your lessons."

And then there was only Miss Gage, sitting rigidly on the sofa, her hands tightly clenched, on the verge of tears.

Louisa knelt at her feet, and gently took one of her hands. "Dear Miss Gage, forgive me for disrupting your life in this abominable way, but truly I could not help falling in love with your brother. He is just too delightful for me to resist. But I promise you I have no wish to overturn all your arrangements, and I wish with all my heart that we can be friends and go on comfortably together. The momentous step I am taking and the responsibilities I am taking on terrify me. Not just Laurence, but Henrietta and Edward, too, and this house… I shall need all the help I can get."

"But you managed Roseacre," Miss Gage said.

"Roseacre managed itself, as it had done for generations, and I was too lazy to interfere. I liked to dabble in the gardens, and I should love to do so here, if you and Laurence will not mind it, but it would be the utmost relief to me to leave the house in your capable hands, and not have to muddle through it myself."

"It is so *difficult!"* she burst out. "And it will be worse with another mouth to feed, and then there will be children, and—"

"No children," Louisa said firmly. "Not for me."

"Even so… you are so *expensive,"* Miss Gage said. "You like everything of the best, and it is so hard to budget as it is, and I could not stay to watch you ruin Laurence, truly I could not."

Louisa sat back on heels. "Is that the problem — money? There is no need for you to worry about that."

"No, indeed," Laurence said. "I shall have the income from Catherine's money again, Vi, I explained all that."

"Only until Henrietta marries! Another two or three years, and that money will be gone, and then were will we be? We shall end up as poor as the Cokelys, I know it, and I could not bear it."

"But I have my jointure," Louisa said.

"Not if you remarry," Miss Gage said. "A widow always loses her jointure if she remarries."

"Not always. My father settled all his money on me that was not tied to the estate, which was a considerable amount, and since I have no children to claim a share of it and my husband was a generous man, it is all mine, with no conditions. I have an income of six thousand pounds a year, Miss Gage."

She squeaked in astonishment.

"Good God!" Laurence said. "You are richer than I am. That makes me a fortune hunter, I suppose."

"Except that you knew nothing of it," she said, laughing, rising to her feet and taking his hands. "You are not going to cry off, I hope? We have been betrothed for less than an hour, and it would be humiliating to be jilted quite so rapidly."

"I would throw you over at once, naturally, except that honour obliges me to marry you, although under the greatest protest, you understand. No doubt I will grow accustomed to the misery of great wealth in time."

"If you truly hate the idea, I can give it all away, and we can live in contented poverty. I should not wish to begin married life by displeasing you."

Miss Gage squeaked again, in alarm this time, and Louisa was instantly contrite. To have all one's monetary worries swept away and then reinstated mere seconds later must be desperately unsettling.

"No, no, no! I am not in earnest, I assure you. I could never live in poverty, not even to please Laurence."

Laurence laughed and said, "Vi, you will have to get used to the way we tease each other."

"Oh, thank goodness! Such a sum! How wonderful! Pray forgive me for saying you were expensive, Mrs Middlehope. I had not the least idea."

"I shall only forgive you if you call me Louisa."

"Oh! Oh, how kind you are, *dear* Louisa. Goodness me, six thousand a year! And Laurence's income, too. Why, think how comfortable we shall all be. Perhaps I shall buy a new bonnet for the wedding. Dear Lucy will make me something suitable. You are not planning to rush off and get a licence, or anything so precipitate?"

Louisa smiled at her. "I promise we shall not marry until Miss Cokely has made you a bonnet."

"Oh good, for I should like to do you credit. It is not every day that one acquires a new sister. Shall we have some tea now? I am sure you are ready for a cup. Laurence, dear, will you ring the bell?"

~~~~~

Laurence enjoyed dinner that evening. Edgerton made an eloquent little speech wishing the betrothed couple a long and happy life. There was champagne, followed by his finest claret in honour of the occasion. He need not conserve his supplies any longer, for he could afford to fill his cellar again. Best of all, he had the pleasure of Louisa sitting beside him, and for once he was permitted to devote all his attention to her without Viola glowering at him.

Captain Edgerton and Mr Chandry were full of amusing anecdotes, the captain managing to raise the occasional smile from Viola and Henrietta blushing furiously under Chandry's gallantry. Laurence could only hope his daughter was sensible enough not to have her head turned by the attention. He would
~~~~~

not be entirely sorry to see Edgerton and his friends leave, amusing as they were.

When the ladies and Edward had withdrawn, Edgerton produced a slip of paper.

"Your estimable future wife has compiled this list of possible murderers for us, Gage. All the single men of the district are listed there. However, we may safely exclude the farmers and the like. Miss Labett has told us clearly that she was to marry a great man with a fine house, and there are not many who fulfil those criteria. Here, what do you make of it?"

He looked at the list, in Louisa's neat handwriting.

'~~Lord Saxby~~ betrothed

John Winslade

~~Luke Winslade~~ in India

Roland Beasley

Zachariah Gage

~~Kenneth Gage~~ in prison

John Brownsmith from the Boar's Head

Several Vale brothers from the farm

Harry Smallwood (the smith before Thomas Preece)'

"Great-uncle Zachariah! Good Lord, but he was an old man and had not two beans to his name, let alone a fine house or unimaginable wealth. He came into a tidy inheritance later, but he was pretty well destitute at the time. Roland Beasley? His house is modest, and he did not even have it, then. It was his aunt's. And if we exclude the innkeeper, the farmers and the smith... we are left with... Winslade. That seems unlikely."

"What about Lord Saxby?" Edgerton said. "He was betrothed but Miss Labett might have thought he would throw over the lady."

"He would never have done so," Laurence said. "No gentleman ever would, and Miss Labett had mingled with the gentry for long enough to understand that. I never particularly liked Saxby, but he was very conscious of his position and the honour of the family name. Besides, he was not the type to plot a murder, I should have said. He was hot-headed and impulsive, so I can imagine him lashing out in a rage, but this was more carefully contrived. Nor do I see Winslade as a murderer, to be frank. Or Beasley, either, come to that."

"There I can only agree with you," Edgerton said. "Having seen both Winslade and Beasley with Miss Labett's remains, and their perfect ease in talking of her and examining her, without the least consciousness, it is inconceivable that either of them might have been responsible for her death. I should very much like it to have been Saxby, if only because the fellow is dead, which would spare everyone a great deal of unpleasantness, but I cannot see it."

"The letter did not actually mention marriage," Chandry said. "She only said that she would be in a position of great wealth. Is it possible that she was Saxby's mistress?"

"That is an interesting thought," Edgerton said. "Was he likely to take a mistress, Gage?"

Laurence frowned, considering. "I would not have said so, for he was careful with his money and the expense would have been high, but who can say? He was some years older than I, so I did not know him well at that time. My father always said that he was wild in his younger days, but that marriage had settled him. Even if it were so, why would he kill his mistress? Why would anyone do so? If she were angling for marriage and he was reluctant, I can perhaps see him becoming embroiled in a violent quarrel, but if she were willing to be his mistress, there would be no need to kill her."

Edgerton heaved a frustrated sigh. "You are right, of course. Murder is such an extreme response that tiring of a lover is hardly sufficient cause. It is a mystery. Shall we join the ladies? Perhaps your delectable betrothed may be persuaded to join us in a rubber of whist."

~~~~~

Louisa saw Laurence every day, and now it was not merely hoped-for accidental meetings but by arrangement. They walked with the dogs, rode together, received the congratulations of their neighbours side by side, and dined together, either at the Grove or at the Dower House. Laurence took her round the upper rooms of the Grove to choose a bedroom, and Viola showed her all the formal rooms and the domestic offices. Chambers inspected his future domain, and deemed it worthy. He and Mrs Rogers eyed each other warily, but Louisa sat them down and drew up a list of responsibilities to prevent hostilities.

"Shall we go and see Truman about the banns?" Laurence said one day as they sat in the secret arbour, the younger dogs racing each other through the undergrowth while Ian sat beside them. "Or would you prefer me to obtain a licence? There is no need to wait, is there?"

Louisa exhaled slowly. "Well… I shall have to go north to retrieve my books first. I cannot settle without them, and Pamela and Thomas have made a complete muddle of the library at Roseacre, and cannot tell what is mine."

"We could marry first and make it part of our honeymoon trip, if you like."
~~~~~

"If you do not object violently, I think this is something I have to do alone. I must make my peace with Pamela and convince her, if I can, that I am not grieving excessively over Ned or my non-existent children, and if I cannot do that, I shall have to learn to accept her ways, trying as I find them. If you are with me, it will be all too easy to hide behind you and not address the problem head on. Do you see? But I shall only be gone for a little while. A week, or two at most. Then, when I have all my books, we can think about a wedding."

He smiled and gently brushed her cheek with one finger, so that she smiled in pleasure at his touch. "It shall be just as you wish, my precious love."

Before she could leave, however, it was necessary to accompany Viola to Miss Cokely's to order a wedding bonnet.

"You have such an eye for styles, Louisa," Viola said. "I can never tell what would suit me, and then I feel obliged to buy something dear for poor Lucy's sake. Will you help me choose?"

Naturally, such an appeal could not be refused, so to Miss Cokely's they went. For a good half an hour, the three ladies set about their appointed task with the seriousness it deserved. Once the style had been agreed upon, however, and the more frivolous matters of ribbons and frills and decorative touches were all that remained, the conversation turned in other directions.

"Is there any news about poor Miss Labett?" Miss Cokely said. "Is there any suspicion as to who may have murdered the unfortunate woman?"

"None at all," Viola said at once. "It is the most shocking thing, for she claimed that she was to marry a wealthy man with a fine house, but no one of that nature would conceivably *kill* her, would they?"

Louisa was struck with a sudden thought. "You must remember her, Miss Cokely. You were in the village at the time."

"Oh yes! I remember her quite well, for she was the last governess here for quite some time... until the girls at the Hall began to grow up."

"Can you think of any bachelors in the neighbourhood that we might have forgotten? We have only Squire Winslade, Mr Beasley and Lord Saxby who fit the picture of a wealthy man of property."

"No... I cannot think of anyone else, and none of them—Well, Thomas Saxby had a temper, but he would hardly *murder* anyone."

"And he was betrothed," Viola put in. "Miss Labett disappeared not two days before his betrothal party."

"Was the betrothal a sudden affair?" Louisa said. "Might he have dallied with Miss Labett and then seized the opportunity to drop her for an advantageous match?"

"Oh, no," Miss Cokely said. "The marriage had been under discussion for almost a year, and he was very set on it. The Makenhams are a most respectable family, you know...an earl, in fact."

"A marquess now," Viola said. "Henrietta Makenham was a great heiress, too, so it was a very good match altogether. Lucy, do you think this is too dark a green?"

Louisa, losing interest in ribbons, wandered over to Mrs Cokely at her usual seat in the window. "Good day to you, Mrs Cokely. You are well, I trust?"

"Mr Birch's boy went past at eleven minutes past twelve, taking the meat to Mr Exton." She tapped the clock on the table beside her with her pencil.

"I still have not met Mr Exton," Louisa mused. "One of two people I have a great interest in knowing, but since the other is dead, I must rest my hopes in Mr Exton."

Mrs Cokely withdrew her gaze from the window to look directly at Louisa. "Dead but not forgotten. He troubles us still, Thomas Saxby."

"What was he like?" Louisa said, thrilled by this sudden lucidity.

"Bad man," she said. "Money... he was only interested in the money. Took him months to convince the earl. So strait-laced, the Makenhams and they saw through him. He would have done anything to get his hands on that money. Ha!" Her head snapped back to the window. "Birch's boy is back again. Three minutes before the half hour." She tapped the clock again, then made a note in the book beside her.

"What would he have done?" Louisa said anxiously, but the moment had passed.

"Birch's boy returned at three minutes before half past twelve." Tap.

"Tell me more about Lord Saxby."

"Birch's boy went past at eleven minutes past twelve." Tap.

Louisa gave it up.

She was almost home, Viola chatting merrily at her side, before she understood. "He would have done *anything* to get his hands on that money," she said, stopping dead.

"Louisa, dear? Are you all right?"

"I must find Captain Edgerton. *At once!*"

30: A Promise For The Future

It was a full hour before Captain Edgerton returned from a ride, and Louisa paced about the Grove library the whole time, while Viola twittered anxiously. Laurence, more amused than concerned, plied her with sherry and macaroons.

Eventually the captain and Mr Chandry arrived, coming straight from the stables.

"Skeates tells us that Mrs Middlehope is in agitation, and we cannot have that," the captain said, bowing to her. "Pray tell us what we may do to help."

"It was Lord Saxby!" she cried. "Because of his engagement to Henrietta Makenham and her fortune. He would have done anything for that money, according to Mrs Cokely. She says he was a bad man. It must have been him."

"But he was betrothed, so—" Mr Chandry began, but Louisa waved that aside.

"Yes, yes, but Miss Labett threatened his marriage. He killed her so that she would not interfere with his plans."

Captain Edgerton accepted a glass of sherry and said thoughtfully, "So you think he got tangled up with Miss Labett, and then he wanted to marry Miss Makenham so he... killed the governess?"

"No, the marriage was in his mind for almost a year. Her family were against it seemingly, but he managed to convince them in the end and there was to be a big party to celebrate the betrothal. Dorothea Labett and her child would have interfered with that. She put him under pressure and he killed her."

"Why not simply pay her off?" Laurence said. "Reprehensible as it is, there are many men who behave in such a way and then shuffle the girl off to a cottage somewhere with an annuity."

"I think she was ambitious," Louisa said. "We know from her previous behaviour that she was set on getting a rich husband for herself. She knew that Lord Saxby would never agree to that, so she set herself to embarrass him. Would that have worked? Would a pregnant governess have destroyed his marriage?"

"Possibly, but what would that achieve?" Captain Edgerton said. "How could she—"

"Blackmail!" Viola said abruptly, then went pink as they all turned to her in surprise. "She was a devious little madam, and she probably cared less for the man than his money. If she could get that another way, she would have. And Thomas would never have given in to that. There would have been no end to her demands, and the constant risk of a scandal, threatening his income from his wife's money. It was all in trust, you know, and the trustees could have turned off the tap at any moment. He loved his money, and I have no idea what he spent it on, for he was never extravagant."

"Blackmail... yes, that makes sense," Captain Edgerton said slowly. "And that is a relief, for the fellow is dead and we need not drag a baron through the ignominy of the Assizes."

"But disappointing that you will not now need to deploy your pistols or sword," Louisa said, smiling.

"That is indeed a disappointment," the captain said solemnly. "One always expects a murder case to reach a spectacular conclusion, with the miscreant cornered and fighting for his very life. It is rather like having the generals lining up their armies for a battle, and then deciding to turn round and go home. Still, no doubt it is all for the best that the culprit is no longer with us. In fact, since we can prove none of it, we may legitimately tell the world that the murder cannot be resolved after so many years. There is no need to distress the Saxby family with any of this, but I think we may set the case to rest now. Excellent work, ladies. If ever you want employment as crime-solvers, do let me know."

"Oh, no, Captain! No, no, no!" Viola cried, taking him seriously. "I hope I never encounter another murder ever again. It has all been most disagreeable. *Most* disagreeable!"

But her eyes sparkled with pleasure as she spoke.

~~~~~

'Bath, 10th August. My dear Gage, I have excellent news from the front to report, for the enemy is routed at all points and the field is ours, or yours, I should say. The magistrates have been most obliging, and the false Mrs Haywood and her devious friends have fled in the night before they were arrested, taking little more than the clothes they stood up in. They seem not to have had the foresight to provide themselves with easily portable funds in case of such an eventuality, having accumulated all their unspent ill-gotten wealth in the High Street Bank against the day when your
~~~~~

daughter marries and claims her inheritance in full. You are now the proud owner of a rather good house, fully furnished and supplied with six servants, and the sum of twenty-two thousand four hundred pounds. I congratulate you, sir. May I thank you for allowing me the very great privilege of acting on your behalf in this matter. I cannot remember when I have last enjoyed myself so much. Your very grateful servant, Pettigrew Willerton-Forbes. Post Script ~ I am delighted to hear that the matter of Miss Labett's death has been resolved to the satisfaction of the good captain, but I regret to inform you that he is fully determined on discovering the fate of Miss Dilys Hughes next, so you will have to suffer our company for a while longer.'

~~~~~

The day before Louisa's departure for the north, Laurence was to dine alone with her for the first time. He arrived well before the appointed time, bearing a bottle of claret in one hand and Cognac in the other. He had expected the house to be in uproar with a whirlwind of packing going on, but he found her stretched out on the chaise longue in her study, book in hand.

"Are you not supposed to be panicking?" he said, between kisses. "Or at the very least, rushing about looking harassed."

"That sounds too exhausting for words. Marie is packing, and what else is to be done? Thank you for lending me your travelling carriage, and your coachman, too. Sarah and I will be most comfortable in it."

"Sarah? You are not taking Marie?"

Louisa shook her head, the curls on either side of her forehead bobbing in a manner he found adorable. "Marie had the most dreadful journey south, and I will not inflict that on her again, poor girl. All the way to Durham and back in that carriage of yours would bring her to death's door, and she is far too good
~~~~~

with my clothes to risk it. Will your people keep an eye on her? And the others, too?"

"Of course, but will you truly be away for two weeks?" he said, aware that his voice had grown wistful. "How shall I manage?"

She smiled and stroked his cheek gently. "It cannot be done in much less. Four days each way, and I do not know how long it will take to sort out these books. But it is the last tie with Roseacre, and once that is severed I shall be free of it. I do not think Pamela will descend upon the Grove as readily as she descended upon me here. I must hope so, anyway."

"She is not quite the monster you like to portray her as, I feel," he said gently.

"A monster? Oh no! Just an irritant, like a persistently buzzing fly. Poor Pamela! I am so hard on her, I know. She means it for the best, and the fault is mine, I am fully aware, so I intend to make my peace with her once and for all. Whenever she rubs me the wrong way, I shall remember that I have you waiting for me at home, and smile benignly at her. I suspect a great deal of her anxiety on my account is guilt. She feels that Roseacre and the title should have been mine, and that she has wronged me somehow. Once she accepts that I am perfectly happy without those things and learns how to manage as a baroness, she will be a great deal less irritating."

"Are you truly happy without those things?"

"Indeed I am. It is very fortunate that there were no children, for just think how lonely I should be now, trapped in that great house with no one but a small child or two for company. No, I am better by far here. And I have you, my love, so how could I not be happy? I am so glad you agreed to dine with me tonight, for two hours over the card table, sharing you with the Beasleys and a dozen others, is not adequate to sustain me through so long a separation."

"I trust Chambers has devised something very special for us," he said.

"You may be assured of it."

Over the first course, the conversation turned to the unfortunate Miss Labett.

"It is still hard to believe that Lord Saxby — a baron, no less — murdered that poor woman in cold blood," Louisa said. "Do you believe it? He was a friend of yours, after all."

"Not a friend," Laurence said cautiously. "Never that, but naturally we had many years of acquaintance... of parish meetings and the like, as well as socially, although we had little in common. He was a sportsman through and through — riding to hounds, shooting, driving that curricle as fast as he could. Did you know that he paid personally to maintain that straight stretch of road to Astley Cloverstone, purely so that he could stretch the legs of those horses of his? It was no great surprise that he met his end there, although it could just as easily have been jumping his hunter. He never did anything in moderation. Whereas I am perfectly happy with a bit of rough shooting, just me and the dogs, or spending all day at the river to put some fish on the table. He had a temper, too, when roused. But murder... it is hard to imagine. The need must have been desperate."

"He does not sound like the sort of man who would be cornered by a governess," Louisa said. "How would he even meet her? She would hardly have been in society."

"She only had Ursula in the schoolroom then, but she used to chaperon all three of the girls around the village, and sometimes to evening engagements when Mama had one of her turns."

"Ah, of course, and no doubt she threw herself at his head. She does not exactly sound like a demure miss. Yet she must have known that he would never marry her, so it was a foolish risk, unless she intended to blackmail him all along."

"You think she planned it?" Laurence said, startled. "An ambitious woman who miscalculated, perhaps, but—"

"There was no miscalculation," Louisa said. "Now that I consider it carefully, I am certain of it. Lord Saxby's marriage was under discussion for a long time, and he was determined to succeed. Miss Labett intentionally entrapped him, knowing that he would never marry her. Then, just before his betrothal was made official, with all the arrangements made, she told him that she carried his child. No doubt she threatened to reveal her condition to his betrothed's rather starchy family unless he paid her a large sum of money."

"He would not have liked to be out-manoeuvred in that way," Laurence mused. "That would definitely have angered him. Nor would he have wanted to pay her off, for very likely she would not have been satisfied with a single payment, but would have returned again and again to drink from the same well. There would have been no end to it. And so he told her he would take care of her, arranged for her to bring all her things to the Dower House, where he murdered her. Poor woman! What she did was very wrong, but she did not deserve such a fate. And now I wonder if the same thing may have happened to Dilys Hughes. She was a housemaid at the Hall, remember, so she could have been another of Lord Saxby's victims."

"Except that she took the stage to Shrewsbury," Louisa said, reaching for another helping of the artichokes. "Whatever became of her, she did not die at Lord Saxby's hand."

After dinner, they strolled along the road to the Beasleys' house, waving to Mrs Cokely as they passed the cottage.

"She is still at her post," Louisa said. "I daresay our passing is noted in her book. *'Mr Gage and Mrs Middlehope, hand in hand, at fourteen minutes before eight.'* Poor woman."

"She was used to be so clever, too," Laurence said. "Cokely was a well-meaning man but dreadfully shatter-brained, and Mrs Cokely and Lucy ran the parish between them. I hate to see them so sadly reduced."

"Miss Cokely is an excellent milliner, and I plan to buy a great many bonnets from her," Louisa said firmly.

It was after eleven o'clock before they left the Beasleys' card party, a fine, clear moon guiding their steps and rendering Laurence's lantern unnecessary.

"Will you come in for a Cognac?" Louisa said with her warm smile, as they walked up the Dower House drive.

He could not resist, of course. William opened the door for them, unsurprised to see Laurence follow Louisa into the study.

"You may lock up downstairs and go to bed, William," Louisa said. "I will bolt the front door. And tell Marie I shall not need her again tonight. There is no point in her waiting up for hours."

Laurence poured the Cognac, while Louisa lit more candles.

"There, that is better," she said, settling on the floor, her back against the chaise longue. "So what will you do with yourself while I am gone?"

He sat beside her, wrapping one arm around her, and she snuggled against him in a way that warmed him to his core. Oh the bliss of loving, and being loved in return!

"Tomorrow I am to spend the evening at Exton's."

Louisa raised an eyebrow. "The mysterious Mr Exton. Do tell me what is wrong with him that he hides away in his house all the time."

"There is nothing at all wrong with him, except grief for his dead wife that makes him unequal to company. And guilt, perhaps, since his wife died in childbirth, just as Catherine did. He knows I understand that, so he has made me something of a friend. His only friend, in truth. He is a very sad man."

"Ah, the sting of guilt," Louisa said. "Yet a husband can hardly be blamed if his wife dies in that dreadful manner."

"The rational mind agrees with you, but a man's heart is not rational, my dear, not on such a subject. He has caused his wife's condition and therefore must carry his share of the blame. So his conscience whispers. It is an almost intolerable pain, and keeps a man only half alive until he is so fortunate as to find a reason to return to the living world. I had the children, and now you, my precious Louisa, but Exton has not yet emerged from his darkness."

"Then I sincerely pity him, and hope that your company will alleviate his despair for a few hours. Guilt is a dreadful companion. Do you know, I think it was guilt which led to my supine behaviour with Ned. Because I could not give him the son he needed, I felt unable to do as I wished, even though he urged me to be free."

Laurence smiled and kissed her gently. "Guilt kept you at Roseacre after he died, as well. Why else stay so long, when

Pamela irked you so? You could have left at any time. And I was guilty about taking Catherine from my brother, when he wanted her so badly. I had never denied him anything before, and I felt dreadful about it. But guilt is a great deceiver, my love. It distorts everything it touches, so that the eye can no longer see clearly, nor the mind accept reason. I hope we can both set it behind us at last."

She snuggled into his arms with a contented sigh. "My marriage was not terrible, and I was never unhappy, but it was not all it could have been."

"It was so for me too," he said. "We will do better this time."

"We will, but Laurence, you must promise me something."

"Anything."

"You must always tell me what is in your heart. There must be no secrets between us, no unspoken wishes, no feelings kept tightly wrapped. Every hope, every fear must be brought into the daylight to be shared and driven away like mist, instead of hanging over us like a heavy blanket, snuffing out all joy. Promise me!"

"I swear it, and let me begin at once by telling you that I love and adore you, but I also see you for the warm, living woman that you are, and not as a goddess come to earth. Regretfully I have no pedestal for you to stand upon, my precious one."

She chuckled, her face alight with mischief. "Thank goodness for that! It must be so tiring, being perfect. I have never put anyone on a pedestal, since I am by far too cynical, but I shall do my very best to see the good in people as well as the bad. Even in Pamela," she added, although the pained expression on her face made Laurence smile. She went on, "But in you, dearest Laurence, there was never any bad to see."

"Ah, my many charms, which you may describe at length."

His arm was so wrapped around her that he felt as well as heard her ripple of laughter. "Idiotic man! But that is one of your greatest charms, it is true, that you are so much fun. I suppose that must be why I love you so much."

He squeezed her tight and buried his face in her hair. But then she lifted her face to his, and for a long time there was no talking, only sweet kisses and the glow of happiness inside him.

Eventually, he sighed. "It is gone midnight. Time for me to leave you to sleep. You have a long day ahead of you."

They both got to their feet, but for a while they simply stood, hands clasped. He gazed at her face, memorising every soft curve, every tiny imperfection, to carry him through the two week separation.

"I shall miss you," she said simply, giving him one last kiss. "Now off you go."

"Do you know, I have forgotten my key," he said, patting his pockets. "I shall have to knock on my own front door, probably rousing half the house before the boy wakes up. How stupid of me."

She giggled. "You could always climb a drainpipe to an upper window."

"What, at my advanced years? I dare not risk it."

"Then you will just have to sleep here tonight," she said softly.

He froze, torn between terror and longing, then cast a glance at the chaise longue. "There?"

"It looks very uncomfortable."

"The guest room?"

"The bed is not made up. There is only one bed available, but there is room for both of us and I shall do my best not to snore."

"Louisa..." he said huskily.

"It is Friday, after all," she said, smiling innocently at him. "It is past midnight, so it is now Friday. Do you not remember? On Mondays and Thursdays, we are friends, but on Tuesdays and Fridays we are lovers. We began the evening as friends, but now we are lovers... if we wish to be."

"Do you wish to be?" His voice sounded odd to his ears.

"I wish us to begin our lives together as we mean to go on, as both friends *and* lovers," she said, holding out her hand to him.

"That sounds wonderful."

He took her hand, and together they blew out the candles and went upstairs.

THE END

The next book in the series is *Stranger at the Grove*, when Laurence's estranged brother is forced by the terms of a will to return to the family fold. Malcolm is not happy about it, but there are intriguing compensations, like pretty French lady's maid Marie Fournier whom he quickly realises is not what she seems. You can read a sneak preview after the acknowledgements or find out more at my website at http://marykingswood.co.uk/.

Thanks for reading!

If you have enjoyed reading this book, please consider writing a short review on Amazon. You can find out the latest news and sign up for the mailing list at the Mary Kingswood website at http://marykingswood.co.uk/.

Family trees and maps: Hi-res versions are available at my website at http://marykingswood.co.uk/.

A note on historical accuracy: I have endeavoured to stay true to the spirit of Regency times, and have avoided taking too many liberties or imposing modern sensibilities on my characters. The book is not one of historical record, but I've tried to make it reasonably accurate. However, I'm not perfect! If you spot a historical error, I'd very much appreciate knowing about it so that I can correct it and learn from it. Thank you!

The great houses: Most of the houses I describe in the books are creations of my imagination, or 'generic' styles of a particular era, but sometimes I base them on real houses. In this series, Maeswood Hall, home of the Saxby family, is based on Stourhead House in Wiltshire, designed by Colen Campbell. Lower Maeswood Grove, where the Gage family lives, is loosely based on the Queen's House, Greenwich, designed by Inigo Jones. The Squire's home, Cloverstone Manor, is based on Hatfield House, another Inigo Jones project.

Isn't that what's-his-name? Regular readers will know that characters from previous books occasionally pop up. Lawyer Mr Willerton-Forbes, his flamboyant sidekick Captain Edgerton and the discreet Mr Neate have been helping my characters solve murders and other puzzles ever since *Lord Augustus*. Michael Chandry, now a crime-solving partner to Captain Edgerton and his pals, was first seen helping after the shipwreck in *The Clerk* and more recently in *The Duke*.

About the *Strangers* series*:* There's a famous saying attributed to John Gardner that authors like to quote: that there are only two plots - a stranger arrives in town, or a person goes on a journey. Most of my books have been based on the latter, in its loosest sense (sometimes a journey of discovery, rather than a literal journey, but a major change, of death or misfortune or even good fortune which propels the main character in a new direction). So I wondered what the other side of the coin would look like - a stranger arriving in town. And there was my series title - Strangers.

Book 0: Stranger at the Parsonage: a new parson arrives at the village of Great Maeswood, and tragedy strikes the baron's family. *(a novella, free to mailing list subscribers).*

Book 1: Stranger at the Dower House: a widow moves into the long disused Dower House and makes a horrible discovery in the wine cellar.

Book 2: Stranger at the Grove: an estranged brother is forced to return to his home and face up to his past.

Book 3: Stranger at the Villa: a new physician arrives in the village, but is he all he seems?

Book 4: Stranger at the Manor: a destitute man comes looking for help from his cousin, and uncovers some mysterious goings-on.

Book 5: Stranger at the Cottage: an out-of-work governess tries to start a school in the village.

Book 6: Stranger at the Hall: the newly discovered heir to the barony arrives to claim his inheritance.

Any questions about the series? Email me at
mary@marykingswood.co.uk - I'd love to hear from you!

About the author

I write traditional Regency romances under the pen name Mary Kingswood, and epic fantasy as Pauline M Ross. I live in the beautiful Highlands of Scotland with my husband. I like chocolate, whisky, my Kindle, massed pipe bands, long leisurely lunches, chocolate, going places in my campervan, eating pizza in Italy, summer nights that never get dark, wood fires in winter, chocolate, the view from the study window looking out over the Moray Firth and the Black Isle to the mountains beyond. And chocolate. I dislike driving on motorways, cooking, shopping, hospitals.

Acknowledgements

Thanks go to:

John Gardner, whose alleged saying about strangers and plots inspired these books.

Allison Lane, whose course on English Architecture inspired me.

Shayne Rutherford of Darkmoon Graphics for the cover design.

Andrew K Lawston, world famous translator of the Chantecoq books, for French language advice.

My beta readers: Tod Crouter, Barbara Daniels Dena, Amy DeWitt, Quilting Danielle, Rosemary Paton and the readers of Rachel Daven Skinner at RomanceRefined

Last, but definitely not least, my first reader: Amy Ross.

Sneak preview of Stranger at the Grove: Chapter 1: The Funeral

MARCH

The rain dripped over the brim of Malcolm's hat as he followed the little procession to the graveside. Why was there always rain at a funeral? As if it was not enough that a man had died to cause the participants to sink into despondency, without the dispiriting grey misery of relentless rain.

The parson began the familiar words. *"Man that is born of a woman hath but a short time to live, and is full of misery. He cometh up, and is cut down, like a flower; he fleeth as it were a shadow, and never continueth in one stay."*

Four working men in their Sunday best, no doubt paid a shilling apiece for their time, laboured to lower the coffin into the ground.

"In the midst of life we are in death: of whom may we seek for succour, but of thee, O Lord, who for our sins art justly displeased?"

Apart from the parson and Malcolm himself, only six men stood around the grave, silently watching. Two were his great-uncle's servants, almost as old and stooped as he had been. Three others were his great-uncle's university colleagues, paying their respects. The sixth was Colville, the attorney.

"Yet, O Lord God most holy, O Lord most mighty, O holy and most merciful Saviour, deliver us not into the bitter pains of eternal death."

Some little distance away, and sensibly sheltering in the lee of one of the yew trees, a small group of neighbours and acquaintances, paying their last respects but not encroaching on the burial itself, since they were not invited. It amused him that they came anyway. How like his great-uncle to specify the precise details of his own funeral, down to the style of the coffin — plain wood, for economy's sake — to the refreshments to be offered the mourners afterwards. Only the official mourners, naturally. But the local people knew what was due to an Oxford man of renown, and so there they were, almost as wet and cold as the smaller group beside the grave.

"We therefore commit his body to the ground; earth to earth, ashes to ashes, dust to dust..."

Several of the mourners stepped forward to cast earth onto the coffin. Symbolic, they would say. Superstitious nonsense, Malcolm thought it. As soon as the clergyman began to move away, Malcolm strode off, glad that the whole business was over.

"Gage? May we offer you a lift?" One of the academics, spider-like in his black, pointed to a waiting carriage.

"Thank you, Monk, but I prefer to walk."

Malcolm's long legs carried him swiftly out of the churchyard and along the road. By the time the academics' carriage and the attorney's gig overtook him, he was already turning into the drive of Maitland House, past the high hedge that hid it from the world, or perhaps hid the world from the house. With Great-uncle Zachariah, either was equally likely.

The cook-housekeeper had the front door open already.

"Well, Mrs Staines, that is the old fellow settled in at the churchyard," Malcolm said.

She smiled at him, patting his arm in a motherly fashion. "Just the will-reading to get through now, Mr Malcolm, and then it will all be over. Goodness, you're wet! Go and have something to warm you up. It's all laid out in the parlour."

All over… that was true enough. The coming night would be his last under the roof of Maitland House, and when he left it, the connection would be severed absolutely. There would be no one left in his life. No family.

The two manservants came rushing in, puffing rather, to receive the gentleman mourners. The hall was already crowded, with a strong smell of damp wool, as they bustled about with dripping hats and greatcoats. Malcolm waited his turn, then followed the others into the parlour.

"Here," the attorney said, pushing a glass into his hand. "I sent Bird out to buy a couple of decent bottles this morning. There are pastries and meat on the sideboard, too."

Malcolm shook his head. He had long since lost his appetite for wine, and never wished to regain it.

"I insist. You will need something to fortify you before... well, it would be best."

For the first time, Malcolm felt a flicker of interest. Before what... the reading of the will? He had no expectations there. Great-uncle Zachariah had a son, after all, and although he had been a ne'er-do-well and a common thief in his youth, no doubt he was a respectable burgher now, and would inherit the house and whatever money had been hoarded away. Not much, he supposed, for the old fellow had never splashed it around.

He took the glass of wine, pretended to take a sip and then ambled over to the sideboard. Tucking the glass behind a bowl of fruit, he found himself a plate and loaded it with as much as it would hold. He might have forsworn intoxicating drink, but food was always acceptable.

"Well, Gage! No doubt we will see more of you during Trinity," Monk said, clapping him on the back so hard that Malcolm almost choked on the meat ball he was eating. "Another of your talks to the Society would be well received."

Swallowing hastily, Malcolm said, "I cannot say when I shall next be in Oxford, sir."

"Now, now, no need to pretend, is there? Surely the house will be yours, and you will be settled here."

"My great-uncle has a son," he said stiffly.

"Fell out, I thought. The boy was worthless and Zachariah cut him off without a penny, so I heard."

"You are misinformed, sir. When Kenneth came out of prison the last time, my great-uncle paid his passage to India and set him up in business out there. He long since forgave him for his youthful follies."

Monk's bushy eyebrows rose in surprise, but he made no further comment, and Malcolm retreated to a quiet corner to eat in peace, and consider that odd quirk of his great-uncle's character. For a man who never attended church, and had told his servants never to allow a man of the cloth across the threshold, he had held to remarkably Christian principles. Forgiveness, he had always said, was the mark of civilisation, above any other virtue. But they had never seen eye to eye on that subject and never would, and eventually they had spoken of it no more.

After a while, Mr Colville called the company through to the drawing room for the reading of the will. Two rows of chairs were set out, but Malcolm sat on the window seat, a little apart. The gentlemen took the front row, and behind them Mrs Staines, the manservants and the wizened old gardener, stiff in his Sunday best, who was older than his master but still put in six full days of work every week, and would no doubt continue to do so until he dropped down dead in the asparagus bed.

The attorney sat behind the mahogany card table. If the old man had left Malcolm anything, and surely he must have done, for he would not have been invited else, he hoped it would be that elegant little table, with its interchangeable tops inlaid with mother-of-pearl to mark out chess or backgammon or cribbage boards. Today it was the plain baize, with Colville's papers laid in a neat pile.

The reading began. The small bequests came first — to the servants, to several charitable institutions, to the Society. A bursary to the college, to support a promising local boy. Then an odd one — *'To my son, Kenneth Gage, last known address Madras, India, my watch, engraved with my name, given to me by my father, but only on the condition that he comes to collect it himself. If he should be dead, then to his heir, if any, with the same condition. If the watch is unclaimed on the fifth anniversary of my death, then it may be given to whomever resides at Maitland House or otherwise at the discretion of my executors.'*

Malcolm had to smile at the old boy's eccentricity. Would anyone travel all the way from India to claim a watch? It seemed unlikely. But when did he lose touch with Kenneth? Quite some time ago, perhaps, for he had not mentioned him for years.

Mr Colville removed his spectacles. "The remainder of the will concerns only Mr Malcolm Gage, and Mr Monk and I, as executors, are agreed that no other person needs to be privy to the contents at this time."

That was unexpected. As everyone shuffled out except Colville and Monk, Malcolm weighed up the possibilities. The house... yes, it must be the house and whatever money the old fellow had. But there was some catch, he knew it. Colville's manner beforehand, suggesting he fortify himself... yes, there must be a condition. Marriage, perhaps, for his great-uncle had been nagging him on that score for years. Or was it more complicated than that? Had his great-uncle left other illegitimate children, besides Kenneth? He was a secretive old buzzard, so anything was possible. But he had left Malcolm *something*, that much was plain. Something to lift him out of this dreadful grinding poverty. A bubble of hope arose inside him.

"Will you not come a little closer, Mr Gage?" Colville said, gesturing towards the now empty seats in the front row.

Reluctantly, Malcolm lounged across the room and took one of the front seats, arms folded and legs stretched out before him.

Colville looked pained at such casualness, but he replaced his spectacles and picked up his papers again. But then he laid them down, and removed the spectacles.

"Mr Gage, I would ask that you listen carefully to the entirety of what follows and not... hmm, not arrive at any precipitate conclusions. The requirements are complicated, and I must insist that you hear the *whole* of your great-uncle's dispositions. Then we may discuss the matter."

"You terrify me, Colville," Malcolm said, amused. "What can possibly be so dire in a will? I presume that there are some devious conditions, but what is that to me? Either I will accept them or I will not. Let me hear the worst."

"But you will not... storm out? Or anything of that nature?"

"I will make every effort not to do so."

Colville stared at him for a moment, as if trying to assess the likelihood that he would or would not. Eventually, with a sigh, he replaced his spectacles, and began to read.

"'To my dear great-nephew, Malcolm Augustus Gage, formerly of Lower Maeswood Grove, in the county of Shropshire, and lately master at Harrow School, in the county of Middlesex, I make the following stipulation, that he should make arrangements with his brother, Laurence Adolphus Gage of the said—"

Malcolm jumped to his feet, fists clenched, boiling with rage.

"'—Lower Maeswood Grove...' Do please resume your seat, Mr Gage. There is a great deal more, and it is very much to your advantage."

Yes, he should hear it all, every last miserable word of his great-uncle's betrayal. *Then* he would walk out. Slowly he sat.

"'...of Lower Maeswood Grove in the county of Shropshire, to instruct his son Edward Henry Gage of the same place of

residence such that the said Edward Henry Gage shall be admitted to the Society of Gentleman Linguists of Oxford, this task to be accomplished within three months of its commencement and in such a manner that the said Malcolm Augustus Gage resides at all times under the same roof as the said Laurence Adolphus Gage. If the task thus described is successful and the said Edward Henry Gage is admitted to the said Society within one year of my death, I bequeath to the said Malcolm Augustus Gage my dwellinghouse, known as Maitland House, together with all my household goods furniture plate linen china and personal effects of whatever sort such as may be found within the said dwellinghouse, for his own absolute use and benefit together with nine tenths of all monies held and invested on my behalf by Fletcher and Parsons of Oxford, and the said Edward Henry Gage shall receive the remaining one tenth part of all the monies so described. If the task thus described is not accomplished successfully, the said house and all monies shall be disposed of in charitable bequests at the discretion of my executors.'"

The silence was absolute. Malcolm sat unmoving. A house… nine tenths of the money, which must be worth a few hundred, at least. Independence, the life of a gentleman… he would never be poor again. He should have howled with rage, but oddly he was now calm. Icy calm. The slimy, devious, scheming, *treacherous* old devil.

"Do you understand, Mr Gage?"

Oh, he understood, all right. He understood perfectly.

"It is a considerable sum," the attorney said, in a wheedling tone. "Above five and twenty thousand for you and almost three thousand for the boy, even after the other bequests. An income of twelve or thirteen hundred a year."

So much! That was a shock. The sly old fellow had been hoarding his money then, for he had never spent so much. He had written several books, of course, or perhaps those ships he liked to invest in had been more profitable than he had suspected. Malcolm would have been a wealthy man…

"It is only three months, Mr Gage, and the boy is very able, by all accounts. It should not be a difficult task, and you would have your house and a good income. Enough to live on quite comfortably. Enough to enable you to marry, should you wish."

Another silence.

"Is it so impossible to spend three months under your brother's roof?" Monk said. "Come, Gage, what do you say?"

Malcolm rose, looking down on the two men disdainfully.

"No." He turned and walked towards the door.

"Mr Gage, I think you should—"

"No. A thousand times no. *Never.*"

He left the room, shutting the door quietly behind him, and went to sit in his room until the dinner hour. Colville left him in peace. They were bound to dine together, for that, too, had been decreed by the dead man, but then Colville would leave and Malcolm would be alone again, as he had been, in truth, for almost half his life.

~~~~~

MAY

The morning had been a rather more enjoyable one than many. A dull Greek lesson had devolved into a long discussion of the Peloponnesian War, with particular reference to the Megarian decrees, which led him to the astonishing but inescapable
~~~~~

conclusion that one or two of the scholars had a modicum of intelligence between their ears after all.

One of the porters was awaiting him as he left the room. He gave the discreet cough which all the porters used when they were required to address a master.

"Dr Butler respectfully requests your presence, sir."

Malcolm grunted an acknowledgement, and made his way directly to the head master's office. As soon as he entered, he groaned aloud, for there was Colville sitting in front of Butler's desk, half-smiling in a rueful manner.

"What the *devil* are you doing here?" Malcolm said, too annoyed to moderate his language. "As if it were not enough to torment me with your letters, now you must approach me here?"

"Do sit down, Gage," Butler said in pleasant tones. "You make me nervous looming over us in that glowering way."

Heaving a disgusted sigh, Malcolm took the chair beside Colville.

"I was not aware of the existence of your brother, Gage," Butler said. "He is older than you, I take it?" Malcolm nodded. "So he got the estate. Was that what the quarrel was about — the inheritance?"

"Good God, no! As if I cared about that!"

"What then? Was it a long time ago?"

Reluctantly, Malcolm said, "Sixteen years."

"Then it must have been a serious matter, I surmise. Not some trivial boys' tiff."

"Not trivial, no," Malcolm conceded. Then, because Butler looked at him expectantly, he added, "A woman. He stole her from me, and then he *killed* her."

"No, no, no," Colville said, in some agitation. "Such intemperate language, Mr Gage. Your great-uncle told me all about it when he drew up his will. They both wished to marry the same lady, Dr Butler, and Mr Laurence Gage was the one who carried off the prize, so to speak. And later, she died in childbed. A great tragedy, but hardly worth sustaining a feud for so many years, I should have thought."

"You know *nothing* about it!" Malcolm said savagely. "She was forced into it! She—" He stopped abruptly. "The details do not matter, but there was no honour in my brother, that is all you need to know. The rift is as much his doing as mine. He would no more welcome me back in his life than I would wish it."

"Now there you are wrong," Colville said triumphantly. "I was obliged to write to him, you know, to apprise him of the terms of Mr Zachariah Gage's will, and he responded with the utmost civility. Let me read you some of it, for it was quite lengthy. Let me see... ah, yes. *'You may be sure that I will place no obstacle in the way of the proceeding, given the benefit to my son.'* There, you see! He places no obstacle in the way."

It was hardly a resounding welcome, however, but it mattered not a whit. "Irrelevant, since I have no intention of complying with these outrageous terms. If I wish to quarrel with my brother, then I shall do so, and no effort of Great-uncle Zachariah will prevail upon me to change my mind."

"Then let me see if my effort will meet with better success," Butler said placidly. "You are relieved of your post here, Gage. If, in the fullness of time, you return here having attempted your appointed task and assure me as a gentleman that you used your best endeavours, I will offer you your position again. Otherwise, I am afraid I cannot employ a man who displays such a grim example of implacable resentment to the boys. I have never concerned myself with your sense of morality, Gage, nor worried that you were not in Holy Orders like the other masters, but I cannot condone such an unchristian attitude. Attempt to overcome it and you may return here, but otherwise my doors are closed to you. You may stay here tonight and leave tomorrow."

Malcolm rose and walked out of the room, but it took every ounce of effort not to slam the door behind him.

END OF SAMPLE CHAPTER of *Stranger At The Grove.* For more information or to buy, go to my website at http://marykingswood.co.uk/.

Manufactured by Amazon.ca
Bolton, ON

43313180R00224